read

BETWEEN THE

lies

Lori Bryant Woolridge

WARNER BOOKS

A Time Warner Company

WARNER BOOKS EDITION

Cover design by Elaine Groh

This Warner Books edition is published by arrangement with Random House, Inc.

Warner Books, Inc.
1271 Avenue of the Americas
New York, NY 10020

Visit our Web site at
www.twbookmark.com

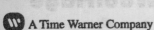 A Time Warner Company

Printed in the United States of America

First Paperback Printing: October 2000

10 9 8 7 6 5 4 3 2 1

This book is lovingly dedicated to my family.
Austin and Eva, in my attempt to leave
a mark on this world,
you have proven to be the greatest gifts
I can give to those whose lives you touch.

To my life partner and soulmate,
Craig, whoever I am now, whoever I become
in the future, it's all because of you.

Acknowledgments

Numerous people, more than I can name here, have assisted in making this dream a reality. Spirit has blessed me with many lights who, with their love and support, have helped illuminate my search for self—both as a woman and as a writer. I am so thankful for you all. In particular, I would like to extend my heartfelt gratitude to:

My parents, Albert and Mable Bryant; my brothers, Albert, Kermit, Gregory; and especially my sister, Susan. You believed, so I did, too. Judy Jenkins, Joyce Gordon, and Jonathan Wafer, this marathon could not have been run without you.

Francesca Neilson and Cynthia Bagby, my "soul" sisters. Thank you both for being such a positive and spiritual force in my life. Saba and Branko, Lee and Lisa, you were there from the beginning. My wonderful friends in Mothers Off Duty: Heather, Angelique, Lynne, Dianna, Ruthanna, Benita, Jackie, Faith, Shelia, Rita, Gina, Mikki, Beverly, Trish, Sandy, Lisa, and Connie. Thanks for your love. You are truly fabulous women.

Benilde Little, thanks for all your advice and support. Patrik Henry Bass, you are an incredible writer and friend. Mark Ulrich, graphics designer extraordinaire, you're always there when I need you. Pam Needles and Wanda Geddie, thank you for your insight into the modeling industry. Meredith Sue Willis, your encouragement made a difference. Rupert Hinds, musician, poet, friend, thanks for sharing your immense talent with me. Your words beg for reality.

Marie Dutton Brown, my literary guardian angel, how blessed I am to flourish under the caring wings of such a legendary agent. Janet Hill, my editor and friend, thank you for "getting it" and caring enough to make this the best book possible. Please know how much I appreciate the uphill climb you two trek daily for authors like me. Andy Elder, the man with the voice, thank you for all your help.

To the millions of new readers in this country, your courageous stories provided much of the inspiration for this book. I tried hard to capture the heart and dignity that shines through each of you. I hope that those of us who take our literacy for granted may read this novel and reap.

And to you, who so kindly purchased this book and gave a new author a chance, enjoy the journey with my best wishes. I trust this will be a long and rewarding relationship for both of us.

Self

What is self?
And what should I find
Do I seek a universal oneness or the mirror kind?
Alone unto itself with utter devotion
Or many, afraid, full of fragmented emotions

I live with a myriad of selves
They take space in my mind
Some easy to see, some hard to define
There is much of myself, some I keep, some I lose
But more important to me is the self I can use

There's the self that is selfish—that one I deny
I don't always win, but I always do try
To be self-fulfilled seems an honorable goal
Though I must achieve without selling my soul

To give thought, word, and deed is self-sacrifice
So that others may have I will pay the price
My heart guides my mind to the self I perceive
For the worse self of all is to be self-deceived

To live, love and laugh is a blessing on earth
To experience true joy you must have self worth
More precious than gold or material wealth
Is a prosperous soul with a true sense of self

RUPERT HINDS

read

BETWEEN THE

lies

Part One

Part One

March 11, 1994

Gabrielle stepped away from the curb and began to wave. Broadway, in midtown Manhattan, was a blur of activity. Up and down the street the sidewalks were crowded with native New Yorkers and visitors from around the world scurrying to their appointed destinations. Impatient pedestrians spilled over the curb waiting for a break in the traffic. Messengers on bikes, driving fast and recklessly, arrogantly wove in and out of traffic like piranhas swimming in a crowded sea of cabs, buses, and limousines.

As the light changed and the confusion momentarily ceased, Gabrielle glanced at her watch. It was five-twenty on a Friday afternoon, a bad time to find an empty cab. On the other side of the street she noticed a well-dressed black man carrying a briefcase and waving frantically. Gabrielle leaned farther into the street and saw the object of his attention—a vacant cab. Quickly she raised her arm again and whispered a silent prayer.

There was no need to pray. Ahmed Ali, spotting the gyrating hands immediately after rounding the corner of Fifty-third Street, had already made his decision. He instantly eliminated the businessman. Ali rarely picked up black or Hispanic men. During the day, maybe, and only if they wore suits because that made it a safe bet that they were staying in Manhattan. He avoided picking them up during rush hour or at night because a lot of them lived in Harlem or Brooklyn, buying up brownstones in dangerous areas that were classified as up-and-coming. Until they up and came, Ali stayed away.

Today he would pass by Gandhi to pick up the woman standing on the corner. Praise Allah! She was one of the most beautiful American women he'd ever seen. She was tall, with enticing long legs accentuated by high-heeled pumps and a short black skirt. Her jacket was fitted, revealing an ample bust and a narrow waist.

The light changed, and Ali zoomed past the black man, who managed to hit the trunk of the cab with his fist while swearing at him for not stopping. Ali paid no attention as he carelessly maneuvered his cab to the other side of the street and pulled up near the curb. Gabrielle opened the door and slid into the backseat. The cabbie turned around and looked into the face of an angel. Her skin was flawless, with the kind of clean glow that clashed with the dirt and grit of New York City. Her long, bronze-colored hair was slightly disheveled and framed a perfectly oval face. The eyes that looked into his were the color of liquid blue lapis, the generous lips that spoke framed an impeccable porcelain smile. Ali felt a pleasant stirring in his pants.

"Thanks for stopping. The New York Hilton Hotel, please."

After traveling ten feet, the cab came to a screeching halt.

"This a joke, lady?" Ali asked, his erection withering away. "One block to Hilton."

Gabrielle cringed as she realized her error. She'd been walking around the West Side for hours and had gotten totally lost. After unsuccessfully trying to follow the directions given by passersby, she'd given up and hailed a cab.

"I'm so sorry," she said, scurrying out of the cab.

"Dumb bitch," Ali called out after her.

Gabrielle wandered back onto the sidewalk and was immediately absorbed into the sea of people hurrying home, eager to begin their weekend. *How could I have been so stupid?* she chastised herself. She inhaled deeply and held her breath long enough to keep from bursting into tears. Gabrielle was afraid that once she started crying she might never stop.

She disengaged herself from the crowd, walked to the nearest trash can, and discarded her latest batch of blank job applications. She expelled a deep breath, trying to rid herself of the tension that had invaded her body since today's job hunt began.

She'd started early that morning, hitting all the little shops that populated Amsterdam and Columbus avenues and all the numbered streets in between, asking for work. But the answers were always the same. Either they weren't hiring or they'd hand her an application to be filled out and filed away.

Why am I in New York? Gabrielle asked herself for the umpteenth time. She'd been in the city for less than a week, but each day the question seemed to surface. There were several answers: to bury the pain and secrets of her past, to start a new life, to fulfill her mother's dreams. But the reason that loomed the largest, the one that terrified her the most, was that she had nowhere else to go.

It was a sad fact that on this, her nineteenth birthday, Gabrielle Donovan was completely alone. She had no family or friends, no home, no money, and was qualifi nothing. It had been six weeks since her mother had died suddenly when a blood vessel burst in her brain. Gabrielle had moved to New York with $347.33 and her mother's dream that she come to the city to find a life of fame and fortune.

Gabrielle's childhood was spent preparing her for that life. She never took a formal dance lesson, never enrolled in charm school or entered any beauty pageants. She was never a cheerleader or homecoming queen, as her mother's ever-changing marital status kept her from attending any one school long enough to become popular. According to her mother, Helene, there was no need for any of those things. Gabrielle had two of the best "stage mothers" in the business. As Mother Nature adeptly guided her transformation from a lovely baby into a stunning beauty, Helene stayed busy grooming her child's mind. Throughout the years mother and daughter often talked late into the night about the fabulous life they would lead. They discussed this starstruck future so often that Gabrielle had no idea at what point her mother's desires had become her own.

Prompted by the aggressive sales pitch of the homeless man panhandling for donations, Gabrielle decided to head back to the hotel. It was too early to retire, so she settled into one of the many plush sofas scattered around the elegant lobby of the New York Hilton. She loved the way the fluffy softness of the cushions engulfed her body. She loved everything about this hotel—the thick, luxurious carpets, the gleaming wood, and the low circular fountain that gurgled near the front doors, demanding attention like a spoiled mistress.

Out of the corner of her eye Gabrielle noticed an attractive young man approaching. She quickly picked up *The Wall Street Journal* from the coffee table and immediately became immersed in the front page. Gabrielle sat behind the newspaper daydreaming about baked chicken, candied yams, key lime pie, and a hundred other favorite dishes she'd rather eat than the stale peanut butter crackers in her pocketbook.

"Uh, pardon me. I, uh, I couldn't help noticing—"

"Yes?"

"The paper. It's upside down."

"I confess. I was trying to get your attention," she said, smiling and extending her hand. "I'm Gabrielle Donovan."

"Doug Sixsmith," he answered, taking her hand in his. "I have to admit that's the most novel approach I've seen in a long while. Now that you've got my undivided attention, may I join you?" he asked, settling down beside her. "What brings you to New York?"

"I'm looking for a job."

"What do you do?"

"Model—or at least I'd like to. If I have what it takes."

"I'm no expert, but with your looks, what else could you need?" Doug said, hoping his compliment didn't sound like some asinine pickup line.

"Well, for starters, two hands." There was a pause as the meaning of her comment penetrated Doug's brain.

"Sorry," he said, releasing his grip.

"Do you live in New York?" she asked, eager to turn the subject away from herself.

"No. Boston. I've been here doing some interviewing myself."

"What kind of job are you looking for?" Gabrielle asked.

"Not job interviews. I'm a reporter."

"Really?"

"Why don't I tell you the tricks of the trade over dinner?" Suddenly Doug was very glad he wasn't a prisoner in some war-torn country. With Gabrielle interrogating him he'd take one look at that incredible face and spill his guts—name, rank, serial number, the secret ingredient in his red-hot chili—anything, everything.

Gabrielle hesitated only briefly. She was starving, and this stranger looked like the perfect meal ticket. Any misgivings she might have had about Doug Sixsmith were being eaten alive by the growling monster in her empty stomach.

"Please," he prompted. "I hate eating by myself. It's so lonely. What do you say? I buy dinner, you supply the company."

What do you know about being lonely? I can keep you company at dinner, but can you keep me from being alone for the rest of my life? Can you take care of me and teach me how to live on my own? she thought.

"Why not?"

"Great." Doug smiled, his excitement obvious. "Do you like Italian?"

By the time Gabrielle returned to the hotel, both her appetite and loneliness were temporarily satiated. Her birthday had been special after all, as Doug Sixsmith had turned out to be an entertaining and thoughtful dinner companion. He'd even arranged for a slice of cake complete with candle and a serenade by the waiters. Before stepping off the elevator on the seventeenth floor, he'd gallantly shaken her hand and thanked her for a great evening. He would have liked to prolong their evening together, but the shock and disappointment of learning just how young she was had not yet worn off. Though Doug could sense that Gabrielle was someone special and well past the age of consent, the word "teenager" wouldn't stop echoing through his head.

The elevator doors closed, and Gabrielle rode back down to the third floor. It was quiet. A good sign. As she walked down the hall, she was confused by the mix of emotions she was feeling. She felt both disappointed and thankful that Doug had ended their evening together. She'd enjoyed his company, but at the same time was tired and wanted to get to sleep. Tomorrow she would have to get up and out early. Gabrielle opened the door and gingerly called out, "Anybody here?" No answer. She walked into the room and headed straight to the utility closet. She recognized the words OUT OF printed on the yellow plastic sign peeking from behind the cleaning supplies. Gabrielle pulled it out and placed it on the floor outside, closed the door and locked it behind her. Just as the sign announced, this bathroom was out of order until morning.

It was his warm breath on the back of her neck that woke her. Stephanie, too terrified to move, lay motionless, listening to the syncopated rhythm of his breathing.

Oh, shit, she thought, panicked. *I can't get caught—not here, not now.*

Slowly, so not to disturb the slumbering body next to her, Stephanie turned to look at the clock. It was 6:47 A.M. Thank God Jack was still asleep. How had she let this happen? If he saw her now, everything would be over before it even began.

Jack stirred, releasing Stephanie from her paralysis. Gently, she lifted the sheet from her naked body and cautiously eased out of his bed. She pulled her jeans over her narrow hips and her shirt over her small breasts. She paused before retrieving her panties. Granted, black lace undies hanging daintily from the TV antenna were an interesting forget-me-not, but these were her Victoria's Secret seduction panties. A brief note would suffice, Stephanie decided, and shoved them into her purse.

Shoes in hand, she padded out of his bedroom and downstairs to the studio area. On the back of his unopened

electric bill she jotted, "Thanks. You were great. Stephanie."
Wait. I'm a writer. I can do better than this. Before she could
think of something coyer and more suggestive, the shrill
sound of Jack's alarm sent her flying across the room and
through the front door.

She'd almost blown it. Seducing him into bed had been
her game plan, not waking up with him in the morning. Another fifteen minutes and all the illusions she'd worked so
hard to create these past three weeks would have been shattered.

Morning was definitely not Stephanie's best time of
day. She was convinced that each night little gangs of trolls
came out and beat her up, transforming her from a relatively
attractive twenty-three-year-old woman into an unsightly
beast.

Her short brick-red hair, which crowned her head in
thick Miss Clairol–enhanced curls when she climbed *into*
bed, was matted and sticking up every which way when she
climbed *out*. Her jade-green eyes were puffy and brown now
that her tinted contact lenses were tucked away in their case.
Her glowing skin, devoid of all makeup, looked splotchy
and uneven. Worst of all was her breath. During last night's
pillow talk her mouth smelled minty fresh, but overnight it
had turned into a toxic-waste dump, emitting fumes that
could easily drop a herd of elephants, let alone a mere mor-
tal.

Oh, no, not the kind of sight you wanted the man you
were trying to draw into your lair to see before your relationship was solid—rock solid. Stephanie had big plans for
Jack Hollis. She wasn't about to spoil them now.

Stephanie suppressed the urge to burst into song as she
slipped quietly through the front door of the Fort Greene
brownstone and upstairs to her rented room. The last thing
she wanted to do was to alert her landlady, Beatrice Braid-

burn, that she was just getting home. It wasn't as if there were actual house rules that precluded her from staying out all night. It was just that Beatrice, self-appointed captain of the morality police, always managed to make her feel guilty as hell.

Congratulations, Steph, she told herself. *Finally something in your life is going right.* Delicious, sexy Jack was the perfect remedy for what ailed her. There was something about him that made her forget how disappointing her life had been lately.

Among other things, having Jack around helped ease her frustration and anger over the constant stream of rejection letters that flooded her mailbox. It irked her no end that she was unable to make a living at the one thing she loved to do. Her bank account was once again running on empty, and now she was forced to job-hunt—using up time she could better spend writing.

Stephanie pushed all thoughts of her sputtering literary career into the "pending" file at the very back of her head. She didn't want anything to bring her down. Last night had made her too happy. Jack Hollis was *the* one—the man who was going to turn her life around.

From the moment she spotted him sitting on a barstool at the Mad Hatter, Stephanie had become the hunter and Jack her unwitting prey. She had sat at the very end of the bar, shrouded in the shadows of the dimly lit room waiting for a blind date that never showed. At the time she was livid, but in hindsight, if she ever met the imbecile who stood her up she'd have to thank him for delivering her to this cleverly disguised promised land.

Writing had made Stephanie an expert observer, and what she saw pleased her immensely. Even in the dim lights she could tell he was attractive. The constant flow of women flocking to his side was also a dead giveaway. After a few moments of close scrutiny Stephanie noticed that none of the women managed to keep his attention for more than a couple of minutes. This could mean one of two things: He was either heartbroken or homosexual. The thought of his being gay was just too depressing, and Stephanie had immediately pushed it from her mind. Hey, for anybody else, fine. But not this man. Not Mr. Right. That would be too cruel. *He must be heartbroken,* she'd decided. *Yes, some bitch has broken his heart and he needs me—the Krazy Glue of love.*

While her eyes watched the pencil-thin blonde with gigantic boobs giggle in his face, her mouth called to the bartender, "What is he drinking?"

"Sidecar."

"That's a new one."

"Not really. We don't get too many requests for it. Shall I send one over?"

"No, I think I'll handle this myself." Stephanie took a minute to freshen up her makeup before making her move. She slipped off the barstool just as the buxom blonde vacated the coveted chair. Stephanie rounded the bar and breathlessly slid onto the seat next to the object of her desire.

"Matt? I'm Stephanie. Sorry I'm so late." She hoped she sounded genuine. From the description she'd been given of her date, getting these two mixed up would be like mistaking Danny DeVito for Johnny Depp.

"Sorry, wrong number."

"How embarrassing. I was sure you were somebody I'm *supposed* to meet," she explained, perfectly pitching her voice between irony and sincerity.

"No problem."

"What can I get you?" the bartender interrupted.

"My usual—a sidecar," Stephanie requested with a conspiratorial smile.

"You got it."

"This guy, Matt, he's a real loser," Jack announced. "Any woman who drinks a classic should never be kept waiting."

"Six-fifty's the damage," the bartender announced, setting down her glass.

"This one's on me."

"Thank you . . ."

"Jack Hollis."

"Nice to meet you, Jack Hollis," Stephanie said, enjoying the taste of his name in her mouth.

"To sidecars," Jack said, raising his glass in a toast.

"And the sidekicks that fill them." Stephanie lifted the amber-colored drink to her mouth and took a sip. *THIS TASTES LIKE SHIT,* screamed every taste bud on her tongue. Smiling weakly, Stephanie drained the contents of her glass—partly for courage, but mainly because she didn't want to sip on that vile concoction all night. She closed her eyes as the alcohol blazed its way down her throat. When she opened them, Jack was smiling at her.

"Whoa, slow down. These things are pretty potent. You know, most people have never even heard of a sidecar, let alone tasted one. How is it that you're so enlightened?"

"It's my father's favorite drink," Stephanie lied, smiling broadly.

Two hours later, Stephanie and a very drunk Jack were in a cab headed for Greenwich Village. Immediately after arriving at his studio, Jack excused himself and stumbled up the narrow stairs to the loft, which doubled as his bedroom. "Have a sheet. I'll be right down," he told her, slurring his words. Stephanie sat on one of the two oversized leather chairs that dominated the studio area. Busy checking out her surroundings, it was several minutes before Stephanie realized that all movement upstairs had ceased.

"Jack, are you okay?" She climbed halfway up the ladder and peeked into the loft. Jack, having parked one sidecar too many, was passed out, leaving Stephanie alone to explore his abode.

In less than twenty minutes, having peered into every closet and cupboard in the place, Stephanie learned everything she needed to know about this thirty-one-year-old graphic artist she'd decided to make her own. He was self-employed, a sports enthusiast—namely golf, windsurfing, and the New York Rangers—loved Chinese food and the James Bond films starring Sean Connery. He appeared to be single, and if he *was* involved with another woman, he wouldn't be for long. Whatever it took, Stephanie would transform herself into his perfect woman, his soul mate. She wanted Jack Hollis, and come hell or high water, she was going to have him.

3

"Invitation, please," the man requested, stopping Felicia as she turned into the Potomac, Maryland, driveway.

"I don't need an invitation. I live here," Felicia informed him, stepping on the gas. Technically, she had lied. She hadn't actually lived in the residence since graduating from Georgetown University six years ago, but Bedside Manor, as the house had been dubbed when her father was named Holy Cross Hospital's chief of neurosurgery, would always be home.

Instead of following the circular driveway that led to the brightly lit front doors and into the waiting arms of the valet team hired for the evening, Felicia sped her rental car past the tennis court and parked behind the house. She walked through the tall black iron gates that separated the parking area from the pool.

"Hey, Coltrane, Miles," she called out to the two barking Doberman pinschers confined in the dog run. Though the guests had already begun to arrive and she should be upstairs getting dressed, Felicia paused by the gurgling goldfish pond and enjoyed the familiar surroundings. The pool was lit just under the cascading waterfall. Steel drums were set up to the left of the hot tub, signaling the entertainment yet to come. The doors to the cabana were thrown open, and the rich, smoky voice of Sarah Vaughan overflowed softly onto the patio. Plush towels, monogrammed BEDSIDE MANOR, were stacked neatly by the bar waiting for any guest wanting to dip into the hot tub's warm, inviting waters.

Felicia took a deep breath and let the sweet night air invade her lungs. It felt good to get away from New York's hustle and bustle, the trash-ridden streets, from her husband, Trace, and their marital problems. But as good as it felt, Felicia knew it was only a matter of time before she would miss the excitement and exhilaration of the city's frenetic pace. And eventually she'd have to come to a decision about her marriage. But not tonight. *Tonight belongs to Papa*, she reminded herself as she headed into the house.

Walking through the mudroom, Felicia could smell the delectable aromas of Caribbean cuisine wafting from the large kitchen. There was a flurry of activity going on as the catering staff, dressed in colorful island garb, concentrated on preparing her father's favorite dishes. As the doorbell chimed and the welcoming cries of her parents' guests rang out, Felicia hurried up the back stairs to the second floor and straight to her old bedroom.

"Licia, is that you? I was getting a little worried," her mother said, coming out of her room to give her eldest daughter a warm embrace. Jolie Wilcot looked positively regal in a fuchsia Isaac Mizrahi evening gown. Her youthful appearance belied her fifty-five years; tennis, swimming, and a busy social calendar kept her mind and body fit.

For as long as Felicia could remember, friends and relatives had commented on how much she resembled her mother—a charge Felicia couldn't deny. From the five feet, six inches of lean build to the large, doelike eyes and intense passion for sourdough bread, Felicia was proud to acknowledge that she and her mother shared the same designer genes.

"Sorry, Mama. My flight was late."

"It doesn't matter. You're here now. Where's my handsome son-in-law?"

"Trace sends his apologies. He's tied up with an important client this evening."

"You two are always so busy. It's no wonder I don't have any grandbabies."

"I still have a few good years left, Mom. So, who's on tonight's guest list?" Felicia asked, wanting to change the subject.

"Colin and Alma Powell, though the general will probably be late. Vernon Jordan and Ann are coming and bringing Congresswoman Maxine Waters. I've been dying to meet her. Jesse and Jackie Jackson said they'd try to stop by. Kweisi Mfume RSVP'ed. Then there's the Neilsons, the Strains, and Susan Mitchell. She's bringing her latest find—some hot new film director, Richard something. Susan says he's the next Spike Lee, so he might ultimately be a good contact for you. Other than that it's just the usuals."

The "usuals" were an eclectic mix of family and old friends, many of whom constituted the wealthy and influential members of the country's black elite. "Is Lindsay here yet?"

"Your sister is downstairs rummaging through your father's music collection and hiding all the Frank Sinatra CDs. And downstairs is exactly where I need to be." Mother and daughter shared a smile before Jolie floated out of the room, leaving a whisper of her signature scent, Chanel No. 19, lingering behind.

Felicia crossed the hall into the bathroom she and her sister had shared since they were children. She showered quickly, not giving in to the temptation to linger under the hot, relaxing spray. Pushing aside her sister's makeup, she took a minute to enhance her flawless skin. With practiced expertise, she applied blush to her high cheekbones, shadowed and lined her light-brown eyes, and set her full lips aglow with fire-red lipstick. In one deft move she swept her copper-colored hair into an elegant French twist. Pleased with the face smiling back at her, she hurried back to her room and slid into her dress for the evening. Another thing Felicia had inherited was her mother's love of beautiful clothes. Tonight she was wearing a black fitted slip dress, accented with three strands of pearls that crisscrossed in the back. Diamond and pearl studs adorned her ears, and Felicia wrapped her slender wrist in a cuff of pearls before heading downstairs to surprise her father.

Drifting through the hall toward the main staircase, Felicia stopped to admire her parents' prized art collection. The wall was lined with a brilliant display of the artistic efforts of the Wilcot children. Framed as elegantly as any Romare Bearden were handprints, finger paintings, family portraits, and other "impressionist" art whose emotional value far exceeded that of any priceless museum piece.

Descending the staircase, Felicia immediately spotted her father among the party guests. He was standing near the ficus tree chatting with a well-dressed woman, his arm draped amicably around her shoulders. Dr. Albert Wilcot was a handsome man, with broad shoulders and an athletic build. His salt-and-pepper hair, short-cropped beard, and small wire glasses gave him a distinguished, intellectual look.

"Happy birthday, old man," Felicia laughed, sneaking up on her father with a hug.

"Bright Eyes," he called out, his delight in her presence obvious. "I thought you were in Atlanta meeting with those producer folks."

"Papa, nothing could have kept me away tonight."

"Well, I couldn't have asked for a better present. Licia, let me introduce you to Councilwoman Mable Lun. Mable, meet my eldest daughter, Felicia. This girl abandoned her father and ran off with some big-time lawyer to start her own Madison Avenue firm."

"Are you in advertising?"

"Public relations."

"How exciting. You must be doing quite well, and Al, you must be very proud."

Both father and daughter acknowledged the remark with a polite smile. Albert Wilcot was indeed proud of his enterprising daughter. Felicia, on the other hand, knew that while people who heard her address had visions of luxurious office space and a thriving business dancing in their heads, the hole in the wall that housed the office of Wilcot & Associates didn't quite live up to the avenue's lofty image.

It might be small now, but Wilcot & Associates was definitely growing. In just one year she had gone from renting a mailbox address and working out of the apartment to having actual office space. She was also in the process of hiring her first part-time employee. Right now she was just squeaking by, but Felicia was determined to make it. She was going to prove to Trace that she didn't need his money to buy her success. She could make it on her own. But once out of his controlling grasp, what kind of state would her marriage be in?

"Where's Trace? Why didn't he come with you?" her father asked, following the councilwoman's departure for the buffet table.

Because I'm being punished for putting my work ahead of his.

"His biggest client flew in unexpectedly, and he couldn't get away. He sends his best, Papa."

"That's too bad. We haven't seen much of the two of you as—"

"Where did you park your walker, you old fart?" boomed a familiar voice.

"Uncle Joe! I thought you were still in France," Felicia cried, giving her godfather a heartfelt hug. "Where's that fabulous wife of yours?" she asked.

"Libby's over there laughing with Jesse. Honey, you know we wouldn't miss your daddy's sixtieth-birthday celebration. We were taught to respect our elders. Lindsay, is that you?" Joe interrupted himself to pull Felicia's sister to his side. "You two girls get prettier every day."

"Uncle Joe, you know I was always the pretty one. It was Licia that Mama wouldn't take out in public."

Felicia laughed as she studied her younger sister. Although the traditional elegance of Felicia and her mother had escaped Lindsay, in its place was an unabashed uniqueness. Tonight her lithe dancer's body was sheathed in a purple silk body suit with matching harem pants trimmed in gold thread at the waist and ankles. Flat gold sandals adorned her feet, and her chosen jewelry for the evening was a wide gold cuff and three small hoops in each ear.

"Oh, Lord, there's Scooty Ross. Joe, come let me introduce you," said Albert as he spirited his friend off.

"How's business? Are you still working on that black rodeo thing?" Lindsay asked.

"Yes. Things are slowly coming together. I'm still looking for a major sponsor. I'm also working on a pitch for the Montell Spirits account."

"As in 'The Wine of Our Times'?" Lindsay asked, referring to the company's popular slogan.

"That's the one. They're about to introduce a new wine cooler, and we're one of three minority firms being considered."

"And naturally they want to target the black market," blurted out a combative and distinctively male voice.

"Not exclusively. That's just one market they're after," answered Felicia, turning to face her unknown inquisitor. Her eyes came to rest on an unfamiliar black man. Short dreadlocks covered the crown of his head, and his mouth was framed by a well-groomed goatee. His tall, lean body was dressed in jeans, a faded denim shirt worn open to reveal a white T-shirt, and sneakers. Around his neck he wore an encircled X the size of a quarter. He was conspicuously out of place in this room of elegantly dressed guests, but the fact that he was so inappropriately attired seemed not to concern him in the least.

"And you want this job?" he asked in an accusing tone.

"Well, I'd much rather have the entire pie, but I'll settle for this one slice," Felicia said while frantically trying to think of a reason to excuse herself.

"You don't think it's odd that the liquor they target toward black people has names like 'Silver Bullet' or 'Mad Dog' or features wild, crazy bulls tearing up everything? Doesn't that tell you something about the poison they're trying to shove down our throats?"

"Those are beers. This is a wine cooler."

"It's all the same. Alcohol or gunpowder—it's just another bullet they got aimed at black people's heads."

"Do we know you? You keep jumping in our faces without so much as a how-do-you-do—" Felicia asked.

"Yeah, well, black folks like you have a tendency to pluck my last nerve."

"Maybe you should leave, to avoid being plucked any further," Lindsay suggested.

"No. I'd like to hear exactly what you mean by 'black folks like us,'" Felicia said.

"I mean all you *Forbes*– and *Town and Country*–reading

folks. As long as Mr. Charlie signs a contract and throws thirty pieces of silver your way, you're happy being his paid assassin," he said, ready for combat. "Hey, if you want to be a sell-out, cool. Just don't walk around here trying to pass yourself off as a sister."

"Who *are* you?" Lindsay asked. There was something wildly sexy about this rebellious stranger. While she found him vaguely appealing, it was painfully obvious that Felicia thought him to be a first-class asshole.

"Lexis—"

"And what in your *expert* opinion do I need to do to prove that I'm a sister? Wear dreads and drape myself in kente cloth?" Felicia asked sarcastically. She was having difficulty keeping a lid on her anger.

"Beats that Malibu Barbie thing you got going."

Felicia, not wanting to cause a scene at her father's party, counted to ten before quietly answering this obnoxious stranger. "Let me tell you something. It takes more than dreadlocks and Malcom X paraphernalia to make you black," she said through clenched teeth. "Half the kids walking around wearing X T-shirts and hats don't know a damn thing about the man or what he stood for. If they did, they wouldn't be killing each other over leather jackets."

"Oh, like you Taittinger-drinking, Porsche-driving, Armani-wearing wannabe tokens have a clue. I don't know why I'm bothering to explain this to a bourgeois Black American Princess. I knew I shouldn't have come here tonight."

"That's the first thing uttered out of your miserable mouth this evening that I agree with. How dare you come to my house and insult me and my family." Shaking with full-blown fury, Felicia turned to leave but was waylaid by Susan Mitchell.

"Lexis, there you are. I see you've met Felicia Wilcot, the daughter of tonight's guest of honor."

Wilcot, Lexis thought. Great. He had just insulted beyond repair the daughter of the man he had hoped would help finance his next movie. This was the only reason he'd let Susan talk him into coming to yet another one of these ridiculous affairs. Despite the anticipated success of *Southeast,* his first, soon-to-be released film, the two-picture, six-million-dollar deal with MarMa Pictures didn't begin to meet his budgetary needs. Supplementing the studio's money with individual financing was the only way he could make his next films and stay true to his creative vision.

He'd really blown it big time. Susan had warned him to keep his opinions to himself, but after two consecutive days of kowtowing to these uppity black folks, the challenge Felicia presented could not go unmet. And now, in less than ten minutes, he had met and slaughtered his cash cow.

"As I'm sure he's mentioned, Lexis Richards is president of In the House Filmworks and one of our up-and-coming directors," Susan continued. "In fact, his first film comes out next week. Felicia owns a PR business in New York. She could be a real help to you."

"The only help I could possibly give to Mr. Richards is in the form of a little advice," Felicia said, wearing a Nutrasweet smile.

"This ought to be good," Lexis retorted.

"If your social skills are any indication of your directing expertise, your best bet at success would be to find yourself a busy street corner and help keep traffic moving."

Before Lexis had the chance to respond, their conversation was cut short by the rhythmic beats of the steel drums coming from the pool. Libby Hobson, arms around the waist of the dean of Howard University's law school, began a conga line that eventually snaked itself around the living room and outside into the cool March night.

"Hey, you three—join the party," encouraged Felicia's laughing mother as she headed out the door.

"In a minute." Felicia smiled back. "Excuse me," she said and made a beeline to her father's study. The conversation with Lexis had put a damper on her previously good mood. *Wannabe white girl. Black American Princess.* His biting accusations clung to her, bringing to the surface feelings Felicia had pushed deep inside.

After all these years she was accustomed to outrageous comments from whites, like "You don't really *act* black" or "You don't look like a *normal* black person." What she never got used to, however, was having to defend herself against her own people for "not being black enough." This form of self-defense was not only frustrating but extremely painful.

Despite what Lexis thought, Felicia was proud to be a black woman. What he didn't seem to understand was that it went beyond simple pride. It was an issue of being caught in the middle—trapped between the black activism of the early sixties and the recent resurgence of Afrocentric pride. Felicia's generation grew up in the glow of Martin Luther King's dream. Her parents had pushed aside the dashikis for business suits, moved from the lunch counter into the executive dining room, and raised their daughters to believe in "being judged not by the color of their skin but by the content of their character."

Assimilation was the marching order of the times, and Felicia's parents took their mission to heart. While the Wilcots surrounded their family with progressive and accomplished people of color, they also worked hard to give their daughters the finest of everything European culture had to offer—the best private schools, classical dance and music lessons, travel abroad. Even Felicia's marriage to Trace Gordon managed to keep her privileged and color-blind lifestyle intact.

Felicia glanced at the family photograph on her father's desk. It was taken on her wedding day. The Wilcots were indeed a beautiful family, and by all appearances Trace, with his brooding good looks, fit right in. He was the son of a prominent family in Atlanta, his father a well-connected judge and his mother a social icon known for her energetic efforts on behalf of several local charities. The Gordons had raised an intelligent, ambitious young man who believed he could do anything—regardless of race. With degrees from Emory University and Harvard Law School, he was a firm believer in the "economics of color." Trace believed that once one reached a certain level of social and economic status, race ceased to be an issue. Black and white no longer mattered—green was the only color that counted.

On the surface Trace and Felicia seemed the storybook, happily-ever-after couple. But were they and the rest of their well-to-do friends, as Lexis had implied, simply a group of selfish, black urban professionals enjoying the good life while so many others lagged behind?

Felicia laid her head on the large walnut desk. Lately she was always tired. It seemed as if she was engaged in a constant struggle these days. A struggle to build her business, to save her marriage, to find herself.

She could hear the collage of happy voices and steel drums, but she had no desire to rejoin the party. She had to get up early to catch the first shuttle back to New York. She was interviewing a new receptionist, and Trace insisted she be back in time to have lunch. Felicia slipped unnoticed from the study and headed upstairs. Right now she just wanted to go to bed. She needed to rest for the struggle that would begin anew tomorrow.

4

"Stephanie?" Beatrice called through the closed door.

"Come in."

Beatrice opened the bedroom door holding Barclay, the house cat. Unlike Beatrice, who took one step forward and stopped, Barclay leaped from Bea's arms into a chaotic playground. As usual, Stephanie's room was a mess. Clothes draped the furniture and littered the floor, both singularly and in piles. Shoes and socks were scattered around the room, and hats hung haphazardly on nails lined the walls. The bed was lost under a pile of twisted linen. In the far corner a bookcase overflowed with books crammed every which way, while cheap knickknacks sat on the shelf collecting dust. In the eye of this hurricane sat Stephanie at her makeshift desk, dressed in a suit.

"You're going out?"

"I have an interview at ten-thirty." Stephanie intentionally left out the word "job," giving Bea and others the impression that she was constantly working on one article or another. The truth of the matter was she hadn't written a word since meeting Jack. "Why? What's up?"

"I was wondering if your friend had decided on the vacant room?"

"Connie told me last night she's going to move in with her boyfriend."

"That's too bad. She seemed like a nice girl. Well, if you think of anyone else . . ."

"I'll let you know," Stephanie promised, conveniently forgetting that her friend Gina was looking for a place. She had no intention of helping Beatrice find a new boarder. Ever since the last girl left to be married, Stephanie's living arrangement had been ideal. For four hundred dollars a month she enjoyed the use of the front parlor, kitchen, and bathroom and even had a clean bedroom at her disposal if she chose to engage in more intimate entertaining. Stephanie never had to wait to do her laundry, and the phone in the hall was always available. Other than a bit of unwelcome advice and a raised eyebrow or two, her living situation was perfect, and she found absolutely no reason to tamper with perfection.

"Hello," Stephanie called out as she stepped inside the small reception area and closed the door behind her. There was nobody available to return her greeting. Glancing around, Stephanie was surprised. Instead of the Madison Avenue–chic decor she'd imagined, this had more of an "early relative" look to it. The small reception area, with its heavy walnut desk, dark bookcases, and worn leather chairs, resembled a man's study. Government-issue-looking file cabinets lined the walls. Adding the only real color to the room and separating the reception area from what must be the boss's domain was a beautiful Oriental screen. Curious, Stephanie peeked behind and found a round antique desk of blond wood and its accompanying chair, upholstered in peach. As she reached out to inspect the framed photo sitting on the desk, the phone rang. Following several unanswered rings, she picked up.

"Wilcot and Associates. I'm sorry, Ms. Wilcot isn't in at the moment. May I take a message? Anita Baker, the singer? Of course, who else? I'll tell her you called." *I just talked to Anita Baker,* she thought as she hung up the phone and walked back into the main office area. *This could be a fun gig. Maybe I could write some celebrity profiles.* Just as she sat down, the phone rang again. "Gary Taylor, Keep the Faith Records, in until noon. Okay, I'll let her know."

Three messages later, the door opened and Felicia walked in from the ladies' room. Stephanie was in the middle of a phone call, and Felicia was impressed by her professional manner and comfortable phone presence. "Stephanie Bancroft?"

"Yes."

"I'm Felicia Wilcot. I'm sorry I wasn't here when you arrived. Thank you for covering the phones."

"You're welcome. I'm here for my interview."

"That won't be necessary. Based on this impromptu trial by fire, you're hired. When can you start?"

5

"Today I will find a job. Today I will find a job." Gabrielle repeated her mantra as she turned the corner of Fifty-fourth Street and walked up Sixth Avenue. It was early, and most of the shops along the street were still closed. Gabrielle's empty stomach directed her into Muffin Mania, where she gazed hungrily into a glass case filled with a mountain of bakery delights.

"What will it be?"

"A blueberry muffin and a small coffee."

"That'll be three fifty-seven."

Three dollars and fifty-seven cents for a muffin and coffee? Gabrielle wanted to tell her to forget it, but she was too embarrassed. She paid the cashier and sat down at one of the small tables by the window.

This was not turning out to be such a great day. After more than a week of successfully dodging the hotel staff, she'd almost been caught. Shortly after six this morning, while retrieving the OUT OF ORDER sign from outside the bathroom door, she saw the cleaning woman approaching and barely had time to grab her bag and hide in one of the toilet stalls. Once the woman gathered her cleaning paraphernalia from the storage closet and left, Gabrielle quickly dressed and slipped out of the bathroom. Hotel workers were busy setting up for morning meetings and men and women in business suits sat coffee-klatching in various corners of the floor. And now, because she hadn't been able to grab a roll from one of the catering tables, she'd been forced to spend nearly all of her daily food allowance on a bitter cup of coffee and a blueberry muffin. Plus her back and neck were killing her. She *had* to find a job today. She could not continue sleeping on the bathroom sofa in the New York Hilton Hotel.

"Is the manager in?" Gabrielle asked.

"Louie, somebody's looking for you."

Gabrielle stood at the counter silently repeating her mantra—*Today I will find a job, today I will find a job*—until the manager stepped out from the back office.

"Who's looking for me?" he challenged.

"Hi, Louie. I'm Gabrielle Donovan," she said arming herself with a foolproof, buttery smile.

Every bone in Louie's body told him that this girl wanted something. They also insisted that he give it to her.

"I need a job."

"Who doesn't these days? You ever worked a cash register before?" he asked, surveying her body. Gabrielle had the distinct impression that he was judging much more than her ability to sell muffins.

Gabrielle simply shook her head no while biting her bottom lip in an irresistible and vintage show of "damsel in distress."

"Do you have *any* retail experience?" Louie asked, after nervously clearing his throat.

"No, I haven't. But I know, with someone like *you* teaching me the ropes, I'll learn very fast," she answered, slowly lowering her eyelashes before looking Louie straight in the eye.

"Well, you seem like an all-right enough kid. Okay, I'll give you a try behind the counter. You've got one week. If things work out, the job's yours."

"Thank you, Louie. Thank you so much."

"Yeah, yeah. I'm a saint," Louie responded, blushing slightly. "You start Monday. Be here at seven-thirty *sharp*. Don't be late. And you need to fill this out," he said, handing her a job application.

"Now?"

"Yeah, now. You can't work till I get all your particulars—address, phone, age. You are eighteen, aren't you?"

"Nineteen. Can I take this and drop it back by this afternoon? I'm late for another appointment."

"Yeah, okay, but you don't work till I get your information."

"No problem, I'll see you later. Thanks again, Louie." She smiled as she took the application and headed out the door. *Everywhere you go somebody's handing you a stupid piece of paper,* Gabrielle thought as she walked back toward the hotel.

"Okay, looks like I have two possibilities here," she murmured to herself as she canvassed the crowded eatery. Gabrielle wanted to sit and get the paperwork for Louie done, but with the lunch hour in full swing, only two seats were available. One was located across from a young man whose entire face was punched full of holes and adorned with a variety of hoops, rings, and studs. Her only other option was to sit at the table situated in a cramped little corner by the kitchen. The heavyset woman sitting there looked perfectly normal; it was just that Gabrielle was carrying her luggage, and the path was narrow and winding.

Slowly she made her way to the back, her progress punctuated by the steady screech of chairs sliding across the floor to accommodate her baggage. "May I?" Gabrielle asked, pointing to the empty seat with her right hand, revealing a thumb splinted and bandaged with white gauze.

Beatrice Braidburn smiled, indicating her approval. She watched as Gabrielle settled into her chair before pulling a pen and form of some sort from her leather-look handbag. After several attempts to put pen to paper, it was obvious to Beatrice that the girl was having trouble maneuvering the pen with her left hand.

"It looks like you could use some help," Beatrice offered. "Would you like me to fill that out for you?"

"Would you mind? I slammed my thumb in the bathroom door. It really hurts."

"Not at all. In fact, I used to be a pretty good secretary in my day. I just retired a few years ago. I'm Beatrice Braidburn. My friends call me Bea."

"I'm Gabrielle Donovan."

"Is that two L's or one?" she asked, jotting down Gabrielle's name on the application.

"Two."

"Date of birth?"

"March eleventh, 1975."

"A Pisces. Happy belated birthday. My late sister, Helen, bless her soul, was a Pisces."

"My mom's name was Helen—well, really Helene."

"Where is your mother, dear?"

"She died recently," Gabrielle answered softly.

"Oh, I'm so sorry."

"Are you from New York?"

"No, I came here from Terre Haute, Indiana, after she died."

"What's your address, dear?" Bea asked, filling in the silence.

"I'm at the Hilton Hotel."

Beatrice gave Gabrielle a quick once-over. Judging from her neat but inexpensive attire and tattered bag, the New York Hilton Hotel seemed beyond her price range.

"Maybe we should list your room number," she suggested.

Gabrielle took a good look at the woman sitting across from her. She had a protective, grandmotherly presence about her. Maybe she should tell her the truth. Maybe Beatrice could help. Maybe Gabrielle had no other choice.

"I'm living in the bathroom on the third floor," she answered softly.

"We can't have that," Bea declared. For the next few minutes Gabrielle watched Beatrice complete the rest of the application without asking her a single question. "There you go," she said, smiling and very pleased with herself. "You have an address, phone number, and reference—mine. Now, gather your belongings. You're coming home with me."

"But you don't even know me."

"Sure I do. You're from Indiana, you're a Pisces, and you're alone. What more do I need to know?"

Nothing. But I can't keep this secret forever. If I move in with you, you're bound to find out. But what other option do I have? she asked herself as she reached for her bag.

"And this, my dear, is your room," Bea announced at the final stop of their tour.

Gabrielle stepped into the room and glanced around. It was sparsely furnished, with a twin bed covered in a yellow flowered spread and an old bureau taking up the majority of space. A table and stuffed chair sat in the corner. It was simple and small, but who cared? This morning she'd been living in a bathroom. This afternoon she had a home.

"I love it. Thank you. There's just one thing. I won't be able to pay you for a while, not until I start my job."

"Honey, don't you worry about that. This house is bought and paid for. When you can afford it, we'll talk. Now, you get settled in. I'm going downstairs to finish writing some letters. If you get hungry, help yourself to whatever is in the kitchen. Stephanie Bancroft, the girl that stays in the room next door, should be home soon. She's rather quirky, but she's okay."

It didn't take Gabrielle long to unpack. Besides her clothes, she'd brought few personal items. On top of the table she placed a picture of herself and Helene, taken on a merry-go-round when Gabrielle was four. Gabrielle placed a Raggedy Ann doll in the chair and threw her mom's favorite shawl across the back. She put the box containing the pieces to her favorite jigsaw puzzle—the New York skyline—in the bottom drawer of her dresser. The last thing she unwrapped was a cheap dime-store snow globe. She shook the globe and watched the plastic snow fall around the feet of the *Wizard of Oz* characters. She'd debated over bringing it. The memories it evoked were strong and painful. It reminded her of Tommy, and no matter how desperately she wanted to forget, he'd always be a part of her.

The rumbling in her stomach reminded Gabrielle that she hadn't eaten since this morning's muffin. She headed down to the kitchen for a late lunch. She hit pay dirt in the first cabinet she tried, pulling from it a small can of tuna. She opened the tin and spooned its contents into a bowl. Gabrielle looked into the refrigerator and located some mayonnaise and relish. Before she had a chance to mix the ingredients, the front door opened and a large cat darted into the kitchen, hopped up onto the counter, and began eating Gabrielle's lunch.

"I swear, that cat can smell an Amoré tuna dinner a block away," Stephanie informed her. "Who are you?"

"Gabrielle. I'm the new boarder," she explained weakly. Gabrielle felt like vomiting. She'd been making tuna salad out of cat food.

"Thanks for feeding Barclay. Usually I get stuck doing it," Stephanie said, curiously examining the condiments lined up on the counter. It looked as if the girl was making lunch. *Nah, it couldn't be,* Stephanie thought, dismissing the notion from her mind. She couldn't help staring at Gabrielle through skeptical eyes. The woman had a body like a centerfold and a face that could stop rush-hour traffic. And in all probability her eyes were truly blue. "By the way, his bowl is out by the back door."

"Ah, my cat . . . back home . . . ate tuna . . . the way we did," Gabrielle explained weakly.

Why aren't you here to help me? Gabrielle screamed in her head at her mother. *You promised you'd always be here to take care of me. I almost ate cat food. There was no cat on the label, only words. How was I supposed to know? Why did you leave me?*

"So, where did Beatrice find you?" Stephanie asked. "Hello. Gaby? Anybody home?"

"What?" She hadn't heard a word.

"I asked you where you met Beatrice."

"I—we— I'm sorry," she cried as she ran out of the room.

"Oh, great," Stephanie said to the cat. "Beautiful and flaky."

6

"Damn it, it's been six years. Just when *do* you think you'll be ready?"

Felicia grimaced. Now was not the time to get into this touchy subject. In just one hour she was due in Peter Montell's office. If the presentation went well this morning, at least two of her professional problems would be solved. The last thing Felicia needed on her mind was Trace and her untried reproductive system.

"How many times do we have to go over this? We decided to wait until I got the business up and running before we started a family."

"No. *We* didn't decide anything. It was *you* who decided that your little PR business was more important than having our baby."

"That's not fair, Trace. W and A is not more important than having a baby with you, but it is important to *me*." Felicia was trying not to sound as annoyed as she felt. Just as Trace could not understand her reluctance to start a family, neither could she understand his hurry. She was only twenty-eight. What was the rush?

"If *Wilcot* and Associates is not more important," Trace

challenged, emphasizing his displeasure at the use of her maiden name, "then why did you move your office out of the apartment?"

Felicia was trying hard to maintain her cool, but her husband was making it very difficult. Trace knew perfectly well that he was the reason she'd moved her office. As long as their home was also her place of business, he saw her work as a hobby, something to occupy her time after the housework was done, his dinner cooked, and his shirts retrieved from the laundry. While she worked at home, Trace had refused to take her seriously. "I needed more room," she said, reluctant to reopen that delicate topic.

"So for a few more square feet you've put so much pressure on yourself to bring in business just to pay your bills, it could be years before you make any money. Your Madison Avenue address is eating up all your profits. Here you may have been more cramped, but your overhead was nil. I paid all your bills *and* gave you an allowance."

Trace had a point. With her overhead so much higher, Felicia had placed herself in the uncomfortable position of merely trying to survive, let alone grow. "I've told you how much I appreciate your *monetary* support, but this is something I want to do on my own."

"I can't believe how selfish and spoiled you can be. It's all about what Felicia wants. What about what I want?"

"Trace Gordon, don't you dare talk to me about being selfish. This whole argument is taking place because you're not getting what you want, when you want it. You're looking for a nice little wife whose only function in life is to cater to you and your whims." Felicia grabbed her briefcase and headed toward the door. "I'm not that woman, Trace. Not anymore."

"What's so wrong with wanting a wife who puts her husband first?"

"What's so wrong with wanting a husband who doesn't live in the Stone Age? I don't have time for this, I have a meeting."

What the hell is happening to us? Felicia thought, slamming the door behind her. She and Trace couldn't go for one week without having a major argument, to say nothing of the minor spats that peppered the days in between. Felicia felt as if she were suffocating under his constant demands and chauvinistic attitudes. She hadn't vocalized it, but wanting to get her business solidly off the ground was the least of her reasons for not getting pregnant. Bringing a child into the instability of their marriage was not only unfair, it was crazy. Until she was sure she and Trace could get back on track, there would be no baby.

"Ms. Wilcot, please come in," Peter Montell said, ushering her into his plush office.

"Thank you, Mr. Montell."

"Call me Peter. I understand that yours is one of the best minority firms in the business."

Inwardly Felicia cringed at his words. She did not want to be known as a good *black* firm, just a good firm. Period. She was tired of the large companies thinking that a business like Wilcot & Associates was capable of working only on minority-related accounts. She wanted to work on the major-market pushes. But she had to get her foot in the door somehow, so she smiled and let the comment slide.

"Can I get you anything before we begin? Coffee? Tea?"

"A glass of water would be nice." Suddenly the inside of her mouth had turned to dust. Felicia had heard through the grapevine that hers was the last presentation. While creating the campaign, she had thought it was unique as well as effective, but now, standing in this office, her confidence waned.

"Thank you," Felicia said, accepting the drink. "I know what a busy man you are, so if you're ready to begin . . ."

"The floor is yours."

Felicia took a sip of her water and began her presentation. "Peter, your goal is to expand Montell's share of the black market. Your idea of beginning this expansion with the introduction of your new wine cooler is a good one, but you're caught in a rather delicate situation. You could run into problems if it's not handled correctly. My firm is prepared not only to help you successfully launch your product but to enhance your company image as well."

"To what kind of problems are you referring?"

"The kind that several years ago caused G. Heileman Brewing Company to pull Power Master, a malt liquor aimed at the black community, off the market. They spent a lot of time and money defending their honor. In fact, as you may recall, the company eventually went bankrupt."

"Go on."

"What Heileman saw is the same thing you do—a large, profitable consumer base. What they didn't seem to understand is that it's socially irresponsible to target low-income populations who already suffer disproportionately higher rates of alcohol-related problems." Felicia paused to take another sip of water and to assess Peter's interest in what she was saying. She knew she was taking a big chance, but—like him or not—Lexis Richards's argument made a lot of sense. This was the only way she could work on this account and live with herself.

"What Wilcot and Associates is proposing is an integrated advertising and public-relations campaign targeted at the *middle-class* African American community. We will position your product as the champagne of wine coolers. When people hear the name Montell, not only will they associate it with good times on the finer side of living, they'll know they're supporting a company that cares about them."

"And how will we do this?"

"By sponsoring The American Spirit Celebration, an exhibition tour of the National Black Rodeo."

"A rodeo? With black cowboys?"

"Most people don't know that in the Old West one out of three cowboys was black. Ever heard of Bill Pickett?"

"Can't say that I have."

"He was the first black rodeo star and the originator of steer wrestling," Felicia revealed.

"Interesting. Let's hear the rest of your idea."

"We'll target five cities—Los Angeles, New York, Washington, D.C., Atlanta, and Chicago—all cities with a considerable population of well-to-do African Americans."

Felicia observed Peter's thoughtful nod and continued her pitch.

"One month before the tour Montell would sponsor an art exhibit showcasing black participation in the settlement of the American West. The evening before the rodeo we'd hold a fund-raiser at the gallery, inviting the city's elite—both black and white. All proceeds would be matched by the company and go toward the Montell Spirits Pioneer Scholarship Fund, a fund we set up to award outstanding young minority students studying math and science."

"A very ambitious plan, Ms. Wilcot, but I don't see how we could pull off something of this magnitude and still meet our target date."

Felicia hesitated a moment and quickly reviewed her options. No matter how she sliced it, she had only one. "Peter, I must be candid. The tour is already in place. I have been working with the National Black Rodeo for over six months, but without the benefit of a major sponsor like

Montell, we aren't able to move ahead. And while I've spent untold hours working on a separate and unique presentation for your product launch, in the end, no other idea seemed as ingenious or potentially successful."

Peter Montell sat at his desk, his face devoid of expression. Felicia couldn't tell if she had made any kind of impression at all—good or bad. He took a deep breath, exhaled loudly through his nose, then removed his glasses and began to clean them. "It's not exactly what I had in mind."

Felicia's heart dropped. She'd failed.

"But I like it. It's innovative, it combines the worlds of art, sport, and education, and it shows the community we care. Give me a day or two to run the idea past some of my vice presidents," Peter said, enthusiastically shaking her hand. "I'll be in touch."

Felicia felt like screaming as she hung up the phone. She wanted to do back flips and sing a song. Instead she settled for a quick victory lap around her desk. Less than an hour after she'd returned to her office, Peter Montell had called with the good news: The account was hers, and the budget was just the way she liked it—big. To top that off, Keep the Faith Records had also decided to retain her services. With these new accounts she would be able to afford Stephanie full-time, thus allowing Felicia to concentrate on bringing in new clients.

"Felicia, your husband called while you were on the phone. He wants you to call him back."

Felicia debated returning Trace's call. She decided against it, preferring to savor her good news alone. Trace seemed to become increasingly difficult with every new account she picked up. The fact that she was reluctant to share even *good* news with her husband struck Felicia as a sad commentary on the state of their relationship.

"Okay. And Steph, we got the Montell account."

"I figured as much when I heard you running around. Congratulations."

"Thanks. This means we have a lot of work to do. I'd like to talk to you about coming on full-time."

"Let me think about it," Stephanie said, getting back to her desk to deal with the messenger walking through the door. Working a few hours a day was one thing, but being Felicia's full-time flunky was an entirely different matter. Stephanie had people to see and places to go, and unless Felicia was going to help her with that, she saw no point in subjecting herself to this drudgery on a nine-to-five basis.

7

Stephanie swore as she crushed this latest rejection letter in her hand. Out of six simultaneous submissions, she'd received in return six letters saying "Thanks, but no thanks" to her story on city bartenders. It was time to face the fact: Without any writing income, she was going to have to work full-time with Felicia.

"Now what?" she murmured, hearing a knock on her door. *Can't my life fall apart without an audience?* "It's open."

"Hi. Have you seen Bea?" Gabrielle asked.

"No, but I haven't been looking," Stephanie barked.

"Are you okay?"

"Read this," Stephanie said, thrusting the crumpled sheet in Gabrielle's face. "If this were the third kiss-off letter you'd received this week, would *you* be okay?"

Gabrielle glanced at the letter. By all appearances, she looked sincerely interested as she perused the brief communication. Inside she was shaking.

"What's wrong with these stupid editors?" Stephanie raged. "Don't they know insightful prose when they see it? Obviously not, judging from these fill-in-the-blank form letters they send out. They don't even have the imagination to reject me with style. Whose ass do I have to kiss to get something published?"

"No wonder you're upset," Gabrielle said, mentally thanking Stephanie for supplying her with the necessary clues to continue this conversation. "You really love to write, don't you?"

"Have you ever wanted something so bad that it consumed your entire life? No matter how hard you tried to forget about it and let it go, it just kept coming back—strong as ever."

Every time I look at a book or a magazine, a street sign, or the label on a can of food. Each time I think, This is it. This will be the day when all these letters come together and make sense. But they never do. "I always dreamed about being a model."

"I've wanted to be a famous writer since the first time I picked up a pen. I published my first story when I was eight years old. I wrote about my dog, Brewski, and the *Sunday News* published it. The first time I saw my words in print, I was hooked. I knew right then I wanted to be a writer."

"Your parents must have been very proud."

"Oh, yeah. They were real proud, all right," Stephanie remembered bitterly. "My dad never got around to reading my story. Said he would, but then a fight came on, and that was that. And my stepmother was so proud, she used my story to wrap the garbage."

Gabrielle could see that Stephanie's memories were painful. "You want to go to the movies with Beatrice and me?" she asked.

"Can't. Jack will be here soon. I'm cooking dinner for him. Which reminds me, we're almost out of soy sauce and it's your turn to do the household shopping tomorrow."

"Oh, come on, Stephanie, trade with me. I'll do the laundry again," Gabrielle pleaded.

"Forget it. I'm not schlepping around the grocery store while you sit back with a book waiting for the spin cycle to finish. Why is it such a big deal?"

"I just hate grocery shopping," Gabrielle said, not willing to reveal the difficulty shopping presented her. Buying for herself was easy because she'd learned to recognize the labels and logos of her favorite foods, and her list rarely varied. Gabrielle was a loyal brand shopper. Since she couldn't read the labels, generic store brands were out as far as she was concerned, even though years buying name brands had cost her hundreds of dollars.

Shopping for others presented a whole myriad of problems. Many items, like pasta or bread, she could pick out through recognition, but choosing others was much more complicated. Often the pictures on labels helped, but sometimes—say, trying to distinguish Campbell's minestrone soup from Manhattan clam chowder, or Minute Maid's tangerine-orange from its original orange juice—the task was much more difficult.

"Sorry, but I'm not food-shopping three weeks in a row. Besides, we only need a few things, like more toilet paper. And don't get that Marcel brand again. It's like using sandpaper."

"I grabbed it by mistake." Gabrielle swallowed back the embarrassment of another time when she'd mistakenly brought home a bottle of Lestoil cleaner thinking that it was olive oil because of its similar color and container.

"Yeah, and you got the wrong juice, too. I like cran*apple* not cran*raspberry*. In fact, here," Stephanie said, grabbing a sheet of memo paper and handing it and a pencil to Gabrielle. "Make a list."

"I don't need a list. I'll remember."

"Who was it that forgot the coffee and flour the last time? Write it down."

Gabrielle accepted the pencil and paper, unwilling to argue and raise any suspicions. While Stephanie walked around rattling off the names of various sundries and food-stuffs, Gabrielle recorded them by using symbols and letters to represent each item. For bread she quickly sketched a rectangular loaf, then drew an egg, two rectangles with a B on top to represent butter, and a steaming cup of coffee. The list grew without problem until Stephanie stumped Gabrielle by mentioning cumin.

"What's wrong?" Stephanie demanded to know, noticing she'd stopped writing.

"Cumin?"

"It's a spice. For Mexican dishes."

"How do you spell that?"

"I don't know. C-U-M-I-N. Now I forgot what else we need. Let me see your list." Before Gabrielle could protest, Stephanie had grabbed the paper from her. "What the hell is this?"

"I just felt a little . . . I don't know—creative," Gabrielle explained with a nervous laugh. "You as a writer should understand that."

"Yeah, I understand creativity, but if your lists always look like this, I understand why you never get the shopping right. I have to go get dinner ready."

"Have fun tonight," Gabrielle said, taking the shopping list back.

"I will. With Jack, I always do."

"Damn it!" Stephanie screamed as she dropped the hot lid and rushed to the sink to cool her burning skin. Running the cold water on her hand, she surveyed the mess surrounding her. Never mind that the kitchen looked as if the food fight of the century had just taken place in it. It was the withered fruits of her labor that depressed her. The rice was hard and undercooked, the vegetables oversteamed and mushy, and instead of tender nuggets of juicy poultry, petrified chicken rocks sat at the bottom of her new wok. *Well,* she told herself, *dinner is ruined and Jack is due in forty-five minutes. Now what?*

Why had she promised him a home-cooked Chinese dinner, particularly when she could barely scramble eggs? Why? Because she wanted to impress Jack. She'd spent an untold amount of time these past three months finding out what he liked and then learning to do it. She was determined to transform herself into his perfect woman and convince Jack that he'd made the ideal love connection.

What to do? What to do? she thought as she drained her wineglass. Bea was at the movies with Gabrielle. She'd have to figure this out on her own. *Voilà! What a clever girl you are,* Stephanie congratulated herself. She'd call the Szechuan Palace and order dinner. It was so easy. She could throw the food into that stupid wok in an attempt to look authentic and serve it up with a smile. Just to be on the safe side, Stephanie put a third bottle of wine in the refrigerator to chill. Once she got Jack's taste buds good and drunk, he'd never be the wiser.

He was already half an hour late, but Jack decided to get out of the cab three blocks from Stephanie's place. The walk would do him good. He had to cool down. This afternoon with Nicole had been particularly volatile—as evidenced by the scratches on his face and wrists. Their relationship was finally over. Her incredible face and impressive body had ceased to compensate for the fact that she was just too demanding. So different from Stephanie, who couldn't seem to do enough for him.

Every time he turned around, Stephanie was making some sort of effort to please him. Like tonight's invitation—a note attached to a tin of supposedly homemade cookies. He'd bet a hundred bucks that they were from Mrs. Fields's kitchen, not Stephanie's. But what the hell. It was vintage Stephanie—indiscretions and half-truths, from those fake green eyes to her bottled red hair. She was creative and inventive and she lied like the proverbial rug, but she was a harmless diversion after crazy Nicole. Besides, he didn't want to marry her. He wanted to sleep with her. Bar none, Stephanie Bancroft was the best fuck he'd come across in a very long time.

Not only was Stephanie great in bed, she was a cheap date. Jack knew he was using her, but she was so willing to be used. Stephanie was like an amusement park where the rides were free and the lines were short. Who wouldn't take advantage? He also knew that the ride would have to come to an end soon. Lately Stephanie had become increasingly possessive and clingy, two qualities he found deadly unattractive.

When it came to women, Jack loved what every red-blooded male with an ego and an ounce of confidence loved—a challenge. Throw in a little friendly competition, and Jack was at his best. Sure, you won some, you lost some. But in the big scheme of things—as for a greyhound at the racetrack—the real fun was in the pursuit. For Jack, the things that followed—love, commitment, marriage—could never compete with the thrill of the chase.

Jack Hollis had no intention of being tied down to one woman. He was a good-looking heterosexual male who made enough money with his business to live a comfortable life. Why throw all that away for the drudgery of monogamy? He'd settle down when he was ready to have kids—maybe in another ten or twelve years. Maybe.

Stephanie watched from the parlor window as Jack climbed the stairs leading to the front door. The sight of his well-built torso caused her to bite her lip in anticipation. No matter how many times she'd seen it, naked or otherwise, Jack's body never failed to make her catch her breath.

"Hi," she purred, looking up at him, her eyes full of lusty promise. She pressed her body to his in a welcoming hug. Right away he knew that before any food passed his lips he had a more urgent appetite to satisfy.

"Sorry I'm late," he said, kissing her long and hard.

Stephanie felt Jack's erection through his jeans. His kiss became more urgent as his lips devoured hers and his tongue tickled the inside of her mouth. Her breath became short as she clung to him both with her arms and mouth. She felt his fingers swiftly undo the buttons on her shirt and peel it away, dropping it to the floor. Jack's mouth began a seductive journey down her neck and across her shoulders, until his lips came to rest on her waiting nipples. He nibbled them with practiced expertise until Stephanie heard a lazy groan escape her lips. Hearing her excitement, Jack lingered there, rolling her erect nipples gently between his teeth. Stephanie continued to moan, arching her back and pressing herself against him.

Suddenly Jack pushed her against the foyer wall. He pulled up her skirt, only to find the treasure he sought unobstructed by panties. He slid his hand between her legs, coaxing apart the lips of her moist vagina with his finger. He began massaging her, teasing her into madness. Jack looked directly into Stephanie's eyes and found them heavy with desire. "I want to fuck you *now*," he whispered urgently in her ear. Stephanie could only smile in agreement, her entire being locked in his gaze as he dropped his pants.

Taking him into her hands, she guided Jack into her waiting body. Effortlessly, he lifted her off the floor, and

Stephanie wrapped her legs around his hips. Together they rocked vigorously, his hands on her behind, their lips locked in a hungry kiss. She came almost immediately, feeling momentarily suspended in a pool of delightful sensations. Finally Jack's body shuddered, and he held Stephanie so tightly against his hard sweating body that she could hardly breathe.

As Jack withdrew from her, he could feel his heartbeat slowly returning to normal. "That was one hell of an appetizer." He smiled, pulling up his pants.

"Just wait till you see what I've cooked up for dessert."

8

Gabrielle emerged from the Fifty-ninth Street subway station and into the summer sun smiling. It was a beautiful June morning, and for the first time in a very long time she felt happy. The pain of losing Helene had dulled to a manageable ache, mainly due to Bea's unwavering love and attention. She'd even grown accustomed to Stephanie and her ever-changing moods. Yes, things were going better than she could have ever wished. True, she wasn't a model yet, but at least she had a job—a job that for nearly four months she'd proven to be very good at.

Gabrielle was proud of herself. She was succeeding without anyone realizing her secret. With her co-workers' help it had taken her only two days to memorize the placement of every variety of muffin and bagel the shop sold. While the rest of the staff read the handwritten signs, Gabrielle developed her own system of counting over, down, and up to arrive at the requested item.

"Hey, wait up," a familiar voice called. Gabrielle turned to see one of her co-workers.

"Hi. Marta, you're in early today."

"I need at least two cups of java before feeding time."

"What's this?" Gabrielle asked, pointing to the huge banner hanging above the shop's doors. "Free—" she said, reading aloud the only word she recognized. Through the years she had acquired a small vocabulary of words she identified on sight. Words like "stop," "exit," "in," "out," "women," "men." For Gabrielle, trying to decipher the rest of the banner's copy was like trying to solve one of her favorite jigsaw puzzles without all the necessary pieces.

" 'Free coffee with every purchase. Today only,' " Marta recited, cutting Gabrielle off. "Has Louie lost his mind? There's going to be a stampede in this joint."

"Marta, Gabrielle," a new voice called out to them as they entered the shop. "I'm Paul, your new manager," he told them, his voice cracking slightly. Paul had recognized the two from Louie's description.

"Where's Louie?" Marta asked.

The new manager. Gabrielle's heart sank. A new manager meant new rules and new problems.

"Uncle—I mean Louie's opening up a franchise on the East Side, so I'll be running this place. We've got a lot to do before the store opens, so shall we get started?" he asked, trying to sound authoritative, but failing miserably. "First off, Marta will help in the back with the inventory. Gabrielle will stay out front with Chuck, who'll work the cash register," he said, avoiding her eyes.

"What's up with the free coffee?" Marta asked, dreading the idea of spending the day counting flour sacks with this geek.

"It's just a promotional gimmick to get us some attention. There's a new gourmet bakery opening up down the block. By the way, I added five new muffins and reorganized the trays this morning. I don't know what system you've been using, but I think you'll find that by arranging everything alphabetically, things will run more efficiently."

Reorganized the trays! Gabrielle felt light-headed. It would take her days to memorize the new arrangement. But she had no other choice. Doing inventory was definitely not an option. She'd have to stay out front and do her best. She just hoped it was good enough.

"Paul, would you write down the names of the new muffins?" Gabrielle asked. "That way I can push the new flavors right away until I get them memorized."

"Now, that's the kind of thinking I like."

Marta coughed to get Gabrielle's attention and with a smile began rubbing the tip of her nose. Gabrielle smiled and stuck out her tongue in response. Marta might be teasing her for being a brownnoser, but she wasn't after brownie points. If Gabrielle had the letter combinations in front of her, she could match them with the words on the tray cards.

I can do this, Gabrielle told herself as she took her position behind the counter and began trying to sort out the stock in front of her. She was able to locate the first two flavors on the list before being interrupted by a customer.

"Morning. Carrot muffin, please."

"Sure." Gabrielle's eyes scouted the trays until they came to rest on C-A-R-R-O-T. The orange bits of color confirmed her find.

"There you go. Hi, Denny."

"Good morning, Gabrielle. I'll have my usual, please."

Gabrielle knew that Denny's usual was an apple-oat-bran muffin with cream cheese. The problem was, she just didn't know where to locate it. They sold apple, banana, and just plain oat-bran muffins. They all looked the same with white oats sprinkled on top. *How can I tell which is which?* Gabrielle was beginning to feel flustered. Paul's coffee incentive was working. There were at least a dozen people standing in front of her, and they were obviously in a hurry.

"You wanna get a move on? I got a job to get to," someone yelled out.

"Over here. To the left," Denny prompted, pointing to the correct tray.

"Thanks. I'm sorry. We reorganized this morning. Everything is in a different place," she apologized loud enough for the others to hear.

"Do you think you can find me two pecan muffins?" the next man in line asked.

Gabrielle looked over the baked goods in front of her, hoping that the pecan muffins would somehow make themselves known to her. She looked at Paul's list again in search of a clue. Nothing.

"Look, honey, are you going to stand there all day or what?"

"Forget this. Free coffee or not, I don't have time to wait," declared one woman as she departed the store in a huff.

"Read the signs, honey. Everything's marked."

Read the signs. Read the signs. The words paralyzed her.

"Hello. Can I get some service here? I'd like my damn muffins."

READ THE SIGNS, she commanded her brain. Gabrielle stood frozen behind the counter, staring in vain at the trays in front of her. Panic and shame washed over her. She really thought she could pull it off—work in the real world, like a normal person. Who was she trying to kid? She wasn't normal. She was a freak.

"Hey, what the hell? What about my order?"

"Can we get some help here?"

Hearing the commotion, Paul stepped out front in time to see a small mob of hungry customers waiting noisily to be served and the back of Gabrielle's head as she ran sobbing out the door.

9

Think, Stephanie. Don't you know any place that's hiring?" Beatrice asked.

"Really, Bea, I don't know of anything. All my friends are either bartenders or waiters. Gaby's too young to work in a bar, and these days the good restaurants only hire experienced people." She was dying to point out to Beatrice that Gabrielle was obviously no rocket scientist. She couldn't even keep a job peddling muffins.

Stephanie was finding it difficult to squash her growing resentment over the way Gabrielle had come in and taken over the household. Ever since she'd moved in, Bea had basically ignored Stephanie, spending all her time and energy hovering over Gabrielle, catering to all her needs and trying to help solve all her problems.

Who's going to help me? Stephanie had her own problems. Forget that it was becoming painfully clear that her career as a writer was in the toilet just waiting for someone to flush it down. Stephanie's most pressing quandary at the moment was Jack. He was sending her distinct signals that he was losing interest in their relationship. Not only had he stood her up again last night, he was effectively dodging her phone calls.

"Well, what about this big rodeo thing you're organizing? Surely you can find something for her?"

The first leg of the Montell American Spirit Celebration was about to kick off in New York. She and Felicia had spent months finalizing the logistics for the five-city tour. The gallery exhibit, featuring the work of a Philadelphia sculptor, Phil Sumpter, was scheduled to open next Friday at Harlem's eminent Studio Museum, followed by an all-black rodeo on Saturday and Sunday. Felicia had done a yeoman's job in getting press coverage, and the rodeo had been sold out for weeks. The RSVP list for the preview party had grown long with enthusiastic responses. Folks without invitations were lobbying hard to get on the exclusive guest list. By all indications, this was going to be a blowout success.

Felicia was certainly excited, but Stephanie was less than thrilled. Yes, she was going to one of the biggest parties of the year, but she was relegated to roaming the room, passing out engraved wineglasses stuffed with gift certificates. An idea clicked in Stephanie's head. Maybe there was something Gabrielle could do after all. If she could persuade Felicia to hire Gabrielle, Stephanie would be free to eat, drink, and be merry with the beautiful people.

"Maybe I do have something for her."

"Wonderful!" Beatrice said, clapping her hands in delight. "Why don't you go tell her now, so she has something to look forward to."

"Let me make a phone call first."

Stephanie called Felicia and then walked downstairs to find Gabrielle stretched out on the couch, reading a book and listening to her Sony walkman.

"What are you reading?" Stephanie asked.

"The Firm."

"You're *always* reading and listening to music at the same time. I don't know how you can concentrate. That's not one of my tapes, is it?" Stephanie asked, reaching for the headphones.

"No, it's *mine*," Gabrielle said, jumping up quickly. She didn't want to have to explain to Stephanie why she was listening to *The Firm* on tape while pretending to read the book.

"Just checking. I came in to see if you'd be interested in a modeling job?"

"Really?" Gabrielle asked, definitely intrigued.

"Kind of. It's only one night, mind you. I need someone at this party I've been putting together to hand out gift certificates."

"I can do that, but—"

"If you're going to ask about money, it was strictly volunteer, but I did manage to get you fifty bucks. Besides, it's a great opportunity for you to mingle and be seen. You never know who you might meet at a party like this."

"But what am I going to wear?"

Good question, Stephanie thought. After all, she was responsible for convincing her boss to hire Gabrielle. Stephanie couldn't chance Gabrielle's being a bad reflection on her judgment. On the other hand, she couldn't afford to have Gabrielle upstage her either, not with Jack in attendance.

"Don't worry about it. I'll help you find something."

"The problem is—well, I don't have much money."

"You really are from small-town U.S.A. You don't need much money. You go to the store, buy a dress, and wear it to the party. Just don't take off the tags, and whatever you do don't spill anything on yourself. The next day, you return it."

"You can do that?"

"Honey, you can do whatever it takes to get what you want."

Felicia looked at her watch. It was six-thirty, and the florist had just placed the last of the huge silver milk cans filled with sunflowers. She and Stephanie had been here since four o'clock, checking on the art exhibit and overseeing the final arrangements for the evening. The gallery looked splendid. The rodeo theme had been played up throughout the space, from the bales of hay artistically stacked in the corners to the cowboy hats and yellow kerchiefs worn by the waiters. With the help of the Studio Museum's curator, she'd managed to amass an amazing collection of art that validated the vast contributions of African Americans to the Old West.

Felicia decided to take her own private tour of the gallery before the crowd rushed in. Among the art decorating the cool white walls were prints by Frederic Remington, considered by most to be the greatest cowboy artist of the last Western frontier. But the stars of the show were the powerfully detailed and authentic sculptures of black cowboys by artist Phil Sumpter. The gallery spotlights danced off the dozen or so terra cotta pieces covered in bronze patina. Some of Sumpter's work was modeled after real people, like Bass Reeves, the first black appointed a U.S. marshal. The majority were representative figures including *The Wrangler, The Brander,* and a series of three Buffalo soldiers. Each sculpture, through Sumpter's command of detail, brought to life the pride and pain of black people in the Old West.

Felicia's eagle eye surveyed the room. This was the biggest client event she had ever thrown, and she wanted everything to be perfect. In one hour this place would be packed with an eclectic group of politicians, athletes, and other celebrities—from Whitney Houston and Bobby Brown to Eddie Murphy and Patrick Ewing.

Television crews outside in the August heat were setting up their equipment to catch the arrival of the guests. Alongside were the paparazzi and adoring fans standing on alert, waiting for a glimpse of the famous faces scheduled to attend. Dozens of New York City's finest were taking their positions up and down the block, keeping the inevitable party crashers at bay and providing extra insurance that the evening's guests would arrive and depart safe and sound.

"Stephanie, please keep an eye out for Tremaine. I don't want our first scholarship recipient to get lost in the crowd."

"Okay."

"And remember, when the mayor arrives—"

"I go up to the curator's office and bring Mr. Montell down into the gallery. And I've asked them to turn up the air-conditioning so the guests don't melt in this heat. Don't worry, Felicia, everything is under control."

"I know I'm being a pain, but I just want everything to work out."

"It will."

"What time is your friend supposed to arrive?"

"Gabrielle will be here at seven sharp."

"Good. What did you tell her to wear?" Felicia asked, unwilling to let even the slightest detail slip by her.

"I told her to pick out something that fit with tonight's western theme. I can only assume she found something appropriate," Stephanie said, a sly smile tugging at her lips. The dress she'd pulled from the Macy's summer clearance rack reeked of bad taste without turning Gabrielle into the evening's joke. It was a patchwork of red, white, and blue bandana print, complete with fringe dripping from the underside of its sleeves. The dress was much too large, but at Stephanie's insistence, Gabrielle had brought it home for

Bea to alter. Stephanie had yet to see the outcome of Beatrice's handiwork.

"Good. Okay, now let's go over these additions to the guest list. Who is this Harry Grain? His name sounds vaguely familiar."

"He's on the press list, but it doesn't say what paper he's with," she said, knowing full well that Harry Grain was a gossip columnist for the tabloid *Star Diary*. Stephanie also knew that Felicia would flip out knowing that she'd invited this "dirt-disher" to the party, but Stephanie, intrigued by his tart-tongued gossip, wanted to meet him.

"Lexis Richards! How did that idiot get invited?"

"He called and said he was going to be in town and wanted to come to the party. I didn't think you'd mind, since he's really big news now that *Southeast* has premiered to rave reviews."

"I don't know why. That movie is garbage. I walked out after the first five minutes. Just be sure to keep him as far away from me as possible. Who is Jack Hollis?"

"I believe he's the photographer's assistant," Stephanie lied. She had her fingers crossed, praying that Felicia wouldn't ask any further questions. At the last minute she had included Jack's name on the guest list, knowing that Felicia had strictly forbidden any further additions. Stephanie was hoping like hell that the magnitude of the evening, combined with her outfit—a sexy suede halter dress adorned with Navajo-inspired beading—would help light a fire under their fizzling relationship.

"Omigod! The photographer—"

"Don't worry. I told him to be here at seven as well."

"Thank you," Felicia said, calming down slightly. *When this is over, I have to find a way to give Stephanie a raise.* In so many ways Stephanie had been a real find. She worked well without supervision, was resourceful, and took the initiative to get things done, allowing Felicia to concentrate on expanding and serving her clients. With W&A showing signs of continued growth, there was no way Felicia could operate with maximum efficiency without Stephanie Bancroft backing her up.

"Phone for a Mrs. Gordon," the caterer's voice interrupted.

"That's me," Felicia answered, knowing it was Trace. She walked to the desk located in the entry of the museum and picked up the phone. "Trace, where are you?"

"I'm still at the club. Our match ran long, and we're just sitting down to dinner. I'm sorry, baby, but by the time I get finished eating, shower, and change—"

"The party will be over."

This is just like him, Felicia thought, not wanting to hear the rest of his lame excuse. Last month when he'd needed her at that blasted company dinner, where was she? Right by his side, even though she had to catch the red-eye from Los Angeles to be there. And when the senior partner and his wife insisted that she and Trace be their guests for the weekend at their Southampton home, hadn't she made it, even though it cost her the Bostic account? Now, on the biggest night of her career, where was he? On the goddamn tennis court.

"Felicia, you know if Curtis wasn't my biggest client I'd leave right now."

"Don't bother. Your biggest client needs you more than I do," Felicia said, slamming down the receiver and mentally cursing her husband. He knew how important this evening was to her. He knew and simply didn't give a damn.

"Is everything okay?"

Felicia looked up only to see one of the most beautiful women she'd ever set eyes on. *The guests can't be arriving already.* She peeked at her watch. It wasn't even seven o'clock yet.

"Everything is fine. I just wasn't expecting any guests so early. Your name, please."

"I'm not a guest. I'm Gabrielle Donovan. Stephanie asked me to help out this evening."

"Felicia, the caterer needs you, and—" Stephanie stopped in midsentence. She stood in wide-eyed, open-mouthed amazement as she looked at the stunning creature in front of her. She couldn't believe how incredible Gabrielle looked. On the hanger the dress looked like something straight from Elly May Clampett's closet. Yet, on Gabrielle, it might have been snatched off a Milanese catwalk. With her honey-bronzed hair piled high on the top of her head in a sexy tousle of curls, Gabrielle looked as if she'd stepped off the pages of some fashion magazine. Forced by shock into total honesty, Stephanie had to admit, though never aloud, that Gabrielle Donovan was born to be a model.

By eight o'clock the gallery was bubbling with the lively chatter of people enjoying themselves. The room was in constant motion, as guests walked around the gallery admiring the fine art. Felicia circled the space, keeping a critical eye out for the smallest detail that might need her attention. She was well aware that the success of this entire Montell Spirits campaign rested on rave reviews from tonight's affair, from both the press and the positive word of mouth passed along this exclusive network.

Felicia smiled as she looked around. By all indications the evening was proceeding smoothly. She watched as Phylicia and Ahmad Rashad engaged in an animated conversation with former congressman and now president of the United Negro College Fund, Bill Gray. While actor Wesley

Snipes stood solo admiring the sculpture *Yahoo,* a beautifully detailed bronze piece of two cowboys, their black faces thrown back, mouths open wide, howling at the moon, a gaggle of female fans stood checking out his artistic lines.

"Ms. Wilcot? Aubree Stephens, Black Entertainment Television. This is quite a history lesson you've got here."

"Most Americans only know the Old West through stories of cowboys and Indians where whites are the heroes, Native Americans the villains, and black people nonexistent. Peter Montell and his company thought this would be a perfect opportunity to begin to set the record straight."

"What do you think the public will get out of seeing this exhibit?"

"Besides the opportunity to experience some great art, any person seeing this exhibit will walk away having learned that there is a lot more to black history than slavery. Take the Buffalo soldiers over there. There were four black regiments formed after the Civil War to patrol the West. They were called 'Buffalo Soldiers' by the Cheyenne Indians because of their heavy winter coats, curly hair, and fierce fighting. They helped capture Geronimo and track down Billy the Kid. Eighteen of these soldiers won Medals of Honor for their actions in the West and the Spanish-American War. They were legitimate black heroes. So if you come see this incredible exhibit, you're going to walk away with a new understanding of the vast and varied contributions African-Americans have made to this country."

Leaving the reporter, Felicia decided to have a quick glass of wine in hopes of calming her nerves. In fifteen minutes she'd introduce Peter Montell, who would make the scholarship presentation.

"You're Felicia Wilcot, aren't you?" asked a well-dressed black woman.

"Guilty as charged."

"This is absolutely fabulous. So nice to see our history on display. I'm Ruthanna Beverly from ABW Publishing. I'd love to do a fashion shoot as well right here in the gallery for one of our magazines. The Western look is going to be very big next season. Who could ask for a better backdrop? Let's have lunch and talk about it. Give me a call," she said, handing Felicia her card.

And who could ask for better publicity for the tour, Felicia thought, immediately seeing the public-relations potential. "I'll call you next week," Felicia promised, slipping the card into her pocket with the dozen others she'd received.

"Felicia, there you are," Stephanie said, rushing up to her boss. "You'd better get up front," she said with quiet urgency. "We have a little problem."

Felicia deposited her wineglass with the nearest waiter and hurried toward the front of the gallery. As she approached, she could hear angry voices that had previously been drowned out by the music and cocktail chatter. She was confronted by a small mob of press people, including a camera crew from the local ABC station. In the middle of the hubbub Lexis Richards, once again dressed in his "I don't give a damn what the invitation says" uniform of jeans and a T-shirt, stood arguing with an impeccably groomed older man. Felicia had seen him earlier wandering around the gallery.

"Man, what part of 'No comment' don't you understand?" Lexis asked angrily.

"You have nothing to say about the fact that two gang members were shot in the theater parking lot where *your* movie is playing?"

"Please lower your voices," Felicia asked, rushing into the fray. "Now, will someone tell me what is going on here?"

"This jackleg reporter is trying to tell me that because of my picture, some kind of gang war is about to erupt."

"You feel no responsibility at all for the violent behavior that your movie is causing? Even though, as I hear it, the picture is just one big shoot-out," the reporter continued.

"Man, get out of my face with that bullshit."

"Be quiet. I'll handle this," Felicia demanded.

"I don't need you to—"

"I said I'll handle this," Felicia shot back in a steely voice that left no room for discussion. "Mr. . . ."

"Harry Grain. *Star Diary.*"

No wonder his name sounded so familiar. Harry Grain was infamous for his weekly gossip column, which one celebrity described as a collection of "something old, something new, something borrowed, nothing true."

"You write for that rag?" Lexis asked with obvious disdain. "You're no reporter, you're a damn storyteller."

Felicia shot Lexis an icy look that resulted in his immediate silence. "Mr. Grain, you just said, as you heard it. Did you see *Southeast?*"

The expression of discomfort on Harry Grain's face, along with his silence, confirmed Felicia's suspicion. The man hadn't even seen the film. He was making an uninformed judgment and trashing another man's reputation based on hearsay and misinformation.

"You're talking all this yang and you haven't even seen my movie?" Lexis asked in disbelief.

Ignoring Lexis, Felicia continued, "Mr. Grain, I'm sure if you checked your facts you'd find that the incident you are referring to took place not because Mr. Richards's movie provoked it, but because the movie theater had oversold tickets, causing these kids to congregate in the parking lot, where, unfortunately, tempers got out of hand and the shooting occurred. I'm sure you will agree that to blame Mr.

Richards for this unhappy incident is doing him a huge injustice. Why, that would be like blaming Julia Roberts and her movie *Pretty Woman* for prostitution."

There was a twitter of laughter from the small crowd that had gathered. Harry, embarrassed by the absurdity of his allegations and the obvious allegiance of the crowd to Richards, turned and walked out of the gallery without uttering a single word. *You bitch. Nobody makes me look like a fool. You haven't heard the last from me. Not by a long shot.*

"Miss Thing to the rescue." Lexis smiled. "Go 'head, girl!" he said, congratulating Felicia as he followed her into the curator's office. He was genuinely impressed by the way she had taken control and quickly defused what could have become an ugly situation.

Felicia turned to him, eyes flickering with contempt. "The only thing I was interested in rescuing was my party. No one—not some sleazemonger and certainly no street urchin—is going to ruin my professional reputation."

"Street urchin?"

"And in the future, if you want the media to treat you like an intelligent black man, start acting like one. Your combative attitude does nothing for your image. You might think about that as well when you're trying to finance your next project," Felicia hissed as she turned and headed toward the door.

Lexis followed behind and grabbed Felicia by the arm. "So my 'attitude' is why your father and his friends refused to invest in my next movie?"

"That and the fact that based on your description, your next film, just like your current one, is boring and the worst form of black exploitation."

"What the hell are you talking about?"

"If a white director had made *Southeast,* with its stereotypical black males and blatant disrespect toward women, he'd be branded a racist. But because a black person wrote, produced, directed it, and is making *big* money off of it, it's not considered exploitation? I don't think so."

"I'm not exploiting anybody. *Southeast* is about real life in the 'hood. It's a story seen and told by someone who's been there, who's lived it. Sorry, princess, we all didn't grow up in the 'burbs eatin' grits out of a silver spoon."

"True, but now *you* can afford to roll out of the ghetto in the back of a limousine," Felicia retorted sarcastically.

"That's beside the point."

"You're right. Here's the point: Why not make a film that glorifies the other side of black life? The good side—the side the evening news never sees fit to show."

"Did *you* see my flick?"

"I saw enough."

"Obviously not, because if you'd stuck it out you'd know that *Southeast* is about family and self-love. Yeah, there's a lot of cussin' and fussin', but the message is positive."

Felicia felt warm as embarrassment replaced the smugness of her earlier posture. "And what about the messenger?"

"What about him?"

"If you're all about positivity, why can't you be in the same room with me without insulting me or my family? What is it about me, Mr. Richards, that irritates you so much?"

"Maybe if you didn't always feel the need to huff and puff and blow the brother down, we'd be cool."

"And maybe if you knocked that boulder-sized chip off your shoulder, you'd realize that disagreeing doesn't mean disrespecting. It doesn't really matter, because I am blowing you off for the last time." Felicia turned and walked away. *Men! First Trace, now Lexis Richards—the hell with 'em!*

Lexis felt a smile tugging at his lips as he watched Felicia gracefully maneuver herself through the crowded room and to the podium. He was perplexed by the reaction she caused in him. She was attractive enough, if you like the thin, redbone type. The Jada Pinketts and Halle Berrys of the world did nothing for him. He preferred his women the color of dark chocolate, with natural hair and a generous behind. With her light skin and long hair, Felicia epitomized the coveted, wanna-look-white image of many black women— an image he was out to destroy. Additionally, the lifestyle Felicia represented—summers in Martha's Vineyard, BMWs in the driveway, and perfect pedigrees—repelled him. No, it wasn't her looks or her lifestyle that intrigued him. It was Felicia's spunk and mental agility that impressed Lexis the most.

"Hi, sexy, can I interest you in a quickie?" Stephanie offered, pulling Jack into an isolated corner and kissing him with erotic desire.

"Not now. We're in public," Jack said, gently pushing her away.

"You didn't say that in the bathroom at Le Bar Bat three weeks ago."

"We were both pretty wasted. Steph, we need to talk."

"Talking is not quite what I had in mind," Stephanie cooed.

"Look, you're a great girl. I don't feel right keeping you all to myself," Jack said, trying to let her down gently. "Maybe we should see other people."

Stephanie winced at the rejection. "You don't want to see me anymore?"

"We can still go out from time to time. I just think we need to slow things down."

"But I . . ." *love you*. The words died in her throat. "What if I don't want to see other people?"

"Steph, you deserve more than take-out food and a wild romp in the sack."

Stephanie felt her world spinning apart. *He doesn't mean it. Even if he does, I can make it all right again.* "Jack, tell me what I did wrong and I can fix it."

"You didn't do anything wrong. It's me. Look, maybe we should talk about this later," he suggested. Stephanie looked as if she was about to lose it, and he didn't want her making a scene. He stepped aside as a young man wearing a black suede jacket brushed past them. Jack followed the man with his eyes, mainly to avoid looking at the tears welling up in Stephanie's.

"Can we get together after the party? Jack?" she pleaded.

"What? Sorry. That woman, the one over in the corner. She looks familiar."

You just broke up with me and already you're on the prowl, Stephanie thought, turning around to see who was captivating Jack's attention. She couldn't believe it. With all the big names occupying the room, Jack's eyes were glued to the one corner that held Gabrielle Donovan. She was standing there looking statuesque and perfect with an attractive, European-looking man. He was doing most of the talking, while Gabrielle stood listening and smiling bashfully. Nearby was the man in the suede jacket who appeared to be listening intently to their conversation as he studied one of the sculptures.

"Oh, her. Isn't that dress a scream," Stephanie said, hoping her eyes had played a nasty trick on her, but knowing by Jack's appreciative stare, they hadn't.

"Do you know her? Is she a model?"

"No, she's just some girl we hired for the night. Let's go

get a drink," she suggested. Stephanie wanted to get him on the other side of the room before Gabrielle wandered over.

"Steph," Gabrielle called out as she hurried over to join them. Excitement radiated from every pore on her face. In her hand she held a business card.

Too late, Stephanie thought. "Hi," she answered flatly. Almost immediately Stephanie could once again feel herself developing an acute case of the "terrible too's." It happened every time she was around Gabrielle. No matter how good she felt about herself, once Gabrielle appeared she immediately felt *too* short, *too* fat, and *too* terribly average.

"Hi. You must be Jack. Stephanie has told me a lot about you," Gabrielle said, smiling broadly. "I'm Gabrielle."

"*You're* Gabrielle? The same Gabrielle that lives with, uh . . ." Jack lost his train of thought, his attention drawn to her mouth. Her succulent lips framed a pearly-white smile that was absolutely devastating. It was the kind of smile that, once bestowed, would make you forget things—like what time it was, what state you were in, or your current lover's name. This woman was nothing like the naïve country bumpkin Stephanie described.

"Stephanie," Stephanie interjected flatly. She could see the twinkle of adoration in Jack's eyes and the way he gave Gabrielle that half-cocked, sexy-beyond-belief, you're-the-only-woman-in-this-room grin. Stephanie felt the bile rising in her throat. He was giving it to Gabrielle with both guns loaded, and right in front of her no less.

"Is there something you need?" she asked with a smile that didn't quite reach her eyes.

"Not at all. In fact, everything is great. I wanted to tell you first. See that guy over there, the one with the ponytail talking to Susan Taylor? He's a photographer. He said he knew some people in the business and could help me get started modeling."

"That's great," Stephanie said with phony verve, "but I wouldn't get my hopes up if I were you. This kind of thing happens all the time in New York. Who was that other guy, standing next to you?"

"I don't know. He didn't say anything. He just stood there."

"Probably his partner in crime. They must be some kind of flimflam artists." Stephanie took great pleasure in watching Gabrielle's bubble slowly deflate.

"Did he mention money? Any kind of fees?" Jack asked with concern.

"Not at all. He just asked if I ever thought about modeling and said he'd love to take some test shots of me."

"Really, Gabrielle, I can't believe you fell for that old line. Let me guess, he wanted you to come over to his place and pose for some lingerie ads."

"No. He gave me his business card and told me he'd call to set up a session at his studio."

"May I?" Jack asked, reaching for the card in Gabrielle's hand. After a quick look he smiled broadly. "You just met Miguel Reid."

"Yeah, so?" Stephanie said, annoyed by his enthusiasm.

"Mig Reid is one of *the* biggest fashion photographers in the world. He's right up there with Herb Ritts and Steven Meisel. Ever heard of Tatiana Krmpotic?"

"Who hasn't? She just signed some big deal with Revlon."

"Yeah, like a five-million-dollar big deal. Mig discovered her, too."

Gabrielle let out an audible gasp of excitement.

"If you want to be a model, you've impressed the right man," Jack told her, reveling in her delight.

"Then he's on the up-and-up?"

"Miguel is as up as they come. Hey, why don't we all have a drink and I can tell you all about him," Jack suggested, flashing his rejection-proof, come-hither smile.

"Maybe another time," Stephanie chimed in, eager to break this twosome apart. "Gabrielle is here to work, not socialize. Besides, she's not old enough to drink." *And wipe that fucking drool off your chin, you dickhead. Better yet, let me grab the nearest chair and do it for you.*

"Stephanie's right on both counts. I don't drink alcohol, and I do have to get back to work," Gabrielle admitted, looking the photographer's way. Now that she knew he was legitimate, she intended to work her way right back over to Miguel Reid's corner and seal this deal.

"After the party, then," Jack insisted. "Stephanie and I would love to buy you a Coke," he added, smiling.

Two hours ago she would have sold her right arm to hear Jack speak of the two of them as a couple, but tonight it was clear that the woman putting the gleam in his eye and the bulge in his pants was Gabrielle.

"Jack is right. A night like tonight calls for a drink. Let's go find the bar," Stephanie said, thinly masking the bitterness welling up inside her.

10

Stephanie shoveled another teaspoon of sugar into her third cup of morning coffee and returned to her chair at the kitchen table. The table's surface and the floor below it were covered in newspapers. The coffee was an attempt to jump-start her body after a sleepless night spent obsessing over Jack, and the papers were meant to keep her mind off the many questions infiltrating her brain. Why had he left her? What had she done wrong, and how could she get him back now that Gabrielle had her hooks in him?

Just thinking about last night caused Stephanie to shudder in disgust. After the party when Jack had insisted they go have drinks at—of all places—The Mad Hatter, Gabrielle had played it cute and coy, deferring to Stephanie, practically ignoring Jack, knowing all the while that every man loves a chase. And Jack, that prick-for-a-brain son of a bitch, you'd think the way he was stepping all over himself trying to be charming that he was in the presence of Christy Turlington or Amber Valletta. Somebody famous. Somebody worth fawning over. Not a dimwitted former muffin maven. Jack had spent the entire evening playing the un-abashed fan, filling Gabrielle's brain with illusions of grandeur. *He's mine. She can't have him. Oh, stop it,* Stephanie commanded her brain. *It will work out. I'll make sure it does. Because one thing is for certain: There is no way in hell Gabrielle is going to take Jack away from me.*

She forced herself to concentrate on the task before her. She'd spent the last hour combing the papers looking for press on last night's party. From the *New York Times* to the *Daily News,* the reviews thus far were very positive. Nearly every reporter in attendance gave the affair, with its historical and philanthropic twists, two thumbs up.

Stephanie picked up *Star Diary.* She peeled away the paper's outer pages, like the leaves of an artichoke, until she reached its heart—"The Grain Harvest." She skimmed through the first column and was halfway through the second when she spotted what she was looking for. Her eyes grew large with amusement as she read Harry Grain's account of the previous evening. He had saved the best for last.

> What excuse did film director **Lexis Richards** have for his sloppy, grungy attire at last night's opening of the Montell Spirits art exhibit? Richards showed up at the Studio Museum in Harlem wearing a washed-out T-shirt and torn jeans. This man, whose movie, Southeast, is making tons of money despite the fact that it's raising havoc on city streets, was either too cheap or too tired from cleaning out his garage to change.
>
> Tinseltown's newest darling was definitely outfitted to match his disposition, as he launched into an angry tirade when asked by this reporter to explain the shootings and violence that have occurred in several theaters where his movie is playing. In fact, his harsh verbal assault would clearly have turned physical if not for the interfer-

*ence of **Felicia Wilcot**, proprietress of the little-known public-relations firm Wilcot & Associates. Ms. Wilcot was retained by the Montell Spirits Company to coordinate last night's exhibit, which highlights African American participation in the Old West.*

*Despite many famous faces in attendance—including diva songstress **Vanessa Williams**, megastar **Bill Cosby** and wife **Camille**, tapmaster **Savion Glover**, and Oscar winners **Denzel Washington** and **Robert De Niro**—the party was DOA. Masquerading as a scholarship benefit, this "gala" event was merely a tacky attempt (and I do mean tacky, darling, from the dreary Western theme to the brown-and-serve hors d'oeuvre) by Wilcot to sell wine coolers. One has to wonder how Ms. Wilcot was able to convince the "wine of our times" mogul **Peter Montell** to take part in this fiasco. Perhaps her power of persuasion is one of the two talents she possesses. The other being her ability to pick out the help.*

"Felicia's going to have a cow," Stephanie snickered aloud. She, on the other hand, was fascinated by Harry's professional audacity. He wasn't hamstrung by the concept of journalistic impartiality. The fact that he had a national byline gave him carte blanche to call things exactly as he saw them. *I want the power to influence people's opinions. I want folks dying to know what I think about something or someone.* Stephanie felt a new surge of purpose course through her body as she continued to read.

*The big buzz going around town is that fashion photographer **Mig Reid** has found his latest dia-*

> *mond in the rough, an unnamed working girl hired*
> *by Ms. Wilcot. Mig, who can spot a megamodel-in-*
> *the-making, is famous for picking and plucking*
> *(read into it what you will, darling) new talent for*
> *the mannequin market. As with his past discover-*
> *ies, Tatiana Krmpotic, Roya Kirsten, and the*
> *showstopping Eva G., the man has mined gold*
> *once again. Trust me on this one, my dears, Miguel*
> *Reid's newest gem is pure Tiffany.*

"Pure Tiffany my ass," Stephanie said angrily. Wasn't it enough that Gabrielle had obviously caught Jack's attention last night? Did Harry Grain have to torture her wounded ego further with his enthusiastic remarks?

How did the reporter know about their meeting any-way? she wondered. *Felicia had already kicked him out by the time Gabrielle met the photographer. Who told him? Who was Harry Grain's spy, and how much had he got paid for this piece of fantasy?*

"Good morning," Gabrielle said, heading straight for the coffeepot.

"Hey."

"Why all the newspapers?"

"I'm looking for press clippings about the party."

"I thought it was the most fabulous party I'd ever seen. All those famous people, the television cameras—it was wonderful. My mother would have loved it," Gabrielle added wistfully. "What did the papers say about the party?"

Stephanie thought about telling Gabrielle about her mention in "The Grain Harvest" but quickly decided against it. Why make her head bigger than Jack and that Mig character already had?

"For the most part everybody thought it was great."

"It *was* great, and I can't thank you enough for asking

me to work. If it wasn't for you, I would never have met Miguel."

"Look, it was no big deal. I needed help, you needed a job. There's nothing to thank me for," Stephanie remarked impatiently. "Now can you leave me alone so I can finish clipping these articles before I leave for work?"

Gabrielle was taken aback by Stephanie's hostility. She'd been like this since last night when the two of them went out for drinks with Jack Hollis. Poor Jack, he'd tried to keep the evening light and upbeat, but Stephanie's dour mood kept it from being anything but long and painful. Tired of trying to understand her moody housemate, Gabrielle went back to fixing her breakfast. Their uneasy silence was broken by the ringing phone.

"I'll get it," Stephanie volunteered, hurrying into the hall. *Please be Jack.*

"Hello."

"Stephanie, hi," Jack said. *Shit!* He'd hoped Gabrielle would answer the phone.

I knew he'd change his mind. "Hey, Jack."

"Uh, thanks for inviting me last night," Jack said, sounding as awkward as he felt.

"I'm glad you could come."

"I've been reading the papers, and the reports look very positive."

"Yeah, everything went off pretty well."

The two lapsed into momentary silence, Jack not knowing how to ask for Gabrielle and Stephanie reluctant to bring up last night's discussion.

Enough of this trivial chitchat. Just come out and say it: You made a mistake and you want us to stay together.

Enough of this crap, Jack told himself. "Ah, Steph, is— uh, I'd like, um . . ."

This is so cute. He really is nervous.

"Is Gabrielle there?" Jack braced himself for Stephanie to erupt in an avalanche of emotion.

She didn't dare utter a single word. Stephanie pulled the receiver from her ear and tightened her grip until her knuckles turned white. The receiver shook uncontrollably in her hand as she glared with rage at the instrument of betrayal. Her breath came shallow and fast, and soon she began to feel light-headed.

Stephanie fought to keep her voice steady. "It's for you," she said, walking back into the kitchen. Her eyes, full of resentment, followed Gabrielle out into the hall.

Jack held on in amazement. He'd expected hysterics or at least a good tongue-lashing. Instead he got controlled politeness. Before he had a chance to ponder Stephanie's reaction further, Gabrielle's eager voice was singing in his ear.

"Hello."

"Morning, this is Jack Hollis. How are you?"

"Oh, Jack. Hi."

"You sound disappointed."

"I'm sorry. I don't mean to be rude. I thought it might be Miguel Reid."

"Understandable. Don't worry, he'll call. Like the paper said, he's found his next diamond in the rough."

"Paper? What are you talking about?"

"There's a write-up in Harry Grain's *Star Diary* column about you and Mig Reid."

"My name is in the paper?"

"Not exactly, but there's no mistaking Harry was talking about you."

As Jack read the "Grain Harvest" clip aloud, Gabrielle's excitement bubbled up within her.

"So what do you think? You're famous."

"An unnamed working girl could be anybody."

"Ah, but we both know it's you—a Tiffany gem. I'll save the paper for you."

"Thanks."

"I could give it to you when we have dinner tonight."

"The three of us?" Gabrielle asked, sounding confused.

"I guess Stephanie didn't tell you. We broke up last night."

"She hasn't mentioned it yet, but that explains her mood."

"She'll be fine. Stephanie Bancroft is one tough lady. So how about dinner?"

"Jack, I can't. Stephanie would be very upset if she thought we were dating."

"But we're just two pals breaking bread together."

"I don't think it's such a good idea."

"Another time, then?"

"Maybe."

"A definite maybe. It's a start." Jack laughed, despite his disappointment.

When Gabrielle walked back into the kitchen, Stephanie was still at the table.

"That was Jack."

"I know. I answered the phone," Stephanie answered curtly.

"He called to tell me I was in the newspaper. Have you seen anything?"

"Nothing," she lied. She'd ripped the tabloid to shreds while Gabrielle was on the phone. "Which paper?"

"*Star Diary.*"

"Nobody reads that rag."

"The reporter said that I was Miguel's latest find. They compared me to Tatiana and Eva G. If that were only true."

Stephanie was having a hard time keeping her coffee

down amid all of Gabrielle's excitement. "Is that all he wanted?"

Gabrielle looked into Stephanie's eyes for a moment and decided to tell her the truth. "He invited me to dinner. Just as friends," she quickly added.

"What did you tell him?"

"I told him *we* were friends and I didn't think it was a good idea. Stephanie, Jack told me you two broke up. I'm sorry."

"Did he tell you why we broke up?"

"No, just that you had."

In a flash, Stephanie's entire demeanor changed. She looked at Gabrielle and smiled. "I'm sorry about my bad mood. It's just that I've been really upset about Jack. It's so sad. He was crushed when I told him we should see other people. I think he thought I was the one."

"He wanted to marry you?"

"Well, I wouldn't go that far. Gabrielle, may I share something with you? Something you swear you won't breathe a word of to another living soul?"

"Sure. You can trust me."

"I know I can, and that's why I can tell you that Jack Hollis is gay."

"No offense, but if he's gay, why does he care if you two are together?"

"That's what I asked. He said he thought that I could help turn him around, but I know I can't. I'd always be wondering if the next guy he meets will be the one who comes between us. I had to break it off with him. To be jealous of another man is a very weird thing."

"Don't forget AIDS," Gabrielle added.

"Exactly. I just can't deal with it. That's why when he called this morning begging me to reconsider, I suggested he talk to you. I thought since you two hit it off so well last night, that maybe you could help him get over me. But I couldn't let you get involved without letting you know the complete truth."

"Stephanie, this must be so hard for you. I know you really liked him a lot."

"I still do. Promise me you won't mention any of this to him. He'd be mortified if he knew you knew."

"I won't say a word. You can count on it."

"I knew I could." Stephanie smiled slyly. "Thanks. Now, let's drop this sad subject and get going. I have to be at work in an hour."

"And I have laundry to do. I'll be in the basement if you need me."

"Okay," Stephanie answered, still smiling. As soon as Gabrielle was out of the room, her smile turned into a menacing grimace. She was beside herself with resentment and fury. How dare Gabrielle feel sorry for her. She didn't need her pity. And how dare Jack call up and ask Gabrielle out one day after ending their relationship. *Well, I fixed your little wagon, Mr. Hollis. Try to get next to her now that she thinks you're a flaming fag.*

Stephanie headed upstairs to her room to get ready for work. As she fished through a pile of clothes in search of a pair of pantyhose, the phone rang. *This better not be that bastard calling to talk her into seeing him,* Stephanie thought as she picked it up.

"Hello," she barked.

"Gabrielle Donovan, please," a male voice requested.

"Who's calling?"

"Miguel Reid. She's expecting my call."

She certainly is. It took Stephanie only a split second to plan her course of action.

"I'm sorry, Mr. Reid, Gabrielle can't come to the phone right now. She's in bed with a terrible headache—well, to be honest, a raging hangover. She was so excited about meeting you that she stayed out all night celebrating. But not to worry, this happens all the time. She bounces right back."

"Really?"

"I don't know how she does it. She can party all night long, every night, and it doesn't seem to affect her looks at all. Of course, for the rest of us mortals it's a mystery we're dying to figure out. Would you like to leave a message? I'm sure she'll be up and around by two or three this afternoon."

"Tell Ms. Donovan I've had a cancellation, so I can shoot her at my studio tomorrow morning at nine." Stephanie could hear the disapproval in his voice. "Tell her that if I don't hear from her today by three, I will assume she's coming."

"Tomorrow at nine, call by three. Anything else?"

"Yes, please inform Ms. Donovan that if she's serious about becoming a model to lay off the booze and night life."

"Gotcha," Stephanie said, smiling broadly as she hung up the phone. Immediately she wrote down the photographer's telephone number and the message "Call today, before three, about a shoot," omitting the advice about partying, and headed to Gabrielle's bedroom. She walked across the room and stood in front of the mirror.

"She deserves it," she convinced her reflection. Before she could change her mind, Stephanie dropped the note behind the dresser.

Payback is a bitch, ain't it, Ms. Donovan?

11

"I'll have her get back to you," Stephanie said, trying not to yawn into the phone. She was exhausted. To avoid Gabrielle and any opportunity to relay Miguel Reid's message verbally, she'd stayed out last night until well after 2 A.M. and was out of the house this morning before seven. She was tired as hell, but what was a little missed sleep when she had the sweet satisfaction of revenge?

Stephanie leaned back in her chair and smiled. The clock on her desk told her it was 9:47 A.M. If all was right, Gabrielle was sitting in the doctor's office with Beatrice, blissfully ignorant that she was missing the opportunity of a lifetime, while Miguel Reid was writing her off as a beautiful but irresponsible lush.

Eye for an eye, Gaby. You took my boyfriend. I stole your chance at fame. Stephanie was still smiling as she answered the phone.

"I need to talk to Ms. Wilcot."

"May I tell her who's calling?"

"This is Lexis Richards. If she's there, could you put me through?"

"Okay, Mr. Richards," Stephanie replied. "Felicia, line two."

"Felicia Wilcot."

"Lexis Richards here, calling to apologize."

"You don't say," Felicia said before hanging up the receiver. Whether he was sorry or not, she had no desire to talk with Lexis Richards. She was still fuming over his behavior at the Montell Spirits party—behavior that had landed her in the tabloid press. Granted, *Star Diary*, with its band of storytellers loosely referred to as reporters, wasn't taken seriously by anyone in her line of work, but still—calling her event tacky? That kind of publicity she did not need.

The phone rang again. "Stephanie, if that's Lexis Richards, I'm not in," Felicia shouted through the room divider. After three unanswered rings, Felicia peeked around the screen to find Stephanie's chair vacant.

"Damn," she said as the phone continued to ring. She considered letting the answering service pick up, but she was expecting an important call from Atlanta.

"Felicia Wilcot," she answered, hoping not to hear Lexis's voice.

"Don't hang up. Just listen to me for a minute."

"You have nothing to say that I want to hear."

"Give me one minute."

"Thirty seconds."

"Look, I'm sorry about the other night. I didn't mean to embarrass you or screw up your party."

"Don't flatter yourself, Mr. Richards. Your outburst did not ruin my party. Other than your equally rude sparring partner, no one really gave a damn that you were there."

"Why are you so bitchy? I did call to say I'm sorry."

"And you think calling me a bitch is the way to apologize?"

"I did not call you a bitch. I said you were *acting* bitchy."

"Whatever. Your thirty seconds are up."

"Wait. I want to talk to you about repping me. I've been catching much heat over these gangbangers cuttin' up at my movies, and I need some damage control. These studio clowns don't know what they're doing. I need somebody on my side. I need you. What do you think?"

"I think you've got to be kidding. It's pretty obvious that we can't be in the same room together without arguing. How in the world do you think we could have a productive working relationship? So look, I accept your apology, no hard feelings, and good luck."

As Felicia hung up the phone, she couldn't help wondering if she was acting a bit too hastily. After all, he did call to apologize and was actually very civilized until she'd started acting, well . . . bitchy. And if she was honest with herself, she'd have to admit that Lexis was the inspiration behind the entire Montell event. Had he not challenged her that evening at her father's birthday party, she would have never thought to combine her two clients. Still, there was something about Lexis Richards that got her defenses up. He was such an arrogant, opinionated, egotistical jackass. How could she work with a man like that? It was enough that she was married to one. Speaking of Trace, she'd best get going. She was having lunch with him following her meeting at Asylum Records, and he didn't like to be kept waiting.

"Damn, she's cold," Lexis said, smiling as he dialed her office number again.

Stephanie, back from the mailbox, answered the phone.

"Hi. Lexis Richards again, can you get me your boss?"

"What did you say to her? She didn't look too happy walking out the door."

"How can she be gone? I just talked to her."

"Honestly. You just missed her. She left for a ten-o'clock meeting."

"What time will she be back?"

"Not until later this afternoon," Stephanie said, checking Felicia's calendar. "She has a lunch appointment at noon."

"Where?"

"You are persistent, aren't you?"

"Yeah, when I want something."

"May I be frank? You're already on her . . . shall we say poop list. If you show up and interrupt lunch with her husband, you're going to zoom right to the top. Why not slow down? I'll just leave her a message that you called and—"

"Won't work. First of all, in my business if you're slow you blow. You have to go after what you want and *make* things happen. If I wait for her to call back, Willard Scott will be wishing me happy birthday on the *Today* show. So why don't you do me a favor?"

"This is going to get me in trouble, isn't it?" Stephanie asked, chuckling.

Lexis laughed. "Probably. But I'll make you a deal. Tell me where she's eating, and if she fires you, I'll double any severance pay. How's that sound?"

"Not so fast," Stephanie said slowly as a plan hatched in her head. If Lexis Richards was bound and determined to hook up with Felicia and needed her help to do it, she should get something out of it.

"What else?"

"I'm only working here until my writing starts to pay off. So here's my offer: I tell you where Felicia's having lunch and you agree to let me write a feature profile on you."

Lexis's boisterous laugh rang in Stephanie's ears. "As long as you don't dis me or my movie, you have a deal. You can call my publicist tomorrow and set it up. So where can I find your boss?"

"Palio Restaurant on Fifty-first at noon. Now, a deal's a deal," she said as she scrambled to find a pen. "Who's your publicist?"

"Felicia Wilcot. I think you have the number."

Lexis was standing outside Palio's at 11:50 A.M. when he spotted Felicia turn the corner of Fifty-first Street and head toward the restaurant.

"What's up?" he asked, smiling.

Ignoring his presence, Felicia pushed past Lexis and entered the bar area of the restaurant to wait for Trace. To her extreme irritation, Lexis followed her inside. Her first instinct was to move to the other side of the room, but she didn't want to create a scene, particularly when her husband could walk in any minute.

"How did you find me?"

"I browbeat your secretary into telling me where you were having lunch. Don't get mad at her, she really didn't have a choice. When I want something, I have a way of getting it."

"Oh, really. And what exactly do you want from me?"

"Like I said on the phone. I'm tired of getting dissed by the press. All this print on the shootings is making some of the theater owners nervous. Three more are threatening to pull out. *Southeast* is being platformed—"

"Platformed?"

"When a studio platforms a movie, it opens it up in just a handful of major cities to see if it gets good reviews and enough word of mouth to build up an audience. If folks talk it up and the thing makes money, the studio releases it into more theaters. If I don't get this bullsh— sorry, this problem under control, these white-boy theater owners aren't going to want to touch *Southeast*. I didn't work this hard for it to end because of some bad press. I really need your help, Felicia."

Felicia listened, touched by his sincerity and obvious concern for his movie. Lexis was trying to keep his creative vision alive, despite the unfair rap some of the press was putting on him. Maybe she could help him. The truth be told, maybe he could help her, too.

Possessed with the winning combination of marketing, writing, producing, and directing genius, Lexis was touted as a budding talent, destined for the top. Representing him, with his hot temper and outspoken manner, would keep her busy and constantly visible, giving her company much-needed exposure. Lexis could be the one who put Wilcot & Associates on the map. Besides, even with the success of Montell Spirits, she was in no position to turn down a potentially lucrative account.

"Mr. Richards—"

"Lexis. Let's not be so formal—since we'll be working together," he said, flashing a beguiling smile.

"Lexis, I think you're absolutely right, you do need representation. Without it, you're bound to self-destruct before you have the opportunity to fulfill the potential everyone feels you possess."

Lexis smiled at the veiled compliment. They were making progress. He could feel victory within his grasp.

"However," Felicia continued, "I am not convinced that I'm the right person for this job. Let's face it, we don't seem to get along very well. If our short history is any indication, we can't seem to coexist for more than two minutes without getting into a screaming match. That's no basis for a productive professional relationship."

"I'll admit that you do push my buttons, but, hey, we've

been talking now for at least three minutes and you've only insulted me once."

"I push *your* buttons—" Felicia started, but was stopped short by her own laughter. "I'll tell you what, we'll try this on a trial basis. If in ninety days this relationship works out, we'll talk about an extension. If it doesn't, no hard feelings."

"Bet."

"I'll draw up a proposal and contract and have it sent to your office. Oh, and I don't come cheap. My retainer is three thousand dollars per month."

"Cool, but you'll earn every penny," Lexis countered with a grin and extended his hand to consummate the deal.

"I have no doubt," she answered, taking his hand into hers. It was soft and smooth, his grip powerful. "Try to keep your mouth shut for the next few days, just until we can get a plan of action together."

"Well, who have we here?" Trace interrupted.

Felicia felt her heart jump as she turned and looked into her husband's face. It wasn't the acrobatics of a heart in love, but rather a heart put on alert, braced for trouble. Felicia knew that Trace's invitation to lunch was an attempt to break the stony silence that had descended upon their relationship since his failure to appear at the Montell party.

"Trace, I'd like you to meet my client, Lexis Richards. Lexis, this is my husband, Trace Gordon."

The two men shook hands and quickly sized each other up. To Trace, Lexis Richards, with his dreadlocks and goatee, looked like just another hip-hop troublemaker from the projects. In Lexis's opinion, Felicia's husband, dressed in a blue pin-striped Hugo Boss suit complete with a white silk pocket square, looked like one of Uncle Tom's well-to-do relations.

"Lexis is the director of *Southeast*," Felicia told him, hating herself for wanting to impress him.

Trace wasn't. "Can't say I've heard of it."

"It hasn't hit the Angelika, so I'm not surprised," Lexis countered, referring to the café/theater on Houston Street frequented by an artsy, mostly white Greenwich Village crowd.

Touché, Felicia thought, applauding her client's subtle retort. She was ashamed to admit that she enjoyed seeing Trace put in his place—even if it was by a man with whom she had just declared a shaky truce.

"Lexis, I'll have that proposal sent to you the day after tomorrow. Once you've looked it over, we'll talk."

"Bet," Lexis said to Felicia before extending his hand in Trace's direction. "Look, man, it was good to meet you."

Trace nodded and responded with a halfhearted shake. He waited until Lexis was out the door before launching his criticism. "He looks like he needs a parole officer, not a PR person."

Felicia simply looked at her husband. When had he become so pompous and self-righteous? Had he always been this way, and had she simply looked the other way all these years? Ignoring his comment, she replied, "Lexis is the best of the brightest directors out there today. He sought *me* out and asked me to represent him. I feel honored to have him as a client." It wasn't until the words left her mouth that Felicia realized she truly meant them.

"Why don't we forget business and eat?"

"Good idea. We have a lot to discuss," she answered in the same tone she used for client presentations. Felicia had her own menu prepared for lunch. She was planning to serve Trace an ultimatum: Either they seek counseling or their marriage was over.

Felicia and Trace followed the hostess into the elevator and upstairs into the dining room. While Felicia busied herself with examining the menu, Trace studied his wife. She was still as lovely as the day they'd met. Trace remembered their meeting in every detail just as if it had happened yesterday, instead of a decade ago.

She was three weeks shy of her nineteenth birthday when he literally bumped into her on the campus of Georgetown University. He was in town recruiting for his New York law firm, and she was a bright-eyed student, finishing up her freshman year. After almost knocking her down in his search for the administration building, Trace had insisted they meet later for coffee. Coffee turned into dinner, dinner into an all-night conversation, and that conversation into plans to meet again the following weekend.

Over the next three years the two solidified their relationship, and following Felicia's graduation they were married in a large, traditional June wedding. After a two-week Hawaiian honeymoon they moved into Trace's Brooklyn Heights brownstone.

Early married life settled into a comfortable, easy pattern. Trace left home for Manhattan every day to further his career at the law firm, while Felicia found a job in the public-relations department at nearby Methodist Hospital.

Trace progressed quickly up the ladder at the prestigious law firm. Last year, at age thirty-five, he became a partner. Now that he could afford to have his wife at home, he went along with—and bankrolled—Felicia's idea to start her own public-relations firm. That's when things really began to change between them. Felicia was no longer the same inexperienced twenty-two-year-old girl he'd married and their life was not working out quite the way he'd planned, but the bottom line still remained: He loved his wife.

"You really are a beautiful woman," Trace observed tenderly.

Taken aback by his compliment, the first in as long as

she could remember, Felicia could only respond with a demure "Thank you."

"Feli," Trace said, calling her by his special nickname, "I know things have been rough between us lately, but I love you. You do know that, don't you?"

"Sometimes I have to wonder," Felicia said, surprised by her candor.

"You think I don't love you simply because I missed your party the other night?"

"Trace, you just don't understand. It isn't simply that you missed the party. It's that you didn't *care* enough to be there. That party was important to me. I wanted to share the experience with my husband, but you were nowhere to be found."

"I told you, Curtis—"

"It doesn't matter what excuse you offer. In the end the only thing that counts is that you put your client and your business before your wife."

"Don't make it sound so calculated. My absence was due to circumstances beyond my control, not because I didn't want to be with you."

"If it had been only this incident, I'd agree with you, but ever since my company started to show real viability, you've gone out of your way to be as unsupportive as possible."

"That's not true," Trace countered indignantly. "I've been behind you since the beginning. Who put up the money to get you started? Who gives you free business and legal advice? Don't tell me I'm not supportive."

"I don't feel supported. I feel guilty for being successful. Tell me, Trace, are you jealous of Wilcot and Associates?"

Trace would not admit that jealousy was the motive behind his behavior. It was just that things had changed so much these past few years. Felicia was so hell-bent on being an independent career woman, she'd lost touch with what was important to him—a woman who put her home and family first. That's how it had been in his house growing up, and that's how he expected it to be in his own household.

"No, I am not jealous of your company. But the truth be known, I am tired of having to compete with Wilcot and Associates for the attention of my wife."

He is jealous. The confirmation of her suspicions angered Felicia. Why did Trace feel that he needed to compete with her work? Particularly when she was killing herself trying to appease him. She felt like a circus performer, constantly jumping through hoops as he cracked his demanding whip. She wanted to be able to share with him her success and get his opinion when she had problems. Instead of being a source of strength and support, he was behaving like a jealous two-year-old with a new sibling.

"It's not just my work. You have expectations of me that I can't fill," Felicia said.

"You were able to fulfill them when we were first married."

"We can't go back there, Trace. We're not the same people. We both want and need different things."

"What exactly do you need?"

"To begin with, I need us to be equals, to share our life and our life decisions together. I don't want to be your little wife anymore. I want to be your partner. I'm a capable, intelligent woman. I have my own mind."

"I know that. Your mind is one of the things I'm most attracted to."

"If that's true, stop treating me like a child. I want you to listen to me, Trace, really listen to me. Stop turning our important conversations into monologues."

"This isn't fair. You're changing course in midstream. For years you've expected me to be the one who made the decisions for us, and now you're complaining as if I'm some kind of dictatorial tyrant."

"You're right. I haven't been forthright with my feelings in the past. The truth is, I'm not satisfied with simply acquiescing to every decision you make or letting you have the last word, despite how I feel, just to keep the peace."

"You're that unhappy?"

"Aren't you?"

"Not enough to end our marriage."

"Neither am I, but we need help. I think we should see a marriage counselor. Somebody who will listen to us objectively and help us find our way back to each other."

"I don't want some therapist in the middle of my marriage. Let's give it some time and try working it out on our own."

Trace was convinced that they didn't need to seek outside assistance to repair their marriage, but he wasn't going to kid himself. Getting things back to normal would be no easy task, not when he considered the woman his wife had become.

"Okay, Trace, if you're really willing to work at it," Felicia agreed. She had her doubts that they could succeed without help, but she was willing to try. "But this can't go on indefinitely. If we aren't able to make some progress on our own in two or three months, we go for counseling. Agreed?"

"Agreed," he said, squeezing her hand. "Truce?"

"Truce," Felicia answered with a tentative smile.

"We *will* make this work, Feli." Trace was determined to save his marriage. Not only because he loved her, but also because he refused to lose her. Trace Gordon was a man who did not know failure, and he was not about to get acquainted now.

12

"Hello," Gabrielle said breathlessly into the telephone. She'd run into the house, leaving her key in the door, knowing that Bea was right behind her.

"Hey, it's me. How did it go?" Stephanie asked gleefully into the receiver.

"Bea is fine. The doctor told her that losing weight would help reduce the strain on her back and gave her a prescription for a muscle relaxer."

"Not that. How did things go with Mig Reid this morning?"

"I've been with Beatrice all morning."

"Don't tell me you didn't get the note," Stephanie cried, feigning shock and concern with great success. "Miguel wanted to see you this morning at nine."

"You left me a note? Where?" Gabrielle asked, hysteria rising in her voice.

"Right on your dresser mirror."

"The dresser," Gabrielle whimpered as the situation became clear. She pushed her hand into the pocket of her jeans and pulled out the message she'd found under her bureau this morning. If she hadn't dropped her brush, she'd have never noticed the note written on Stephanie's personal memo paper. She'd shoved it in her pocket, making a mental note to have Beatrice read it to her later. It had remained there—forgotten—until this very moment.

"This is all my fault. I should have called earlier or woke you up last night when I came in. I'll never forgive myself if you lost your big chance because of me," Stephanie replied, hoping Gabrielle could not detect her ever-widening smile over the phone. She wished she could witness, face to face, the devastation Gabrielle was obviously feeling.

"It's not your fault. You left me a message. I just didn't see it," Gabrielle said, as she slowly crushed the paper in her hand and dropped it onto the floor.

Hearing the pain in Gabrielle's voice, Stephanie almost felt sorry for the girl. "Ah, look, I have to run. The FedEx guy just walked in."

"Sure. I'll talk to you when you get home." Gabrielle hung up the phone and dashed up the stairs, her sobs putting Bea's maternal instincts on alert.

Beatrice picked up the crumpled note and trudged up after Gabrielle. She could hear the violent cries emanating from her room. She stepped in the doorway to find Gabrielle slumped on the floor at the side of her bed.

"Honey, what on earth is wrong?" Bea lowered her girth to the floor, and Gabrielle collapsed into the older woman's soft and fleshy arms, sobbing wildly. The tears came fast and furious.

Beatrice rocked Gabrielle against her breast and allowed her to expel her grief. As she stroked Gabrielle's hair and tried to console her, Bea felt a surge of maternal love overtake her. Never in her sixty-four years had she felt so needed.

As the minutes passed, Beatrice took the time to reflect on her life. She'd always intended to marry and have children, but the right man just never seemed to materialize. When she was twenty-three, she was engaged briefly to a sailor in the merchant marine. They'd met while he was in port in New York, and after a six-day, whirlwind romance she agreed to marry him. On the seventh day he shipped off, leaving her with the promise of a ring and a spring wedding. Their engagement lasted exactly two months, long enough for him to sail to the Philippines and marry a local barmaid.

Bea's greatest regret was not that she'd never wed or never explored the world as she had once dreamed, but that she'd never had a child. It appeared, however, sitting here with her arms wrapped around Gabrielle, that the Lord had intervened.

After several minutes, when Gabrielle's sobs had evaporated into an occasional whimper, Beatrice gently pressed her into revealing the cause of her grief.

Gabrielle spoke in a low monotone. "I blew it. I had my big chance, and I blew it. Everything my mom and I dreamed about, I ruined. All because—" Gabrielle's voice broke as the tears resurfaced.

"Sweetie, calm down and tell me, is this what has you so upset?" Bea said, smoothing out the discarded note.

"The photographer I told you about called yesterday. He wanted to take some pictures of me this morning. Stephanie left me that note, only I didn't know. Now I've missed my chance."

"Honey, you don't know that. We'll call him and tell him you didn't get his message. I'm sure he'll reschedule."

"I did get it. It fell under the dresser, but I found it."

"I'm confused. If you got Stephanie's message, why didn't you call?"

"Because I couldn't read it."

"You couldn't read Stephanie's handwriting?"

"No. You don't understand. I can't read *anything*."

"What are you saying?" Beatrice asked, trying to make sense of what she had just heard.

"I'm saying I never learned how to read or write."

"You mean, you don't read very fast."

"No, I mean that other than a few small words like 'the' or 'at,' I can't read."

Beatrice sat silently. It was inconceivable to her that this bright, beautiful child in front of her was illiterate.

"Your mother? She knew you couldn't read?"

"Not until I was twelve."

"How could she not know until then?"

"My mom was a waitress. She worked at night—the tips are bigger then—so she wasn't home much with me. When she was, we'd do other stuff, like work on puzzles or go to the movies."

"But once she knew, why didn't she get you some help?"

Gabrielle had no way of explaining to Beatrice what her mother had never clarified for her. Helene impressed on her daughter a thousand times over the years that she was smart in plenty of other ways—that being book smart wasn't everything. Gabrielle accepted her mother's subtle insinuation that whatever was keeping her from learning to read, while not fixable, was indeed tolerable. The child had no way of knowing that it was Helene's blind ambition that was the real culprit. Helene was determined that Gabrielle's beauty, not her brains, was their ticket out of their miserable existence. She could not take the chance that a literate Gabrielle might make some other, less compelling career choice. Helene was sure that once her ex-husband, Nick, saw his "famous" daughter he would change his mind and they could finally be a family.

"She helped me a lot, mainly by not making me feel like something was terribly wrong with me. She always said we should emphasize the positive, because the negative parts were irrelevant," Gabrielle explained.

"What about school? Somebody must have known."

"We moved a lot—every year, sometimes twice. By the time I was in high school I'd been to seventeen schools. I was always the new girl. I was quiet and shy and just kept to myself. It's like the teachers never really noticed me. Even if they had, it wouldn't matter, I'd be gone by the end of the year anyway. They just kept passing me along."

"How long did you stay in school?" Beatrice asked.

"I graduated high school last year."

Shock was written all over Beatrice's face. "You have a high-school diploma and you can't read or write. How?"

"My mom helped me with my schoolwork by reading the textbooks to me and writing out my reports. I would memorize the work and copy the papers letter by letter and turn it in like everyone else. In class I'd figure out some way to get help on tests." Gabrielle looked at the expression of disbelief on Beatrice's face.

"How could your teachers or classmates not know?"

"I guess I was good at hiding it. In class I'd watch when everyone else was reading silently and would turn the page when they did. I'd scribble in my notebook when the others were taking notes and then rip them out in case anyone asked to see them after class. When we had assignments to finish in class, I'd ask someone questions, like 'What do they mean here?' or 'What does this mean to you?' Working in teams was the easiest, because I could walk around thinking out loud and leave my partner to do the reading and writing."

"Did you cheat?"

"Sometimes, but only when I didn't have a choice," Gabrielle admitted.

"But you did manipulate people. Like you did me when

we first met. Your hand wasn't hurt at all, was it?" Beatrice accused, her emotions fluctuating between anger and pity.

"It's not really manipulation, it's more orchestration," Helene had told her. "Getting people to help you when and how you need it. There's nothing wrong with that, Cookie. You're not hurting anybody."

"No," Gabrielle admitted. "I hated being dishonest, but I had no other choice."

Beatrice sat contemplating Gabrielle's shocking revelation. She didn't look illiterate. But then, what does an illiterate person look like? She was far too smart and productive to be illiterate. But not being able to read, does that make you stupid? Beatrice looked away from Gabrielle, focusing hard on the details in the small room. Her eyes were immediately drawn to the pile of paperback books stacked on the table in the corner. "I've heard you discuss those very books with Stephanie. How can you do that if you can't read?"

Gabrielle stood up, her heart pounding. Feeling sad and defeated, she walked to the dresser, bent over, and opened the bottom drawer. Gabrielle reached in and pulled out a bundle of audio cassettes. "By listening to them on tape while pretending to read."

"And the way you speak. Your vocabulary isn't that of an illiterate person."

"You don't have to be able to read to have a big vocabulary. You just have to listen and ask questions."

"Why didn't you tell me this before?"

A familiar wave of shame washed over Gabrielle. "I wanted to tell you. I needed to tell somebody, but I was too ashamed. Can you imagine what it feels like to be a high-school graduate but unable to read a little kid's ABC book? Or to walk away from your job selling muffins just because somebody rearranged the shelves? I didn't want you to hate me, or think I was stupid, because I'm *not* stupid . . ." Gabrielle's voice trailed off into a new onslaught of tears.

"Sweetheart, I know you're not stupid. I think you're the brightest and bravest person I know. Don't worry, you're not alone anymore. I'll help you. Stephanie will help you, too. I'm sure together we can teach you to read."

"No!" Gabrielle screamed fiercely. "Promise me you won't say a word, not to *anyone,* especially not Stephanie. Beatrice, you must promise me."

"Honey, calm down," Beatrice said. "This will stay between me and you, I swear. Nobody will ever know. When you're ready, we'll get you some help."

"Thank you," Gabrielle whispered as she sank back into Beatrice's arms. *No one can ever know. Not about this, not about anything,* she thought as her eyes settled on her *Wizard of Oz* snow globe.

Stop it! Gabrielle commanded her thoughts as she fiercely wiped away her tears. She didn't have time to dwell on yesterday's mistakes. Right now she needed to concentrate on rectifying today's. Miguel Reid must be persuaded to give her another chance. There had to be something she could do, and Gabrielle was determined to do it.

Part Two

Part Two

13

October, 27, 1994

Your nose is wide, and your cheeks are too full," Miguel noted as he gently turned Gabrielle's face from side to side. "And your chin—your chin is weak."

Gabrielle sat stiffly in her chair, crushed by the weight of his words. She felt embarrassed and confused by Miguel's disparaging evaluation of her facial features. All her life people had praised her lovely face. Now, when it really mattered, the man who cradled her future in his hands found it flawed. Gabrielle bit her lower lip and frowned with despair, certain that Miguel was reevaluating her future as a model.

"Baby, why the frown?" Mig asked with obvious concern.

"My face—you said it's not—"

"Perfect? Is that the word you're searching for? Perfection is a man-made concept, Gabrielle. Most of this business is smoke and mirrors."

"But if my nose and my cheeks are too full—"

"Then I'll light you from the side so your face will look

thinner. Trust me, baby, I am going to take you beyond the high board," Miguel promised, using the term that categorized the supermodels of the industry. "You'll be in a class all by yourself."

Mig had put aside two entire days for Gabrielle's test shoot and had gone to great expense to hire top people to work with him. This was highly unusual for a photographer of his stature, particularly when it was all being done for a virtual unknown. Miguel's intention was not only to produce a variety of shots of Gabrielle but to teach her the rudiments of the profession before sending her out into the fierce world of modeling. He knew that this was just the beginning. Gabrielle's lessons would be ongoing—a progressive transformation from raw talent to polished skillfulness. Miguel also knew that he was in the process of creating a legend.

He'd known it from the first time he set eyes on her. He could tell by the lyrical movement of Gabrielle's body as she roamed the art gallery the night of the Montell Spirits party. He was impressed with her ability to transform that hideous dress into an awe-inspiring work, leaving every woman in her wake wondering where to buy one. If she could do that with a polyester nightmare, what could she do for the designs of Ungaro, John Galliano, or Calvin Klein? And that face, despite its imperfections, was exquisite. Gabrielle was the proverbial needle in a haystack.

Miguel shuddered to think how close he'd come to writing her off. If it wasn't for Gabrielle's frantic call, explaining the mixup with his phone message, she'd be history in his eyes. This young woman was certainly persuasive, because after she'd stood him up, Mig had dismissed Gabrielle Donovan as an unfortunate waste of talent.

It had taken another two months before he could clear his jammed schedule to accommodate her again, but now the test of that potential was at hand. Today would be the first trial of the qualities that separated the supermodels from the mere mannequins—patience, reliability, and perseverance. She definitely had the necessary "magic," but only time would tell if Gabrielle had what it took to excel in this demanding and sometimes treacherous business.

The studio was buzzing with activity. Alf, Miguel's photo assistant, was standing high on a ladder holding a light meter against the seamless white backdrop. While he worked to make sure the illumination was soft and flattering, Pam, the prop stylist, was busy polishing the vintage white Corvette sitting in Miguel's massive studio.

Tucked away in the dressing room, Gabrielle did not recognize the woman in the mirror staring back at her. Miguel's crew had changed Gabrielle into a young Ann-Margret. Jenny, a magician with makeup, skillfully pruned Gabrielle's thick eyebrows into a dramatic arch and with the magic of her contour brush made her nose and cheeks appear more chiseled.

Zeke, the wardrobe stylist, clad Gabrielle's body in a sleeveless butterscotch crepe de chine sheath. The rich color complemented Gabrielle's hair, and the fit of the simple design emphasized her shapely figure. Topping off the outfit was a long chiffon scarf of the same buttery yellow. Jenny gently draped the whisper of silk over Gabrielle's hair and, careful not to crush her Rodeo Drive bouffant, wrapped it around her neck. Dark glasses completed the ensemble.

When Gabrielle walked into the studio, there was an audible sigh. Even Miguel, who had seen, photographed, and made love to an international bevy of gorgeous women, was left breathless by the potential of this raw beauty.

"Baby, you look magnificent," Miguel told her.

"I feel like a female impersonator," Gabrielle joked.

The photographer laughed. "Seeing you in that dress, even RuPaul would be jealous." Not wanting to undercut her confidence, he did not reveal his reasoning for the Ann-Margret look-alike approach. For this first set of pictures Miguel had provided Gabrielle with a defined look that could be enthusiastically imitated. By removing the necessity of being herself, Miguel was relieving much of the pressure on the young model. Later, when Gabrielle was more comfortable in front of the camera, he would begin to tap her individual personality.

"Ready to roll?"

"Ready," she answered, eager to begin living her dream.

"Then let's go," Mig said, taking her hand and leading her to the white sports car. The top and windows were down, waiting for the addition of Gabrielle to grace the leather seats. He opened the driver's-side door and helped the young model behind the steering wheel.

"You must sit tall and straight," he told her, pressing his hand to the small of her back. "Good. Now, tilt your head slightly to the left. Chin up. You *must* keep your chin up so the light can hit your face. Fantastic. We'll start here," he proclaimed as he stepped back behind his camera and took a look through the viewfinder.

Gabrielle sat in the car processing all of Mig's instructions. Already her back was beginning to ache, and one of the straight pins used to mold the dress perfectly to her body was making its presence known.

Mig stopped after snapping about forty frames. Gabrielle was stiff and shy, but he was not discouraged. She had what it took, he was sure of it. He just had to find the way to draw it out and then teach her to perfect it.

Music is what this shoot needs, Mig decided. Something to make her feel loose and easy. He had the perfect tune.

"I want you to relax and just groove with the music," he said as he popped in a Prince CD and selected the track "U Got the Look." "Listen to what the man is telling you. You've got the look, he wants it, and you know it." Soon the hot and funky sounds of Prince and Sheena Easton were blasting out over speakers mounted high on the studio walls.

The change was immediate. Gabrielle let the music transport her to another place. She was no longer in Miguel's Union Square studio. She imagined herself out in Los Angeles, cruising Sunset Strip and enjoying the sunlight and attention she and her car were attracting. It was no longer the hot studio lights, but the warm California sun kissing her face. She thought about all the Ann-Margret movies she'd seen with her mother. The woman had a coy, sex-kitten quality about her that was lusty yet wholesome. She tried to project this coquettishness through her facial expressions and body language. It appeared to be working, because Miguel was snapping himself into a frenzy.

"Yes, yes. Fabulous. Go, baby," he called out to her as he moved around the floor capturing her image from different angles. As her confidence grew, so did Mig's enthusiasm. Gabrielle had a natural vibration. Her poses were playful and innocent, while at the same time alluring and suggestive. There was a spark in her eyes—a light that challenged, drew you in, and held you captive. This girl was going to be big—very big.

By the following afternoon Gabrielle was feeling much surer of herself. She also felt more confident in Miguel's desire and ability to make her look and feel good. Over the last day and a half Miguel had begun to manipulate the young model's image bit by bit. Under his tutelage Gabrielle was learning many critical lessons that would serve her well in the future. Miguel taught her to keep her mouth slightly opened when she was photographed; that way her teeth showed attractively, her cheekbones appeared more prominent, and her chin line more angled. In between shots she would practice thrusting both hips forward, shooting one hip out to the side, and balancing her legs, one behind the other. Gabrielle found this position to be quite uncomfortable, but the stance gave her a shapely curve and minimized her already small waist even more.

The greatest trick to master was to do all of these things and manage to look naturally serene. This was a lesson Gabrielle found easier in theory than in practice, but she was learning quickly. It didn't matter if her back ached, her feet hurt, or her eyes burned from the ever-present wind machine. As Miguel constantly stressed, the camera must never pick up any discomfort or pain.

"Your outfit for the next photo is in your dressing room, lovey," Zeke informed Gabrielle as she sat having her hair styled. It was pulled high on her head into a ponytail, and Jenny was busy applying a thick coat of cobalt-blue gel before pinning it into half a dozen sausage curls. The blue gel stood out dramatically against her honey-bronze-colored hair and complemented her eyes. Next Jenny applied Gabrielle's makeup, making her face stark and pale, a burnished orange lipstick providing its only color.

"Thanks, Zeke," Gabrielle answered, curious to see what setting Miguel had chosen for this next set of photographs. Gabrielle noticed that the photographer was getting progressively more daring with each setup.

Gabrielle walked into the dressing area to find a wispy white dress hanging on the wardrobe rack. Wearing nothing but a pair of skimpy black panties, she slid into the body-hugging slip dress and pulled the thin spaghetti straps over her shoulders.

"He's ready for you," Zeke announced.

Gabrielle followed Zeke into the studio and was surprised by the sparseness of the set. There were no props visible, only a seamless white background. Once again, Alf was checking out the lighting, while Mig was preoccupied with a slide projector that was apparently jammed. After several attempts he was able to dislodge the culprit slide, and a rainbow of color splashed against the stark whiteness, spilling a collection of words diagonally across the screen.

The blood in Gabrielle's head began pounding against her temples. She could only hope that Miguel was not going to ask her to read them. She could see that they were the same words written over and over again, but the question remained: What did they say? *Calm down,* her inner voice cautioned her. *This is a still-photography shoot. Why would you need to read anything?*

" 'The future belongs to those who believe in the beauty of their dreams,' " Miguel recited. "It's a quotation by Eleanor Roosevelt."

"I like it."

"I consider them words to live by. Come, let me explain how this shot will work," he said, taking her hand and leading her onto the set. He positioned Gabrielle in the center of the backdrop, where the words melted onto her body. Miguel had conceived the idea for the photograph shortly after meeting Gabrielle. His intent was to use Gabrielle as a human movie screen by projecting the words right onto her torso.

"I'd like you to stand here, very still, with your hands by your side. Great. Beautiful. You are so gorgeous," he praised her as he snapped away with his Polaroid. After shooting an entire box of film, he put down his camera and studied the pictures. Frustration replaced his earlier excitement. Something wasn't working. Aesthetically speaking, Miguel could tell he was headed in the right direction. The composition was interesting, but not exciting. He wanted more drama, more flair. "It's the dress," he muttered under his breath.

Gabrielle relaxed and waited. She was growing accustomed to her clothes constantly being refitted, readjusted, and realigned.

After several minutes of studying the Polaroids, Miguel knew what had to be done to achieve his goal. He was sure that if he changed the lighting and projected the slide onto her naked torso, he'd get the artistic punch he was after. But would Gabrielle do it? Miguel debated over asking her to pose topless for the shot. After all, this was only her second day in front of a camera, and she was obviously a young and naïve girl. But he was a breakthrough photographer, and this was a breakthrough concept. If Gabrielle wanted to be a breakthrough model, she was going to have to lose her inhibitions. That was the bottom line.

Quietly, in as matter-of-fact a tone as he could muster, Mig called Zeke into the room and requested the wardrobe change.

Gabrielle's face said it all as she overheard Miguel's request. Her eyes opened wide, while a thousand thoughts played pinball in her head. Nudity was never mentioned when they went over the different shots. Why was he springing this on her so suddenly? Was Stephanie's prediction coming true? Was Miguel really some kind of flimflam artist? Would this photo come back to haunt her?

Instinctively Gabrielle clutched the dress tighter around her breasts. "I—I can't," she stammered.

"Gabrielle," Miguel said sternly. "You are a model. I'm

a photographer. And this is not some nudie-magazine photo session. Now, please, go with Zeke and let him adjust your wardrobe." Seeing her obvious fear and discomfort, he added gently, "It will be okay. I promise."

Gabrielle followed Zeke back to the dressing room. Slowly, with great reluctance, she slipped out of the dress.

"Here," he said, handing her a white robe to cover her near-naked body.

"Thanks," she answered in a small voice.

"Lovey, don't worry. Miguel is a professional. You can trust him," the stylist said in an effort to comfort her.

"But this isn't even a real job. These photos are just for my book. Why do I have to take my clothes off?"

"All I can tell you is that Mig is an artist. If he wants you to undress, it's only to make the shot work, nothing more."

"Zeke, I can't do this."

"Girl, you don't know how lucky you are. Do you know how many women would kill for the opportunity to have a master photographer spend this kind of time, money, and creative energy on them?" Zeke said, losing his patience. "Don't blow this," he advised before turning and leaving.

Gabrielle faced her image in the mirror. "Zeke is right," she scolded herself. "You *are* fortunate. And what is the big deal anyway? The big-time models pose practically naked all the time. So what's it going to be, Gabrielle? Miguel Reid is offering you the chance to make your dreams come true. Are you going to be a wuss and blow the chance of a lifetime, or are you going to march in there and take the damn picture."

Gabrielle decided to take a chance and trust Miguel and her instincts. But now, having made her choice, how was she going to face all those people in there?

Posing in front of a crowd was not going to be a problem. She and Mig were alone. On his orders, the room had been cleared, and only Jenny stood waiting in the wings for any necessary touch-up. The usual buzz of activity generated by Mig's assistants had ceased, replaced by the soothing sounds of the New Age musician Kitaro. A nervous Gabrielle appreciated the effort.

"I want you to relax," he told her. Slowly, deliberately, and with complete reverence, he untied the belt to her robe and placed his hands on her bare shoulders. Gently Mig slid the robe off her body, allowing it to drop to the floor. His action was innocent and at the same time very seductive.

Miguel was gentleman enough not to give any outward reaction to the tantalizing physical beauty he'd just unveiled. A quick intake of his breath, however, made his feelings clear. Without saying a word, he took her right arm and draped it across her breasts, resting her hand just below her left shoulder. He crossed Gabrielle's lower torso with her left arm, placing her left hand across her right thigh. The pose effectively covered her nipples, while leaving exposed the fullness of her breasts.

Gabrielle, too embarrassed to move, stood motionless. Unable to look at Mig, she closed her eyes and let the music wash over her body. As he did with every setup, Miguel first shot a box of Polaroid film. Standing there with a rainbow of color and words sprayed across her body, she was an awesome sight. The woman had become, in all her splendid nakedness, a living, breathing poem. Checking over the instant pictures, the photographer felt a sexual charge surge through his body. Miguel knew that while 50 percent of his desire was due to the close proximity of this incredibly beautiful woman, the other half was due to the artistry of the shot. For Miguel, making art and making love were one and the same.

Pleased with the Polaroids, Miguel picked up his Nikon

and began to shoot. The model and photographer worked in silence—Miguel concentrating on the aesthetics of the picture, Gabrielle on giving the outward appearance of being comfortable and tranquil. Six rolls and two hours later, after capturing the image from every angle imaginable and with several variations in the lighting, Miguel approached Gabrielle. She opened her eyes as he kissed her gently on the forehead.

"You are remarkable," he whispered softly, helping her on with her robe. "And I am going to make you a star."

14

Gabrielle stopped in front of the ABW Publishing building
on Madison Avenue and quickly pulled off her gloves. Leaving the brisk February air behind her, she breezed through
the revolving door, checked in at the lobby desk, and was directed to the sixteenth floor by the security guard.

The room was already crowded when Gabrielle arrived.
There were at least twenty young women packed into the
small waiting area outside the casting director's door. She
gave her name to the receptionist and watched as the woman
located and crossed it off the list.

"Take this casting sheet, fill it out, and return it with
your composite," the receptionist requested. After four busy
months as an emerging newcomer, Gabrielle knew exactly
what information the form requested—name, agent, height,
weight—it was the same at every go-see.

"I rushed right over from the manicurist, and my nails
aren't quite dry yet. Would you mind filling it out for me?"
she asked sweetly.

"Sure," the receptionist said with just the slightest bit of
aggravation in her voice. She was used to this kind of behavior. Wet nails, runs in their pantyhose, with beauty

queens it was always something. "What was your name again?"

"Gabrielle Donovan."

"Agency?"

"First Face," Gabrielle answered proudly.

Miguel had advised Gabrielle to start with a small agency, one that would have the time and incentive to finesse her budding career. His suggestion was First Face, the newest and hottest agency going at the moment. It was small, Eva G. and Veronica Gillian being its only stars. But with two supermodels on its roster, along with an up-and-comer like Gabrielle, First Face was hot on the heels of the bigger and more established agencies like Ford, Elite, and Click.

Thanks to an enthusiastic recommendation by Miguel, Gabrielle was able to bypass the open-interview process and meet personally with the agency's president, Gregory von Ulrich. He took one look at her test shots and signed her on the spot. Recognizing talent and potential income when he saw it, Gregory assigned her to the agency's best booker, Jaci Francis.

"Do you think your nails are dry enough to leave me a composite?" the woman asked with a dry twinge of sarcasm. Gabrielle handed her card to the receptionist, taking great care not to smudge the polish on her nails that had been dry now for at least thirty-six hours.

"Thank you. Have a seat. Ruthanna will call you when she's ready."

Gabrielle found a seat by the door. Despite the crowd, the room was quiet enough to hear the hum of the water cooler. This was a big job, and every model in the room wanted to be the cover face chosen to launch this new magazine. Except for two women conversing in the corner, the models sat nervously leafing through magazines and sizing up their competition.

"Gabrielle Donovan," a voice called out before its owner appeared in the doorway. Gabrielle stood up, aware of the forty or so eyes picking her apart. She walked across the floor and into the office with an enthusiastic stride. Smiling brightly, she shifted her black leather portfolio from her right to left hand and extended her arm. "Hi, you must be Ruthanna Beverly. I'm pleased to meet you."

"Please sit down," Ruthanna said, shaking Gabrielle's hand politely. The editor, a former model herself, sat down and got right down to business. "You brought your book?"

"Yes, of course," Gabrielle answered, handing the casting director her thin but impressive portfolio, containing Miguel's pictures and tear sheets of her first modeling assignment.

Within just two weeks of making the rounds to meet the magazine crowd, Jaci was able to secure Gabrielle's initial booking with *Elle* magazine—a fashion spread that began to get her noticed by the casting directors from various magazines, catalogues, and advertising agencies.

Because Gabrielle had refused to move to Europe to get experience, Jaci and Greg mapped out an alternative strategy for managing Gabrielle's career. They'd decided to ignore all but the most prestigious catalogue and editorial assignments. With great care, Jaci and Gregory selected every appearance, making sure the job supported the image they wanted to portray—that of an innocent yet sensual young woman.

"You have a huge fan in Mig Reid," Ruthanna commented as she studied Gabrielle's tear sheets.

"He's the best," Gabrielle answered sincerely.

Seeing her test shots had been quite a revelation for Gabrielle. She was especially pleased with the topless photo, particularly given her reluctance to participate. Miguel still held the negatives and prints at his studio. He was planning to use that photo and others from an upcoming session in a brochure promoting his photography. It was the least Gabrielle could do, considering all the work and expense he'd gone through on her behalf. And, as Jaci had adroitly pointed out, it couldn't hurt that this brochure would find its way to the desks of the most influential editors, designers, and art directors in the business.

Ruthanna's only comment before closing Gabrielle's model book was a polite but noncommittal "Very nice."

"Thank you," she replied, not quite sure if the interview was over.

"I'd like to take a Polaroid."

"Of course." Gabrielle knew that taking instant photos was standard practice. They were clipped to her casting sheet and used later in the final selection process.

"Could you stand over there in the corner?"

Gabrielle walked over to the designated area and turned to face Ruthanna. There was a baby spot light illuminating the area sufficiently to accommodate a quick photo.

"Right there is perfect," Ruthanna instructed. "I'll be with you in a minute."

While she waited, Gabrielle casually ran her fingers through her hair. Within seconds she heard the snap of the camera.

"That's great. Thank you very much."

"Thank you," Gabrielle answered, disappointed she'd been caught off guard. She shook the editor's hand goodbye and left the room not knowing if she was any closer to having the job than when she'd entered.

Ruthanna closed the door behind Gabrielle and returned to her seat to study the Polaroid. Gabrielle's candid pose reeked of wholesome seductiveness and sensuality. Even for this quickie photo her eyes were alive and engaging. Ruthanna could definitely see this playful enchantress on the cover of the magazine, inviting readers to pick it up and share all the wonderful news inside. The editor's original intent had been to use an established face—Bridget Hall, Niki Taylor, or Claudia Schiffer. But after careful discussion, the decision was made to find a fresh face—a new face that was beautiful but approachable. A face that defined the philosophy and intent of *Appeal* magazine.

The creators of *Appeal* wanted a different kind of fashion magazine, a publication that sorted through the barrage of fads and minitrends and urged readers to revel in their own individuality. Models of all sizes would be featured, and each issue would be a reflection of the cover model's actual personality. Each girl would act as her own fashion editor, choosing the designer clothes and accessories that enhanced her personal sense of chic beauty.

Ruthanna broke out into a huge smile. Her work was done for the day. She'd found the cover girl for this all-important premiere issue. Clutching the photo in her hand, she also knew that not only was she launching a new magazine, she was launching Gabrielle's career and her own.

"You have a tentative with *Glamour* magazine for Friday at eleven-thirty," Jaci informed Gabrielle. "As soon as they let me know, I'll let you know."

"Friday the twelfth at eleven-thirty—tentative *Glamour,*" Gabrielle recited into her microcassette recorder.

Jaci waited as Gabrielle recorded her appointments. She was accustomed to the model repeating her words, but never realized that instead of writing her schedule down in her leather Filofax, Gabrielle was recording an audio calendar.

The idea to use a microcassette to keep track of her bookings came to Gabrielle after seeing Stephanie use one to transcribe her boss's notes. Her method was simple: Gabrielle recorded her schedule and any changes directly into the tape recorder while Beatrice jotted the information down later in both her and Gabrielle's Filofaxes. Gabrielle insisted on carrying and "using" her appointment book imprinted with the First Face logo. The book was more than just a prop. If something ever happened to her tape recorder, Gabrielle would simply invent an excuse and have someone read it to her.

"Anything else?"

"Monday you have the brochure shoot with Miguel, but you've also got a request from *Self*."

"Book me out on Monday," Gabrielle instructed Jaci. "I promised Miguel."

"Okay. Monday belongs to Mig, but the rest of next week is going to be particularly hectic. I have you booked on two shoots—Tuesday in San Francisco for the North Beach Leather catalogue. Then on Thursday you're in South Beach for the *Allure* spread. Congratulations. Your first two out-of-town jobs."

"Are these bookings tentative or confirmed? If they're tentative, maybe we should pass," Gabrielle suggested.

Jaci stopped sorting vouchers and gave her full attention to Gabrielle. Since they'd begun working together, she'd never once heard Gabrielle complain about her growing workload.

"You okay?" she asked with genuine concern. It was easy for these young girls to burn out, and a girl with Gabrielle's potential was only going to get busier. If she was having problems, it was best they come out in the open now rather than later.

"I'm embarrassed to tell you."

"Don't be. I'm here to help."

"I'm afraid to fly," Gabrielle revealed.

"You're not serious, are you? A model lives half her life—hell, three quarters of her life—on an airplane."

"I can't do it," she said, unable to tell Jaci the truth. It wasn't the actual flying she feared, it was the traveling through strange airports, checking in and out of hotels, reading itineraries—reading anything—that scared her.

"I'm going to have to noodle this one around."

"Can't I ask Beatrice? I'll pay for her travel expenses myself."

"I don't see how anyone can argue with that. Wait. Hold on."

In a few short seconds Jaci returned to the phone. "Good news, you got the *Appeal* cover! Congratulations!" The two women shrieked together on the phone.

"I can't believe they picked me!"

"Believe it. And not only do they want you on the cover, there's a guaranteed six-page fashion spread," her booker revealed.

"I can't wait to tell Mig. He'll be so psyched that I've gotten this far."

Jaci knew that this was only the beginning. The new magazine was all the buzz in both the publishing and fashion businesses. Rumor had it that the parent company, ABW Publishing, was sinking millions into the magazine to ensure its success. This meant that the exposure leading up to the magazine's debut would be extensive. It also meant that Gabrielle's career as a model was officially about to hit the big time.

15

Stephanie was livid when she saw the contents of the envelope. Inside was a check—her kill fee from *Strive* magazine. Now, if this didn't add insult to injury. Not only had it taken her months to finally get her story on Lexis Richards accepted—and by a tiny, almost anonymous bimonthly at that—now the bastards were paying her *not* to publish the story.

"They could have saved the paper and paid me with a roll of quarters," Stephanie said, crushing the check in her hand.

Not that others weren't interested in the explosive young director's story. It was simply that none were interested in *her* story. Thanks to the media blitz Felicia had managed to whip up, six weeks had passed before Stephanie was able to sit down with Lexis. By the time she'd gotten her promised interview, it was too late. Stories about the director had already run in the major daily papers around the country, and profiles were scheduled in *Ebony, Esquire, Rolling Stone,* and *Playboy* magazines. Still, an interview with a hot commodity like Lexis was too good for Stephanie to pass up.

At the top of their discussion, the director had been completely open and forthright, talking to her in depth about his business and his art. It wasn't until he inadvertently mentioned that his first project had starred his twin brother, Lewis, that the interview took a quick slide downhill.

"That's off the record. Nothing about my family goes in this story," he said brusquely.

"Come on, Lexis. The public wants to know about your childhood."

"I don't give a damn what people want to know. This article is about me, not my family."

Later, when Stephanie wrote her profile, she took great care to paint a positive picture of Lexis, dwelling on his childhood fascination with making movies. Other than a quick mention of the director's twin brother, she honored his condition that the Richards family remain off limits. And what was the thanks she received? A story she couldn't sell.

How selfish could Felicia and Lexis be? After all, if Stephanie hadn't directed Lexis Richards to the Palio Restaurant, Felicia would have never signed him on as a client, thus leaving him and his movie to be swallowed up by a sea of bad publicity. In saving her client's first shot at fame, Felicia had effectively killed Stephanie's.

Why is life always kicking me in the ass? Stephanie asked herself bitterly. This article was to be her big launch into the world of magazine reporting. The story that put her in the Rolodexes of important editors around the city. But once again, instead of the glory she expected, she got zilch—nada. *Nothing ever works out for me*, Stephanie thought, full of self-pity. *Not school, not writing, not Jack.*

She missed Jack. Even though he had turned out to be just another dog who treated her like his personal fire hydrant, time and distance had not put an end to her obsession with him. When the pain of not having him with her became too much, Stephanie resorted to sophomoric tricks like calling his number late at night and hanging up after he said hello. Once, when a female voice answered, Stephanie claimed to be calling from the Gay Men's Health Crisis with the results of Jack's HIV test. She had no way of knowing if her insinuation had had any effect on the woman, but Stephanie took the chance that it would work on her just as it had apparently worked on Gabrielle.

She was sure that the story she'd concocted about Jack's sexuality had everything to do with Gabrielle's initial resistance to Jack's advances. But even if it hadn't done the job, Gabrielle's burgeoning career left no time for Jack or any of the other men beating a path to her door.

Gabrielle Donovan. Now, that was one lucky bitch. Everything worked out for her. *Everything.* Not only was she beautiful, but she was well on her way to being rich and famous, the three things that Stephanie wanted most out of life. Sure, any one of the three was powerful enough to open doors, but in Stephanie's mind it was the sacred trinity of beauty, wealth, and fame that all but guaranteed a fairy-tale life.

By now Stephanie had come to terms with the fact that great beauty was out of the question. It just wasn't in the cards, let alone the gene pool. As for being rich and famous, Felicia had effectively shot Stephanie's current opportunity to hell, and Stephanie had the minuscule paycheck to prove it.

Damn it. Felicia's getting paid, Gabrielle's getting paid, and here I sit with barely enough money to buy breakfast. It's not fair!

"Life's not fair, so why should I be?" Stephanie asked herself out loud as an idea fermented in her head. She rustled through the crumpled magazines and newspapers. Finding what she, needed, Stephanie picked up the phone and dialed the number listed in the ad.

"'Grain Harvest,'" proclaimed a smooth voice.

Stephanie immediately recognized Harry Grain's voice from his public confrontation at the gallery. "My name is Stephanie Bancroft. I'm calling you about Lexis Richards, the director of *Southeast*."

"Oh, yes. Mr. Hip-Hop, Does His Mouth Ever Stop," Harry answered dryly, amused by his attempt at snide humor. "I doubt there is anything that you could say that could possibly be of any interest to me."

"I know one thing he likes to keep his mouth shut about."

"And what would that be?" he asked, taking the bait.

"The ad says that I can supplement my income."

"It also stipulates accurate and *interesting* celebrity gossip."

"This information is both."

"We'll see about that."

"Lexis Richards has a brother."

"Really? So do about a billion other people in this world."

"But this is a *twin* brother that I get the distinct impression he's trying to hide."

"Go on," Harry said with renewed interest.

"I interviewed Lexis recently, and he accidentally let it slip out that he has a brother named Lewis. When I tried to get more details, he angrily cut the interview off, saying that his family was off limits."

"It does sound rather mysterious, doesn't it? I'll tell you what. I'll give you fifty dollars for this initial climb up Mr. Richards's family tree. If you can find out anything more about his secret twin, I'll give you another fifty."

"Why don't we say fifty dollars for this and we'll leave

the rest negotiable, depending on what I come up with," Stephanie countered. She had a hunch that Lexis's secret was big, and if she was right, she didn't want to sell herself short. This time, come hell or high water, somebody was going to pay her for delivering Lexis Richards.

"No, ma'am, I'm looking for a Lewis Richards, not Lamar. Thank you anyway." Stephanie hung up, crossed the name off the list, and began dialing the next number. This was her twenty-third phone call this morning and, while she was intent on calling every Richards listed in the Washington, D.C., phone book until she found Lexis's brother, she sincerely hoped it wouldn't come to that.

"Lewis Richards, please," Stephanie requested after the third ring.

"He's not here," volunteered a female voice. "Who's calling?"

Stephanie immediately put a cap on her growing excitement. "My name is Beatrice Braidburn and I'm calling from the Hecht Company department store," she lied with great conviction. "Lewis was apparently in the store a few weeks ago and entered a drawing in our men's department. He's won a two-hundred-dollar gift certificate. When will he be back? I'd like to congratulate him personally."

"I'm sorry. I'm afraid you have the wrong person. Lewis could not have been in your store, and Lexis has been out of town for weeks," the woman explained.

Lexis! Stephanie could feel the adrenaline start to pump through her body. She felt like Indiana Jones on the dig of a lifetime, just hitting pay dirt. "No, the card definitely says Lewis."

"Miss, it is *impossible* that Lewis was in your store. He can't even cross the street by himself, let alone shop. My son has been a quadriplegic for over twenty years."

"I'm so sorry. How did it happen?" Stephanie felt a twinge of shame for asking, but polite tactfulness was no match for her growing curiosity.

"Why do you want to know all of this?" Mrs. Richards asked, her guard up.

"Forgive me for all the questions, it's just, well, I have a sister who was paralyzed in a car accident," Stephanie said, not missing a beat. "I guess I got a little excited talking to someone who understands what I've been through. You know—the guilt, the blame, messed-up family life . . ."

"Blame and guilt are a deadly combination," Mrs. Richards philosophized. "And life after a tragic accident is never the same for *anyone.*"

"Please forgive me for being so inquisitive, but what actually happened?"

Ten minutes later, Stephanie hung up the phone, amazed by the story she'd just heard. With one shot, Lexis Richards had destroyed his entire family, and Stephanie couldn't wait to tell.

"This is even juicier than I imagined," Harry commented after Stephanie filled him in. Harry Grain loved digging up dirt on people. His philosophy about fame and privacy was simple: When you make a living demanding that people pay attention to you, you deserve for people to pay attention to you. If that meant people digging into the clothes hamper of someone else's life—so be it. Nothing made him happier than finding out and revealing all the dirty laundry these spoiled celebrities thought they could keep hidden. "I applaud your resourcefulness."

"I am *very* resourceful, Mr. Grain. I talk to a great many people. Famous people your readers would love to read about."

"I see. And how do you know so many celebrities?"

Stephanie didn't dare reveal her source. If she played her cards right, her job with Felicia could turn into a nice little bread-and-butter gig, particularly if Wilcot & Associates continued to grow at its current rate. "I told you, I'm a writer with lots of friends in the public-relations business."

"You're sure you can deliver?"

"I think my handling of Lexis Richards is adequate proof."

"All right, I will make any substantive, verifiable news you give me well worth your while, but only if you give me complete exclusivity. No running to Cindy Adams or Liz Smith."

"And you'll guarantee that my name will never be mentioned?"

"Darling, if I revealed my sources, I'd be out of business in fifteen minutes."

"In that case, I'll be in touch."

16

Is this a new coffee?" Trace asked, returning his cup to its saucer. He and Felicia were sitting at the breakfast table, reading the Sunday *New York Times*.

"I thought you might like to try something different," Felicia explained. *Something different to spice up this regimented routine we call our life,* she added silently.

"What happened to the kind we always get?"

"Your regular brew is in the freezer," Felicia replied, a tint of resignation painting her words. This was so like her husband, unable or unwilling to try anything new. She was trying, as they'd both agreed to do at their lunch détente last summer, but Trace was still so anal retentive. From the time he got up in the morning to the order in which he read the newspaper, unless there were extenuating circumstances, nothing could shake Trace from his prescribed routine. Over the years Felicia had come to realize that Trace thrived in the comforting confines of habit. Always knowing what came next gave him the feeling of control. But now they were stuck in a rut—a rut so deep that Felicia had to wonder if they'd ever climb out.

"No, this is fine," Trace told her. He really wanted his

regular coffee but was unwilling to break the fragile truce. Much of the tension that was eating away the love between them had lifted, replaced by a cordial air of cooperation. For the past seven months both he and Felicia had made a concerted effort to improve their relationship, though with his wife's being constantly on the road with the Montell Spirits promotion, trying to save Lexis Richards from himself, and her new magazine account, it had been impossible to make any drastic changes in their life pattern. Still, as long as Felicia thought he was making an effort, Trace was confident that soon they'd be right back into their regular routine.

That's why he wanted to readdress the subject of starting a family. Felicia's reluctance to get pregnant was infuriating, but, as with everything in his life, Trace had a blueprint to reach his goal.

"I have an idea. Instead of spending Easter this year with your folks, let's book the villa in Aruba," Trace suggested.

"Why don't you let me find some place new?" Felicia replied. His timing couldn't be worse. Easter fell on April 17 this year, smack dab in the middle of her first *Appeal* event.

"I thought you liked Aruba."

"I do, but we always go there."

"Okay, you decide on a destination. As long as I'm with you, any place will be perfect," Trace said as he leaned over and kissed his wife.

He really is trying, she thought, surprised by his uncharacteristic flexibility. Felicia smiled and patted his cheek. Trace wasn't perfect, but then again he was no monster. Perhaps if she concentrated on the good things, the things that she initially fell in love with, she could get back the feelings she so desperately wanted to recapture. In a rush of affection, Felicia pulled her husband's face toward hers and gave him a kiss that made her intentions clear. Any doubts or disappointments she felt about her marital situation were temporarily replaced by desire.

Without unlocking their lips, Felicia stood, bringing Trace up with her. She wrapped her arms around him in a passionate, almost desperate embrace. She wanted to want Trace—to need him. If that was lost, what did they have left?

Trace's lips stretched into a slight smile. He felt great. He had things under control again. It was just a matter of time before he and Felicia were back in sync with each other. Trace opened his eyes to look at the kitchen clock. *Perfect timing,* he thought. *I can make love to my wife and still get to my tennis match.*

Gently Trace pulled away from Felicia, took her hand, and began leading her upstairs to the bedroom.

"No, let's stay here in the kitchen," Felicia suggested, enjoying the excitement of their sexual spontaneity.

"But, Feli," Trace protested softly, nibbling on her earlobe, "this is where we eat."

Felicia could feel her excitement level drop a notch. They always made love in the bedroom, or occasionally in the living room by the fireplace. Right now she was feeling sexy and adventurous. She wanted her husband to feel the same. For once Felicia wanted Trace to get caught up in the moment and—practicality be damned—make love to her right here on the kitchen table, even if it meant spilling his untouched coffee. *I'm not going to ruin this by getting mad. That's just the way he is. I have to keep trying.*

"Then we're in the perfect place, because breakfast is served," she announced. Just to make certain he got the full scope of her message, Felicia took her hand and reached inside Trace's tennis shorts. Even Felicia was shocked by her own risqué behavior. Sex between the two of them was generally a quiet affair. Physically Felicia was never left unfulfilled, but spiritually and emotionally their lovemaking lacked the fire and imagination she craved.

First the coffee, then the vacation planning, and now this. What's happening to my wife? Trace wondered. Felicia rarely took this kind of initiative. Granted, it was a turn-on to know that she obviously wanted him, but he was usually the one who made the sexual advances. Now Felicia seemed to be taking control of their sex life, and Trace wasn't sure if he liked it. Before he could sort out his feelings, the doorbell rang.

"Damn," Trace said as he disengaged himself from his wife. This unwelcome interruption was going to throw off his entire schedule.

"Forget it," Felicia pleaded, trying to hold on to her desire.

"It might be important. I'll get rid of whoever it is and meet you in the bedroom." Trace winked as he gave her a hungry kiss and sent her upstairs. That he had once again managed to get his way was not lost on Felicia.

Trace straightened up his shorts and opened the front door to find an angry and upset Lexis Richards at his doorstep.

"Where's Felicia? I need to talk to her *now*," Lexis barked as he pushed his way into the exquisitely renovated brownstone.

"What the hell . . . ?" Trace said with a glare. "Look here, you can't come bursting into my home demanding to see my wife. Felicia is not at *your* beck and call, client or not. Is that understood?"

"My bad. I'm sorry for busting in on you like this," Lexis apologized, "but this is an emergency. I need to talk to your wife."

"Well, whatever it is can wait until tomorrow when Felicia is at her office."

"Lexis, what's wrong?" Felicia asked, rushing downstairs still dressed in her sapphire-blue silk robe. "Come sit down. You look terrible."

"Felicia," Trace said in a stern tone that was both inquisitive and reprimanding.

"Excuse us a minute, Lexis." Felicia piloted Trace up the stairs and into the bedroom. "Honey, I'm sorry, but you can see how upset he is. I can't just ignore him."

"Felicia, we were about to make love."

"I'll make it up to you tonight," Felicia promised as she quickly got dressed. "Lexis is my biggest client. *You* can understand that."

Trace recognized Felicia's subtle dig, and it did not set well with him. Damn skippy that *his* clients came first. He was the provider in this house. Everything they owned—the brownstone, the car, stocks, art—everything was bought and paid for with *his* paycheck. This business of hers could not begin to compete with his law practice, which is why he couldn't believe that Felicia was putting some client's needs above his. This little public-relations company of hers was getting out of control. Once things were back to normal, Felicia was going to have to make a choice. She was going to be either Felicia Wilcot of Wilcot & Associates or Mrs. Trace Gordon, wife and mother. It was obvious she couldn't be both.

"Why do you have to talk to him now?" he asked, still unwilling to concede.

"Because *you* insisted on answering the door. But isn't it time for you to meet Derek anyway?" For once his routine was coming in handy.

Felicia was right, it was time for him to go. Besides, he was no longer in the mood for sex. "Just make sure he's gone by the time I return," he demanded as he pulled on his jacket and stormed past Lexis without saying a word.

Felicia shook her head as she walked back out into the living room. If it had been the other way around, there would be no discussion. She'd be expected simply to accept the situation. She might as well face the fact that Trace was never going to change. Felicia was going to have to either learn to deal with that fact or make some drastic changes in her life.

"How could you let this happen?" Lexis asked wildly, waving a newspaper in her face.

"Let what happen? Calm down for a minute and tell me what's got you so upset."

"You mean you haven't seen this?" he said, thrusting a copy of the *Star Diary* into her hands. "Tell me again, Felicia, just what the hell am I paying you for? I was under the impression that it was your fucking job to keep shit like this from happening."

"Hold on a minute, Lexis. I don't know what you're ranting and raving about, but I suggest you get a grip on yourself before I finish what my husband started and throw you out of my house."

She was furious. How dare he come in acting like a complete and utter fool, accusing her of not doing her job? *Men are all alike,* she thought in disgust. *When something goes wrong, blame the woman.*

What the hell are you doing? Lexis admonished himself. He knew that none of this was Felicia's fault. In the months since he'd hired her, she'd been a public-relations godsend, creating so much media attention over him and his movie that *Southeast* was now a box-office smash. Felicia was a damn good publicist, and he trusted her instincts, which was exactly why he had re-signed with her at the conclusion of their trial run.

But seeing Felicia half dressed, looking all sexed-up and hot, cozying up with that Oreo-cookie, Clarence

Thomas—lovin', chino-pants-and-Docksider-wearin' husband of hers, caused something inside him to snap. What the hell did she see in that asswipe? And to top it off, here was this bullshit story by Harry Grain. How much was a man supposed to take in one morning?

"I'm sorry. I didn't mean to dis you, it's just— What are we going to do about this?"

Felicia smoothed out the mangled tabloid, revealing its bold headline: HOMEBOY DIRECTOR SHOOTS TWIN. The subhead read, "As Lexis Richards Sits in Lap of Luxury, Quadriplegic Brother Languishes in the Projects." Accompanying the explosive headlines was a picture of Lexis in a friend's lavish Tribeca loft, borrowed for a recent magazine photo session. In juxtaposition was an exterior shot of the Clifton Terrace projects, located in southeast Washington, D.C.

"Oh, no," Felicia said, her anger displaced by concern for her client's obvious pain. "Come have a cup of coffee while we sort out this mess."

"Where did he dig up this stuff?" Lexis asked, pouring a cup of coffee.

"Not only does a slime like Harry Grain have sources all over town, but he also couldn't care less if what he prints contains a 'grain' of truth—pardon the pun."

"Some of it is true," Lexis admitted.

"Well, then you better tell me about it. It looks like we're going to have to do some damage control."

Lexis pulled off his wire-rimmed sunglasses and rubbed his eyes. Judging from his body language, it was clear that all the anguish and guilt that had eaten away at him these past years were rising to the top, replacing his characteristic confidence with remorse.

"It happened when we were ten years old," he began softly, his voice almost inaudible. "My uncle had given me an old home-movie camera, one of those eight-millimeter things. I decided to shoot a Western called *Shoot-out at the LA Corral.* Pretty original, huh?" Felicia saw Lexis smile slightly at the bittersweet memory. He paused and let loose a heavy sigh. She reached over and took his shaking hand in hers.

Lexis squeezed her hand slightly and continued. "We had all the props—hats, lassos—everything we needed, except we were short one pistol. It was Lewis's suggestion that we use my father's gun. It seemed like a good idea at the time," he said, his voice growing momentarily faint. "Anyway, we both wanted to use the real gun, so we flipped a coin. It was heads. I won," Lexis said, his face expressing the irony of his last statement.

"We staged the shoot-out, just like a real Western— standing back to back, counting to ten as we walked away from each other. Lewis must have miscounted, because when I turned around and pulled the trigger, he was still walking. When the gun went off, I was shocked. I had no idea there were bullets in that gun." Lexis looked Felicia in the eye, imploring her to believe his story. She did. There was no question in her mind that Lexis was telling the truth.

"At first, when Lewis fell down, I laughed, thinking he was really getting into this acting thing, but he didn't say anything. I noticed he wasn't moving, so I went over to him. That's when I saw the blood. The bullet hit Lewis in the lower back and severed his spinal cord. He hasn't been able to walk or use his arms ever since. . . ."

Felicia could hear the guilt and regret in Lexis's voice as his words trailed off. He hung his head in shame, like a child who has inadvertently broken some treasured heirloom. But in Lexis's mind he had damaged much more than some porcelain vase. He'd broken the very heart of his family.

"Lexis, you were playing a game," Felicia offered gently. "You didn't intentionally shoot your brother."

"Yeah, that's what my mom said, but that game caused much grief. I ruined everybody's life—my brother's, my folks', mine. Sometimes I think Lewis would have been better off had he died, because the way he is now, the brother has *no* life. He's stuck in a wheelchair, unable to do anything for himself."

"He lives with your parents?"

"My folks split up a couple of years later. My father dropped out of sight, leaving my mom alone to raise the two of us. I don't know, maybe he felt guilty, too. Mom had been after him for years to get rid of that gun. I think she blamed him, which was wrong. It was my fault, not his."

"Why are your mother and Lewis living in the projects?" Felicia asked. If she was going to rectify this situation, she needed to know all the details, no matter how distressing they might prove to be.

"They're still there because the new house I bought them isn't ready yet. They're making it wheelchair accessible. And contrary to what that asshole Grain has to say, I've always done whatever I could to help with my brother's medical expenses. Now that I'm finally making some cash, I'm taking everything over so my mom doesn't have to work so hard."

"What about you and Lewis? Are you close?"

"No."

"He never forgave you?"

"Lewis forgave me. I just can't forgive myself."

Felicia didn't know what to say to her client. His anguish was palpable. Her heart ached for him. At a complete loss for words, she simply pulled him into a sympathetic hug. Lexis leaned into her body, drawing comfort from her supportive embrace. He felt better for telling her the truth, and he trusted Felicia to explain his story in a way the public would understand.

Felicia closed her eyes and allowed herself to breathe in the provocative scent of his cologne. She immediately recognized the citrus smell as Armani. An appropriate choice, she thought. Definitely indicative of the man—bold, compelling, and, if not applied in correct measure, overpowering.

Perhaps it was the cologne, the intimacy they'd just shared, or being in such close proximity to this complicated man that sent a sexual charge surging through Felicia's body. She was confused. How could he infuriate her one minute and leave her feeling tipsy and light-headed the next? *This is ridiculous,* she thought, refusing to acknowledge her attraction to Lexis. Felicia decided that her feelings were the remnants of her earlier, unconsummated seduction with Trace and pulled away.

"We'll straighten this thing out," she promised.

Lexis said nothing, simply smiled slightly and shook his head. Tenderly he reached up and caressed Felicia's cheek with the back of his hand. With a whisper of a touch he ran his finger gently across her full lips. Their eyes locked, each searching for a clue to what was happening between them. He bent his face down toward hers, and for a fleeting moment Felicia thought, wished, and feared that Lexis would kiss her. Instead his lips found her ear and he simply whispered, "Thank you," and turned to leave.

"You're welcome," she called back softly, still touching her cheek as the door closed behind him.

17

Beatrice didn't notice her error right away. It was only after she put the red six on the black seven did she realize her earlier mistake of placing two red cards together. Now her morning game of solitaire was thrown totally awry. Defeated by her inattention, Beatrice gathered the cards back into the deck and stifled a yawn. She was tired but determined to stay awake. Her future was riding on the outcome of Gabrielle's meeting. Sleep could wait.

Another yawn prompted Beatrice toward the kitchen for a cup of tea. This past week had been particularly hectic. As Gabrielle's official chaperone, Beatrice now accompanied the young model to all location shoots. Because Gabrielle was a model in demand, the two of them were now genuine frequent fliers, hopping a flight every three or four days headed for a different part of the country. It was no longer an uncommon scenario for the two to be on the pink-sand beaches of Bermuda one day, only to leave that evening for a two-day shoot in the cactus-strewn deserts of Arizona. It was a job that, despite the wear and tear the high-speed pace caused her aging body, she wouldn't trade for a king's ransom.

Bea loved every minute she spent with Gabrielle. Nothing could compare to the joy she felt knowing how much Gabrielle depended on her. Because Gabrielle had successfully convinced the people at First Face that she was afraid to fly, they had no reason to suspect that away from familiar surroundings Gabrielle became a foreigner in her own land and Bea her tour guide in a world she couldn't understand.

Beatrice was fully aware that this dependence was reciprocal. Gabrielle had become her lifeline. Being around this young girl added years to her life, effectively saving her from the despair of growing old alone.

For this reason Gabrielle's sudden desire to get literacy tutoring alarmed Bea. Her decision came immediately following a series of embarrassing and frightening incidents that took place while they were on location in Florida on Miami's South Beach.

The photo shoot had been a particularly tough one, thanks to the weather's refusal to cooperate. Gabrielle and Claire, the job's makeup artist, decided to have a leisurely dinner at a nearby Cuban restaurant to unwind and relax. They invited Beatrice to join them, but, exhausted from the long day, she declined and opted for room service.

While she and Claire waited to order, Gabrielle excused herself and headed downstairs to the bathroom. She stopped in her tracks, confused by the signs marking the two doors in front of her. The door on the left said "Señoras," while the sign on the right read "Señores." These unfamiliar letter combinations threw Gabrielle into confusion. Where were the familiar words "Men" and "Women"? These were words she recognized on sight. She looked back and forth at both doors, searching for some sort of hint. Finding none, she walked over to the pay phone, picked up the receiver, and waited for someone to come into or out of the restroom.

After a few minutes Claire rounded the corner. She saw

Gabrielle at the phone and stopped to wait for her. Gabrielle mouthed the words "My booker," and motioned for the woman to go ahead. Claire walked into the door marked "Señoras" and disappeared. Gabrielle counted to ten and rushed in behind her.

Back at the table Gabrielle pretended to study the menu, wishing Beatrice were there to read it for her. When the waiter approached, Claire, unable to decide, prompted Gabrielle to go first.

"I'll have a hamburger," she ordered.

"I am sorry, señorita, but we do not serve hamburgers," the waiter informed her.

"Well then, I'll just have a salad," Gabrielle requested nervously. She was starving, but she didn't want to risk making another mistake.

"You models are always watching your weight. Come on, Gabrielle, this place is famous for their Cuban cuisine. Try something else."

"There's so much to choose from. I can't decide. Why don't you order for me?" Gabrielle suggested.

Happy to oblige, Claire proceeded to place their dinner order.

After dinner Gabrielle returned to the suite she and Beatrice shared and headed directly for the bathroom. Her stomach, unaccustomed to spicy Cuban food, was upset. Gabrielle found what she was looking for, poured herself a glass of Evian, plopped the tablets into the water, and waited for them to dissolve. Gabrielle picked up the fizzing glass and was about to drink when Bea wandered into the bathroom.

"Upset stomach?" she asked gently.

"Too much *ropa vieja*. Alka-Seltzer to the rescue," Gabrielle said, lifting her glass. "Cheers."

Noticing the discarded foil wrappers on the bathroom

counter, Beatrice shouted, *"Don't!"* and grabbed the glass from Gabrielle's hand. Her action caused the foamy liquid to spill across the tile floor. "Sweetheart, this isn't Alka-Seltzer. This is Polident."

"The stuff you clean your dentures with?"

"Yes. If you drank that, you would have made yourself very ill."

"But it's wrapped like Alka-Seltzer," Gabrielle argued, her voice dropping. "How could I be so stupid?"

"You're not stupid. Don't let me ever hear you say that again," Beatrice said sternly.

"Then why do I *feel* like I am at least a hundred times a day? When am I going to stop feeling like I'm two years old?"

"Did something happen tonight? You haven't been yourself since you got back from dinner."

Bea listened as Gabrielle ruefully recounted her evening at the restaurant.

"Gabrielle, look at me," Beatrice demanded. "Stop upsetting yourself over this. It will be okay. I promise."

"How do you know it will be okay?" Gabrielle snapped fiercely. "Do you know what will happen if people find out about me? They'll laugh me out of the business."

Gabrielle began crying, and Bea held her for a moment, stroking her hair. "You don't understand how it feels. Being illiterate is like being at the bottom of a dark well." She sobbed. "You feel totally alone and helpless, and all you can think about is 'How am I going to get out of this?'" Following a fresh series of sobs, Gabrielle abruptly pulled away.

"Teach me how to read," she demanded.

"Honey, I tried to with those learn-with-phonics tapes, but you quit."

"I just didn't get it."

"Don't worry, I'll still read to you whenever you want."

Gabrielle went over to the coffee table and picked up several magazines. "I want you to teach me so I can read these myself. I'm not a child."

"Honey, I can't teach you to read."

In an uncharacteristic fit of anger, Gabrielle threw the magazines across the room. "Yes, you can. You just won't," she shouted.

"Gabrielle, listen to me. You need a professional tutor."

"How can I see a tutor with the kind of schedule I keep?"

Beatrice was glad that Gabrielle had brought up the point herself. She didn't want it to look as if she was trying to dissuade her from seeking help, but she was selfishly grateful that Gabrielle was putting up her own argument against finding a tutor.

"Honey, don't worry. I'll always be here for you," she promised.

Instead of having the soothing effect she'd hoped for, Beatrice's words unleashed a torrent of fury from Gabrielle. "Just like my mother? She also promised to always be here for me. Where is she now? Dead and buried. Are you going to swear never to die on me, Beatrice? Can I count on you outliving me? Shall we draw up a contract—one that you can read to me, because I can't do it for myself?" Gabrielle demanded as she stormed out of the room.

Beatrice was stunned by the vehemence in her voice, but she understood Gabrielle's anger. She was angry herself. It was tragic and inexcusable that this girl was allowed to slip through the cracks and graduate from high school knowing little more than her alphabet and how to sign her name. Since Gabrielle's astounding revelation, Beatrice had researched the illiteracy problem in this country, and the facts had left her dumbfounded. Gabrielle was one of more than forty million American adults who either could not read or write well enough to vote, understand a legal document, or even read a young child a simple story. She shuddered to think what toll so many illiterate adults were taking on this country's well-being—present and future.

Later that evening Gabrielle came to her, not only to apologize but to inform Beatrice of her decision to seek help. Gabrielle's determination to learn to read and write left Beatrice with mixed feelings. She could see the emotional damage that being illiterate had done to the girl. In many respects she was an outlaw, manipulating her way through literate society by any means necessary. Sometimes that meant lying and cheating, behavior that went against her natural goodness and inclination to do right. This constant collision between honor and survival left the girl confused and struggling to maintain some semblance of self-confidence.

Any fault Beatrice attributed to Helene for not seeking help for her daughter was tempered by the wonderful job she had done in making Gabrielle feel special and important in spite of her reading deficiency. By continually stressing her magnificent career potential, Helene had allowed Gabrielle to grow up convinced that her future held marvelous things. Still, with Gabrielle held hostage by her illiteracy, her emerging success offered only a temporary buffer from potential disaster.

Bea's dilemma was clear: A literate Gabrielle, with all her accumulated wealth and fame, would be capable of living and functioning on her own. The very idea of not being a crucial part of Gabrielle's life scared and saddened her. Beatrice was fully aware that someday it would happen. She even *wanted* it to happen, but not now. The Almighty had just sent Gabrielle to her, and she wasn't ready to give her up.

* * *

"Hi," Gabrielle called out to the receptionist as she made her way back to Jaci's desk. She was nervous and scared, yet amazingly hopeful. After this meeting she'd be on her way to the Brooklyn Library to see a literacy tutor and, she hoped, on her way to a more peaceful life as well.

Jaci motioned to Gabrielle to take a seat while she finished up a phone call. "Another call from *Appeal* about you," she said when she was done, spinning her chair around to face the model.

"What now?" Gabrielle asked.

"They want to know if you've chosen your favorite designer because they need your 'personal style' selections by the end of the week."

"I guess I'd have to say whoever designs for the Gap and Maynard Scarborough," Gabrielle revealed. On her last shoot for Saks Fifth Avenue she'd worn several Scarborough outfits and was impressed by the simplicity of his designs and the quality of his workmanship.

"I love his clothes, too. His lines are clean and slick-looking. You don't get lost in the extra frills some designers find it necessary to include."

"I guess I never thought about it like that. I just like the way I look and feel in his designs. Jaci, I don't know if I can do this. I can wear the clothes, but I don't know if I can talk about them."

"Which is exactly why God created PR people. Felicia Wilcot is handling the publicity for the launch. She'll have you so well briefed that by the time your interview comes around, the whole thing will be a piece of cake."

Gabrielle felt a slight sense of relief. Her experience at the Montell Spirits party had left her with a good impression of the woman. Judging from the huge success of the party and those that followed in other cities, Felicia was obviously very skilled at her job. Gabrielle knew that she was in good hands.

"Now, I know you're afraid of flying, but do you get seasick as well?" Jaci asked, crossing her fingers, toes, legs, arms, and eyes. She hoped not, because if Gabrielle did, this big launch would literally be dead in the water.

Gabrielle laughed at the spectacle her booker was creating. "I don't think so," she said as Jaci uncrossed her eyes and appendages. "Why?"

"Because the great majority of this shoot takes place on a cruise ship. The fabulous *Costa Classica* to be exact."

"The *Costa* who?"

"The *Costa Classica*. It's only the most sensuous and most *Italian* cruise ship sailing the Caribbean. I wish I could go with you on this one—good food, luxurious accommodations, and an entire ship filled with handsome Italian men at your beck and call. What more could a woman want out of life?"

"How do you know that all the men on board are handsome?"

"Because they're Italian, you silly girl. But physical features are the least of what makes Italian men handsome. It's mostly in the way they make a woman feel—adored, sexy, and oh, so feminine."

"You obviously speak from experience," Gabrielle observed through her laughter.

"Absolutely, but we don't have the time to delve into that now. Back to the business at hand. You'll also do some location work in Martinique and Barbados. Oh, did I mention that you leave in two weeks?"

"I take it I won't be working much until then."

"Except for the *Harper's Bazaar* shoot, you're booked out until your bon voyage. Enjoy the break, because with all these major publicity events centered on you, once this magazine hits the newsstands, you won't be able to go anywhere without people recognizing your face," Jaci informed her as she picked up her ringing phone. "Beatrice, hello. Tell me, do you get seasick? I'll let Gabrielle explain," the booker said, handing Gabrielle the phone.

"I called to wish you luck at the tutoring center," Beatrice said.

"I'm not going."

"What made you change your mind?" Bea asked, trying to keep her relief in check.

"According to Jaci, people all over are going to recognize me once this magazine comes out," she explained, hoping that Bea would understand. There was no way she could get literacy tutoring now. Word would get out so fast that her newfound fame would turn to instant infamy. She was trapped. Whatever bubble of hope she had walked in with had quickly burst.

"I understand completely, dear, but don't you worry. We'll straighten this thing out somehow. Now, what's this about getting seasick?"

"Pack your sunscreen. We're going on a cruise."

18

When I find the bastard who's holding the voodoo doll with my face on it, I'll string up the little shit by his balls, Stephanie thought, reacting to Felicia's news. With *Appeal* magazine as a new client, she now had not only to live with Gabrielle but work for her as well. It was bad enough she had to watch the girl flit around the house with glee ever since she got this stupid cover. Promoting Gabrielle was going to be pure, unadulterated torture.

Nothing could be as torturous as this stupid staff meeting, Stephanie decided. *Who other than Felicia "Work Till You Weep" Wilcot calls a staff meeting for two people?*

"The *Appeal* magazine account has added a considerable amount of work to our already full plate," Felicia was saying. "To deal with that, I've hired a new receptionist slash office manager. Her name is Deena Lacey. I'm also promoting you to account executive. You'll get a pay raise and have much more client interaction. How does all this sound?"

"Terrific."

"You deserve it. I couldn't have gotten through these hectic months without you. Now, that's it for new business.

As for our other accounts, The American Spirit Celebration Tour is officially over, and from all reports it was a smashing success in all five cities. So smashing that the winecooler sales are double the company's initial projections and Peter Montell is keeping us on retainer for future events."

"That's great. What's going on with Lexis Richards? That awful story about him was picked up by a lot of newspapers after it ran in *Star Diary*."

"Tell me about it. I feel like a California fireman desperately trying to put out a wild brushfire. Every time I smother the flames of one, another one breaks out. I'd love to find the little arsonist who lit the match on this blaze."

"Any clue how Harry Grain got his information?" Stephanie asked, assuaging her guilt by reminding herself that she had only reported the truth.

"I'm sure he paid for it."

"He *buys* news?" Stephanie asked, feigning surprise and outrage.

"They all do. These tabloids are notorious for doling out dollars to people who swear they know something about somebody. The more sensational the news, the bigger the payoff."

"Journalists can't pay for their stories, can they?"

"That's the point, Stephanie. Harry Grain is *not* a journalist. He isn't interested in reporting unbiased news. Anything goes—fact or fiction. It's not all his fault, though. If people stopped buying this garbage, filth like 'The Grain Harvest' would cease to exist."

Stephanie disagreed totally with Felicia's assessment of why these papers not only survived but flourished. It wasn't the readers who fueled the tabloids, it was the celebrities themselves. Stars like Roseanne, Madonna, Michael Jackson, and Europe's spoiled royalty were the drum majors in the great tabloid parade—marching the public straight into their wild sexual exploits, bizarre antics, and volatile relationships. How dare they have the audacity to whine and cry about invasion of privacy?

"If I can do anything to help clean up this mess, please let me know," Stephanie offered for good measure.

"Thanks, but I think I have it all under control."

"For our sakes, I hope Lexis isn't hiding anything else," Stephanie probed gently.

"He assures me that there are no other skeletons in his closet. If anyone asks *anything* about Lexis Richards, refer them to me. I want to avoid at all costs a repeat of this current catastrophe. Look at the time," Felicia said, glancing at her watch. "I have a conference call with Gabrielle in five minutes. While I'm on the phone, I need you to pull together a list of feature writers we've used in the past. Ruthanna wants to handpick the reporter to do the *Appeal* story on Gabrielle, and I promised her a few suggestions."

A story on Gabrielle? Stephanie's heartbeat quickened. *Who better to do a story on Gabrielle than me?* Stephanie tried to restrain her smile. Gabrielle Donovan's story was hers to tell. Now she just had to convince Felicia.

"Felicia, I would be perfect to write that story. I do know Gabrielle very well."

"Don't you think it would be a conflict of interest for the same firm that represents Gabrielle to write a story on her?"

"But this is Gabrielle's first big interview," Stephanie went on, ignoring Felicia's argument. "Don't you think she'd be more comfortable with a friend than some stranger? I know I could do a good job."

"Stephanie, I'll give your name to Ruthanna for consideration," Felicia offered, "but you do understand it's *her* decision?" Felicia found it pointless to argue the facts with Stephanie. Not only did she think Stephanie was the wrong writer for the assignment, Felicia was counting on her to take care of things in the office while she was away on the cruise.

"I know, but with *your* recommendation I might have a chance," Stephanie said, making her expectations clear.

Gabrielle answered her cellular phone on the third ring. She was on location in Vail shooting a layout for *Harper's Bazaar.*

"Gabrielle, how are you?" Felicia inquired.

"Great. Sorry we couldn't have this meeting face to face."

"Not a problem. So, are you excited about all this hoopla?" Felicia asked. "According to Ruthanna Beverly, you're a star on the rise."

"We'll have to see about all that," Gabrielle replied modestly.

"With everything we have planned for the launch of this magazine, it will be impossible for you *not* to be noticed."

"I guess that's the way it has to be," Gabrielle said with resignation. Her comment had an understandably nervous edge to it.

"I thought this is what you wanted? Am I hearing something different?"

"No, it's just that I had no idea modeling would be like this. I hadn't factored in all this public-relations stuff."

"That's because you think of yourself as just another model, but the people promoting you see you as a superstar."

"Why do they have to know so much about me?"

"For girls in your category, fame brings with it a lot of tedious and sometimes annoying consequences—the press being one of them," Felicia explained. It was clear that Gabrielle was apprehensive about her impending fame. She had every reason to be. Beauty, celebrity, and large amounts of money could be a deadly combination for any person, but particularly for someone so young. Gabrielle had to be 100 percent sure that this was the life she wanted. If not, the time to get out was now, before things went too far.

"Gabrielle, I know all this attention seems pretty intense, but I'm afraid that it's inevitable for someone with your potential, and it will probably get much worse. So before we go any further, you have to ask yourself: In your heart of hearts, do you really want all of this?"

Felicia's question caught her off guard. Everyone assumed, herself included, that not only did she *want* this life but that she *would* have it. But things were different now, Gabrielle reminded herself. Helene's death was never factored into the equation. Her mom was gone, and Gabrielle stood alone on the threshold of her dream.

"Yes, this is exactly what I want," Gabrielle said, casting aside any doubt. Nothing was going to stop her from fulfilling her mother's vision. Gabrielle had to take the chance that things would work out. They had so far. It had been just over a year since she'd arrived in New York, and only Bea knew her shame. And perhaps, with Beatrice and Felicia running interference, her secret life would remain just that—a secret.

19

"*Benvenuto a bordo,*" the cruise hostess greeted Doug Sixsmith as he reached the end of the gangplank. Her smile was
second nature—a grin that came automatically after years of
nonstop pleasantness in the company of strangers.

"Your cabin number, sir?"

"Sixty-thirty," Doug replied, stepping into the ship's artistically appointed lobby. "I'm here with the *Appeal* magazine shoot."

"Of course," the woman said. "If you go with Paolo, he
will escort you to your stateroom."

"Thank you," Doug said as Paolo picked up his carry-
on bag and led him into the elevator. Following his white-
gloved escort, Doug still could not believe he was boarding
a cruise ship. He hadn't been on a proper vacation in at least
six years, and when he did get around to taking one, cruising
would not be present on his list of things to do. He'd often
heard about these seafaring amusement parks—the ridiculous amounts of food, the unparalleled pampering, and, of
course, their "Love Boat" reputation—but the idea of being
held captive aboard a floating hotel did not appeal to him.

Cruises were for honeymooners and old folks. Single and thirty-four, Doug Sixsmith did not belong in either category.

You could find him, however, listed under the heading "workaholic." An accomplished journalist with a reputation for always getting his story, Doug was known among his peers as a resourceful and forthright reporter. His work was informative and provocative, and he had the awards to prove it. The Peabody, Du Pont, and Pulitzer prizes that lined his bookcase were nice, but Doug wrote not for the acclaim but because he truly loved his work.

As his readers' eyes to the world, Doug traveled around the globe, witnessing and writing about everything from the crumbling of the Berlin Wall to the suffering of the people of Somalia. He had his own unique style of combining description and fact into a compelling must-read story for millions of people. What really set Doug apart from the rest of his colleagues, however, was his unmatched ability to link what was going on in the rest of the world to the everyday lives of common individuals. From the separation of Siamese twins to the bloodshed in Bosnia, Doug made his readers stop, think, and care about the people and events he reported.

After nearly a decade of covering world-altering events, writing about a day in the life of a human clothes hanger was a long way from his idea of a challenging assignment. When Doug's college friend, Ruthanna Beverly, had called him about writing the article, his first notion was to turn the assignment down, but, as they say, timing is everything.

Recently Doug had come to a startling realization: Outside of work, he had no life. Five months shy of thirty-five, Doug determined that while he had the admiration and respect of his colleagues, he owned no property, had few close friends, no children, and only his journalism awards to wrap his arms around at night. Having reached this sad conclusion, he decided it was time to take a real vacation and get his head together. Four days on the open sea seemed as good a place as any for such a major soul search. And even though technically he was working, how demanding could this assignment be? It wasn't exactly a day in the life of Fidel Castro, for God's sake. Doug was certain that he could write this fluff piece and still have three days and twenty-two hours left to figure out his future. He might even have time to work on his novel.

"Your stateroom, *Signor* Sixsmith," Paolo announced, unlocking the door of Doug's cabin. "Your luggage will be delivered within the hour. Your stewardess will be here shortly to acquaint you with your room. Enjoy your cruise."

"Grazie," Doug responded, closing the door behind Paolo. He was embarrassed to admit even to himself how impressed he was by these luxurious accommodations. As in the rest of the ship, every detail in his spacious stateroom— from the cherrywood cabinetry with chic leather pulls to the handwoven tapestries gracing two of the sandcolored walls—was *molto italiano.* "Okay, a *five-star* floating hotel," Doug conceded aloud.

On his bed Doug found the ship's itinerary for the rest of the evening—dinner at six-thirty, safety briefing at eight, and set sail at ten, which was also the hour the *Appeal* bon-voyage party began. He wasn't hungry and decided to get some sleep before the briefing. Making himself comfortable, Doug couldn't push the thought from his mind that, yet again, he was going to bed alone.

Priority number one, he decided, was finding a good woman when he returned to Boston. *Wait,* he told himself, stopping his thought short. There had already been *two* good women in his life, both lost because of his crazy self-imposed schedule. Doug quickly amended his thinking to include letting his personal life take priority over his professional one. *This sea air is making me delusional,* he observed. *I'd love to meet the woman who can make me forget work.* Settling into his nap, Doug was unclear if he was issuing himself a challenge or simply making a wish.

"I think I'll shave before dinner," Trace informed Felicia.

"Dinner isn't for another two and a half hours."

"I thought maybe we could have a little fun, and I know how you hate scratchy stubble."

"Mmm. Well, you go right ahead and shave while I finish unpacking. Who knows what I might find in here to put on?" Felicia answered with a voice laden with promise. Trace was being a good sport about tacking their Easter getaway onto her business trip, and lately he'd been particularly attentive. Rather than question his motives, she decided to enjoy these good feelings while they lasted.

"Or for me to take off," Trace suggested as he stepped into the small European-style bathroom. His five-o'clock shadow was well over an hour away, but he needed the time alone to put his plan into action. Coming on this damn cruise, a working event for Felicia no less, was not his idea of a romantic vacation. He had agreed to come only when she promised that they would disembark in Martinique and continue the rest of the trip alone.

Trace needed his wife's full attention. It was time for Felicia to turn her focus away from her work and toward building a family. Trace was tired of waiting for Felicia to come around. It was up to him to get things going. This was the perfect opportunity for them to get pregnant—before Lexis Richards got himself into more trouble or Felicia picked up yet another new client and became even busier.

While Felicia continued to unpack, Trace searched the bathroom. His hunt was brief. In her cosmetic bag he found the red-satin pouch he was looking for. He unsnapped the bag and pulled out the plastic container holding Felicia's diaphragm. Trace picked up the molded rubber cap and squeezed it together several times. For years he'd considered this simple contraption a friend, protecting him from the responsibility of premature parenthood and freeing him from the burden of using a condom. But now that he was ready for a child, the tables were turned.

Pulling the needle out of the sewing kit, he quickly punched thirty or so minuscule holes into the rubber device. Trace felt no guilt over his actions, convinced that he was merely giving his wife a push in the direction in which they both wanted to go. Confident that his work was invisible to the naked eye, Trace replaced the diaphragm and, smiling broadly, proceeded to slap on some cologne.

Trace returned to the cabin to find Felicia dressed in a black-lace teddy, reclining suggestively on the bed. She'd turned on the radio, and soft Italian love songs filled the air. Trace felt himself becoming aroused. His wife was an incredibly beautiful woman, and she was going to make an even more beautiful mother.

Trace pulled Felicia from the bed and kissed her hungrily. His tongue probed her mouth deeply as his hands moved swiftly to remove the thin straps of her teddy from her shoulders. He pushed her lingerie away from her body as his hands followed the contours of her small waist and hips.

Felicia let out a soft groan as Trace rolled her stiff nipples between his fingers. *How luscious these will be when they're swollen with milk,* Trace thought, bending down to suckle her aroused breasts.

"Wait, baby," Felicia requested, pulling away. "I have to go put in my diaphragm. It's my dangerous time of the month."

Trace commanded his lips not to betray him with a

smile. "Fine, but you might as well leave it in for the duration. We're going to christen this ship with style."

When Felicia slipped back into Trace's arms minutes later, he was barely able to contain himself. As his kisses grew more demanding, he climbed on top of Felicia and entered her with urgent desire. The constant friction of their bodies caused Felicia to moan loudly as she reached her climax.

"I'm—I'm coming," Trace called out, the intensity of his orgasm causing his voice to break. The two collapsed onto the bed, both still throbbing from their encounter. Felicia rolled out from under Trace, and instead of basking in the glow of lazy contentment, she lay back analyzing the situation. This was the lustiest romp she and Trace had shared in a very long time. For whatever reason, her husband had been so demanding of her body. He'd loved her with the intensity and passion she'd been aching for. But if this was the case, why then, just as she was experiencing the most intense orgasm she'd had in years, did she think of Lexis Richards?

"That dress is perfect," Bea assured Gabrielle. "But then again, so were all the others."

After trying on nearly everything in her suitcase, Gabrielle finally chose a flocked-velvet jacquard slip dress designed by Maynard Scarborough. The claret-red dress, cut on the bias, flowed over every curve, ending just above Gabrielle's ankles. The low scoop neck, held up by thin satin straps, dipped just enough to reveal the fleshy tops of her voluminous breasts.

"I've never been so nervous about going to a party," Gabrielle admitted.

"It's because you're the guest of honor. Relax. You look sensational."

"That's not it, Bea. I'm afraid to meet all these reporters. What if they start asking a bunch of questions I can't answer? And what about the reporter who's doing the 'day in the life' story? What if I do something that makes him suspicious and he finds out everything? I should have never agreed to this."

"It will be okay. Remember, you're in control. You alone call the shots."

"Then we'd better go get this over with."

The two women headed downstairs to the Puccini Ballroom. They were greeted at the door by both Ruthanna and Felicia. "We were just on our way down to get you," Felicia told Gabrielle. "Everybody wants to meet our cover girl."

"Okay, ready or not, here we go," Ruthanna said as she took Gabrielle's arm and the two plunged into the crowded room. Bea found a comfortable chair near the dance floor as Ruthanna ushered the young model around the ballroom. The ballroom surrounded Gabrielle, cloaking her in warm flickering candlelight. A three-piece band provided an entertaining array of popular tunes, and several couples were already out on the floor dancing with an uninhibited giddiness brought on by free-flowing champagne. The majority were milling around the room enjoying themselves, while several of the other models booked for the shoot were fanned out across the room, each creating her own little pocket of havoc among the admiring passengers.

One by one, Ruthanna began introducing Gabrielle to the men and women whose companies had committed advertising dollars to the first six issues of *Appeal* magazine. It was Felicia's idea to invite them on the cruise as a way to say thank you for their support and to ensure future business.

"*Buona sera,*" interrupted a handsome gentleman dressed in a crisp white nautical uniform. "I am Captain Gianni Di Angelo. It is my pleasure to welcome you personally aboard the *Costa Classica*."

"How nice of you, Captain. And I'd like to thank you for lending us your beautiful ship," Ruthanna said, smiling.

"With you ladies on board, her beauty pales considerably," he flirted. Captain Di Angelo was gracious and polite, including both of the women in his compliment. It could not be mistaken, however, where his interests lay. Ruthanna, understanding immediately, took the opportunity to mingle with the other guests.

"Signorina, do I know your name?"

"Gabrielle," she answered shyly, mesmerized by the captain's charming demeanor.

"Ah, the name of an angel. You know, Signorina Gabriella, I must now rechristen my ship. With *you* aboard, she should be named *Bellezza del Mare*, 'Beauty of the Sea.'" Gabrielle found herself blushing as Captain Di Angelo's eyes roamed her body with admiration.

"Unfortunately, I am headed back to the bridge, but tomorrow evening you will join me at my table for dinner, *si?*"

"Thank you, I'd like that."

"Even one day is an eternity to wait for one so lovely," he said, kissing her hand again. *"Buona sera, bella."*

"That was no Captain Stubing," Beatrice remarked, appearing from nowhere. "That was one handsome man."

"He was, wasn't he?" Gabrielle agreed dreamily. "He's so charming. Jaci was right. These Italian men are something else." She chuckled. "All this flattery has made me hungry. Let's visit the buffet table before I get dragged off to meet someone else."

Before Beatrice could answer, an older, distinguished-looking gentleman approached. *"Buona sera, signora, signorina.* Pardon me for interrupting, but would the signora like to dance?"

Bea, pleasure erupting all over her face, took his arm and headed off to the dance floor. Gabrielle, happy for her friend, headed for the buffet. The layout was awesome. Dominating the table was a huge ice sculpture carefully chiseled into the shape of three leaping dolphins. Surrounding it were bite-sized hors d'oeuvre artistically arranged into mosaics of starbursts, peacocks, and other fanciful shapes. Everything was so elegantly displayed that Gabrielle was reluctant to eat anything, unwilling to destroy such works of art. Conversely, everything looked so succulent and delicious, it was impossible to pass up the opportunity to taste such treats.

She reached across the table for the fattest, juiciest-looking chocolate-covered strawberry nestled among the almond cookies, but before she could grab it, another hand bumped hers.

"I guess the gentlemanly thing to do would be to let you have my strawberry," an American male's voice remarked. "But let the record show that I did see it first."

Gabrielle turned to find herself looking into a vaguely familiar face. "Do I know you?" she inquired.

Returning her gaze, Doug felt his stomach flip. He was stunned to see her. Gabrielle had crossed his mind several times since their meeting over a year ago. She'd impressed him that night, not just with her outstanding physical attributes but also with her genuine interest in his work and her shy but sharp sense of humor.

"We always seem to meet over Italian food. I think the last time—well, the only time—we ate together, you tried to steal my focaccia," Doug told her, unable to keep a smile from overtaking his face. "Doug Sixsmith. In case you don't remember, we met at the Hilton Hotel in New York a little over a year ago."

"I'm Gabrielle Donovan, and I believe that it was *my*

focaccia that you tried to sneak onto *your* plate," she responded, causing them both to laugh.

"I assume that since you're here, your interviews with the modeling agencies worked out."

"They did. I was picked up by a great agency, and I've been working pretty steadily. Now, you were working on a story about the death of Communism when we met, so I'm surprised that the rise and fall of hemlines is within your area of expertise."

"It's definitely not. I'm here doing a last-minute favor for a friend. Ruthanna and I went to Penn State together. Apparently the original writer got the chicken pox, so she asked me to fill in and write one of those 'day in the life' pieces on one of your colleagues."

"You don't sound like you're looking forward to this assignment."

"Watching a beauty queen have her picture taken isn't exactly my idea of a formidable assignment," Doug responded before realizing what he said. "No offense, it's just, that I'm used to writing about more important—I mean, challenging— Well, not that your work isn't challenging . . ." Having babbled himself into a corner, Doug simply shut up. *Try to take your foot out of your mouth without chipping any teeth, asshole.*

Gabrielle smiled broadly. Doug was obviously too embarrassed for her to take offense at his remark.

"Doug, there you are," Ruthanna called out as she approached. "I was beginning to think you'd missed the boat. Bad puns aside, I'm so happy to see you."

"Ruthie," Doug answered, his arms enveloping his friend in a warm hug. "You haven't changed a bit. You look terrific. God, how long has it been?"

"Too long. I see the life of the roving reporter agrees with you."

"There you two are," Felicia said as she pulled up to the trio, Trace by her side. "This is turning out quite nicely don't you think?"

"It's wonderful," Ruthanna agreed. "Felicia, this is Doug Sixsmith. Doug is the fabulous writer I literally begged to do our first cover story. Doug, this is Felicia Wilcot. She is one of the best PR people in New York, and we've hired her to help us launch *Appeal*."

"Hello, Doug. I always enjoy your work. I'm glad you could join us on such short notice."

"So am I. I think this is going to work out for all of us," Doug responded, thinking of Gabrielle. He hoped that once he was finished interviewing the cover model, he and Gabrielle would have an opportunity to spend some quality time together.

"Everyone, this is my husband, Trace Gordon. Trace, meet Ruthanna Beverly, Doug Sixsmith, and Gabrielle Donovan."

"Good evening," Trace said, shaking everyone's hand. He was impressed with Ruthanna's introduction of his wife. Felicia was obviously developing quite a reputation in her profession. Good for her. Perhaps after their kids were older and in school, she could return to her business.

"And, Doug, I see you've met our cover girl," Ruthanna said.

"It's true. I'm the beauty queen," Gabrielle revealed, laughing at Doug's pained expression.

"Ruthie, you may need to find another reporter for your story. I wouldn't be surprised if I've insulted Gabrielle into not speaking to me. My foot is so far down my throat, it's tickling my intestines."

"I think we'll let you two work this out. Just remember, *your* day in *her* life begins tomorrow morning at seven," Felicia said. "Now, if you'll excuse me, I'm going to dance with my husband."

"Oh, I'll be there," Doug promised. The way he saw it, he and this young lady were going to have to spend all four days and three glorious nights getting to know each other. How else could he write an in-depth profile about the day in the life of a model? Any story worthy of carrying his byline had to be thoroughly researched. If that meant conducting interviews on fabulous pink-sand beaches or walking the deck at all hours of the night under star-filled skies, so be it. He'd made it through the Los Angeles riots and the Persian Gulf War. Somehow, some way, he'd get through this as well.

"Why are you smiling like that?" Gabrielle asked.

"I was just thinking how much I liked cruising. You know, Felicia has the right idea. Would you like to dance?"

"Sure, but first . . ." she said, turning back to the buffet table. As Doug looked on, Gabrielle plucked the forgotten strawberry and took a big, satisfying bite. Her action set them both off, and, laughing, they headed out to the dance floor.

20

"Okay, that's a wrap, kids," Austin shouted seven hours and five costume changes later. The photographer, known for the sex and humor he infused in his work, was pleased. "Good work. I'll see everybody back here bright and early for the sunrise shot."

Doug had spent the entire day observing Gabrielle. Before he began his interviews, he wanted to get a feel for the woman and the way she operated. Tomorrow he would begin talking to her about her work. Tonight, however, he was not interested in the model. Tonight Doug hoped to have the opportunity to learn about Gabrielle Donovan, the woman.

"So, what do you think?" Gabrielle asked.

"I had no idea you girls work so hard. I'm impressed by how easy you make it look."

"Some jobs are easier than others. I have my share of horror stories."

"I'd love to hear them. Why don't we grab a bite together—for the story," Doug added, not wanting to put her off by sounding as if he was asking for a date.

"I can't. I'm having dinner with the captain."

"How about a quick drink afterward?" *Don't beg, stupid.* Doug couldn't help himself. He had to have some one-on-one time with this delicious woman.

"Okay, as long as it's not too late. I have such an early call in the morning."

Finally she throws me a bone. Be cool, don't show your relief. "No problem. How about the Alfresco Café, say eight o'clock? Though even a few hours is an awfully long time to wait for you." *That was good—rather James Bond–esque,* Doug congratulated himself.

To his dismay, Gabrielle responded with a polite laugh.

"Did I say something funny?" Doug asked lightly.

"It's just that Captain Di Angelo said something very similar."

"That's because men all over the world have the same training manual," Doug quipped, forcing himself to laugh, though he was feeling like a complete idiot. Compared to the suave, debonair, accented Captain Di Angelo, he was sure he'd sounded less like 007 and more like Maxwell Smart.

"I'll see you at eight," Gabrielle said, chuckling as she walked away.

Well, Dougie, you're on a roll. Last night you insult her work, today you toss her a line another man has already used. Smooth, real smooth.

"Hi. How's it going?" Felicia asked, taking a minute while Trace was working out to check in with her office.

"Things are just fine. Deena and I are holding down the fort quite nicely," Stephanie answered, her irritation plain.

"Are you okay? You sound a little angry?"

Why should I be angry? Is it because instead of letting me write the story on Gabrielle that would jump-start my career, you have me here writing public-service announce-

*ments on weather stripping—a subject that nobody with a
life gives a rat's ass about? Or maybe I'm mad because after
screwing me royally you keep calling instead of having the
common courtesy to leave me the fuck alone!*

"I'm fine, Felicia. It's just that this LILCO account is
being difficult about this copy."

"Do I need to make a phone call?"

"No, I can handle it."

"Good. Is Deena around? I want to get my messages."

"She's on the phone. Hold on, I'll get them for you."

Waiting for Stephanie to return, Felicia found herself
hoping that Lexis had called. She felt confused and ashamed
when it dawned on her that she wanted an excuse to call
back and hear his voice.

"Not much here, since everybody knows you're on vacation. Your mother called; Faith Taylor called about Fred 2
Fine, but says it can wait until you get back; and a Lois Jourdan left a message for you to call when you return."

"What a surprise. Lois is a friend from Georgetown. I
wonder what she wants. Anybody else?" Felicia asked lightly,
not wanting to mention his name.

"Yeah, Lexis called. He wanted your number in Martinique."

"I'll call him when I get to the hotel tomorrow."

"I guess that's it."

"Okay, then. I'll see you in a few days."

Lucky me, Stephanie thought, hanging up the phone.

Felicia was still smiling when Trace walked through the
door. "How was your workout?" she asked.

"Great until I called my office."

"Why? What's up?"

"Tom has totally screwed up the Acey Newit case, and
they need me back pronto to pull it out of the toilet. Sorry,

Feli, I'm going to have to cut our trip short and catch the first flight out of Martinique."

"Can't somebody else take care of it?"

"I'm afraid not."

"Trace, you could work something out if you wanted to. I did. Instead of working this entire trip as I should be, I arranged to leave midway so we could spend some time together. I compromised; can't you do the same?"

"This is an *important* case. It's a bit more involved than holding some glamour girl's hand while a reporter asks her inane questions about her beauty secrets, or playing hostess at some client party. For Christ's sake, Felicia, millions of dollars are at stake."

"So we're back to this, are we? Your work is platinum and mine is cheap nickelplate?"

"I didn't say that."

"Not in so many words, but your meaning came through loud and clear. If this were me interrupting our vacation because of work, you'd serve my head on a platter, but because it's you, I'm supposed to smile and understand."

"We haven't been able to even *begin* our vacation together because of *your* work," Trace lashed back. "Have I said anything about that? No. I've been following you around like some lapdog while you try to keep everybody else happy."

"You haven't changed at all, have you? All your nice talk and sweet playacting these past months was just sugarcoating. You're the same self-involved, egotistical bastard you always were," Felicia accused her husband angrily.

"And you, my dear wife, are a spoiled, unsupportive bitch. The next time you want to accuse someone of being self-involved and egotistical, take a good look in the mirror."

"You have a lot of nerve—"

"I'm not going to argue about this, Felicia. I have to go back to New York. Now, are you going to start packing?"

"No. Frivolous or not, I have a job to finish, and then I am going to Martinique tomorrow to relax and unwind—with or without you."

"Fine, Felicia, you go to Martinique and have a good time," Trace said calmly. He was angered by her reaction, but he refused to fight with his wife. His energy was focused on the big picture. Soon all this bickering would end, replaced by the pitter-patter of his son's little feet. *Yes, you go to Martinique. All mothers-to-be need their rest.*

Doug stood outside in the Alfresco Café at the ship's stern waiting for Gabrielle. He took a refreshing breath as he observed the magnificent view. The sun had set hours ago, leaving in its place a dark sky packed with bright, twinkling stars. The moon was full, and its silver glow rippled over the waves of the Caribbean Sea.

He peered out into the perfect night and, pushing away his usual propensity to engage in rational thought, allowed himself the luxury of daydreaming about Gabrielle. Doug found himself basking in the delicious edginess brought on by the anticipation of seeing her again. He hadn't felt like this in years. The giddiness he was experiencing was as refreshing as it was embarrassing. At his age he should be well past sweaty palms and nervous butterflies, but there was something about being with Gabrielle that brought out the unsophisticated high-schooler in him. If he didn't know any better, he'd swear he was falling in love.

Don't be ridiculous. How could you be in love with someone you just met? Ah, but technically we met over a year ago, he quickly reminded himself. *And Gabrielle Donovan is no mere someone.*

"Are you okay? You look like you're lost in space," Gabrielle told him, appearing at his side.

"It's amazing how this sea air can clear your head," he told her. Gabrielle looked so exquisite standing before him. There was a sparkle in her eyes that lit up her face when she smiled. It took all he had for Doug not to bend down and kiss her.

"Isn't this an amazing experience?" she asked dreamily, totally ignoring his comment. "Out here on the ocean, the moon and stars creating a perfect mobile above this floating cradle."

"That was very lyrical."

Gabrielle laughed, which sounded like falling rain to Doug's ears. "It must be this sea air. It's bringing out the poet in me."

"Would you like to take a walk?" he asked.

"Sure."

They leisurely climbed the stairs to the Capri deck in silent awe of this lovely night. They walked to the ship's rail and stood silent in the moonlight for several moments. There was a light breeze blowing, and Gabrielle felt herself shiver.

"Cold?" Doug asked.

"A little bit, but it's too beautiful to go inside."

"Here," Doug said, removing his cotton sweater and tying it around Gabrielle's shoulders. "Better?" he asked as their eyes met, their gazes welded together by the innocent but compelling intimacy of his action.

Doug smiled slightly as he felt a tug at his heart. Deep down he knew that he and Gabrielle were obviously meant for each other. Why else had they been thrown together again? Last night at the bon-voyage party Doug could feel a strong current flowing between them. The way they danced and laughed together all evening, the easy banter that flew back and forth between them—all proof, in his mind, that Gabrielle was at the very least intrigued by him. Even back when they'd first met in New York, hadn't Gabrielle used that upside-down-newspaper ploy just to get his attention? What was that, if not interest? And now, as she stood before him, her skin flushed not with lunar glow, but, he hoped, with the same delicious current that was surging through him.

"You know, Ms. Donovan, I could have predicted that we'd meet again," he announced, breaking the tension.

"Are you some sort of fortune-teller?" Gabrielle asked with a flirty lilt to her voice.

"I have been known to read a palm or two," he admitted, taking her hand into his. "Now, this is your life line," Doug said as he gently traced her palm with his index finger. "I'm glad to report that you have many long and happy years ahead of you. And this is your love line . . ." he said, not bothering to continue. Smiling directly into her face, Doug slowly placed his hands against Gabrielle's, matching each of his fingers with hers.

Once again their eyes locked as they stood silently, palm to palm. Gabrielle was mesmerized as Doug folded and refolded his fingers into hers. For several intensely sweet moments he tenderly massaged and caressed Gabrielle's hands with his own. With a featherlike touch, he seductively explored the contour of her exquisite hands, visiting each valley between her fingers. Doug paid equal attention to both front and back, while occasionally curling his hand around her slender wrist in a loving handcuff. There was strength in his gentleness, and possession in his touch.

Unable to contain himself, he brought her right index finger to his mouth, first to kiss and then gently suck. The sensation of his action was gentle and erotic, causing Gabrielle to respond with a soft moan and a slight tremble.

Confounded by this pleasant yet unfamiliar sensation, she slowly pulled away.

"Still cold?" Doug asked, trying to regain his composure. Their encounter had been the single most sensual experience he'd ever had, and though the sexy spell was broken, a thick, lusty fog still enveloped them.

"Something like that."

"Why don't we go inside?"

"So this 'day in the life' article includes a report on my nighttime activities as well?" Gabrielle asked with a smile.

"Absolutely."

"Well, then follow me."

Doug paused and momentarily watched Gabrielle's long, shapely legs carry her away from him. Oh, yeah, there was definite interest brewing here. With a cock of his head and a broad smile, he followed her down to the Portofino deck and into her suite.

"This should be more than enough light for what I have in mind," Gabrielle remarked, turning on the small bedside lamp and casting a low, soft light around the cabin. "I'm going to get comfy. Don't go away. I'll be right back."

Doug could only guess what was on Gabrielle's mind, but whatever it was, he was up for the challenge. He stole a glance in the mirror, combed his fingers through his shaggy mane, and wished like hell he had a breath mint. He heard the bathroom door open behind him and turned to find Gabrielle dressed for a night of one-on-one.

"Nice outfit," he commented with a laugh. She stood before him in a gray sweatsuit, socks, a ponytail, and instead of a basketball she was holding a large felt roll in her arms. His laughter was directed less at her outfit and more at his totally mistaken expectations.

"I said I wanted to get comfortable. What did you think I meant?" she asked, a sly smile tugging at her lips.

"Whatcha got there?"

"My passion." Gabrielle led him over to the small round table under the porthole. They sat down, and she proceeded to unfurl the felt tube, revealing a yet-to-be-completed jigsaw puzzle. "You look shocked," Gabrielle observed with a laugh.

"I am. Who would think that a young woman with your looks and lifestyle would be sitting around at night putting together puzzles?" Doug was surprised but also impressed. Gabrielle's chosen pastime said a lot about her personality—her tenacity, patience, and love of a good challenge.

"It may not be glamorous, but it's fun," Gabrielle revealed. "They can be frustrating, and you have to approach each puzzle differently, but I love the idea of taking a pile of cardboard rubble and turning it into a beautiful picture of someplace in the world I'd like to visit."

"And this would be the floral carpets in front of the Grand-Place in Brussels, Belgium," Doug said after a quick examination. He picked up one of the loose pieces and after a few moments of searching, placed it in its correct spot.

"You've actually seen them?" she asked with excitement. "Of course you have. You have such a great life—one full of interesting and important people."

"I know it sounds good, but the truth be known, my life is a lot more like one of your puzzles. Without all the proper pieces in place, it's rather incomplete."

Gabrielle smiled shyly, picked up another puzzle part, and searched for its location. Doug followed suit, and soon the two found themselves once again chatting and laughing amicably. The longer they worked to complete the picture, the more intimate their conversation became. Slowly they began to reveal the safe inner parts of their lives. Doug explained how he'd felt growing up with three older sisters. How at times he'd felt isolated, being the youngest and only boy and how writing became his instrument for attention. Gabrielle divulged to Doug how lonely and disconnected she sometimes felt without her mother, and how her success seemed less sweet without Helene there to share it. It was after 1 A.M. before Doug placed the final puzzle piece.

"A perfect fit," he announced, staring not at the table but soulfully into Gabrielle's eyes.

21

21

It would not be difficult to fall in love with a woman this devastatingly attractive both inside and out," Doug wrote in his notes as he waited for Gabrielle to return to the set. He knew that those exact words would never make it into his story, but they precisely summed up his feelings. He was looking forward to their lunch together this afternoon, anxious to better know this fabulous woman.

Gabrielle emerged from the wardrobe tent looking angelic in a white gauze trapeze dress that fell from her shoulders with a loose swing. She walked to her mark in the area designated by a border of light reflectors and stood in the surf between the small, silvery panels.

"Let's roll," Austin said, satisfied with the Polaroid samples.

As the photographer worked, Gabrielle transported herself into another place. In the movies of her mind she found herself reliving the evening before—with all its magic, mystery, and promise. She drew her hands through her hair in a lazy, sexy stretch, thinking of Doug's touch. Next she cupped her face in her hands and, putting the tips of her two little fingers into her mouth, gently sucked her fingertips, trying to recapture the sensation of Doug's actions. Slowly, tilting her face to the sun, she drew her hands down her neck and shoulders, stopping just short of touching her breasts.

"Whoa. This is some great stuff. Very hot, Gabrielle. Keep it coming," the photographer called out to her. The entire crew appeared mesmerized by her simple but very seductive poses. Whoever she was thinking of was one lucky guy.

Doug, sitting nearby under a tree, could only hope that he was the impetus behind her sexy mood. He'd never felt like this before—so possessive, his emotions so out of control. On one hand, Doug was enjoying this newfound sensation, realizing that his wish had come true—he'd found the woman who could make him forget work. On the other hand, unless his feelings were reciprocated, he was setting himself up for an extended stay at the Heartbreak Hotel.

The entire crew was so caught up in Gabrielle's suggestive poses that nobody noticed the huge wave until it crashed on the beach. The giant curl wiped out the set and left Gabrielle sputtering in its wake. When she came forth, she was soaking wet, her gauze dress clinging to every beautiful curve, outlining her breasts and nipples with absolute clarity and revealing the lines of her tiny panties. To the small group of people who stood by watching, it was as if suddenly the world had stopped revolving; all sound ceased, and total attention was focused on the lovely creature rising from the sea.

"Makeup," she requested lamely, pulling seaweed from her mouth.

The mostly male crew, laughing at her weak joke in an attempt to cover their sexual arousal, rushed in to help Gabrielle. Doug, however, could not move. Seeing Gabrielle looking wet and so exposed had left him with an enormous erection the size of a California redwood. His penis felt tight and ready to explode as it strained against his khaki shorts. He wanted to take Gabrielle right here in the surf, to feel her body melt into his as the soothing ocean waters kept the heat of his desire from igniting. Finally Doug managed to pull himself into an upright position and make his way over to the scene.

"Hey, Jigsaw, you didn't tell me you were a surfer," Doug quipped. "Are you okay?"

"I'm fine. I just feel a little silly. I didn't see that wave coming at all." Gabrielle felt herself blush, embarrassed by her sexy thoughts.

"That was one hell of a shot. We'll wrap till after lunch," the photographer declared, sending his model in to change.

"I'm starving," Gabrielle announced as she reappeared in dry clothes.

"Then you're in luck. I have lobster tail, a lovely Caesar salad, some incredible marinated olives, French bread, and—if you're very, very good and answer all my questions—an extra-special dessert."

Gabrielle followed Doug up the beach about one quarter of a mile to a secluded cove with a spectacular view of the ocean. He pulled a blanket from the picnic basket and smoothed it out on top of the sand. Gabrielle stood by as he set up lunch—complete with china, wineglasses, and one perfect bougainvillea flower set in a Perrier bottle.

"Lunch is served," he announced as he helped settle Gabrielle on the blanket.

"All this for an interview," she observed, secretly pleased by his efforts.

"Well, if I don't ply you with great food and good wine, how else can I pull all your deep, dark secrets out of you?"

The smile and witty reply he expected were not forthcoming. Instead Gabrielle's demeanor changed from cheery and playful to quietly apprehensive.

"Hey, I was just joking. I don't know if you've read any of my work, but I have a pretty good reputation out there. I won't embarrass you or misrepresent you in any way. I promise."

Gabrielle forced herself to relax. She wanted to believe that Doug would not hurt her. She was merely being overly sensitive—something she must stop if she was to avoid drawing suspicion. "I'm sorry. It's just that I know a lot of girls who've gotten burned by reporters who were disappointed by the facts and decided to make up their own."

"You don't have to worry. If you say something that you don't want repeated, simply tell me it's off the record. I promise, it will go no further."

"That makes me feel much better."

"Good. Now let's eat."

Together, Doug and Gabrielle hungrily devoured the lobster and salad. Conversation during their meal was light and friendly. For the second time Gabrielle found dining with Doug Sixsmith to be an enjoyable experience, while Doug found her to be a delightful enigma—sophisticated and bright one second, cute and self-deprecating the next. Doug was pleasantly surprised by the depth of this young woman. Her casual ease and comfort made Gabrielle seem much older and more mature than her age would indicate.

"Time for dessert. Close your eyes and open wide," he coerced her, placing the tip of a fat strawberry between her full lips. The erotic vision made Doug squirm slightly in his seat. "Now take a bite."

Gabrielle bit down on the strawberry, causing the fruit's juice to run down her chin. "Chocolate-covered strawberries! You've thought of everything."

"I tried," Doug told her, happy to see that his effort had

impressed her. "We'd better get to work," he said, pulling out his tape recorder and notepad. *Before I follow through on my impulse to lean over and kiss that strawberry juice from your face.*

"Let me start by telling you that I'm a little uneasy about this assignment," Doug admitted. "Following Boris Yeltsin around is more my style."

"I'm just as nervous. I've never had anyone follow me around asking questions and writing down my every word. The way I see it, we're even."

"Great. Here's my first official interview question: After watching you these past few days, I can see that you seem to really enjoy your work. Is there anything about this business that you don't like?"

"I hate that some people think that because models are attractive, they're lazy and spoiled. That's not true. We work very hard. The worst are the people who think that we're not very smart."

"Why do you think people have that impression of you?"

Gabrielle's lip stiffened. "You think I'm stupid?" This was the one thing about her business that Gabrielle despised—the idea that people thought models were vacuous Barbie dolls and not intelligent human beings. It was hard enough trying to convince herself that she was merely illiterate, *not* ignorant. Fighting that particular demon had become doubly hard now that she was immersed in a career with an unjust reputation for hiring pretty faces with empty heads.

Doug was waylaid by Gabrielle's defensive tone. "Absolutely not. I find you to be very bright and incredibly aware for someone so young," Doug answered, his tone soft and complimentary. "How do you feel knowing that people have pegged you to be a big success?"

"Like I've stepped out of the rain and into the sun. My future now seems very bright, and I didn't always feel that way," Gabrielle answered.

"So what would you say is your secret to success?"

"Focus and faith. My mom always told me that if you focus on your goal and truly believe in what you're doing, success will come. It works."

"Tell me about your upbringing," Doug asked, his reporter's sixth sense aroused.

Gabrielle took a long swig of her Evian water before answering. Her thirst quenched, she began telling the story that she and Beatrice had concocted about her background. This was her first time going public with the story, and she hoped Doug wouldn't ask too many probing questions.

"So your mom was a surgical nurse, your dad was in the military, and you moved around a lot while you were a kid. You're an only child, and your mother died last year," Doug summed up. "You've told me all about your mom—how close you two were, how much she wanted this career for you. What about your dad? Is he still alive?"

"No, he died about five years ago."

"Tell me about him."

Tell Doug about Nick? What could she say? That she never really knew her father because he'd never loved her? Should she tell him that had she not been born, her mother would have led a much more charmed life than the one she had—traipsing around the country chasing a man who obviously didn't want her or their child? What could Gabrielle tell Doug about her father? Certainly not the truth.

Gabrielle's father and the great love of Helene's life, Nick Tate Donovan, with his muscular build and dark, brooding manner, was a sexy man's man. Helene fell for Nick the first time she set eyes on him. She was a seventeen-year-old waitress, he was a twenty-seven-year-old truck driver who pulled into the Bakersfield, California, truck stop for dinner and, after a lusty romp in the back of his rig, pulled out with Helene. They were married two days later in Las Vegas.

For six months they roamed the country together. Helene had never been happier. She worshiped her new husband. And he, in his own way, loved Helene. But Nick was a loner who lived his life in search of something. He had no idea who or what that something was; he knew only that he had to have complete freedom to find it. Helene, young and insecure, was quite willing to let Nick live his life without demands or ultimatums.

It never occurred to him that Helene would ruin everything by getting pregnant. It happened almost immediately, and Helene was ecstatic. But once Nick learned the news, everything changed. As her belly swelled, Nick's desire for Helene decreased to the level of disgust. He could not stand to look at her, let alone touch her.

Helene went through the duration of her pregnancy ignoring his coldness, assuring herself that he would turn around. The day she went into labor, Nick dropped her off in front of the hospital and went to park the car. He never came back.

For thirteen years Helene followed her husband around the country begging for another chance. He always said yes, with one condition—no Gabrielle. Helene, refusing to leave her child, would give up and marry her current suitor. It was never long before her insatiable desire for Nick became overwhelming and she, child in tow, was off again like a junkie in search of a fix. The chase ended when Nick died in a truck crash two days after Gabrielle's fifteenth birthday.

"Basically I was a daddy's girl. I think he felt guilty for being away so much of the time, so when he was home, he spoiled me rotten," Gabrielle said, sticking to her script.

"I'll bet whatever you wanted, he would give you."

"Something like that."

"So, besides puzzles, what else do you do to relax in your spare time?" Doug asked in a shameless attempt to satisfy his own curiosity.

"Catch up on sleep, listen to music, go to the movies. What about you? What do you like to do when you're not chasing down a story?"

"Pretty much nothing. I love reading—biographies, Tom Clancy novels—listening to music—jazz, reggae, bossa nova. And one of my favorite pastimes—don't laugh—is baking pies. I can make a mean apple pie, and I've nearly perfected the art of the light, flaky crust."

"So you're sort of a homebody."

"Sounds pretty boring, huh?"

"Not at all. When you spend all your time traveling, staying home is a luxury."

"So why aren't you running around with some rock-star boyfriend?" Doug asked, not sure if he really wanted to know.

"I don't have time for serious romance—with rock stars or otherwise."

"Is that because of your work?"

"Partly. Most guys act kind of weird around me."

"Gabrielle, I don't think you have any idea the effect you have on men. Your looks can be rather intimidating to the average guy."

"Are you intimidated?"

"Immensely."

"I'm a little intimidated by you, too," she admitted.

"Me? I'm not exactly Jean-Claude Van Damme or Arnold Schwarzenegger—more Ron Howard when he still had all his hair. What about me could possibly be intimidating? Not my debonair good looks," Doug fished.

"For an old guy, you are kinda cute," Gabrielle teased. Doug was a slightly hipper version of the guy next door. His face was kind and intelligent, round tortoiseshell glasses framing his hazel eyes. Light freckles were strewn across his nose, and his mouth was constantly breaking into an endearing lopsided smile. Debonair? Not exactly. But adorable? Appealing? Absolutely.

"Then I don't see your point. Cocker spaniels are cute. Pit bulls are intimidating. Mickey Rooney is cute. Mickey Rourke is intimidating. You see where I'm going with this? Cute and intimidating don't go together."

"You make me feel so comfortable that I relax completely, and that leaves me feeling vulnerable and a little intimidated."

"But if you feel comfortable and relaxed around me, how can you still feel vulnerable and intimidated?"

"I don't know. It's hard to trust people, uh—in this business," she added quickly.

"I told you, you can trust me," Doug said, taking her hand in his.

The simple touch of his hand brought up the powerful feelings of last night. The flow of emotions between them set off a panic alarm in Gabrielle's heart. "I need to get back to work," she said, abruptly cutting off the conversation. She felt too defenseless around Doug. Gabrielle needed to get back to work, back to safe ground. "Could I leave you here to clean up alone? Laslo works himself up into a tizzy if I'm late."

"No problem. I'll catch you later."

Gabrielle wasn't in danger of being late, but she needed time alone to think. Last night and lunch today had been wonderful, and she was confused by the contradictory emotions she was experiencing. She found herself totally drawn to Doug, both physically and emotionally, yet her brain warned her to stay as far away from him as possible.

Gabrielle's attraction to Doug was fueled more by the *little* things. She liked how his eyes danced when he was excited about something he was discussing. It drove her to distraction the way he raked fingers through his thick, sandy curls when he was searching for a word. Doug made her feel safe and at ease. She was beginning to feel that Doug Sixsmith was a man she could fall in love with. He baked pies for God's sake! Doug Sixsmith, Gabrielle decided, was a man to avoid at all costs. Gabrielle had no intention of getting serious with Doug, or any other man for that matter. Not now, not ever.

22

Felicia felt like the defiant child that, even as a youngster, she never gave herself permission to be. Carrying her beach towel, sunblock, and the latest bestseller, she headed for the beach at the Bokaru Hotel and found a chaise away from the water's edge and out of the path of the early beachcombers. Felicia spread her towel on the chair, pulled off her leopard-print pareo, and made herself comfortable. The beaches in Martinique, true to the island's French heritage, were topless. Trace would have a heart attack if he saw her now—wearing nothing but a very small black bikini bottom. With her husband absent, Felicia shamelessly bared her chest in all its glory.

But soon she and Trace would be together again. The ugly exchange between them tortured her. *When did we become so disrespectful?* Felicia asked herself. It was now plain to her that all these years she and Trace had spent building his career and her business might have cost them their marriage. In the beginning she thought she could do it all, but Trace's lack of support and his need for her to be the perfect corporate wife had pushed her further and with more intensity into her own career. Felicia also knew, in all fairness, that she was to blame as well. Her drive to succeed had effectively usurped all the energy she should have put into her marriage.

It was time to face the truth. Her marriage was in a catatonic stupor, limping along on life support supplied in the form of occasional sex and cordial conversation. The intimacy and respect a relationship needs to grow and flourish were dead. Now it was left to Felicia to decide if she had the guts to pull the plug. But that decision was not to be made today.

Felicia opened her book but found she could not concentrate on the contents. She was annoyed that Lexis hadn't returned her phone call, neither here in Martinique nor at the office in New York. *Why should I be disappointed?* she asked herself. *Lexis is just one less detail I have to worry about.* Determined to get some well-deserved rest, she put down her book, closed her eyes, and willed all thoughts of work, Trace, and Lexis Richards from her mind.

Felicia closed her eyes and let nature's sensations invade her being. She listened to the crisp, syncopated rhythms of the ocean tide rushing the beach, the soothing sound lulling her overworked mind into a relaxed state. She felt the heat of the morning sun pouring down on her near-naked body, leaving her feeling sexy and brazen. She wanted to feel the soft contact of hands stroking her hot skin. Unable to stand the absence of touch, she reached down and picked up her suntan lotion. Felicia poured a warm pool of oil into her hand and slowly applied the lotion to her arms, stomach, and bare breasts. Pouring more into her hands, she closed her eyes and imagined her man there with her. As she stroked herself with a soft, feathery caress, she imagined her hands to be his, oiling up her feet and working his way up her legs to her tender inner thighs. Felicia felt as if she were being consumed by heat, both outwardly from the sun and inwardly by her own desire. *Lexis, why aren't you here with me?*

Startled by her error, Felicia sat up and opened her eyes. In all her years of marriage, Felicia had never been unfaithful to Trace—not in thought or deed. Now, for the first time, she found herself fantasizing about being in the arms of another man. She closed her eyes again, shook the thoughts from her head, then reopened them, only to find herself staring into the smiling face of Lexis Richards.

"How long have you been standing there?" she asked, scrambling to cover her bare breasts.

"Not long. Don't do that on my account."

Felicia hoped he was telling the truth. There was no way of knowing how her face had translated her feelings and thoughts. "What are you doing here?" Felicia asked.

"I want to talk to you about my next movie, and I needed to chill a bit myself, so I flew in last night. Why are you out here alone?"

"Trace had an emergency at the office. He flew back to New York this morning."

"What a shame," Lexis said sarcastically. "Though he's not too bright, leaving you here alone, looking like this."

"I can be trusted," Felicia said, trying to convince Lexis as well as herself.

"I wasn't implying otherwise. It's just you sittin' up here on the beach, lookin' all fine. Any man who still has testosterone running through his body is going to have to stop, look, and try to hoopdie-swoop you."

"Hoopdie-swoop?"

"Try to pick you up," Lexis translated.

"I see. Well, so far you're the only one who's come by to stop and look. Are you trying to pick me up?"

"Baby, when I do, you'll know it. Have you eaten yet? I

really do want to run this idea by you. It's hot, Felicia, so hot that I want to start a buzz before we even finish the script."

"Okay. We'll do breakfast. You've piqued my interest."

"Cool. I'll meet you by the pool, say, ten-thirty."

"Fine."

"And Felicia, maybe you should change. I want to be able to concentrate."

By 10:20 Felicia was sitting poolside waiting for Lexis. As she sipped her iced tea, she grew increasingly annoyed with herself. Why in the world was she sitting here, in this place, feeling so excited about having breakfast with Lexis Richards? Lexis was her client and friend—end of story.

Then why were you so concerned about what to wear? the devil on her shoulder baited her. After eliminating most of the clothes in her suitcase, Felicia had chosen off-white linen slacks and a sleeveless silk shell in the same color. Her hair was pinned up, giving her the air of a sophisticated and elegantly nonchalant woman.

"You look great," Lexis commented, as he approached Felicia. "Are you hungry?"

"More curious than hungry. What's your big news?"

"I've decided my next flick is going to tell the story of the New Orleans *gens de couleur libre*. The free people of color," Lexis translated.

"I'm not familiar—"

"They were this whole society of educated, enterprising black folks who lived this bourgeois existence before the Civil War," Lexis revealed.

"You're telling me that there was an entire society of well-to-do, free black people even before slavery ended?" Felicia asked in awed disbelief.

"A society some eighteen thousand strong, livin' it up in New Orleans. They were mostly the descendants of the

Spaniards and French Creoles. The Europeans not only freed the kids they had with their slaves but took care of them, too. So this whole aristocratic society of old families, plantation owners, merchants, artists, poets, and doctors sprang up. It was hella cool, but strange, too, because they kinda existed in this netherworld, not really accepted by black or white," Lexis informed her. Felicia could see the excitement penetrate his body.

"There's so much of our history people don't know."

"Until black history becomes American history, our big contribution to this country will be pickin' cotton and singin' spirituals. Shit, there's only so much you can teach in one month—let alone the shortest month of the year."

Felicia sat back, totally absorbed in what he had to say. Once again, it amazed her how much she'd learned about her people and herself since Lexis had come into her life. One of the things she found so attractive about the man was the way he reveled in his blackness. Lexis told her numerous times over their months together that he was "black by nature, proud by choice." Through Lexis, the feelings of ethnic pride and cultural awareness that had grown dormant inside Felicia were being awakened.

Lexis introduced her to the works of great African American writers like James Baldwin and Ralph Ellison, authors whose books had populated the shelves of her father's library but whom Felicia had disregarded to concentrate on the works of Hemingway, Faulkner, and F. Scott Fitzgerald. Lexis revealed to her that *The Three Musketeers* and *The Count of Monte Cristo,* both staples in libraries stocked with great literature, were written by a black man, Alexandre Dumas. He took her to museums to show her the profound impact African art had on the European masters like Pablo Picasso and his generation of artists. And Lexis's generosity with his CD collection furthered her education on the only true American musical art form—jazz.

"What are you going to call it?" Felicia asked.

"Praline Livin'."

"I get it. A brown, sweet, and rich life."

"Don't be fooled, though. They might have been livin' large, but they were still niggers in the eyes of white people. They had no political power, no free speech, and were considered second class. After the Civil War, many of them became the leaders in the fight for freed slaves' civil and human rights."

"Praline is a long way from the girl-gang movie you pitched to my father," Felicia observed.

"Yeah, well, my films reflect the mood I'm in at the time. I was pissed off by the conditions in the 'hood—hence, *Southeast* and *She Gang.* Part of my inspiration for *Praline Livin'* came from being in the French Quarter during Mardi Gras. I went into one of the shops to pick up something for my mom and ended up checking out these incredible mulatto dolls dressed to kill in period costumes. The saleswoman gave me the lowdown on the history, and I came back and did some more research."

"And the rest of your inspiration?"

"I guess you can pat yourself on the back and take some credit. Even though you totally dogged *Southeast,* you made me think that maybe it was time to do something different. So I scrapped the girl-gang script. So what do you think?"

"I think it's a wonderful idea. It's time people learn that blacks had a long legacy of class and breeding—way before the 'Cosby' show arrived," Felicia admitted, pleased that she'd been a source of inspiration. "Though I'm surprised that *you're* doing a movie on the 'uppity' black elite," she teased.

"Like with most things folks don't understand, with exposure comes tolerance," Lexis said, smiling.

"It's a great idea. One even my father might be interested in investing in. Will it be a love story? It would be nice to see that side of our lives explored."

"Sorry, love stories aren't my thing. I want *Praline Livin'* to focus on the politics of color. Now, here's what I'm thinking. We can do some kind of reception thing during Mardi Gras next year and announce the film. That way we get people talking early."

"Hey, stop doing my job. Ideas like that are what you pay me for. Isn't that why you rushed down here—for my public relations expertise?"

"Oh, yeah—for your PR expertise," Lexis acknowledged, giving her the once-over. "Look, I have to be straight up about this. I came down here, not just to rap about the movie, but because I couldn't stand not being or talking with you for so long. I figured seeing you with your husband was better than not seeing you at all."

Felicia acknowledged Lexis's confession with a silent smile that spoke volumes. It was a smile that conveyed her pleasure at hearing his words, that agreed with his rationale, that encouraged him to continue.

"I know I'm crossing the line here, but when I saw you there on the beach, looking so fine, I wanted to grab you up, carry you off somewhere, and make love to you until you begged me to stop. Felicia, I know I'm probably screwing up this whole business thing we have going here, but I can't front anymore. I want to be with you and for once not be dreaming."

Felicia felt complimented and appreciative of his honesty. She was happy that he hadn't complicated things further by saying that he loved her. All she knew was that she, too, wanted to be with him—no strings, no commitments.

She just wanted to kiss and touch Lexis and feel his body next to hers. Felicia needed him to make her feel like a whole woman again.

"Come," she said softly and headed for her room. She was just about to put her key into the door when Lexis stopped her.

"Are you sure about this, Felicia? I don't want you doing anything you'll regret."

"I'm sure," she said, drawing him into a confirming kiss. "Come in, make yourself comfortable. I'll be right back."

Lexis watched Felicia walk into the bathroom and close the door behind her. He walked over to the minibar and fixed himself a drink. It was early, but he needed fortification for what was ahead. There was a lot riding on this afternoon. If things went well, who knew what pleasant and wonderful things the future held for the two of them? At the same time, this one act of passion could ruin a fruitful professional alliance and crush a friendship that had come to mean a great deal to him. Still, he was willing to take the chance. After all these months of yearning, there was no way that if Felicia was willing, he was going to pass on the opportunity to finally touch the soul of the woman he'd longed for all these months.

Lexis took his drink to the window. Felicia's room had a fabulous view of the ocean. There were at least thirty sailboats dotting the sapphire-colored water. Under a sky speckled with puffs of silky white clouds, windsurfers skimmed the sea, powered by the tropical island breeze. It was a beautiful day to make love to a beautiful woman—a woman who belonged to another man.

Why was it that when he finally found a woman who truly interested him, she was married? Lexis didn't like the idea that he was about to go to bed with another man's wife.

He prided himself on being a bigger, better man than that. But in the end, Trace simply did not matter.

Felicia returned from the bathroom wearing a short kimono robe, her hair cascading down her shoulders. The gold silk clung to her trim, shapely body. She walked purposefully toward Lexis, took the glass from his hand, and drained the remains of his drink.

"Was that for courage?" Lexis asked.

"Something like that." The idea of sharing her body with another man was as frightening as it was tempting.

"If this doesn't feel right, we shouldn't go through with it."

"How do you feel?"

"Baby, nothing ever felt more right to me in my life," Lexis told her as he lightly ran his fingers through her hair. "I've wanted this for a long time. The question is: Does this feel right to you?"

"All I know is that it doesn't feel wrong."

"What about Trace?"

"Shh," Felicia said, touching her finger to his lips to silence him. She did not want to think about Trace now. Any guilt or remorse she might feel would be dealt with later. Right now Felicia simply wanted to satisfy her overwhelming desire to make love to this sensuous man.

Lexis stopped talking and kissed her finger. He ran his hand down her back, roving her spine with a gentle, fluttery touch. His hand came to rest lightly on her behind, drawing up the silky fabric of her robe, revealing her left buttock.

"Follow me," he requested. Felicia followed Lexis out onto the private balcony. He wrapped his arms around her, his chest pressing against her breasts. They kissed long and hard, slowly tasting each other. Lexis eased off Felicia and untied the belt on her robe, revealing matching gold brassiere and thong panties. Lexis drew in his breath in admiration.

"You are incredible," he whispered as his hand found its way to the damp inside of her thigh.

"Is this a swoopdie-hoop?" she asked coyly.

"Without a doubt. And it's *hoop*die-swoop," Lexis corrected her, chuckling.

Felicia stood facing the ocean and allowed Lexis to ravish her body. She was torn between her passionate desire to return Lexis's physical attention and her feelings of betrayal. If she continued to take and not give, would she be less guilty of infidelity? On the other hand, if she did not become an active participant, would Lexis think her to be a terrible lover? Ego and guilt, Felicia decided, made for terrible bed companions.

It was Lexis's hot mouth on her erect nipples that turned the tide. The intensity of her desire made it impossible for Felicia not to respond fully. Only after he'd worked her up into a hot frenzy did Lexis stop to remove his own clothing. Felicia, the sun pouring down on her, watched as Lexis's lean, muscular body was revealed. Unable to stand his mouth away from hers one second longer, she reached up and pulled his lips to hers. Felicia replaced their earlier slow kisses with shorter, more ardent ones.

"Whoa, baby, slow down," Lexis said softly. "I want to make this last. I've waited too long to be with you to let it come and go in a flash." Lexis punctuated his declaration with a long, tender kiss. His tongue softly explored the warmth of her mouth, pausing only to gently lick her raw and swollen lips.

Felicia had never been kissed like that before. The sensuality of the act grabbed her heart and lifted it into her throat. She stood, her buttocks pressed against the sliding glass door, as Lexis covered her body with a string of lingering kisses. His lips traveled south, and on bended knee lustfully explored her with his tongue.

"Baby, you taste scrumptious—how I'd imagine the nectar from the most exotic, most exquisite flower would taste. I don't think I could ever get enough of you."

Felicia felt herself tremble, unsure if it was his words or actions that were the cause. Lexis was so tender, so erotic. The combination of his words, kisses, and touch stirred Felicia body and soul. She wanted to feel him inside her.

"Wait," Felicia said, pulling away breathlessly. "Do you have a condom?"

"No. You?"

"No." They sat facing each other, their chests rising and falling with excitement. It was clear that their bodies ached for each other. "So what do we do now?"

"Baby, I may be a little freaky, but I'm certainly no fool," Lexis assured her. "I am *very* selective. There ain't no booty worth dyin' over. I don't take chances with my life, and I won't with yours."

Felicia was grateful to Lexis for bringing the matter up. She didn't know how to approach the subject with him. She'd been with only one man and wasn't sure how to handle the etiquette of sex in the nineties.

"Thank you."

"What about birth control?"

"I'm wearing my diaphragm. We're safe."

"Then what are we waiting for?"

Lexis carefully lowered Felicia down on the oversized chaise, his body following hers. He pressed himself into her, showering her face, neck, and ears with quick little kisses. His hand rubbed across her breasts, down her flat stomach, and came to rest on her thigh. Lexis could feel Felicia quiver slightly as he slowly entered her. Every nerve ending between her legs tingled, causing Felicia to draw in her breath in a pleasurable moan. She felt herself opening up wide to receive him.

His stroke was smooth and sensual, and Felicia was surprised by his gentleness. Lexis was an accommodating, skilled lover, and he knew exactly how and when to move to afford them both maximum pleasure. He shifted positions so they were both lying on their sides, their bodies still connected. Lexis disengaged his hands from her hair and reached down between her legs. Lubricating his finger with her juices, Lexis fondled her with soft, circular motion. Felicia, mind and body stimulated, quickly climaxed into the most intense orgasm she'd ever experienced. The shake and tremor that consumed her body released itself in a primal, guttural outcry. It was a cry that she couldn't have suppressed even if she'd tried.

Lexis, excited by the pleasure he saw Felicia experiencing, ejaculated inside her with a powerful thrust. Still wanting to give more, he continued to finger her. For Felicia pleasure became pain, and, unable to stand the touch, she pulled back from Lexis and curled into a ball, savoring the delectable sensations.

Lexis curled up next to her and let the physical and emotional satisfaction consume his body. He knew that the two of them would be so right together. Smiling from the miracle that had just happened between them, Lexis gently turned Felicia around to face him. He was greeted with tears streaming down her face. Lexis could not determine if they were tears of joy or regret.

"Baby, what's wrong?"

Felicia could not speak. Her emotions felt as raw and exposed as her body. Lexis had touched a place in her that Trace had never even come close to. She felt as if the fog she'd been wandering in these past few years had finally lifted.

Lexis wiped away her tears, first with his fingers and then with his lips. "Don't cry, Felicia. I don't want you to be sad, not when it felt so right."

Before answering, Felicia took time to consult her heart. It was important that truth prevailed here. She wasn't sad or sorry for her actions. Lexis, with his sweet, attentive ways, had given her back a part of herself she hadn't even realized she'd lost. For so long she'd been someone else's daughter, wife, employee. Making love with Lexis had made Felicia realize that first and foremost she was a woman. A woman who had needs and desires, a woman who didn't have to please everyone else all the time. She was a woman who was capable of making her own choices and facing any consequences those choices might bring.

Lexis waited for what seemed an eternity, hoping he hadn't ruined things between them. Still, even if he had, he wouldn't change a thing. Never before had he experienced a moment of such complete and profound gratification.

"I'm not exactly sure why I'm crying," Felicia admitted. "I know it's not sadness or regret, though."

"Guilt, maybe?"

"Maybe. Probably."

"You don't have anything to feel guilty about," Lexis said.

"What about betraying my marriage vows?"

"You're not the kind of woman who creeps on your man. If things were cool at home, you wouldn't even have been tempted. Maybe your heart was trying to tell your head something it didn't want to hear—like it's time to move on."

"Lexis, I don't want you to get the wrong idea. What happened here was— Well, I can't make any promises."

"Look, I'm not asking for anything that I know you're not ready to give. I promise I won't push things between us, if you promise you won't let fear and guilt pull you away."

"That's fair, *if* you think you can avoid pushing. I know you, Lexis Richards. Look how you ran me down just to represent you."

"Ran you down? Girl, your game of hard-to-get was so transparent it wasn't even funny," Lexis said with a grin.

"What do you think you are, irresistible?"

"I *am* the Mack Daddy. Even *you* couldn't keep your hands off me."

Felicia laughed briefly, grateful for the levity.

"You're sure you're okay? We're still cool?" Lexis asked, turning serious again.

"I'm fine, and yes, we're still cool."

Just as Felicia allowed herself to surrender to the fresh onslaught of Lexis's kisses, the phone rang. She followed, trying to keep the telltale lust out of her voice.

"Felicia?" Trace's voice boomed through the receiver.

"Trace! This is unexpected," she said as she pulled away from Lexis's embrace. "Where are you? Are you in New York already?"

"No, I'm in Miami waiting for my flight. I called because I realized what a jerk I'd been. I'm sorry, Feli, for acting like such an ass."

Why is he being so thoughtful now? Trace never apologizes. "I'm sorry, too, but Trace, we have some major talking to do."

"I know. When you get home, we'll get some professional counseling. You were right, we can't do this on our own," he said. Trace was still against the idea of counseling, but he was willing to say anything to keep Felicia placated long enough for him to get her pregnant. "I do love you, Feli."

"I'll see you when I get home," Felicia said, hanging up, unable to return his words. Lexis reached for her, but the spell between them was broken. She got up, reached for her robe, and walked over to the window. Why did Trace have to call? Their brief conversation had turned everything around. Guilt overcame her, causing Felicia to second-guess her desire to end the marriage and move on with her life.

"Are you okay?" Lexis asked, pulling on his pants.

"Yes, I just have some thinking to do, so if you don't mind . . ."

"I don't mind," Lexis said, trying not to let his frustration show. "But do you mind a little advice?"

"I'm listening."

"Go with your heart. It never lies." Lexis took her into his arms for a good-bye kiss and then left her at the window with her thoughts.

Felicia heard the door close behind him. She fully intended to heed his advice. Did this mean that she and Lexis had a future together? Felicia wasn't worried about that now. She did not intend to get tangled up in another relationship, not when she and Trace had some major untangling to do.

23

"Gabrielle's taking off faster than fat-free potato chips at a Weight Watchers rally," Gregory von Ulrich announced to the others in the room. He had called this meeting with Jaci and Felicia, now Gabrielle's full-time publicist, to discuss strategy for the model's booming career. "The editors love her. Since the *Appeal* job, she's done three magazine covers, including *Vogue*," Greg said, gesturing toward the advance copy that lay on the conference table. "I'd say our young starlet has arrived."

"But it's the August issue," Jaci pointed out. August was notorious for being the least prestigious cover of the year.

"The cover of *Vogue* is the cover of *Vogue*, twelve months out of the year. Just doing a cover shot for them is like a model's debutante ball. Besides, this certainly won't be her last. What's the update on publicity?"

Felicia, lost in her own thoughts, did not hear the question. Though her body was present, her mind was preoccupied with her next appointment. In less than two hours she would go through a life-altering experience—an experience she'd give anything not to go through alone.

Shortly after returning from the cruise, Felicia had begun to suspect that she was pregnant. Though she'd had all the signs of an approaching menstrual period—headache, bloating, cramps—the month came and went without her period making an appearance. Her doctor's appointment last week had confirmed Felicia's suspicions. Now, three months later, she'd run out of time.

How could this happen? she asked herself for the ten-millionth time. She'd always been so careful about birth control. For eight years she'd used a diaphragm without incident. Why did it have to fail the one and only time she'd been unfaithful?

This was all wrong. Not only was this pregnancy unexpected, it came at a time when her personal life was in a shambles. Everything was up in the air, drifting in the stratosphere, unresolved and uncomfortably tenuous. Though she and Trace were now in counseling, Felicia knew in her heart that she was only going through the motions. She often thought about separation, if only to ease the tension and give her time to sort out her confusion and guilt. But if she and Trace wound up living in separate households, she'd then have to deal squarely with her feelings for Lexis.

Since returning from Martinique, Felicia had found herself doing exactly what she promised *not* to do—pushing Lexis away. They talked on the phone constantly but had actually seen each other only four or five times. On each occasion Felicia had gently refused to go to bed with Lexis again. She was afraid it would only confuse her more, and she had too many things on her plate to worry about.

If a failing marriage or the uncertain future of a new love affair were her only concerns, she'd consider going through with this pregnancy. Plenty of children were conceived during bad relationships and despite their parents' divorce grew up to be successful, productive adults. No, a miserable love life was the least of her problems. The overwhelming predicament Felicia was facing was that she had no idea who was the father of her baby.

Neither man had reason to suspect her pregnancy. Lexis was no problem, because he didn't see Felicia on a daily basis, but Trace seemed to monitor her monthly cycle as if it were his own. To throw him off, Felicia went through the motions of having a period and blamed her general malaise on the flu that was conveniently making the rounds.

For a fleeting moment she'd considered having this child, but its dubious paternity made any such thought an impossibility. After a long, heart-wrenching search, Felicia had come to the determination that abortion was her only answer. Terminating this pregnancy was the most difficult decision she'd ever had to make. She was not only snatching fatherhood from one man but cheating her folks out of becoming grandparents as well. Still, Felicia was thankful that she had the right to choose what was best for her, and that a safe, legal option was available.

Despite the emotional turmoil she was experiencing, Felicia's decision was irreversible. She was looking forward to having this ordeal over and done with, so she could get back to putting the pieces of her shattered life together. She knew, however, that things were never going to be the same. *She* was never going to be the same.

"Felicia?"

"Sorry, Greg. My mind drifted off for a moment."

"I asked what kind of response Gabrielle's been getting from the press."

"Folks are clamoring to get Gabrielle on both the inside and outside of their publications. She has a Q and A coming out in *GQ* next week, and *Young Miss* is featuring her in a story on hot young models."

"That's good to hear, but I don't want her associated with those damn tabloids and sleazy gossip columns. I don't want to read about who she's sleeping with or what nightclub she's been seen in. I want her image to stay pure."

"We don't have to worry about that with Gabrielle," Jaci told him. "She's as professional as they come. Everybody loves her—the photographers, editors, casting directors—everybody."

"I can vouch for her, too," Felicia said. "She's a pro."

"Good."

"She is very hot right now, and when her *Vogue* cover hits the newsstands next week, she's going to explode. I know Gabrielle was against the idea earlier, but I think it's time she went international—did some work in Europe, strolled some of the designer catwalks," Felicia advised.

"I agree," Greg said. "It's time for Gabrielle Donovan to be associated with a top designer. Now for the ten-million-dollar question: Who?"

"How about Ralph Lauren? Or Todd Oldham? Donna Karan's practically an American institution," Felicia offered, forcing herself to concentrate on the meeting.

"They're big names, all right. Too big. That's the problem. Too many well-known models are already associated with their clothes. I want a designer who's on the cusp of becoming *huge*. Someone Gabrielle can link stars with and ride to the top. Someone who has insight, ambition, and massive staying power."

"Someone like Maynard Scarborough," Jaci shouted, jumping up from her seat. "He's perfect. Not only is he all the things you mentioned, but by Gabrielle's choosing his clothes for the *Appeal* shoot, they've already established a connection. I'm telling you, Greg, those two are a natural fit."

"I think Jaci's onto something," Felicia chimed in.

"His last show was the talk of the industry. He had the editors and buyers fawning all over him. The word is that the licensers are practically licking his trademark loafers. Putting the two of them together is a stroke of genius. Jaci, send Maynard her file this afternoon and start the ball rolling."

"I think we can get some great publicity out of this," Felicia said, her professional wheels spinning again. "We can blanket the industry with stories about the man and his muse, both in print and on some of those fashion TV programs popping up everywhere."

"Good idea," Greg replied. "We'll do whatever it takes to get Gabrielle to the top. I intend for her to become a giant in this profession. And all the while she's climbing the ladder, she'll be pulling First Face right along with her."

24

Gabrielle picked up the phone on the third ring. The voice seeping through the receiver sent a pleasant shiver down her back. She found herself smiling as she returned Doug's hello.

"I've been busy trying to figure out what I could do to make you go out with me," Doug said, mustering up a light-hearted delivery. "I thought we were friends, but I've asked you out three times now, with no success. So what is it? My aftershave?"

He'd been going over the situation constantly since they'd returned home from the Caribbean, trying to discern what had happened to cause such a complete reversal in her behavior toward him. Each time Doug came to town, he attempted to see her, to no avail. Tonight he was determined to learn what was going on in Gabrielle's head.

"I happen to like the smell of Drakkar Noir, and yes, we are friends."

"If that's the case, you can prove it by going out with me tonight."

"You're in New York again?" she asked.

"Just overnight. I'm meeting with a crusty old assignment editor in the morning, so this evening I'd like to enjoy myself. I know this is last-minute, but would you join me?"

A dozen or so excuses why she couldn't see Doug tonight ran through her mind. Finally she decided to accept his invitation. The truth be known, she missed him. Acting distant and uninterested was one of the hardest things she'd ever done. And as much as she didn't want to risk getting serious with Doug, she found herself unable to once again pass up the opportunity to see him.

"I'd love to."

"Great. Why don't we hang out in the Village? No big plans, just see where the evening takes us?"

"Sounds like fun. Why don't I meet you under the arch in Washington Square Park at six?"

"I'll be there. I'm really looking forward to seeing you again," Doug admitted.

"Same here," Gabrielle told him, grinning as she hung up. She was still smiling when the phone rang again.

"You know if you stand me up I'll be scarred for life," Doug told her with feigned sincerity. He knew he was acting like a total adolescent, calling her up like this again, but he couldn't help himself. "I have your word that nothing short of an act of God can keep you away?"

"You have my word," Gabrielle promised through her rising laughter.

"Not even if Karl Lagerfeld, on the stipulation that you can be in his office exactly at six, offers you a contract that could pay off the national debt?"

"I promise."

"Okay, but remember, my fragile mental health is in your hands."

"Good-bye," she said, laughing. She broke into chuckles again as the phone rang for a third time.

"I told you, I'll be there," she snickered into the receiver.

"Great, but I haven't even told you with whom or why we're meeting," answered Gregory von Ulrich.

"Greg, I thought you were someone else. What's going on?"

"Are you sitting down?"

"This sounds very mysterious."

"It's no mystery that you're the hottest new model on the circuit, which is why Maynard Scarborough would like to have a little chat with you."

"About?"

"About paying you an obscene fee to represent his designs. I sent your file up to him, and he was very impressed."

Greg waited for Gabrielle's fit of laughter to subside. "Did I miss the punch line?"

"A friend of mine predicted that something like this might happen—tonight, as a matter of fact. I guess he must be psychic or something."

"Gabrielle, you don't need a psychic to predict your future. It's all set—fame, fortune, success, all yours for the taking. The meeting is merely a formality. This is a done deal. Maynard loves you. After you dazzle him, we'll meet with the lawyers to go over the contract."

"I can't believe this."

"Believe it."

"When is the meeting?"

"Wednesday morning at eleven in Maynard's Paris office."

"I can't go to Paris tomorrow."

"I know you don't have any bookings until the end of the week and that your passport is valid for another nine years, so what exactly is the problem?"

"Bea's back is still acting up, and there's no way she can sit on a plane for that long. Can't we meet here in New York or postpone it for a week or so?"

"Gabrielle, I know how fearful you are about airplanes," Gregory said patiently, "but this meeting is too important to miss because you're afraid to fly. You just have to hang tough and get there by yourself."

"Couldn't we fly there together?"

"Sure, but you'll have to leave with me tonight. I have other business to take care of in the morning."

Gabrielle wasn't sure what she should do. The idea of flying to France alone petrified her. She should go with Gregory, but leaving tonight meant not seeing Doug, and Gabrielle didn't want to disappoint him or herself. Greg was right, she'd just have to tough it out alone.

"I can't leave tonight. I have plans."

"You're sure?"

"Yes. I'll be okay."

"Good. I'll send the car for you tomorrow evening at five-thirty. You can grab a cab at Charles de Gaulle to take you to the hotel. Don't worry, Gabrielle, you'll be fine."

"I hope so. See you in Paris."

"It's good to see you again. This is for you," Doug said, pulling an exquisite purple iris from behind his back.

"Thank you," Gabrielle replied, appreciation and excitement lighting up her blue eyes. She bit her lower lip to keep her smile from spreading all over her face. The fact that he had not brought her the romantic floral cliché—a rose—pleased her immensely. Doug's choice of the iris, with its deep-purple petals streaked with gold, told her that he was a creative and considerate man who recognized their friendship as something special. From that moment on, the iris would always be her favorite flower.

"You won't believe what happened this afternoon."

"Why don't we start walking, and you can tell me."

Instinctively, Doug took Gabrielle's hand into his and began walking through the crowded maze of students, street performers, and drug dealers that populated Washington Square Park on this warm July evening. As they walked, she told Doug how his earlier prophecy had come true.

"You mean you actually gave up going to Paris tonight just to be with me?" He hoped he wasn't jumping to conclusions, but Gabrielle's decision seemed to him an indication that a relationship between the two of them might be possible after all.

"After you made it clear that you'd be off to the rubber room if I didn't show, how could I not come? Though *I* may be the one to end up in a straitjacket."

"Am I that tough to be around?"

"No. Paris is a long way away, and I'm terrified of flying." Gabrielle felt a twinge of guilt for lying to Doug.

"Doesn't that make things a bit tough in your line of work?"

"Kind of. That's why Beatrice usually travels with me, but she can't go with me this time. I guess one of the Air France flight attendants can hold my hand during the flight, but what am I going to do once we land? How am I supposed to get around? I don't speak French."

"Don't worry. You're an American tourist. No one will expect you to speak the language, and it's not difficult to find someone who speaks English."

For the first time in as long as she could remember, Gabrielle experienced a moment's peace about being illiterate. She found herself looking forward to seeing Paris. In France nobody would think she was stupid for not being able to read or write, because French wasn't her native language. The same applied to Italy, Germany, and most of the rest of the world. With this simple revelation, the idea of traveling and working in Europe became much more appealing.

"Suddenly Tuesday in Paris sounds like a marvelous idea."

Doug and Gabrielle walked the streets of the Village hand in hand, chatting easily. Their words flowed smoothly and fell on mutually interested ears. Like the skilled storyteller he was, Doug magically wove the details of his escapades through Paris into delightful tales of adventure and pleasure. Hearing these wonderful stories left Gabrielle anxious to experience Paris, not only for herself but with Doug as her personal guide.

They ducked into the fashionable Bar 89 on Mercer Street, where Gabrielle was immediately recognized by the maître d' and several of the eatery's patrons. Her growing celebrity status provided them with the best table in the house, upstairs overlooking the entire restaurant. By the time dinner was over and coffee was served, Gabrielle had been approached by two autograph seekers, one a struggling male model, the other a middle-aged woman toting a camera.

"I see I'm dining with a celebrity," Doug commented. Though slightly annoyed by the interruptions, he was amused by Gabrielle's uneasiness at being singled out as someone important.

"Oh, sure, like eating with a model tops lunch with the President."

"With this model it does. Any day."

Gabrielle answered with a warm smile. "I'm really having a good time."

"I'm glad, because I'm enjoying myself, too."

Gabrielle reached over and coupled her hand with his. Many of the physical sensations she'd experienced on the cruise had resurfaced this evening. Doug Sixsmith was like the proverbial quiet storm, gathering up her apprehensions and fears into a swirling funnel and tossing them aside. In its wake was left a heart bursting with emotion. Gabrielle felt herself falling under his sweet control and liking it very much.

Doug reached over and tenderly touched Gabrielle's lips to his own. "Sorry, I couldn't resist any longer."

"Don't be. I liked it."

"I would really like us to spend more time together. To try and build a relationship. If that's possible." Doug sat through Gabrielle's silent hesitation. "Is it?" he prodded.

"I don't think I'm ready to have a serious relationship yet, especially with someone, you know, so much older," Gabrielle said, torn between revealing her true feelings and setting up excuses for why a relationship between them would have no future.

"I think you're worrying needlessly. Both of us are busy people with extremely demanding careers. A serious relationship would be hard to pull off at this point even if it is what we both want. Why don't we take things one step at a time? Let's just enjoy the knowledge that we are two people who are deeply in *like* with each other. Despite my advanced age, we have all the time in the world to see where this thing takes us. Make sense?"

"Yes, it does."

"Good," Doug replied tenderly, sealing their declaration with a sweet kiss.

"As much as I hate to say it, I need to get home. I have to get up early. I have a million things to do before I leave for Paris tomorrow evening," Gabrielle told him, looking at her watch. It was already after eleven. She couldn't believe they'd been in the restaurant talking for nearly three hours.

"I don't think I like the idea that you're off to one of the most romantic cities in the world without me," Doug declared.

"One day I hope we can see Paris together."

"I promise—one day you and I will be strolling down the Champs Élysées. I'll take you to all my favorite places and introduce you to the fine art of café sitting."

Waiting on the corner for a taxi, Doug stood behind Gabrielle with his arms wrapped snugly and possessively around her. His head was nestled perfectly in the crook of her neck, and Gabrielle could feel his warm breath on her skin. Tonight everything had changed between them. They'd become a couple. They had exited the den of friendship and were now standing on the perimeter of something bigger and far deeper.

"I want to go to sleep and wake up in the morning just like this," he whispered in her ear. Not caring who looked on, Doug turned Gabrielle around and took her lovely face in his hands and kissed her again, this time without hesitation or formality. His kiss was warm and loving, his tongue gently probing the sweet recesses of her mouth.

"Promise me you'll call as soon as you return," he demanded.

"And you promise me that we'll see each other again when I get back?" Gabrielle responded. Now that she had allowed herself to go with her feelings, her need to be with him was overwhelming.

Doug answered Gabrielle with another deep kiss. It was a kiss that said hello as well as good-bye. It was a "to be continued" kiss, one that lingered deliciously to remind them both that more would follow.

25

Gabrielle was the only passenger sitting in first class. She picked up the in-flight magazine and absently flipped through it, paying brief attention to any photos that caught her eye. Unable to concentrate, Gabrielle replaced the magazine in the seat pocket in front of her, sat back, and closed her eyes. Things were happening so fast in every area of her life right now. Gabrielle was happily caught up in a whirlwind of good luck, and she was savoring every minute of it.

"Excuse me," said a husky voice as its owner sidestepped Gabrielle and settled into the seat next to her. "Aren't you that model with the most delicious mouth in the business? How about just one kiss for your biggest fan?"

"What?" Gabrielle said, turning to look at the man sitting next to her. "Doug! What are you doing here? I thought you had to be back in Boston today?"

"I promised you we'd walk the Champs Élysées soon, didn't I? Besides, I figured you needed me more than *Newsweek* did."

"I'm glad you came," Gabrielle responded happily as she grabbed hold of his arm.

"So am I. Now, how about that kiss?" The two were interrupted by the flight attendant politely clearing her throat.

"Excuse me, Miss Donovan?"

"Yes?" Gabrielle responded, her face flush with equal parts of embarrassment and happiness.

"Your driver asked me to deliver this. Apparently he forgot to give it to you."

"Thank you. I wonder what it could be?" she said, as she gently shook the long, thin box.

"There's only one way to find out. Open it."

"Too early for Christmas, and it's certainly not my birthday," she continued as she untied the gold bow. Gabrielle lifted the hinged top of the jeweler's box. Inside, nestled on a bed of forest-green velvet, was a fabulous antique bracelet of white gold. The exquisite filigree design was encrusted with pavé diamonds and ten brilliant square-cut aquamarines. The center stone was another aquamarine of at least five carats. Even to the untrained eye the gift obviously cost a small fortune.

"Whoa. That's some bracelet," Doug commented, donning his reporter's hat in order to get the why, what, and, most important, *who* knew Gabrielle well enough to give her such an extravagant piece of jewelry.

"There's a card. Would you read it?" Gabrielle asked, pretending to be too absorbed in examining the bracelet to do it herself.

"It might be personal," Doug said, sounding much more sincere than he felt.

"It's okay."

" 'Dear Gabrielle,' " Doug read aloud. " 'In the old days the aquamarine was always associated with travel. Its sparkling blue color reminded people of the sky and sea, so women wore it as protection on long journeys. It's the perfect stone for the frequent flier, particularly a frightened one.

" 'Please accept this bracelet as token of my affection and best wishes. As it did the travelers of old, may it provide you safe passage as you wing your way across the world and into superstardom. I'm proud of you and extend my heartfelt congratulations on your first endorsement contract with Scarborough Designs. Love, Greg.'

"I assume that this is from Gregory von Ulrich, president of your agency."

"Yes."

"Does he congratulate all his models with such extravagant trinkets?"

"Doug, are you jealous?"

"Should I be?"

"There's nothing personal going on between Greg and me. There are no other men in my life."

"Are you saying that the position has been filled?" His demeanor brightened.

"Maybe. Probably. Yes. At least for the time being," she said, both seriously and in jest.

"Anybody I know?"

"I'm not sure, but he's very cute, extremely smart, and exceedingly sweet."

"Sounds like quite a guy."

"He certainly is," she concurred. This time it was Gabrielle's turn to kiss Doug's lips. She closed her eyes and felt the sensation of the plane taking off, causing her stomach to lurch and her heart to pound. She opened them again to find that the plane was still planted firmly on the runway. Love, Gabrielle was finding, was a truly magical thing.

"Why don't we check into your hotel and then go get breakfast?" Doug suggested after clearing customs.

"I'm too excited to eat. Since we both have only one

carry-on bag, can we just walk around and see some of the city?"

"Works for me. Where would you like to go?"

"Anywhere. Everywhere."

"That certainly narrows it down. Why don't we take a stroll down the Champs Élysées, grab a peek at the Arc de Triomphe, and then we'll ramble by the Eiffel Tower and Notre Dame?"

"Terrific."

"I need to make one quick phone call, and then we'll get moving."

Gabrielle waited as Doug ran into a nearby phone booth. Within minutes he was back by her side and the two were off to discover the incredible city of Paris.

"Called your editor?"

"No. I made a reservation at my favorite hotel. By the way, I booked two rooms, just in case you decide to blow off the Ritz and experience some real Parisian hospitality."

They spent the day walking the city's many cobblestone streets. At every landmark Doug would explain its background, recounting not only historical fact and local folklore but his unique personal commentary as well.

"Let's hop aboard one of the sightseeing boats," Doug said after suggesting that the Eiffel Tower resembled a gigantic erector set.

"That sounds heavenly. My feet are killing me."

"Follow me," Doug said, grabbing her hand and leading her to the boat. Hand in hand, Gabrielle and Doug boarded one of the *bateaux-mouches,* docked and waiting to ferry passengers down the Seine. It was now after seven, and the mast of the barge was strewn with twinkling white lights.

While their fellow tourists listened obediently to the French guide recite the history of the landmarks gracing the banks of the river, Gabrielle could only concentrate on the swell of happiness that was overtaking her body. Never had she experienced such a feeling of magnificent calm, of such tremendous satisfaction. Maybe it was being in this foreign place that had momentarily freed her from her secret prison, or maybe it was the romantic nature of the city; she didn't know. All she was sure of was that for the first time since she'd acknowledged her feelings for Doug, Gabrielle allowed herself to revel fully in the comfortable space he provided her.

They floated down the Seine in silence, Doug's arm thrown possessively around Gabrielle's shoulders. She leaned into his torso and savored the close proximity of his body. Doug reacted by resting his lips on the top of her head.

"I'm so glad you surprised me. I couldn't imagine being here without you," Gabrielle whispered.

They ate a romantic dinner in a candlelit alcove of one of Paris's fine restaurants. Following their meal, the two took advantage of the city's reputation as one of the great jazz cities of the world and headed over to the Left Bank to explore a few of the premiere venues. They left shortly after midnight so that Gabrielle could get a good night's sleep before her big meeting in the morning. Soon they were walking through two huge doors that led into a picturesque courtyard and up the stairs into the Hotel Augustin.

"Monsieur Sixsmith, how delightful to see you again," called out the gentleman behind the reception desk.

"Edouard, my friend, how are you?"

"I am well, and it, appears you are doing quite well yourself," Edouard replied, nodding favorably toward Gabrielle.

"Gabrielle, this is Edouard Augustin, proprietor of this charming establishment. Edouard, Gabrielle Donovan."

"Mademoiselle Donovan, it is a pleasure."

"This is where I stay whenever I'm in Paris," Doug told her. "Edouard and his wife always make me feel more like family than a hotel guest. I wouldn't dream of staying anywhere else."

"You are very kind. I have put you in your usual room, Douglas. And if you still desire, Mademoiselle is in the room down the hall," the Frenchman informed him with a questioning glint in his eye.

"*Merci,*" Doug responded, taking the two keys from his hand. "We'll see you in the morning for coffee. *Bonne nuit.*"

"Sleep well, monsieur, mademoiselle," Edouard answered, thinking what a shame it was that two such beautiful people should spend the night in separate beds.

"Well, here we are," Doug said softly as he turned the key and opened Gabrielle's door. "You're sure I can't interest you in a nightcap?"

"Maybe another time. I think I'm going to take a nice long bath and go to sleep. Thank you again for surprising me," she whispered, staring Doug straight in his eyes.

"It was my pleasure," he said, bringing his lips down over hers. Their kiss was slow and sweet and sent shivers down Gabrielle's spine.

"Gabrielle, I love—" Doug paused, afraid to continue. "I loved every minute of today. See you in the morning. Good night."

"Good night," she replied, backing into her room, not wanting to leave him.

"Sleep tight," he told her, unwilling to let go of her hand.

"Don't let the bedbugs bite."

"See you later, sweet potato."

"Go to bed, you crazy man," she admonished him through her laughter.

"You're supposed to say, 'Bye-bye, cutie pie.'"

"No, *you're* supposed to say, 'See you later, alligator,' and I say, 'After a while, crocodile.' At least follow the script."

"How about I just say I love you?" There, he'd told her. Damn playing it safe. He'd simply have to deal with the fall-out.

Gabrielle's face revealed a multitude of emotions—first surprise, then gratitude, lastly, fear. Her potpourri of expressions was followed by a soulful and heartfelt kiss. It was a confusing and frustrating response that left Doug clamoring for clarification.

"A great man—at least I think it was a man, though it could have been a woman . . . Nobody knows for sure because the author is listed as the ever-popular Anonymous—" Doug babbled on nervously. "Anyway, whoever it was said, 'One kiss breaches the distance between friendship and love.' An appropriate thought right about now, don't you think?"

"It's lovely. It's also getting late. Good night, Doug," Gabrielle told him as she walked through the door and closed it behind her.

Doug spent the next few seconds staring at the wooden barrier that stood between him and the woman to whom he'd just declared his love. He had no way to gauge Gabrielle's feelings. Was she insulted or just scared? Did his spontaneous revelation mean the end of their short relationship, or was it just about to begin?

Something is not right, he told himself as he unlocked his own door. *A man doesn't tell the woman of his dreams that he loves her, only to have her put him in a lip lock that curls his toes and then close the door in his face. This is not how it's supposed to work. Shit, where's that damn manual when I need it?* Doug thought in anguish as he threw himself onto the bed.

What happened to take things slow, you idiot? What happened to giving her time to get over the age thing? Well, you asshole, you've really gone and blown it now. Thoroughly disgusted with himself, Doug headed downstairs to drown his regrets in a bottle of good wine. He paused outside of Gabrielle's door, debating whether to knock and apologize. Deciding he'd done enough damage for one evening, he hurried downstairs to find Edouard.

"He loves. He loves me. He loves me," Gabrielle sang gleefully into the mirror as she soaked in her bath. At first, after Doug had actually spoken those three tiny but incredibly powerful words, she was terrified. That's why she'd slammed the brakes on the wonderful moment. From the beginning, she and Doug had tried to tiptoe around the reality of their feelings, but the oh, so wonderful truth of the matter was that she was a young woman falling in love with a man who loved her.

As fabulous as she felt, Gabrielle also found herself in a genuine quandary. She'd decided long ago that she'd never allow herself to get too serious over a man, because marriage would never be a part of her life. It was her own irrational conclusion that matrimony would eventually turn into motherhood, and she could never be a fit mother for any child. Little Tommy was proof of that.

For the time being, her desire and undeniably strong feelings for Doug won the tug-of-war with her heart. Doug was absolutely right; the nature of their individual work would force them to take things nice and slow. Why deny herself the opportunity to love and be loved? Why not enjoy it while it lasted? As her mother's relationships had confirmed, the bliss of love never endured. When it was time for their relationship to be over, she'd end it, no hard feelings.

But for now Gabrielle planned to revel in the fabulous new sensation of being in love.

Gabrielle, you stupid girl, what have you done? she asked herself, sitting up in the tub. *Doug declares his love and you close the door in his face!*

"I have so much to learn," she told herself out loud as she flopped back down into the warm water and watched the candlelight flicker on the walls. She always took candlelight baths when she traveled. They helped her to relax and unwind after a long day in front of the camera.

Tonight is the perfect time for me to begin my lessons, Gabrielle decided, remembering the way Doug's tender kisses had made her feel. What better way to top off such a monumental day than making love for the first time with the man she loved in Paris, the city of love?

Gabrielle got out of the tub and quickly toweled off. After applying a coat of Coco Chanel body lotion, she paused, unsure what else to put on for her first seduction. Digging through her overnight bag proved to be futile; all she had in there was her very comfortable but very unsexy sleep shirt. She could wear her underwear, but that seemed too clichéd.

Gabrielle surveyed her room looking for something appropriate. As her eye fell across the wet towel lying on her bed, her mouth widened into a triumphant smile. What could be sexier than a freshly bathed woman showing up at her lover's door wearing nothing but a fluffy white towel? Gabrielle ran into the bathroom and yanked the unused towel from the rack. She wrapped it around her body, making sure it was adequately secure. She quickly ran a comb through her hair, brushed on a little mascara, and glossed her lips with a clear shine.

Gabrielle inspected herself in the mirror and smiled at her reflection. Skimpy but effective, she decided. Her bronze hair rippled down her back in unruly waves. Her face was flush with anticipation and excitement. She was nervous, but ready. Doug was the one; every fiber in her being told her so.

She headed purposefully toward the door, only to stop, turn around, and hurry back into the bathroom. She picked up three of the vanilla-scented candles and a book of matches. Candlelight seemed appropriate for the occasion. One last check in the mirror, and she was off again.

She slowly opened the door to her room and cased the hall. Finding the corridor empty, Gabrielle quickly scampered over to Doug's room and knocked softly on the door. Receiving no reply, she knocked again, harder and louder.

Maybe he's asleep, Gabrielle thought. She slowly turned the knob, only to find his door unlocked. She tiptoed quietly over to the bed, moonlight illuminating the way. She expected to see Doug's slumbering body, but instead found the bed neatly turned back, undisturbed but for a few wrinkles.

Now what? So far her big seduction scene was not turning out as she'd imagined. She had two options: She could slip back across the hall and Doug would be none the wiser, or she could wait for him to return. She'd come this far, she decided. She was going to see it through.

Gabrielle lit the candles, found a nice, soft French music station on the clock radio, and then sat down to wait for her man. She sat for nearly twenty minutes before Doug finally came sauntering through the door.

"I must have drunk more than I thought," he commented, a bit tipsy, a lot confused. "Am I dreaming?"

"No."

"You mean, you're actually sitting here in my room, smelling utterly delectable, wearing nothing but moonlight and a towel."

"Yes," Gabrielle confirmed softly.

"And I've been downstairs all this time with my hands wrapped around a bottle of wine, when I could have been here with them wrapped around you?"

"Yes, but we're both here now, though I'm over here and you're way over there."

Doug smiled broadly as he finally moved toward Gabrielle. He picked her up from the chair with one grand swoop and carried her over to the bed. His action caused her towel to peel away. The sight of her completely naked was sobering.

"You are even more ravishing than I imagined," he whispered as his lips crushed hers.

"I want to see you," Gabrielle said, reaching up to unbutton his shirt. She pulled the shirt off his body and reached for the fly of his slacks. Doug stopped kissing her long enough to help remove his pants. His clothes had successfully hidden the lean, taut muscles of his washboard stomach and well-toned arms. She was surprised by the broadness of his shoulders and the slimness of his waist. Mr. Universe he wasn't, but he was far from being a ninety-pound weakling.

"Wow," she remarked.

"I guess I can take that as a compliment."

"Yes, you can, though you are the first totally naked man I've ever seen. At least this close up."

"You mean this is—"

"My first time."

"Then I will do my utmost to make this the most special night of your life."

"You already have."

"I mean it. I intend to show you what it means for a man to make love to you, because I do love you, Gabrielle."

The weight of Doug's hungry kiss silenced any response Gabrielle tried to make. She found herself slowly losing control under the delectable and drugging effect of Doug's actions. He moved slowly and seductively, intoxicating all her senses and liberating her inhibitions. After thoroughly exploring her mouth and face with his lips and tongue, he moved on to her young and copious breasts. Doug took them into his mouth and hungrily feasted on her large, rosy nipples. Gabrielle felt them grow longer and harder with each lick of his tongue. She could feel a delightful nagging sensation in her groin, causing her hips and pelvis to instinctively tilt upward in search of Doug's. A slow, sexy moan escaped from her lips.

The sound of her pleasure was Doug's indication that it was time to move on. Slowly, luxuriously, he bathed her torso with his tongue, stopping to playfully dip it inside the well of her bellybutton, causing Gabrielle to laugh.

"A prime tickle spot," he commented.

"Could be."

"How about here?" he asked, as he lightly ran his fingertips down the length of her inner thigh.

"Hmm," she moaned, her body melting into the bed.

"And here?" Doug inquired again, as this time he parted her lower lips and lightly circled her clitoris.

Again Gabrielle could answer his question only with a seductive moan as her hips rose to meet his fingertip. Doug was anxious to taste her. He pressed his nose up against her silky thatch of pubic hair. Doug targeted her sexual nerve center with a soft steady stream of warm air before circling it with the very tip of his tongue. Gabrielle stopped breathing, and for a brief period time stood still. She was lost in the pleasure of new and delightful sensations. Her breath came rushing back as Doug, like a cat lapping a bowl of warm milk, dragged his tongue in one long, luscious stroke from the bottom of her vagina to the top of her swollen clitoris.

Gabrielle grabbed his curly head and pressed his face against her pelvis. She needed the delicious ache in her groin to be satisfied. Doug was more than ready to fulfill her need but instead held back, wanting to make sure she was truly ready to receive him. His mouth once again searched out her breasts as his hand worked its magic below. Doug tested her readiness with his fingers, pushing first one, then two of them deep inside her. He fingered her gently but urgently, following the rhythm of Gabrielle's subtle bucking motions. Gabrielle instinctively moved with his hand, enjoying the sweet pleasure the friction was creating.

She was so ready—wide open and wet. He momentarily put his desire for her in check and rolled over to put on a condom. His task complete, Doug grabbed his rigid penis and began to guide it into her virgin body. Only entering her halfway, Doug lay above her, his weight resting on his arms, while he began a slow glide toward full penetration. Gabrielle, longing to be skin-to-skin with Doug, grabbed his buttocks and pushed him deep into her waiting body. A brief cry of pain escaped her lips.

"Did I hurt you? Are you all right?"

"I'm okay. It just hurt a little bit. Please don't stop."

She didn't have to tell him twice. He continued to love her in slow motion. Gabrielle's mouth found his, and their tongues danced a lazy, sensual tango. As her hunger for him grew more unbearable, Gabrielle found herself unable to remain silent.

"Oh, this feels so good. Don't stop. Please don't ever stop."

Knowing how much Gabrielle desired him released his pent-up passion, and Doug exploded into a fury of syncopated thrusts. Gabrielle reciprocated his lusty rhythm, their bodies bucking back and forth in a wild, passionate dance.

Doug felt himself grow, swell, tighten, and then burst inside her.

"I'm sorry. I couldn't wait," he panted, holding her close. "We'll do it again just for you. I want you to come, too."

"I can't imagine it feeling any better than this."

"Oh, it can, baby. It definitely can. And next time you'll see for yourself."

The two lay together, enjoying the afterglow of their lovemaking. Gabrielle was in awe of the wondrous thing she'd just experienced. How lucky she was that her first sexual encounter was with such a loving, considerate man.

"I love you," Gabrielle purred, circling his nipples with her index finger.

"I love you, too."

"Doug?"

"Hmm?" he answered, his voice getting thicker and lazier.

"Can we do it again, now?"

"I've created a monster! What a brilliant and lucky man I am," he congratulated himself as he drew Gabrielle back into his arms.

"I see the aquamarine must have worked. You are positively glowing. Your flight was good?" Greg whispered to Gabrielle as they sat waiting for Maynard Scarborough to get off the phone.

"It was wonderful, full of surprises—your generous gift being one of them. Thank you so much. I actually enjoyed myself. Maybe I'm beginning to get over my fear of flying—enough to start working in Europe. What do you think?"

"I think that's a great idea and will be very necessary if things go as I suspect they will today."

"Sorry to keep you waiting," Maynard greeted the two, interrupting their conversation. "Greg, good to see you."

"Maynard, it's great to see you again. Please let me formally introduce you to Gabrielle Donovan."

"If after seeing you in *Appeal* I hadn't already decided that you were exactly what Scarborough Designs needed, I'd certainly have come to the conclusion at this moment," Maynard said, gazing appreciatively at Gabrielle's Scarborough-clad body.

"I knew you two were meant for each other," Gregory said, mentally patting himself on the back as they all sat down. This union between Gabrielle and Maynard was going to increase the visibility of his agency a hundredfold.

"Why don't you tell us exactly what you have in mind for Gabrielle?" Greg suggested.

"After we talked on the phone, my original idea was to use Gabrielle as the lead model during the collection shows and in print ads, but then I saw this," Maynard said, pulling a long, thin brochure from his desk drawer. "You recognize it?" he asked.

"Of course. That's Mig Reid's new promotional brochure," Greg answered.

"It was this brochure, particularly this picture, that changed my thinking," the designer stated, pointing to the living-poem shot. "When I saw this photo, I knew immediately that Gabrielle must also be the image for my new line of jewelry. In fact, I've scrapped the previous ads and have already talked to Miguel about duplicating this very shot in our print ads for the launch this fall."

"Maybe we should discuss some of the finer details," Greg suggested, ready to get down to business.

"Let me cut to the chase. I'd like to offer Gabrielle an exclusive six-year contract to represent Scarborough Designs and Scarborough Jewels. I am prepared to compensate her with the sum of two million dollars for approximately thirty days of work per year. This will mean making the rounds of personal appearances at press conferences and the like. In return, I expect exclusivity on the runway. So, do we have a deal?" the designer inquired.

"Close, but not quite. Six years is an awfully long time for someone with Gabrielle's earning potential to be tied down. We can't possibly agree to this deal for under four million, not when Calvin Klein is expressing interest," Greg bluffed.

"That Calvin, he knows talent. Three million, but that's my final offer."

"Three million is perfectly acceptable, but for three years, not six, and with an additional payment of ten thousand per show," Greg demanded. Underneath his easygoing demeanor, Gregory von Ulrich was a deft negotiator.

"You ask a lot," Maynard responded, making Greg wonder if he'd pushed too far.

"Yes, but she's worth a lot," Greg countered with steely-eyed determination.

The silence was torture as the designer pondered Greg's demand. "Welcome to the House of Scarborough," he announced finally, extending his hand to Gregory before turning toward Gabrielle.

Gabrielle, stunned by the news that in less than half an hour she'd become a millionaire, accepted Maynard's handshake and kiss in silence. She was speechless. She could not believe that he was willing to pay her three million dollars to pose for a few pictures and attend a few parties.

"We'll hammer out the details with our respective lawyers later. But I would like to announce our agreement to the press in a joint conference very soon," Greg told him.

"That's fine. I have only one stipulation. The monetary

terms of our agreement are to remain secret. I do not want any details released to the press."

"I understand."

"One other thing: I would like Gabrielle to begin her public association with us with the holiday ads for the jewelry line and then during show week in the spring."

"I think I should tell you that I've never—"

"That she's never been so excited before," Greg stated, interrupting Gabrielle. There was no need for the man who was going to pay Gabrielle ten thousand dollars a show to know that she'd never strolled a catwalk before. March 1996 was still eight months away. They had plenty of time to teach her what she needed to know.

"I'm excited, too," Maynard said as his secretary walked in carrying a bottle of Dom Perignon and three flutes. "A toast to Gabrielle Donovan. Scarborough Designs has found its perfect ambassador. Together we are going to set the fashion industry on fire."

The delicate clink of fine crystal punctuated the air. Gabrielle, Gregory, and Maynard all smiled as they drank, each of them aware that, by sealing this deal, the best was yet to come for all of them.

Doug stood outside the offices of Scarborough Designs. He'd walked the busy Champs Élysées for the last hour and a half before turning onto the avenue Montaigne to wait for Gabrielle. The time alone gave him an opportunity to examine what was happening between the two of them.

Doug was happy he'd acted on his impulse to accompany her to Paris. The spontaneity of his actions had left him feeling delightfully derelict. Never before had he acted so irresponsibly toward his work or done anything to jeopardize his pristine professional reputation, but he'd do it again tomorrow if it meant spending time with Gabrielle.

Last night had been so incredible. In many ways he'd been just as much a virgin as Gabrielle. Never in his life as a sexually active man had he experienced anything like making love with Gabrielle. It left him feeling profoundly joyous and totally susceptible, both physically and emotionally.

For as beautiful as their union appeared, it was certainly vulnerable for a variety of reasons—one being the differences in their ages. Fifteen years was a big span, not so much in age, but more so in life experience. Doug had traveled the world, broken hearts and had his own broken, but Gabrielle had spent most of her twenty years sitting on the window seat of life, watching the world go by. Now, because of the nature of her work, she was being hurled, ready or not, onto life's fast track and into the fishbowl living of celebrity. Could she cope with the changes her life was about to undergo?

And how would they both cope with the fact that they were destined to spend more time apart than together? Could he expect a girl as young as Gabrielle to remain interested in a man she might see only once or twice a month? And would he be able to handle the demands that loving a young, incredibly beautiful celebrity would bring?

If the examples of her predecessors were any indication, Gabrielle could count on being pursued by royalty, musicians, movie stars, and professional athletes—all anxious to pump up their own egos by acquiring a supermodel "arm piece." The antique bracelet from Greg von Ulrich was just the first of many lavish and expensive gifts men would use to woo Gabrielle.

Could he deal with all this and more? Granted, as a prize-winning journalist with an international reputation, Doug was no lightweight, but he had neither the disposition nor the inclination to join the ranks of the coveted "beautiful people." Doug also had never considered himself to be a jealous man, but this was an entirely different ball game. Did he have a big enough bat to play in the major leagues?

Doug's thoughts were interrupted when an exuberant Gabrielle jumped into his arms. She was flying high. She gave him an excited hug and kiss, her face flush with excitement.

"I take it all went well," he replied with the greatest understatement of the year.

"Can you keep a secret? What I'm about to say is strictly off the record."

"You have nothing to worry about," he assured her.

"Kiss me, I'm a millionaire!"

Doug let out a gigantic shout and twirled Gabrielle around in a circle. He silenced her joyous screams and cries of delight with a long congratulatory kiss, a spectacle greeted by their fellow pedestrians with applause. A street cleaner tipped the fluorescent-green bristles of his broom in a congratulatory salute. *"Aime, et fais ce que tu veux,"* he advised as he swept past the couple. Love, and do what you will.

26

"Good morning, Bright Eyes," Albert Wilcot's voice sang out over the phone.

"Papa! When did you guys get into town?"

"About an hour ago."

"Where's Mama?"

"In the bathroom trying to steam the wrinkles out of her outfit before your lunch. She's really looking forward to seeing you."

"Me, too," Felicia responded, hoping she sounded more sincere than she felt. When Jolie suggested accompanying her husband to New York so mother and daughter could spend time together, Felicia had unsuccessfully tried to discourage her, citing an extraordinary workload as her excuse. As much as she loved her mother, she couldn't bear the idea of setting off Jolie's ultrasensitive maternal radar and having to answer a barrage of questions about her strange behavior of late. "You're sure you can't join us?"

"I'm afraid not, honey. This medical conference has me tied up morning till night, which is why I'm calling so early. I wanted to at least speak with you and my son-in-law while I'm in the same city."

"I'm afraid you're stuck with just me, Papa. Trace already left for court," Felicia informed her father.

"That's too bad. When do you expect him this evening? Maybe I can catch him during the dinner break."

"It's hard to say. You know how Trace is when it comes to his work." She didn't bother to add that his early departure was directly related to yet another heated argument between them. In fact, she and her husband hadn't spoken to each other in days.

"Yes, I do. Both of you work a bit too hard, if you ask me. But since you didn't, I'm not going to butt in. I'll leave that to your mother," Albert said, causing Felicia to chuckle. "Good to hear you laugh, sweetheart. I'll talk to you soon."

"I'm sorry Papa couldn't join us," Felicia told her mother after placing her lunch order with the waiter.

"He is, too, but I'm glad we have this chance to talk alone."

"How is he? Is he sticking to his diet?"

"Reluctantly."

"What's up with Lindsay? She called me the other day, but I haven't had a chance to get back to her," Felicia said.

"Lindsay's busy being Lindsay," Jolie remarked, smiling. "I think she's finally picked a major—two, actually—dance and psychology. She's decided to become a dance therapist."

"And how are you doing, Mama?"

"I'm okay. Just a few worries rattling around in my head."

"What's wrong?"

"Why don't you tell me?"

"What makes you think there's something wrong with me?" Felicia asked, avoiding her mother's inquisitive eyes.

"Maybe because we rarely hear from you these days, or

because you and Trace continually avoid being around us lately. And look how your clothes are hanging off you. Just how much weight have you lost?"

"I've been working very hard, Mama. We both have. There just hasn't been time to eat, or call, or run down to D.C. to visit."

"Does hard work explain away the pain and confusion in your eyes? Felicia, what's wrong? Is everything all right between you and Trace?"

Felicia could feel the tears welling up in her eyes. Just as she knew it would be, it was a futile exercise to try to hide her problems from Jolie. Maybe a little mother's love was exactly what she needed right now. Maybe some maternal TLC could make her feel less guilty and confused about what a mess her life was in. "No, Mama, it's not."

"Honey, why didn't you say something sooner? You know I'm always here to help you."

"I don't know. I guess I was too embarrassed or afraid you'd think I'd let you and Papa down."

"Licia, every marriage has its problems. Your father and I have been married for thirty-six years. Do you really think that all thirty-six were blissful and problem-free? Honey, marriage is hard work. There are peaks and there are valleys. The key is to store the love and respect you gather during the high times to help get you through the low. Tell me, what's going on between you two?"

"We're having some problems. Problems that we're seeing a marriage counselor about," she admitted.

"Is there another woman?" Jolie probed gently. "Is Trace cheating on you?"

Felicia didn't know whether to laugh or cry. Laugh at her mother's assumption that it was Trace who'd been unfaithful, or cry because only she knew the truth. How heartbroken and disappointed would her parents be if they knew that it was their "perfect" daughter who'd made love to another man and then aborted their grandchild because she was unsure of its paternity? "No, Mama, there definitely isn't another woman," Felicia assured her. "It would be so much simpler if there were."

27

"Will we be done soon?" Gabrielle asked nervously. Laslo was putting the finishing touches to her makeup. The press conference to announce her working relationship with Scarborough Designs was scheduled to begin in little over half an hour, and Gabrielle wanted to review her statement one more time.

"All done," Laslo announced, brushing away some excess powder. "Beautiful as usual."

"Thanks, Las."

"Here's your dress," announced one of Maynard's assistants, walking through the door. She helped Gabrielle slip into the short emerald-green dress that Maynard had chosen especially for her. Inspired by his new muse, he had designed a fresh line of outrageously sexy, make-the-most-of-your-body cocktail dresses. The line would be introduced as part of his new collection.

"You look magnificent."

"Thanks. Could you find Beatrice for me?" Gabrielle wasn't concerned about her appearance. Right now she was more interested in how she was going to sound when she stepped up to the podium.

"I'm right here," Bea said, stepping into the room. "What do you need?"

"Could we go over this statement one more time, please?"

"Sure, if you really think you need to. You knew it perfectly last night."

"Just once more."

"Okay," Beatrice agreed. She sat down in the makeup chair and listened as Gabrielle ran through her lines. She recited them flawlessly. Her delivery was easy and fluid and did not sound scripted or rehearsed.

"Perfect."

"Good. I just want this to go very smoothly. I'd hate for Maynard to think it was a mistake to hire me."

"He's lucky to have you," Bea assured her.

"Maynard, good to see you," Greg said, greeting the designer with a strong handshake.

"Hello. Do you know where I can find Gabrielle? I had a brainstorm over breakfast. I want to make some changes in her statement."

"She's in makeup, but we're only a few minutes away from getting started. Are you sure you want to make changes now?"

"She can read them off the cards if necessary."

"Well, if you don't have a problem with that, she shouldn't either."

The two men walked into the makeup room to find Gabrielle, Beatrice, and Felicia huddled together. Gabrielle was again rehearsing her copy.

"Mr. Scarborough, Greg, how are you this afternoon?" Felicia asked. "The house is packed, and the reporters have just about finished their requisite snacks and coffee, so I think we're about ready to begin. Bea, why don't you come with me and I'll help you find your seat?"

"Break a leg, honey," Beatrice encouraged as she lightly hugged Gabrielle and followed Felicia out the door.

"Well, young lady, how do you feel?" Maynard inquired.

"Terrific. I appreciate the opportunity, and I'll do the best job I possibly can."

"I have no doubt you will. I'd like you to add this to your statement this afternoon," Maynard said, handing Gabrielle a piece of paper.

Gabrielle felt herself go pale under her foundation. What was she going to do with these late changes? Beatrice had already taken her seat, and even if she were still around, there was no time to learn these new lines.

"I know I'm springing this on you at the very last minute, but don't worry about memorizing it. You can read it right off the cards."

"Gabrielle, you look positively petrified," Gregory observed. "Are you okay?"

"Just a little nervous about the changes. Could you read this to me, Maynard? Hearing it will help it sink in." There was no way that in this short bit of time that she was going to memorize his words verbatim, but if she got the gist down, she could wing it.

"Sure. It's quite short, so don't be nervous," Maynard said as he began to read. "Epictetus once said, 'One who desires to excel should endeavor in those things that are in themselves most excellent.' This is the philosophy behind every Scarborough design. Our goal is to design clothes that emphasize and flatter the wearer, not just the dream. That's why I'm proud to represent—so on and so on."

"Very nice," Gabrielle commented.

"I'm glad you think so. It's important you believe the words, not just read them."

"I absolutely believe in your clothes and your vision. If I didn't, I wouldn't be here," Gabrielle assured him. "Don't worry, I won't let you down."

"I know you won't."

"Well, kids, it's show time," Felicia returned to inform the group.

"Let's get out there," Greg said as the three left the room. Walking down toward the auditorium, Gabrielle worked hard to compose herself and put a check on her panic. Frightened as she might be, there was no way she was going to blow this now.

Gabrielle took her seat in the first row. As Felicia took the podium and proceeded to introduce Maynard Scarborough, she glanced around the crowded room. There had to be at least forty reporters and photographers in attendance. Among the several television crews set up in the back, she recognized Cynthia Bagby, host of "Fashion Forward," a popular cable-TV show that chronicled the comings and goings of the industry's players. Gabrielle also noticed Stephanie with an armful of press kits standing among the various assistants in the back of the room. Up front, Maynard was still speaking, though Gabrielle had no idea what he was saying. She was too busy concentrating on her upcoming role. All too soon, she heard her name announced. Before leaving her seat, she sent a silent SOS, first to her mother in heaven and then to Doug in Boston. She needed all the help she could get.

"Ladies and gentlemen, I'd like to present to you now the new face of Scarborough Designs, God's most beautiful idea, Ms. Gabrielle Donovan," Maynard said, gesturing Gabrielle to the front.

Gabrielle rose and walked slowly to the podium. Turning toward the audience, she looked out into a pool of reporters, pens and tape recorders poised, all waiting for her to say something, if not brilliant, at least interesting. With television cameras rolling and flashbulbs going off in her face, Gabrielle opened her mouth and found herself unable to speak. She smiled broadly, fighting to maintain control and remember what she was there to say. To her dismay, even the original statement she'd memorized was nowhere to be found in her head. Moments passed, several lifetimes it seemed to Gabrielle, before the words "Good afternoon" finally escaped her lips. Behind the podium she crossed her fingers and began to ad-lib.

"My mother always used to tell me that when life gives you a pimple, make a beauty mark," Gabrielle began, reciting one of Helene's homespun quotes. The folksy humor prompted a friendly chuckle to ripple around the room. It was a sound that put Gabrielle at ease and encouraged her to continue. "She was trying to tell me that every human being has imperfections, that the trick to looking and feeling good is to take what God has given you—flaws and all—and make the best of it. Well, that's the genius behind Scarborough Designs. Maynard Scarborough not only dresses a woman's body in luscious fabrics and creative designs, but her mind and ego as well.

"As every well-appointed woman knows, the secret to great style is confidence. Maynard's clothes give a woman the confidence to be her *own* fashion accessory, to emphasize her positives, and to create a unique look for herself. That's why I am so pleased to be representing Scarborough Designs. I'm *confident* that this relationship will be long and fruitful, because while fashions may fade, style—Scarborough style, that is—remains. Thank you."

The audience, led by Maynard himself, burst into applause. The sound of such magnanimous approval was music to Gabrielle's ears. The designer hurried toward her and embraced her, while the photographers in attendance captured the exuberant moment on film. It was clear that the creative union of this divine woman and this powerful designer was going to be a force to be reckoned with.

God's most beautiful idea, Stephanie thought. *Isn't that going a bit far?* This entire Gabrielle affair was going way too far, in Stephanie's opinion. Why was Gabrielle getting all this adulation, not to mention cash for doing nothing but standing around while someone took her picture? And to really make this entire thing a major Maalox moment, it was part of Stephanie's job to see that the girl went even further.

"Maynard, it's obvious you've picked a very beautiful and able representative for your company, but why a novice? Why not a more famous face?" inquired a reporter from *Women's Wear Daily.*

"At Scarborough Designs we constantly try to dazzle our customers. If we use a girl who is already too famous, we lose our cutting-edge appeal. We weren't looking for a star, but it just so happens that when we found Gabrielle, we found one."

"Gabrielle, how does all this make you feel?"

"Very lucky," she answered, smiling.

"And very wealthy perhaps? Can you tell us the details of your contract?" asked a journalist from the *New York Post.*

"I can tell you that while I hope to be associated with Scarborough Designs for decades, our initial contract is for three years. My salary is confidential, but Maynard has been very generous."

"Generous to the tune of three million dollars," the girl standing next to Stephanie remarked.

"He's paying her a million dollars a year? How do you know this?"

"It's the gossip around the office."

"Whose office?"

"The guy's up front."

"You work for Maynard Scarborough?"

"Not directly. I usually work in personnel, but this week I'm filling in for his assistant who's on jury duty. I heard some people talking about this girl's deal."

"What people?"

"Well, they were secretaries. They were griping about having to bust their behinds every day while he gave this new model a million dollars a year, plus fifteen thousand per fashion show. All for working less than a month all year."

"They have a point," Stephanie answered dryly. Wasn't this just delicious? Ever since Gabrielle had signed this contract, Stephanie had been trying to find out the details. And now she'd managed to scoop every reporter in the room simply because she'd had the dumb luck to stand next to a bigmouthed temp who worked with bigmouthed secretaries.

"Is she lucky or what?"

"Yeah, lucky—real lucky." *How is it that women like Gabrielle get handed the magic wands in life, while I'm left holding a fuckin' pooper scooper?* Stephanie stood up and made her way across the row of seats and out the ballroom. *I'm tired of having nothing and being a nobody,* she decided as she headed for the phone. It was time to call Harry Grain. Stephanie was about to offer up Gabrielle as her sacrificial lamb.

"Harry, this is Stephanie. I want to talk to you about my roommate."

"Who's your roommate?"

"Gabrielle Donovan."

"You live with that delicious little tidbit? The woman who *Vogue* says is going to be the supermodel of the century?"

"That very same tidbit," Stephanie said, unable to keep the sarcasm from coloring her words. She was glad that Harry couldn't see the smirk on her face. She was in no mood to discuss, ad nauseam, the divine Ms. Donovan. This was her dime, and she was planning to turn it into dollars— many, many dollars. "Maynard Scarborough must agree with *Vogue*. He's just announced that he's signed her to represent his clothing and jewelry lines."

"Old news, darling."

"Oh, so you already know the confidential terms of her contract."

"Do tell."

"First things first, Harry. Before I tell you how much Gabrielle is getting paid, I'd like to know how much I'm getting paid."

"Oh, Stephanie, you do cut right to the chase, don't you, darling?" Despite his sometimes crabby attitude toward her, Harry Grain actually liked Stephanie very much. She reminded him of himself. Stephanie was wily, wicked, and desperate to get ahead.

"What exactly is the extent of your access to Miss Donovan?"

"Harry, I can tell you everything from what Gabrielle Donovan craves when she's premenstrual to how messy she keeps her underwear drawer. For a price, of course."

"Of course. I will double what I'm paying you now, but only if you assure me that I'll have exclusive rights to any news about Gabrielle."

"Harry, how could you even think I'd take my gossip elsewhere?"

"We're in agreement, then?"

"Yes indeed."

"Well, let's hear about her contract. I do have a deadline to meet."

After filling Harry in on the details, she hung up the phone, smiling as if she'd won the lottery. Why hadn't she thought of this before? Handing Harry a few innocent bits of gossip about Gabrielle wouldn't hurt. In fact, this could prove to be a real boon to the girl's career. After all, weren't all the big-time models mentioned in gossip columns all the time? Hell, you couldn't pick up a paper without reading about the antics, engagements, divorces, or weight gains of Naomi Campbell or Elle MacPherson. *Something else to thank me for, Gaby. One day you're going to have to return the favor. And when I'm ready to collect, I'm going to collect big—real big.*

28

"Get Greg von Ulrich on the fucking phone *now*," Maynard
barked at his assistant. He was furious. Going through the
clippings from yesterday's press conference, he'd come
across "The Grain Harvest" only to find the details of his
contract with Gabrielle laid out in black and white for the
world to read.

"How the fuck did a sleaze like Harry Grain get the details of Gabrielle's contract?" he screamed in the phone after
Gregory's hello. "Do you know what havoc this will wreak
on other contract negotiations I have going on?"

"What are you talking about, Maynard?"

"We agreed that our deal was to remain confidential,
but not only do I read about it in the paper, I read about it in
a fucking tabloid! How do you explain this?"

"Frankly, Maynard, I don't know how to explain it, but
I will get to the bottom of this. In the meantime, I'll alert Felicia about the leak and advise her not to confirm or deny
anything to the press. I'll also talk to Gabrielle and remind
her that all business dealings are confidential."

"I'll do the same here, and if I do find that the information was leaked from my side, heads will roll."

* * *

"Gabrielle, I read about your deal with Maynard Scarborough. Why didn't you tell me you were a multimillionaire?" Stephanie said.

"Where did you read that?"

"In *Star Diary*. Is he really paying you three million plus fifteen thousand a show?" Stephanie asked.

"No, I'm not making fifteen thousand dollars a fashion show," Gabrielle told her, without offering the correct figure. "That information was supposed to be confidential."

"This isn't going to affect your deal, is it?"

"I'm not sure, but I'd better call Greg and let him know." Before she could pick up the phone, it rang.

"Ms. Donovan?"

"Yes?"

"We'd like a comment on your contract with Scarborough Designs."

"I—uh, I—" Gabrielle stuttered into the phone.

"Are the terms as outlined in *Star Diary* correct?"

"No, not really."

"This is Stephanie Bancroft, Ms. Donovan's publicist," Stephanie said, taking the receiver from Gabrielle's hand. "Ms. Donovan has no comment at this time."

"Can *you* confirm this report?"

"No comment."

Stephanie hung up the phone, only to have it ring again. "Hello. No, this is her publicist, Stephanie Bancroft. That's B-A-N-C-R-O-F-T," she told another reporter. "Ms. Donovan has no comment about the terms of her contract with Mr. Scarborough. Good-bye." Again the phone rang.

"Ms. Donovan has no comment on—"

"Stephanie?"

"Felicia?"

"You obviously already know that we've got a problem."

"Tell me about it. Somebody leaked the terms of Gabrielle's contract with Scarborough Designs. The press has been calling nonstop. Don't worry, I'm handling it."

"I can see that. Excellent work, Stephanie. If you can take care of any calls on the home phone, I'll cover the office. This should all blow over soon. May I speak to Gabrielle, please?"

"Sure," Stephanie said, handing the phone to Gabrielle. She was both grateful and surprised by Felicia's praise. Felicia's behavior had been so quirky and withdrawn lately that Stephanie was beginning to wonder if she noticed anything that went on in the office.

"It's pretty crazy around here, Felicia. How did they find out?" Gabrielle asked.

"I have no idea. Did you tell anyone?"

"Only Bea and—" Gabrielle paused, wondering if Doug could have possibly been the source. How could he be? He'd promised to keep the information off the record. Doug wouldn't betray her, would he?

"And?"

"And I'm sure that she wouldn't tell a soul, let alone a tabloid hack."

"I agree, so don't worry. This won't last long. Harry Grain will soon move on to his next victim."

"What can we do to fix this, Felicia? Can't we call someone and get them to retract the story?"

"Believe me, it's usually best to just ignore these stories. Besides, when you look at the big picture, it's not that huge a deal," Felicia said.

"Only to Maynard, who asked specifically that all this remain confidential."

"I'm sure Gregory will take care of Maynard, and in the

meantime Stephanie will talk to any reporters who might call you at home."

"What did she say?" Stephanie asked once Gabrielle had hung up.

"She told me not to worry and that you'll handle the situation here."

"She's right," Stephanie said, smiling brightly. "I'll take care of everything."

Doug stood in the entryway of his Boston apartment building and sifted through his mail. The pile contained the usual bills and junk mail, plus a small package addressed in handwriting he didn't recognize.

He sprinted up the three flights of stairs that led to his front door. Once inside, Doug threw the rest of his mail onto the table next to the door and carried the small padded envelope into his study. He sat down and tore open the envelope, spilling onto the desk a cassette tape and two Polaroid photos.

The first picture was of a man he didn't recognize, holding a shirt he did. It was his lucky Boston University sweatshirt. This was the shirt that got him through his writer's block and the one he wore whenever he was working on an important story—like his award-winning story on Romanian orphans. This ratty old sweatshirt was the most important piece of clothing he owned, and from the looks of things it was in big trouble.

The man was strangling his security sweatshirt in one hand, while brazenly flicking his Bic perilously close to the frayed right cuff. The second Polaroid was a pinup shot of Gabrielle stretched out across a sofa wearing nothing but his shirt and a pair of black-suede pumps. Talk about torture.

With an expansive smile on his face, Doug popped the cassette into his tape recorder. After several seconds of silence he heard Gabrielle's voice, sounding stern and mysterious.

"Doug Sixsmith, we have your sweatshirt. If you ever want to see it in one piece again, follow these instructions. You must arrive in New York City on Friday, September fifteenth. Be at the New York Hilton by one o'clock and look for a woman sitting behind a newspaper in the lobby. Come alone—and be prepared to be held hostage."

Doug played the tape again and again, each time marveling over his lover's creativity and sense of humor. He missed Gabrielle so very much and was thrilled that she obviously missed him as well. Doug couldn't continue to live like this. Their short, sporadic visits in between work trips were no longer enough. He needed to be with Gabrielle on a daily basis, to go to bed with her wrapped in his arms and to wake up each morning with her beside him. *It's time to make some changes,* he thought as he reached for the phone.

"This is perfect—holding me hostage in the same hotel where we first met," Doug remarked.

Gabrielle replied by snuggling closer to Doug. She smiled and mentally congratulated herself on her luxurious surroundings. She'd come a long way from sleeping in the bathroom of this very hotel. Instead of scrounging off room-service trays, her meals were prepared at the whim of her appetite. And instead of dodging the hotel maids, they were now at her beck and call.

"It would be even more perfect if we could be together all the time," Doug continued.

"That would be heavenly, but impossible with me here in New York and you in Boston."

"It could happen if I moved to New York."

"I'd love it if you were here all the time, but with both

of us on planes as much as we are, it really won't matter much, will it?"

"It would if one of us gave up all the travel," Doug said. "I can't quit traveling."

"How sexist of you to assume that I was talking about you."

"You're going to quit writing?" Gabrielle asked.

"I didn't say I'd stop writing. I said I would stop traveling. I've been thinking it might be time for a career change. And since I finally finished this novel I've been working on for years, and my agent has gotten some serious interest from publishers, now seems like a good time. I can edit my book here in New York and we can be together."

"That's fantastic! When can you move?"

"Just as soon as I find us an apartment."

"Us?" Gabrielle felt like a balloon that had just been pricked, releasing all the euphoria she'd been experiencing.

"I want us to live together, Gabrielle. What do you think?"

"Are you sure you could work with me underfoot?" she asked, stalling.

"Maynard Scarborough is not the only man you inspire," he announced, kissing the tip of her nose. "Hey, where are you going?"

"To the bathroom. Back in a minute," she promised. Gabrielle didn't need to use the toilet; she needed to think. *This is all moving so fast,* she thought as she closed the door behind her and faced the woman in the mirror. There was no doubt that she loved Doug with everything she had inside her. Gabrielle also knew that there was nothing more in the world she'd rather do than to be with this man day and night. The delight she felt in his presence was overwhelming, and the idea of experiencing such joy on a daily basis was tempting. Her heart and body wanted to take him up on his offer, but her brain said no.

There was no way that she and Doug could set up a household together without his finding out all the ugly truths about her. Gabrielle couldn't bear the thought of disappointing him like that. She had to figure out how to make Doug understand that as much as she loved him, she just couldn't live with him.

Gabrielle returned to the bedroom to find Doug staring out the window. He was hoping he hadn't scared Gabrielle off by rushing things between them. He was trying so hard to be patient, but it was difficult.

"So, what do you say? Are we going to be roommates?"

"No, and it's not because I don't love you."

"Then why?"

"I just don't believe in living together. My daddy always used to tell me that a man won't keep what he gets for free," she told him, giving her father credit for her mother's words.

"Not all men."

"Will you still move to New York?"

"I'm already packed."

"Good," she told him, feeling bittersweet. She was in too deep. How would she ever be able to give him up when the time came?

29

S hit," Stephanie yelled, as her thumbnail pierced the silky web of her pantyhose. It was bad enough that she had been summoned to Gabrielle's stupid cocktail party, but now she'd ruined her last pair of hose. There was only one thing left to do—raid Gabrielle's stock. Stephanie hurried into Gabrielle's room, counting on her staying too busy downstairs to come up and find her.

Stephanie headed over to Gabrielle's bureau and opened the top drawer. Not finding any pantyhose, she closed it and opened the next and the next. In the last drawer she found not only several packages of nylons but a supply of cassette tapes as well. Stephanie picked one up and read the label. It was an audiocassette of a recently published novel. She browsed through the rest of the tapes and found several other bestselling titles, including *The Client* and *Waiting to Exhale*, two books Stephanie had seen Gabrielle reading. *She bought the tape and the book? I swear, people with money sure know how to waste it,* she thought, closing the drawer and heading back to her room.

* * *

"Sorry I'm late. Traffic from La Guardia was outrageous," Doug apologized after kissing Gabrielle in the entry of Beatrice's brownstone. "Has the reviewing committee arrived?"

"They're not a reviewing committee, they're my friends."

"Same difference."

"Are you really nervous?"

"Of course I am. Once you introduce me as your boyfriend, the scrutiny will begin." Doug was happy that Gabrielle wanted to share him and their relationship with her friends. It was yet another sign of her growing commitment. Still, he was apprehensive about meeting Gabrielle's makeshift family. He wanted to impress them, particularly Beatrice.

"Don't worry, they won't bite—at least not hard," Gabrielle teased.

With a kiss and a quick hug, the two walked hand in hand into the front parlor where the others were gathered. Beatrice and Felicia stood talking to Jaci, while Stephanie took the opportunity to corner Ruthanna Beverly from *Appeal* magazine.

"Ladies, I'd like you to say hello to a good friend of mine, Doug Sixsmith."

"It's good to see you again," greeted Felicia.

"You, too. Where's your better half?"

"He couldn't make it," Felicia said, offering no further explanation.

"You mean I'm the only male here tonight? I feel like a lamb about to be slaughtered."

"Don't be silly," Beatrice told Doug. "You're among friends."

"Thank you, Mrs. Braidburn."

"Please, call me Bea."

"Doug, this is my booker/friend, Jaci Francis and my housemate/publicist, Stephanie Bancroft. Ladies, I'd like you to meet Doug Sixsmith," said Gabrielle.

"Your article on Gabrielle for *Appeal* was dynamite," Jaci said.

"Thank you."

"I'm surprised that such a hot journalist would even bother to do a piece on a fashion model," Stephanie remarked, still bitter about not getting to write the story. "Nothing against Gabrielle, of course, but you always write about important things. Fashion seems so trivial."

"The truth be known, that's exactly what I thought, but in fact it turned out to be the most important story I've ever written," he admitted before giving Gabrielle a hug. It was impossible to misread their feelings. They positively glowed in each other's presence.

How did Gabrielle manage to fall in love without me knowing? Bea wondered. It disturbed her greatly that Gabrielle had not been totally honest about her relationship with Doug. She was well aware that the two had been seeing each other, but Beatrice had no idea until now that things between them were so serious.

If literacy was her enemy in the fight to hold on to Gabrielle's devotion, love was its ally. Even if Gabrielle never learned to read, there was always the possibility that Bea could be replaced by the insinuation of some horny young man into their lives. Love and raging hormones were no match for an old woman's affections. If it came down to a choice, Bea would much rather lose Gabrielle to a book than to a beau.

Until tonight everything in that department had seemed to be under control. Gabrielle had had little time or apparent desire for men and courtship. Though many had tried to woo her, Gabrielle's reluctance to get involved with any man who showed interest in her had earned her the nickname "Gabrielle the Untouchable" from her peers.

Now, with Doug in the picture, Bea's access to and influence over Gabrielle would be severely limited. Already he had managed to breach the confidential relationship the two women shared. Plus, he was too damn old for the girl. Despite the fact that Gabrielle spent her days dressed up to look like a grown woman, she was still only twenty years old. Bea thought she was too young to really be in love. Apparently Gabrielle felt different, and for right now Beatrice had no choice but to take a wait-and-see posture.

"Doug and I have something we'd like to tell you," Gabrielle told the group. The five women went silent, each expecting an engagement announcement.

"No, it's not what you think." Doug laughed, reading the anticipation on everyone's face.

"Then why have you summoned us all here?" Stephanie inquired.

"I asked you all here tonight because I wanted Doug to meet my friends. And I wanted my friends to get to know the very special man in my life. He's moving to New York, so we'll all be seeing much more of him."

"Does that mean you two will be living together?" Stephanie asked.

"No," Doug replied.

Doug's answer offered great relief to Beatrice. If Doug had asked and she had refused, that could mean only one thing: Gabrielle had not shared her secret with him. As long as Bea was the only one who knew of her illiteracy, she would still continue to play a pivotal role in Gabrielle's life.

"Sweetheart, if you're happy, which you obviously are, I'm happy for you. And Douglas, I'll be watching to make sure you take good care of my girl," Bea said, issuing a stern, motherly warning.

"I stand forewarned, but believe me, I intend to take good care of this incredible woman for as long as she will allow."

Why does every man who crosses her path fall in love? Why don't men ever want me like that? Stephanie wondered, her thoughts turning to Jack.

"Well, I'm really happy for you two," Jaci said.

"This all started at the bon-voyage party, didn't it?" Ruthanna cried out.

"I don't know what you could possibly be talking about," Gabrielle answered coyly, her smile giving everything away. "That trip was strictly business."

"Monkey business," Ruthanna teased. "Well, whenever it happened, I think it's terrific, and I'm even more pleased that Doug's moving to town."

"I think all this good news requires a toast," Felicia suggested, raising her glass. "To Doug and Gabrielle: In both work and play, may you always be happy."

"Here, here," chimed in the rest of the group. Gabrielle and Doug were both too happy to notice both Stephanie's and Beatrice's lack of enthusiasm.

"You okay?" Ruthanna asked Felicia. "You seem rather distracted and withdrawn lately. And to be perfectly honest, you don't look your usual stunning self."

"I caught some bug I can't seem to shake. It's been going on for weeks now, so that's probably what you've noticed." Despite the fact that the two had become good friends, Felicia didn't feel comfortable confiding certain things to Ruthanna.

"Could it be a case of the stork flu?" Ruthanna said, smiling.

"I am *not* pregnant," Felicia said, with more vigor than intended.

"Well, you seem pretty stressed out. Maybe your body is telling you it's time to take it easy."

"I wish I could."

"You have to look out for number one. If you don't, nobody else will."

Ruthanna was right, she needed to look out for herself. Since the abortion Felicia had felt as if she were coming unglued. Everything was a big mess. Concentrating on her clients was the only way for her to get through the day, so Felicia worked harder and longer to avoid having to deal with her personal life. This only aggravated the situation at home. Her counseling sessions with Trace had deteriorated into shouting matches and sobbing spells, brought on not by the condition of their relationship but by all the guilt and emotional baggage she was keeping locked inside. Maybe she should seek counseling for herself. She needed to talk to someone about all this. Felicia felt paralyzed by inaction, unable to make any decisions about her life.

"Why don't you go home, snuggle up with that superfine man of yours, and get some rest?"

"It is time to go," Felicia told Ruthanna, looking at her watch. She *was* leaving, not to go home but to see Lexis. He was back from his latest research trip, and Felicia had agreed to get together to discuss the progress of *Praline Livin'*. She only wished she were ready to discuss the progress of her own life as well.

"Baby, I'm glad to see you," Lexis told Felicia as they embraced in his living room. "It feels good holding you again." Since making love in Martinique, they had not been intimate, and Lexis's body ached to be with her again. While he was making a conscious effort not to push her into a relationship, Lexis wasn't convinced that Felicia was being true to her promise not to pull away. He could understand her reluctance to pursue this thing lingering between them until she'd straightened out everything with that tight-ass she was married to, but in the last few months Lexis had felt a wall go up that had not previously existed.

"It's always good to see you, too," Felicia responded truthfully.

"It doesn't seem like it. Not the way you've been playing me lately. Is everything cool? Trace hassling you?"

"Not really, but things are pretty strained between us."

"Would he be pissed if he knew you were with me tonight?"

"Trace knows nothing about you and me—about anything."

"What does that mean?"

"Things have been difficult for me lately. I just haven't shared much with him, or anybody else for that matter."

"Is it work?"

"No, everything there is fine. Just busy," Felicia answered quickly. Despite all that had transpired between them, Lexis was still a lucrative and valued client. She didn't want him to have any apprehensions about her ability to service his account.

"If you need me for anything, I'm always here for you. Twenty-four/seven," Lexis offered.

"I know, and I really appreciate it." She did value Lexis's willingness to listen. Unlike her husband, he didn't judge her. He didn't assume that he automatically knew what was best for her and try to impose his opinions on her. Instead Lexis always encouraged her to follow her heart.

Maybe she could talk to him about the abortion. Maybe he would understand and help her get through this nightmare.

But then again. Maybe not. She couldn't afford to take the risk—for personal and professional reasons. If she was going to have to support herself and her business, she couldn't afford to lose Lexis's profitable account. Just as important, she couldn't afford to lose his love and respect.

30

Gabrielle stood at the stove waiting for the teakettle to boil. She found herself humming along with the whistling pot, eagerly anticipating Doug's return from dinner with his editor. She was so pleased that not only would he be in town to attend the Scarborough Jewels trunk show at Neiman Marcus tomorrow, but that the two of them would also be eating Thanksgiving dinner with Beatrice next week.

With Gabrielle's demanding work schedule and Doug's being busy editing his novel, neither of them were in the city at the same time more than eight or nine days a month. They talked incessantly on the phone, often calling each other several times a day. When their schedules did coincide, the two stayed holed up in Doug's Tribeca loft, venturing out only when necessary. She still maintained her room at Beatrice's, sleeping there when Doug was out of town, but it no longer felt the same. Going back to Bea's now had the comfortable feeling of an adult's visiting her childhood home. Gabrielle's home was with Doug, in both body and spirit.

Although Gabrielle had declined Doug's invitation to share a place officially, there were traces of Gabrielle everywhere in his apartment. Gabrielle's clothes occupied the closets, while her makeup and toiletries took up residence in the medicine cabinet. The kitchen cupboards were stocked with her favorite foods. Photos of Gabrielle were scattered around the apartment. Doug's favorite—the shot of her as she emerged wet and wild from the waters of Martinique—sat in the coveted position at his bedside.

She loved this apartment. The place was open and airy, with lots of light, exposed brick, a fireplace, and a beautiful rooftop garden. There was no formal decorating scheme—just an eclectic mix of art, old rugs, and comfortable, roomy furniture.

As she headed toward the bedroom, Gabrielle's bare feet padded across the living-room rug that she and Doug had picked out in Istanbul, one of the few trips he'd been able to accompany her on in recent months. She loved when they traveled together. He made each trip an adventure and provided memories that her heart would keep a lifetime.

Bea still traveled with Gabrielle on occasion, but as Gabrielle's schedule intensified, the grind became too much for Beatrice to handle. And with Gabrielle feeling more confident about traveling alone, due to the continuous VIP assistance her growing celebrity status afforded her, Bea's role shifted from that of travel companion to that of personal assistant, helping to keep Gabrielle's professional life in order.

Gabrielle climbed into bed and sipped her cup of herbal tea while listening to the CNN anchor deliver the late news. Hearing Doug come through the door, she flipped off the television and picked up the newspaper, quickly checking to see that the people pictured on the front page were standing upright.

"I'm glad you waited up. This is for you," Doug said, handing her a large gift bag.

"What's the occasion?" Gabrielle asked, touched by his thoughtfulness.

"No occasion. I'm just glad to have you here."

Gabrielle reached around the glittery tissue paper and pulled out a box containing a 3-D puzzle of one of the Seven Wonders of the World.

"Shah Jahan built the Taj Mahal as a monument to his wife. I thought it was a fitting tribute as well to the love of my life."

"You are so sweet. Come get into bed," she requested, patting the pillow next to her,

"If you insist." Doug smiled as he quickly stripped down to his boxers and slipped into bed beside her. "Keep digging, there's more."

Gabrielle once again reached into the bag and this time retrieved a leatherbound book. She opened its cover, revealing blank pages. *How appropriate,* she thought dryly, *a book with no words.*

"I bought one for myself, too," Doug told her. "I thought, since we're apart so much, that we could both keep a journal as a way to preserve all the experiences and feelings we'd like to share with each other. Sort of like a travel journal of the heart."

Gabrielle felt the tears well up in her eyes and slide silently down her face. She couldn't speak, for what could she say? How could she explain that his request, while thoughtful and romantic, was simply impossible? Believing her to be touched beyond words, Doug reached for Gabrielle, and slowly and gently they made love.

The two cuddled together until Doug drifted off, leaving Gabrielle to reflect on her situation. In such a brief time Doug Sixsmith had become the single most important thing in her life. Gabrielle found that every day she was growing more and more deeply in love with him. Most days she reveled in that fact, but at other times, like tonight, she was reminded of just how impossible this situation really was.

Hearing the slight whistle of Doug's soft snore, Gabrielle gently disengaged herself. Clutching the blank book he'd given her, she crept out of the bedroom and walked across the apartment into Doug's office.

"Tonight," she whispered softly in the dark. "Please let it happen tonight."

She leaned over and switched on the floor lamp next to the desk. A soft GE glow lit up a small area, giving the room the clichéd look of a police-interrogation scene. Gabrielle turned and stood before the bookcases. The shelves were lined with his favorite Tom Clancy novels, historical biographies, travel guides, and a wide variety of reference books. Her eyes moved across the several rows of book spines until they fell upon Mother Teresa's kind, wrinkled face. She pulled the publication from the bookcase and, with reverence, moved her fingers across the slightly raised type of the book's title, *Mother Teresa: The Authorized Biography.*

Help me, Gabrielle silently beseeched the nun's image. *You lived your entire life helping outsiders like me. Let it be my turn tonight.* Gabrielle closed her eyes and flipped to a random page in the book. *Please,* she begged again, before opening her eyes and peering down on the print. Her eyes and brain scanned every letter with firm resolve, all the while willing each word to reveal itself. Within seconds of beginning this futile exercise, Gabrielle could sense her determination give way to a familiar wave of disappointment. She snapped the book shut as her tears began to fall.

How much longer was she going to play this game with herself? How many more years of pretending? Of drawing inspiration from her personal motto, "Fake it until you make it." How much longer before Doug found out that the professed woman of his dreams was nothing more than that—a dream, an illusion, a lie? Gabrielle knew that she had to do something to change this and she had to do it soon before it was too late.

Leaving Doug working in the quiet of his office, Gabrielle grabbed her purse and cell phone and headed outside into the early morning air. Last night's resolve propelled her boldly down the street for several blocks before leading her into the outside vestibule of an old apartment building. In silent haste, she retrieved her wallet and pulled the worn and tattered slip of paper Beatrice had given her months ago. Anxiety danced in her stomach as she quickly dialed the toll-free number.

"National Literacy Hotline," a friendly voice answered.

"I, uh, I'd like some . . . in . . . information," Gabrielle stuttered nervously. "I want to learn how to read. Can you help me?"

"I'll certainly try. To get started, I'll need your name, address and phone number," the woman requested.

"Why do you need all that?" Gabrielle asked, hesitation coloring her voice.

"So I know what local contact number to give you, and with your permission, we'll give your name and phone number to the literacy provider in your area so they can follow up. Sometimes it's hard to get started," the operator replied.

"If you'll just give me the number, I can do the rest," Gabrielle said, determined to get the information she wanted and remain anonymous. "I live in Manhattan," she began. Before the operator could reply, a teenage couple joined Gabrielle in the vestibule.

"Hey, aren't you a model? I'm sure I've seen you in magazines," the girl announced loudly.

"I'll have to call you back," Gabrielle said, quickly terminating her call. What was she thinking? There was no way she could learn to read without the public finding out. Not when she was becoming more recognizable with every passing day.

"Gabrielle, right? Can I get your autograph?" the teen asked, holding out her backpack. "It must be so cool to be famous."

"I know," Gabrielle replied flatly, signing her name on the canvas bag. "Real cool."

"It's not over yet, is it?" Doug asked, rushing over to Bea and Felicia.

"Not yet, but they've shown most of the collection already, so Gabrielle's finale should be coming up," Felicia whispered.

As the last model exited the stage, the lights in the tent slowly dimmed. When they came back up, Gabrielle had magically appeared on a circular riser behind a majestic, six-foot-tall rectangular frame. To re-create the original nude photo, she was dressed in a fleshtone body stocking and slightly more elaborate makeup. The original quote by Eleanor Roosevelt had been replaced with one by Oscar Wilde: "One should either be a work of art, or wear a work of art." Gabrielle's face was shrouded in darkness and the total effect was dramatic and masterful.

After giving the crowd time to digest the impact of the presentation, a spotlight came on, illuminating Gabrielle's neck and head and clearly revealing Maynard's most incredible piece of work. A collective "ahh" circulated the room. In the middle of Gabrielle's forehead rested a spectacular South Seas pearl hooked to an eighteen-carat-gold flower encrusted in diamonds and dangling from a silk cord.

"Artfully You. Scarborough Jewels," recited the eloquent voice of the show's announcer. The tag line caused the room to erupt in applause. As the clapping died down, the lights once again dimmed. When they were turned up,

Gabrielle was gone, replaced by Maynard Scarborough. His appearance caused another round of thunderous applause. It was obvious that the Short Hills Mall crowd here in New Jersey, just like all the other wealthy shoppers at high-end malls around the country, loved this theatrical presentation. It was more than just attention-grabbing, it was memorable and provocative.

Doug, watching from the back, was awestruck. Seeing Gabrielle standing there, framed like a priceless work of art for the world to admire, left his heart bursting with pride. She was indeed, like the name of the collection she represented, an "Object of Desire."

"Thank you, thank you. You're very kind," Maynard told the audience when the fanfare had died down. "Please meet the woman you've seen featured in our print advertising for months, the fabulous Gabrielle Donovan." Applause once again filled the room as Gabrielle reemerged wearing a filmy white dress and the flowering pearl.

"You're divine," the designer whispered as they turned and exited the stage together. "I can't wait until the show this spring. We're going to have tongues wagging on both sides of the ocean."

As the crowd thinned and Doug was about to approach Gabrielle, Greg von Ulrich appeared by her side. Doug watched as Greg embraced Gabrielle and fondly kissed her lips and gently caressed her back. Doug tried to calm his jealousy by reminding himself that public displays of affection were quite common in the modeling business. Still, he was beginning to tire of the extra attention Greg paid Gabrielle. He always popped up out of nowhere to share these special moments. Boss or no boss, star model or not, enough was enough.

31

"Honey, if you don't walk right, you are nothing more than a hanger," Diego shouted out to Gabrielle from the back of the room. "Now, keep your head up! Divas *never* look down."

Diego Santana was attempting to teach Gabrielle how to walk the fashion runway. A former model himself, Diego had the distinction of being the first drag queen to work the major designer shows. He was also famous for having one of the best strolls in the industry. Two years after hanging up his pumps and extensive wig collection, Diego was the most sought-after runway coach in the business. Under his tute- lage the new girls learned the fine art of sauntering up and down the catwalk.

"Honey, technique is *everything*. Do you hear me? You've got to *work* those clothes and make them come alive," Diego continued, giving her a generous circle snap to emphasize his point. "Now, do it again, and this time I want to see much 'tude."

Gabrielle once again walked from one end of the makeshift platform to another, trying to incorporate all of Diego's lessons—lead with her pelvis, keep her head up, hands and fingers curved gracefully, and most important of all, give them attitude. Who would have known that walking could be so difficult? This was her third session with Diego in as many weeks, and still, the more she tried, the clumsier she felt. Instead of the graceful glide achieved by her contemporaries, Gabrielle felt like an awkward fawn trying to walk for the first time.

"No, no, that's not it. Let's take a break. In fact, I think that will be it for today."

It was definitely time to stop. His frustration level with this girl was rising out of control. They'd been at this all morning, and she still could not master the simple mechanics of getting from one end of the runway to the other without loping along like a clumsy oaf. And they hadn't even begun to work on removing jackets or carrying props.

Diego left in search of Greg von Ulrich. It was time to break the news to him that there was nothing more he could do for Gabrielle. No matter how much the camera might love her face or how terrific she might appear in a fashion video, when it came to the runway, this girl was bound to stick out like Rodney King at the policemen's ball.

"So you're telling me it's hopeless?" Gregory asked after hearing Diego's diagnosis.

"There is no way that even *I* can perfect that walk. I understand why she's only done print work up till now."

"What am I going to tell Scarborough?"

"I'd tell him that in every other way, the girl is fierce. There's got to be a way to make this work in her favor."

"Well, let me get Maynard on the phone and get this over with. Show Week is in six days," Greg replied, referring to the busy week when the designers show their ready-to-wear collections to the retailers and press. "This is something he has to know."

"Baby, if you roll that piecrust any thinner, we'll be able to see through it," Doug remarked as he added another pinch of cinnamon to the apple slices.

"I'm sorry. I can't seem to keep my mind off this afternoon." Gabrielle swept up the dough, squished it into a ball, and in a fit of frustration dropped it into the bowl with a thud.

"I take it the lesson didn't go so well," Doug commented, waving away a cloud of flour. "You want to talk about it?"

"Let's just say that if Maynard even lets me backstage, Diego Santana will put a handicapped-parking sign at my makeup table. I swear, Doug, you don't know what humiliation is until a man wearing three-inch heels leaves you standing in the dust."

"I think you're worrying too much. This is your first fashion show, after all. Maynard has to know you'll be nervous."

"The show is a week away. How can I not worry?" Gabrielle asked, making another feeble attempt to roll out her crust.

"By switching gears for a moment and thinking about something else—like your twenty-first birthday. You'll be in town to celebrate, won't you?"

"I'll be wherever you want me, whenever you want me."

"Good answer. Now, what would you like for your birthday?"

"A new walk," Gabrielle requested, trying to brush away the flour on Doug's forehead, but only depositing more.

"Seriously. If you could have anything in this world, what would it be?"

"For every birthday from now on, I want you and one of your famous apple pies—preferably one I didn't help bake," she said, poking a finger into her pitiful crust.

"That certainly makes shopping one hell of a lot easier. Here, let me do that," he said, commandeering the rolling pin. "You know, sweetheart, if you're still worried about that walking thing, I think I can help."

"Not that I don't appreciate the offer, Doug, but what do you know about runway walking"

"More than you think. Why don't you take off all your clothes and strut around the room so I can check out your form?" Doug suggested with a wicked smile.

"And that's going to help me?"

"I can't speak for you, but it will do wonders for me."

Greg dialed the designer's office and waited for him to pick up. He hoped Maynard would take the news well. They'd all come too far for this to blow up over Gabrielle's goofy gait.

"Maynard, I need to speak with you about Gabrielle," Greg began.

"She's so marvelous. Have you seen the response to Scarborough Jewels? The holiday numbers were unbelievable, and sales are still so hot we can't keep the stores stocked. It's because of that glorious ad campaign. It was genius to do the ads and trunk shows first. Do you know what a coup it is to have her exclusively working my runway?"

"About the show," Greg began reluctantly.

"Yes."

"We have a little problem. Gabrielle can't walk."

"She's injured?"

"No, just clumsy-looking when it comes to the runway. I've tried to teach her. I even hired Diego Santana to coach her, but she just can't seem to get the motion down."

"I don't care if she isn't perfect. Let her walk like she's on the street. People aren't going to care if she comes down the runway on her hands and knees. Gabrielle Donovan is incredibly hot. Her presence will fill up the catwalk as only a star can."

"I agree with you totally, but I wanted you to know."

"Now I know, so let me get back to work."

Gabrielle hurried through the rear entrance of the white tent set up in Bryant Park. The atmosphere inside was electric, as crews prepared for the annual spectacle of New York's week of fashion madness, known as Seventh on Sixth. The huge tent was divided in two by a lengthy runway, broken up at the end by three low pedestals. On either side of the runway, chairs were set up for the viewing audience. Several assistants from Maynard's office were busy placing a small writing pad embossed with the Scarborough Designs logo and a gold pencil on each seat. On the rear stage wall, visible from every corner of the room, hung the same huge logo.

"Gabrielle, let's go. I want to do a quick run-through," Del, the show coordinator, yelled out.

Within minutes Gabrielle was joined by the other models, still dressed in their street clothes for a short rehearsal. As Del briefed the group about the show, Gabrielle's brain and eyes remained locked on the seemingly endless length of the runway. You could land a 747 on this puppy! How was she ever going to make it down and back without embarrassing herself and the man who'd hired her? She tried to imagine the now-empty tent full of people watching her every step. The image made her stomach flip.

"Everybody understand?" Del asked.

"What pedestal am I supposed to use?" asked Eva G., one of two supermodels booked for the event.

"You, Roya, and Gabrielle, will use the center pedestal every time you go down," Del answered. Eva, Roya Kirsten, and Gabrielle were the designated "stars" of the show and would take solo runs down the catwalk. This would give greater emphasis not only to the clothes they'd be wearing but also to the girls themselves. Though the other two well-known models were hired to lend the show prestige, Maynard had saved his best designs for Gabrielle, ensuring that much attention would be paid to his star.

"Okay, now that everybody understands the drill, let's give it a try."

While the girls practiced, Diego Santana and Gregory von Ulrich stood watching in the back of the tent. Both were there to give Gabrielle moral support, as well as witness with their own eyes this potentially career-threatening situation. Despite Maynard's strong feelings that the quality of Gabrielle's runway strut did not matter, both men knew that in this room full of fashion folks, whose love of gossip was second only to that of the tabloid tattlers, Gabrielle's skyrocketing career could get shot down in a matter of moments.

Stephanie walked through the Forty-first Street entrance of the tent. She scanned the area, looking for Gregory von Ulrich. Felicia had requested that she fax him Gabrielle's interview schedule for the month, but Stephanie had decided to deliver it personally in order to find out firsthand what all the fuss over this week was about.

Stephanie spotted Greg on the other side of the tent speaking with a man she didn't recognize. She made her way over, stopping a short distance away to allow them to finish talking. Their conversation ceased when Gabrielle stepped onto the runway for her practice walk. The three of them stood watching as the young model ventured down the length of the runway, posed, and then walked back and disappeared.

"She definitely stands out," Stephanie overheard Greg say. "What do you think?"

"Let's face it, Gabrielle's walk is absolutely wretched," Diego stated. The mention of the model's name caused Stephanie's ears to perk up. She moved two steps closer in an effort to hear their conversation better. "Compared to the other girls, she's very klutzy, but—"

Wretched? Klutzy? You mean Gabrielle isn't perfect after all? At last, a little justice in this world, Stephanie thought happily.

"But what?" Greg asked, hoping for some salvation.

"But it's an *endearing* kind of klutziness. She doesn't have the clean elegance of Eva G. or the smoldering prowl of Roya, but still, Gabrielle manages to mesmerize you when she moves. Maynard is right, even in her jeans she owns the runway. She has a commanding presence that forces you to notice her, and once you do, the clumsiness just doesn't matter anymore."

"I hope you're right. She's got a lot riding on this show. I hate to say it, but this could make or break her."

Interesting concept, Stephanie thought as she turned around and headed for the door. She decided to fax Greg the information after all. She needed to make a stop by *Star Diary* before heading back to the office. This little discovery was much too juicy to keep all to herself.

Backstage, the models, dressed in their first outfits, walked up to be inspected. One by one, Maynard checked each ensemble against the appropriate Polaroid, to ensure that every girl was wearing the correct accessories with the right outfit and that everything was fastened correctly.

"I thought this was fixed. I need pins," Maynard bellowed, finding one model's dress too big. One of the assistants ran over with a box of straight pins, and Maynard proceeded to take in both sides of the dress.

Before returning to the inspection site, Maynard walked over to Gabrielle. One of the dressers, after consulting the model's "look board," was putting the final touches on Gabrielle's first outfit, a tomato-red knit and suede jumpsuit. Maynard, not wanting to crush the material or disturb her makeup, took her hands into his and brought them to his lips.

"I know you are nervous. Don't worry, you look divine. Go out there and have a good time," he encouraged, sounding like a coach before the big game.

Gabrielle smiled slightly and nodded. She was going to give this her best shot and pray like hell it was enough.

"May I have all the girls in lineup?" Del called out, clapping his hands.

At thirteen minutes past noon the music blared and the production showcasing Maynard's Fall '96 collection began. From the very first group, Maynard's designs were welcomed with loud approval. Gabrielle, the fourth model in line, waited nervously for her turn. She was scheduled to go out behind Brooke, a popular Eurasian-looking model. As Brooke made her entrance, Gabrielle stepped up, only to be snatched back by the stage manager.

"Too soon," Del told her.

"Just forget everything they told you," whispered the model who followed Gabrielle. "Just walk to the music. You'll do fine."

"Thanks," Gabrielle replied, appreciative of the support.

"Now," the manager whispered, releasing Gabrielle's arm.

Gabrielle stepped onto the runway and looked out into the crowd. The excitement was palpable and contagious. She pushed her chin up, took a breath, and began a star's saunter down the ramp. Brooke was zipping down the runway with an easy glide. Instead of trying to duplicate her style, Gabrielle walked naturally, relying on Diego's much-touted "attitude" to get her through. As Gabrielle approached the end of the runway, Brooke was on her way back, leaving Gabrielle standing center stage, commanding the attention of every eye in the room. She stepped up onto the pedestal and posed as flashbulbs and applause erupted around her. With a coy smile, Gabrielle did a sassy pivot with a slight kick, snapped her head around at the last minute, and took herself back up the ramp and backstage to get into her next outfit.

Each time she went back out, Gabrielle felt stronger and more confident. Bolder with every entrance, she played with her audience, appearing openly flirtatious at times, nonchalant and distant at others, whatever the mood of the clothes dictated. The obvious admiration and approval of the spectators was liberating, removing any self-consciousness Gabrielle harbored because of her less-than-perfect stride. Before she knew it, it was time for the finale, and all the girls, wearing silver and cream, walked out onto the stage with Maynard. After taking several bows, he walked back to the group of models and retrieved Gabrielle from the mob. Arm in arm, the designer and his muse walked up to the center pedestal to take a bow. This time Gabrielle glided down the runway, her feet barely touching the ground. She was ecstatic. The fashion show was finally over, and she hadn't fallen, tripped, or otherwise embarrassed herself.

Greg von Ulrich managed to work his way backstage.

The area was a mob scene of well-wishers and press people trying to get a word with the designer. Photographers were busy snapping away as the models and crew people packed up to go home. Greg found Gabrielle standing by her dress rack with tears of satisfaction welling in her eyes.

"You did good, kid," he told her with outstretched arms.

"I'm just glad it's over," Gabrielle admitted as she met Gregory's arms with her own. The two hugged warmly, and Greg gave the model a congratulatory kiss on the mouth, as cameras captured the touching moment on film.

"Harry, you don't look so good," Stephanie observed as she sat in the reporter's office.

"I'm fine," he answered gruffly. "Why did you stop by?"

"I have a little scoop for you. I just left the rehearsal for the Scarborough fashion show this morning. You won't believe the scuttlebutt."

"I'm listening," Harry prompted brusquely.

"According to Diego Santana, Gabrielle's runway coach, she's really wretched on the runway. I heard him tell Greg von Ulrich that, compared to the other girls, Gabrielle is a klutz," Stephanie repeated gleefully.

"What was von Ulrich's reaction to that news?"

"He loves her dirty underwear, so he wasn't too upset, just concerned that the press receive her well."

"Something going on between those two? I thought she was all lovey-dovey with the journalist."

"She is, but who knows what else she has simmering on the side?"

"Interesting. How would you like to write a story about all the behind-the-scenes happenings between Gabrielle and her boss?"

"You got it," Stephanie said, excited that she was going to finally have her own byline. *Wait. I can't write this under my name,* she suddenly realized. *I'll not only get crucified, I'll lose all my sources,* Stephanie thought. "I have to use a pen name."

"You can call yourself Snow White for all I care. Just have my story in by five."

"Okay," Stephanie said, turning to leave. *Why not tease the public with a little romantic speculation?* she thought. Doug, of all people, would know that this was just idle gossip. And if he didn't, Gabrielle would just have to convince him otherwise.

32

"Happy birthday," Doug announced, placing a tray of Belgian waffles smothered in fresh raspberries over Gabrielle's lap. In addition to the food, the breakfast tray also held a pitcher of mimosas, a single orchid spray, and a rolled-up newspaper.

"This smells delicious."

"Thank you. Breakfast in bed happens to be my culinary masterpiece," Doug said, pouring the orange-juice-and-champagne drink into crystal flutes. "Happy birthday to the most fascinating woman I know. May you live a long and wonderful life, and may I have the good fortune to share it with you," Doug said, raising his glass. The two gently touched glasses and slowly drained the contents.

"I brought you *Women's Wear Daily* so you can read the review of yesterday's show," Doug said, unfolding the paper. "You and Maynard are on the front page." Under the bold headline THE EMPEROR'S NEW CLOTHES was a large picture of the show's finale, with Maynard Scarborough and Gabrielle surrounded by the other models.

"You read it. I'm not interested in knowing how badly they skewered me."

"It's not like you tripped or fell down or anything."

"No, but you didn't see me out there. Compared to the other girls—"

"You didn't want me there, remember?" Doug interrupted.

"It's not that I didn't *want* you there. But had you come, I would have been even more nervous. I'd have worried about embarrassing you on top of everything else."

"That could never happen. I'm always in your corner. You should know that. Now, let's see what *WWD* has to say about your walk on the wild side." Doug scanned the article, skipping all the details of the show and collection until he reached the part about Gabrielle. "Looks like you and Maynard were a big hit."

"Really? What did they say about me?"

"'When Scarborough's featured mannequin, First Face model Gabrielle Donovan, took the stage, one had the feeling that at that moment a lovelier creature in New York City did not exist,'" Doug read with pride.

"What a relief."

"Just one more thing to celebrate tonight."

"About this celebration . . . How long am I to remain clueless?"

"Everything will be revealed to you in due time."

"Okay, I won't push. I guess everybody has a right to keep a few secrets."

"Just be back here from your lunch with Beatrice by five. Now, you hit the showers while I do the dishes. Call me if you need help washing your back," he volunteered as Gabrielle disappeared into the bathroom.

Doug picked up the tray and carried it into the kitchen. While he loaded the dishwasher, he mentally ran through his list of things to do. He had plenty to take care of before he saw Gabrielle again later this evening. This was a celebration that he hoped they'd be reminiscing about for years to come.

Once Gabrielle departed, Doug dialed his favorite florist to double-check that his flower order would be delivered promptly at five-thirty. He dictated his message for the enclosure card, directing Gabrielle to meet him at six-thirty in his suite at the Pierre Hotel.

Next he called the hotel to confirm his reservation and to go over his special arrangements. Doug had planned an especially romantic evening, beginning with a sumptuous dinner catered in the privacy of their suite. Dinner would be followed by champagne and birthday cake served in a luxurious candlelight bath. It was there that Doug would propose. Gabrielle had requested only him for her birthday, today and always, and that's exactly what Doug planned to deliver.

Assured that everything was proceeding according to plan, Doug got dressed and left the apartment to run the last of his errands. He headed over to the jewelers to pick up the ring he'd designed especially for Gabrielle. The exquisite five-carat Burmese ruby, bezel-set in white gold with baguette diamonds gliding down each side, was unique and exotic, just like the woman.

Doug slipped the sterling-silver ring box into his pocket and practically skipped out of the store. Waiting at the corner for the light to change, he looked to the newsstand on his right only to see Gabrielle's face gracing the cover of *Marie Claire*. He walked over and picked up the magazine. This photographic image was so unlike the real woman. There was no way that any still photo could capture her essence, and Doug would have it no other way. Knowing that there was a side of her that only he was privy to was what made Gabrielle's ever-increasing popularity palatable.

Doug glanced around the kiosk and counted four other

magazines featuring Gabrielle, including the cover of *Star Diary*. Unable to resist, he paid for the paper and carried it down into the subway station. He jumped onto the train and made himself comfortable in a window seat. Oblivious to his fellow passengers, Doug unfolded the paper and found the blaring headline A MODEL AFFAIR, under which was a picture of Gregory von Ulrich and Gabrielle engaged in a major lip lock. Doug quickly scanned the article, to learn that, according to the sources of writer Visa Lee, Gabrielle and the president of her agency had been carrying on a hot and heavy affair for quite some time.

Doug's name was mentioned as the unsuspecting boyfriend whose head was so deeply buried in his manuscript that he couldn't see the deceit going on all around him. The article also quoted a "friend close to the couple" as saying that Gabrielle liked what dating an intellectual guy like Doug did for her image. According to this source, Gabrielle believed that having a prize-winning journalist madly in love with her helped distance herself from the annoying industry stereotype of the mindless model.

Doug couldn't read any more. Writers like Visa Lee made him ashamed to say he worked in the same profession. When Doug reached his stop, he threw the newspaper into the first trash can he encountered and headed up the stairs into the afternoon sun.

He was angry, and—as much as he hated to admit it— he was worried. Doug battled against the demons in his head, wanting to give absolutely no credence to this garbage, but the words and images were nagging his brain and worming their way into his heart. A disturbing thought crossed his mind, forcing his feet to stop in their tracks. Doug turned around and hurried back down into the subway to retrieve the newspaper.

He stopped midway up the stairs and once again looked

at the picture of Gregory and Gabrielle. Closer examination showed that the photo was taken backstage at yesterday's fashion show.

She didn't want me at her show. Was von Ulrich the reason? Doug asked himself. "Everybody is allowed to keep a few secrets." Those were Gabrielle's exact words to him this morning. Was Gregory Gabrielle's secret? The man was always around, giving her gifts—like that bracelet. That bracelet had been a major vexation to him ever since Gabrielle had unwrapped the damn thing. Doug—and no man he'd ever known—would give a woman he was not intimate with a piece of jewelry that expensive. It just didn't make sense. Or, in light of this article, did it?

Unable to help himself, Doug hungrily searched the rest of the newspaper for any further news on Gabrielle. He found more in "The Grain Harvest."

*According to runway coach **Diego Santana**, the catwalk strut of supermodel-in-waiting **Gabrielle Donovan** is less a golden gait and more a vermeil vamp. In Diego's words, "Gabrielle's clumsy walk forces her to be noticed." And while he had little luck polishing up the model's stroll in time for **Maynard Scarborough's** show yesterday, her boss and rumored playmate, **Greg von Ulrich**, is taking the news in stride.*

Doug once again trashed the paper, forcing himself to banish any crazy thoughts conjured up by the reporter's story. He was not going to give in to insecurities fueled by anything as unreliable as a tabloid story. It was becoming increasingly clear that being in love with a celebrity whose fame and popularity were growing on a daily basis meant accepting the gossip and rumors that followed her. Doug also reconciled himself to the fact that, like it or not, he was going to have to learn to live with it. He headed for the hotel, refusing to let rumors put the brakes on this special day.

Gabrielle was pleasantly surprised to see Bea, Jaci, Felicia, Stephanie, and Ruthanna Beverly assembled at the restaurant for a small, impromptu, surprise luncheon.

Conversation flowed lightly and freely, taking a stumble only when Jaci brought up the *Star Diary* stories. Gabrielle found herself getting upset at this double whammy of negative publicity, until both Felicia and Beatrice made her see the futility of allowing such trash journalism to disturb her.

"It's obvious that this reporter is operating in some sort of fantasy world," Felicia told her. "Besides, who would believe anything from the mouth of someone with a ridiculous name like Visa Lee?" she asked, sharing a good laugh with the others.

"How do you know it's not her real name?" Stephanie asked, trying not to sound defensive.

"How do you know it's a woman? I mean, aren't you giving *credit* where *credit* may not be due?" Ruthanna chimed in, causing the others once again to burst into laughter.

Stephanie had taken great care in choosing her pen name, and she didn't appreciate these pompous assholes making fun of her. If she could, she would have explained that as a reporter she was like the commercial—"Visa. Everywhere you want to be"—and that she'd selected the name Lee because she liked the combination's similarity to the words *vis-à-vis*, meaning "face to face." It was like one friend giving another some exciting news. The whole thing was quite cleverly thought out, though it was obvious that these morons had neither the creativity nor the intellect to appreciate it.

Gabrielle returned to Doug's apartment a few minutes before five. She showered quickly and put on her black, suitable-for-any-occasion Donna Karan pantsuit. So she wouldn't tower over Doug, Gabrielle wore her black-suede pumps with the medium heel covered in leopard skin and finished off the outfit with dangling jet bead earrings.

Shortly after five-thirty the buzzer rang. It was the doorman, informing her that a messenger was on his way up. Soon after, the doorbell rang, and Gabrielle opened the door to find before her an impressive bouquet of exotic blooms.

"The gentleman wanted to make sure you received this," the delivery boy said, placing the large arrangement on the table and handing her a card.

"Thank you," Gabrielle said, accepting the envelope. "This is for you." She handed him a five-dollar bill and closed the door. She opened the small envelope and pulled out a heavy, cream-colored card.

My Dearest Gabrielle,

Your birthday celebration begins at six-thirty tonight in the Pierre Hotel's Grand Suite, room seven two seven.
See you in one hour.

Forever,
Doug

The card was more than just a handwritten note. It was a work of art. The florist had taken great time and care to write out each word in beautiful gold calligraphy. And while she could truly appreciate the beauty of its penmanship and presentation, the only words Gabrielle recognized were her own name and Doug's.

Wanting to respond appropriately when Doug arrived, Gabrielle decided to call Beatrice. She would spell out each word and let Bea translate Doug's message. Gabrielle carried the card into the kitchen and dialed the brownstone. After several unanswered rings, she hung up. Erroneously assuming it to be a loving birthday wish, she decided to sit tight, watch the news, and wait for Doug.

Just after Peter Jennings said good night, the doorman buzzed again, announcing the arrival of Greg von Ulrich. She opened the door to find Greg smiling, holding a bottle of champagne and a spectacularly wrapped package.

"Happy birthday!"

"Greg, come in," Gabrielle insisted. "How did you know I was here at Doug's?"

"Jaci told me I could find you here. I couldn't get away for lunch, but I didn't want this day to pass without personally wishing you a happy twenty-first."

"You didn't have to go through all this trouble."

"It's no trouble at all. Now, if you'll just get me a corkscrew, we can share a toast."

"Here you go," Gabrielle said, returning from the kitchen with a bottle opener and two champagne flutes.

"I heard about the *Star Diary* story. I hope you're not upset," he said as he uncorked the bottle of Cristal.

"I'm trying not to be, but it is annoying."

"You can't worry about these silly gossip columns. Maynard loves you. The legitimate press loves you—"

"Even though the entire world now knows that I can't walk and chew gum at the same time?"

"*I* knew you were destined for greatness from the first time Miguel Reid brought you to me," Gregory announced, handing Gabrielle a glass. "I hope we'll always be connected, both professionally and personally. Happy birthday. Cheers!"

"Cheers!" Gabrielle echoed and drank down her champagne.

"This is just a little something to mark this momentous occasion," Gregory said, handing Gabrielle a package. Like a child on Christmas morning, she excitedly began to rip open the wrapping.

"Aren't you going to read the card?" Gregory asked.

"Sorry," Gabrielle apologized, pulling the gift card from its sheath. She paused a brief moment as she appeared to read the card. "Thank you," she said simply.

"And I meant every word."

Gabrielle opened the box to find a lovely, hand-painted scarf from Italy. The turquoise silk chiffon was whisper-thin and decorated with gold, purple, and green scrolls. "It's beautiful," Gabrielle exclaimed, giving Gregory a friendly kiss on the lips.

"Wear it in good health. So what are you doing to celebrate this evening?" he asked, refilling her empty glass.

"I don't know. I'm waiting for Doug to get here and let me know, but he seems to be running a little late."

"Well, then I should be running along. May I use your phone before I go?"

"Sure, the cordless is in the kitchen. There's only one extension, so if you'd like more privacy, you can take the handset into Doug's office," Gabrielle offered.

"Kitchen's fine," Greg remarked and went to make his call. Almost immediately upon his return to the living room, the phone rang.

"That's probably Doug now," Gabrielle said, hurrying into the next room to pick it up. "Hello."

"Doug Sixsmith, please," the caller requested.

"He's not here right now." She looked at the clock. She

was beginning to worry. It was almost eight. *Where is Doug? Why hasn't he called?* "Would you like to leave a message?"

"This is Mona Samuels from *Gab* magazine. I'm calling for his reaction to the news that Gregory von Ulrich has been doing much more than looking after his girlfriend's career."

"Like I said, he's not here to give you a comment. If he were, however, he'd tell you that lies like that deserve no reaction. And for the record, there is nothing going on between Gregory von Ulrich and me," Gabrielle insisted, walking back into the living room with the cordless phone.

"Oh! Ms. Donovan, it's you. Is it true that the other models at First Face are in a stage of revolt because of all the favoritism shown toward you?" the reporter pressed.

"Where do you get these lies? People like you and the sleaze who wrote this story make me sick!" Gabrielle retorted, turning off the handset and angrily slamming it down onto the coffee table. Almost immediately it rang again.

"Ms. Donovan, is it true that Gregory von Ulrich helped you kick an addiction to diet pills?" Mona Samuels persisted.

"Leave me alone!" Gabrielle yelled, hanging up close to tears. When the phone rang for the third time, Gregory picked up the handset and spoke harshly into the receiver, demanding that the reporter cease calling. Hanging up, he took the handset back into the kitchen and unplugged the base. There was no sense in letting these asinine reporters spoil Gabrielle's birthday. When he returned, Greg took Gabrielle into his arms in a calming hug. "Don't let them upset you. Have some more champagne, and forget these stupid reporters and their inability to sort fact from fiction."

*   *   *

Doug dialed the apartment again. The line rang and rang, but nobody picked up. First the line had been busy, and now there was no answer. He called Beatrice in Brooklyn and got no response there either. It was already after nine. Dinner was ruined, not to mention his plans, and he had no explanation for why she'd never showed up. He was getting more worried by the hour. Shortly after ten, Doug checked out of the Pierre and returned home, frantic that something had happened to Gabrielle.

Doug burst into the apartment twenty minutes later, calling out Gabrielle's name. He immediately headed for the kitchen to check the phone. It was unplugged, and beside it, on top of the counter, was his note. Doug walked into the living room and looked around. An empty bottle of champagne and two glasses sat on the coffee table. Next to the bottle was an opened gift box containing an expensive-looking scarf and a small gift card. Doug walked over to the box and picked up the card. It was from Gregory, with all his love and admiration.

Not sure what to think, Doug went into the bedroom and found Gabrielle asleep in the bed. He turned on the light so he could examine her. She was as beautiful as ever, with no visible signs of illness or foul play. She appeared serene and at peace in her slumber. She was also completely naked. The relief over finding her safe and unharmed was quickly replaced by intense anger. The unplugged phone, the scarf, the champagne, von Ulrich's love and admiration—Doug's worst fears had been realized. And tonight, of all nights, she'd stood him up to be with her lover.

Devastated, Doug went to the closet, pulled out his suitcase, and began throwing his clothes inside. The whirl of activity woke Gabrielle. Her senses, dulled by the alcohol, made her slow to realize what was going on.

"Why are you packing? Where are you going?" she asked through a fuzzy mouth.

"As far away from you as possible," Doug retorted, his anger evident.

"Why? What's wrong?"

"Why don't you tell me? I thought we were spending your birthday together. You apparently had other plans," Doug said, his voice drenched with sarcasm.

"I've been here waiting for you all night. Why didn't you call me?"

"I tried. The phone just rang and rang. But then you should know that, since you obviously unplugged it."

"I didn't unplug the phone. Why would I do that?" Gabrielle asked in bewilderment.

"Evidently you and your lover didn't want to be disturbed."

"Lover? Doug, what are you—"

"I've been waiting for hours for you to show up at the Pierre Hotel," Doug interrupted. "Did you get my note, Gabrielle, or did you just decide to ignore that, too?"

Gabrielle didn't know what to say. If she told him she got the card when the flowers were delivered, she'd have to explain why she thought it was simply a loving birthday wish instead of instructions. But he'd know she was lying if she said she hadn't seen it at all. She hated herself for being deceitful. He deserved to know the truth, but not now, not when he was obviously so furious with her. Gabrielle had no choice; she'd have to concoct some story and hope Doug found it plausible.

"I was late getting back this evening, and I was in a rush to get dressed. When the delivery guy brought the flowers, he gave me the card and I put it on the counter, intending to read it once I finished dressing. But then Gregory came by and—"

Hearing those three words—"Gregory came by"—caused Doug to explode. Every ugly image that had been circling in his head all evening swooped down on him like vultures ready for the kill.

"And you decided to stand me up so you could fuck your boyfriend in *my* bed," Doug said, finishing her sentence.

"Are you accusing me of sleeping with my boss?" Gabrielle asked him, outraged by his allegation. She was trying to understand his pain, but his angry and offensive accusations were getting her ire up. "Look, I don't know what you *think* happened, but the truth is that Greg came by merely to toast my birthday and bring me a gift. We just sat around talking, drinking, and waiting for *you* to come home. Then this reporter kept calling about some stupid story in *Star Diary* and I got upset. Greg must have unplugged the phone when he took the last call, which was after eight o'clock, by the way. If you were really *that* worried, you had *plenty* of time to call," she pointed out snidely. "Anyway, Greg gave me another drink to help calm me down, and by the time he left, I was feeling pretty bad. And since *you* were nowhere to be found, I took off my clothes and went to bed. End. Of. Story."

"Let me ask you this, Gabrielle: Every time Greg brings you some pricey gift, do you fuck him? They have a name for girls like you," Doug said, completely ignoring her explanation. In his hurt and anger, Doug's mouth had taken on a life of its own, spewing out words he neither believed nor meant to say.

"How dare you talk to me like that?" Gabrielle said, horrified that their first serious argument had degenerated into ugly mudslinging.

"And how dare you give me that 'the best defense is a good offense' bullshit story? Don't insult my intelligence,

Gabrielle. Though I have to question it myself, since I was stupid enough to want to marry you."

"Are you saying that you don't want to marry me now?" Gabrielle asked softly. She was no longer angry. Doug's enraged words and hurtful accusations had taken her way past fury. She was devastated. "Well, it doesn't really matter, because I wouldn't marry you anyway."

"Why? Because of von Ulrich?" he asked, swallowing his tears.

"No, because having numerous stepfathers doesn't make you a believer in happily ever after," she said simply.

"You told me your mother and father were together until the day he died."

"Most of the things I told you about my childhood were untrue," Gabrielle admitted.

"You lied about that, too?" he asked, his fury once again rising.

"Yes, I lied to you. I'm not proud of it, but I had my reasons. Doug, I—"

"I was walking around here feeling so lucky because I knew the *real* Gabrielle, not the celebrity face on some magazine cover. I'm such a goddamn sucker."

"Don't say that."

"Who are you, Gabrielle Donovan? Do I know you at all?"

"If you'll just listen—"

"What other secrets have you been keeping from me?"

"There's so much I have to explain—"

"Save it for von Ulrich. He can have you. I'm a patient man, but the one thing I can never forgive is dishonesty. I can't love someone I don't trust, and I refuse to live my life trying to read between the lies," Doug shouted as he stormed out.

Gabrielle let him go without any further discussion. She

could never tell him the truth now. As she knew it would, the time to let go had arrived. It was clear she'd never live a normal life, but it had been so sweet pretending.

"He was going to ask me to marry him," Gabrielle sobbed in Beatrice's arms. Two days had passed since Doug had walked out on her, and she hadn't heard one word from him. She'd called the apartment twice and left messages, but Doug apparently had no intention of returning her calls.

"Do you want to marry Doug?" Bea asked gently.

"Yes. I love him, Bea."

"If you became his wife, you'd have to tell him your secret," Bea pointed out.

"He deserves to know the truth."

"Telling him could be risky."

"What do I have left to lose? I've been lying to Doug since the day we met. He's right. There's so much about me he doesn't know. That's why I have to tell him everything."

"You're sure?"

"I can't breathe without him. Maybe once he knows, we can start all over. The only trouble is, I can't get him to return my calls."

"I wish there was something I could do," Bea remarked sympathetically.

"There is. I want you to help me write him a note explaining everything," Gabrielle announced. "I'll dictate the letter, and you write it. He loves me, Bea, and once Doug knows the truth, everything will be okay again. It has to be. So you'll help me?"

Bea took a minute to think before answering. This was a very delicate situation, and she could not risk alienating Gabrielle by refusing and suggesting that she simply forget

Doug Sixsmith. But Gabrielle was in such obvious pain, she had to do something.

"Of course I will. You go get your stationery and put your thoughts together. I'll make sure he understands exactly what you're trying to say," Bea assured her.

Part Three

33

September 13, 1996

Stephanie was tired and discouraged, and her feet were screaming. More than anything, however, she was incensed. For two days, armed with the real-estate section of the *Times,* she'd been crisscrossing the city trying to find an affordable apartment. But based on the astronomical rents being charged, Stephanie had come to the sad realization that she couldn't afford to lease a shoebox in this town, let alone a luxury duplex like Gabrielle's.

Shortly following her breakup with Doug Sixsmith, Gabrielle and Bea had moved out of the Brooklyn brownstone and into a swank high-rise on Manhattan's East Side. Not only did the place offer an expansive view of the East River, but it also provided its tenants an elegant private lobby with a twenty-four-hour concierge and doorman, valet parking, maid service, and a rooftop health club. While Stephanie could not afford the eight hundred dollars a month it would cost her to live in a studio the size of Gabrielle's new bathroom, Gabrielle had purchased not one but two condominiums. She now resided in a splendid three-bedroom penthouse with a panoramic view and a garden terrace outside her bedroom. Bea, thanks to Gabrielle's generosity, was comfortably tucked away one floor below in her own two-bedroom apartment. They'd flown the coop and were living the good life, leaving Stephanie stuck in Brooklyn, strung out on a financial shoestring, with custody of the cat and a new landlord who wanted her out as soon as humanly possible.

She had to make more money. The way Stephanie saw it, she had three options: one, find a new job that paid more; two, ask Felicia for a raise; or three, put Visa Lee to work. Finding a new job would mean working harder—something Stephanie had no intention of doing. Going to Felicia for a raise was also out of the realm of possibility. Now that she'd expanded the firm to include a new partner and the offices of Wilcot, Jourdan & Associates had moved into a bigger, more impressive office space, Felicia was in no position to increase Stephanie's salary.

Her only choice was to approach Harry Grain about doing more Visa Lee stories. The three stories she'd written thus far had paid her substantially more than her contributions to "The Grain Harvest." She also enjoyed the influence that having her own byline brought. Already she could see that her words had the power to change people's lives. Just look what they had done to Gabrielle and Doug Sixsmith.

Thinking of the estranged couple caused Stephanie to smile with satisfaction. The news that their love connection had been severed came as a pleasant shock. She had expected to cause some friction between the lovers, but never in her wildest fantasy had she thought her story would split them up. Stephanie didn't pretend to feel bad for any part she might have played in the breakup. After all, it was Gabrielle who had come between her and Jack Hollis.

Stephanie was about to step off the curb when she saw

the M6 bus approaching. Quickly she jumped back onto the sidewalk. When the bus stopped at the light, so did Gabrielle. She was laid out on her side on a poster that ran nearly the full length of the bus, advertising a new mascara by Cover Girl cosmetics, the latest in her recent crop of million-dollar endorsement contracts. Nose to nose with the model, Stephanie had no choice but to study the ad. Gabrielle was dressed in a Maynard Scarborough dress that cost more than the two-months' security deposit that Stephanie could not afford to pay, and her hair was combed to windblown, come-fuck-me precision. She was also wearing *that* smile.

It was more of a sexy pout than a full-fledged grin, and the camera loved it. America loved it. Hell, the entire damn planet loved Gabrielle Donovan's stupid smile. Women all over the world stood in their mirrors each day trying to emulate it. *People* magazine had even done a story on the famous Donovan pout, calling it an exercise in sheer seduction and Gabrielle a master in the art of "lip tease."

"I hate that fucking smirk," Stephanie said under her breath. Unable to restrain herself, she pulled a Magic Marker from her purse and had just enough time to black out Gabrielle's front teeth before the bus pulled away. She knew her actions were irrational, immature, illogical, and bordering on desperate, but shit, she didn't care. It felt *so good!*

Stephanie wasn't sure when the tolerance she felt toward Gabrielle had turned to envy. But lately even the jealousy was metamorphosing into a slow, simmering hatred. Stephanie was tired of watching things always work out for Gabrielle while nothing ever seemed to work for her. In the two and a half years she'd known Gabrielle, everything the woman wished for came to pass. It didn't matter in what area—career, finances, love life—success rained down on Gabrielle from massive tubs, while sprinkling down on Stephanie from a thimble.

If people only knew the real deal, she thought, *they wouldn't think you were such hot shit. If they could see you the way I have—wearing baggy sweats, no makeup, your hair dirty—they'd see you as the fraud you are. I should write a book and let everyone know the real you.*

Stephanie felt the excitement of the best idea she'd ever had overcome her body. Writing Gabrielle's authorized biography would be just the thing to put Stephanie's career on the literary fast track and place her squarely among the legitimate biographers and journalists. She crossed the street and hurried toward the subway. For the first time in what seemed to be a very, very long time, she couldn't wait to talk to Gabrielle.

"No thank you," Gabrielle spoke into the phone. She was polite but emphatic. "I don't want my life story written right now."

"It was just a thought. We can talk about it later," Stephanie said, retreating from her request. Completely aware of Gabrielle's skittishness about publicity, she should have known better than to start out so big. But this book was definitely possible; it was just going to take longer than Stephanie thought to convince Gabrielle. She could afford to be patient. She was the perfect writer with the perfect subject. There was no way that anything or anyone was going to stop her from doing this book.

The only problem was that Gabrielle was a bit too perfect. She led such a boring personal life. She didn't party, she didn't have any wacky hobbies or interests, and her private life was lived discreetly and quietly. Frankly, for being such a celebrity, Gabrielle made for dull copy, and editors weren't interested in dull people, famous or otherwise.

The only way to get this book published was for Stephanie to create a media situation in which the publicity was so intense that the public would be clamoring to find out everything they could about Gabrielle Donovan. Once the publishers were busy outdoing each other trying to get their hands on Gabrielle's life story, Gabrielle would be more inclined to turn to a trusted friend to write her biography, and Stephanie would have no problem selling her manuscript for big money.

Creating juicy and enticing publicity on Gabrielle was going to be great fun, Stephanie decided. Thank goodness for *Star Diary*. It was the perfect vehicle to take her where she wanted to go. Stephanie grabbed a notepad and started jotting down ideas. It was definitely time for Visa Lee to get to work, so that Stephanie Bancroft could finally come out and play.

34

"You're still here?" Felicia commented, walking into the office. It was already after six o'clock, and she still had a good three hours of work ahead of her.

"I'm actually about to leave," Deena answered. "Oh, the woman from Jonathan Demme's office called again."

"That's her third call in as many days. They really must want Gabrielle. Are Lois and Stephanie here?"

"Stephanie left a while ago. Lois is on her phone, so it's just the two of you."

"When Lois hangs up, could you ask her to come by my office? Have a good evening, Deena." Felicia walked proudly through the new reception area, feeling a huge sense of accomplishment. In the areas of public relations and talent management, Wilcot, Jourdan & Associates was fast becoming recognized for its professional acumen, and they now had the office space to go along with it.

Felicia had just settled in behind her round desk when her intercom buzzed. "What's up?" Lois asked.

"Can you come in for a minute? I might have a new client for you."

"Anybody I know?"

"Gabrielle Donovan."

"Ching, ching," Lois said, giving her impression of a cash register.

"What's that supposed to mean?"

"Just adding up my fifteen percent. I'll be in in a minute."

Thank goodness for Lois, Felicia thought, laughing. Her addition to the firm was a blessing on several levels. Personally, Felicia was thankful to have her old friend working with her. Even after years of separation, the two women had stepped right back into the same comfortable, companionable friendship they'd shared in college. Her humorous, tell-it-like-it-is attitude was contagious, and her mere presence added a certain levity to the office.

Financially, Lois was also a godsend. She came on board with a roster of clients that was growing quickly. Thanks to her savvy and aggressive business sense, Lois also brought to the firm a plentiful infusion of cash. This money allowed them to move into their new offices and relieved much of Felicia's worry that a divorce might topple her business. Together they were building a powerful alliance.

It was less than a minute before Felicia heard a tap on her door, followed by Lois's familiar, "Hey, girl. What's all this about Gabrielle?"

"Jonathan Demme wants her for a small part in his next movie."

"If she's interested in the part, she'll need an agent."

"That's exactly what I was thinking. Is your client roster full?" Felicia asked.

"There's always room for a potential star. Why don't we take Gabrielle out to lunch and discuss the idea with her?"

"I'll set something up when she gets back from Europe."

"Just let me know when and where," Lois said, as she turned around to leave.

"Don't go. Come on in and take a load off."

"That sounds like you got some juicy dirt to dish, sistafriend. What's up? And start with where you were all afternoon," Lois requested as she made herself comfortable.

"At my lawyer's. I filed for divorce, and I'm telling Trace tonight."

"What made you go ahead with it?"

"I've let Trace drag this separation on for months. I don't want to live in limbo anymore. Our marriage is over, and it's time to let go."

"You're sure?"

"Yes. That's not to say that I'm not scared as hell. I've never lived on my own before, but this just isn't working. A part of me still loves Trace and probably always will, but I can't be married to him anymore."

"I have to be honest with you. I always thought you could do better. Trace was a tight-ass when you met him at Georgetown, and his butt is even tighter now. Hell, he even managed to suck most of the life out of *you*."

"We had our problems, but Trace is a good man. He'll make some woman very happy, but I'm not that woman."

"I have to give it to you, you're a lady to the very end. I've never seen a more graceful kick to the curb. I hope, for your sake, that Trace is as understanding and cooperative as you are."

"Why wouldn't he be? I don't want anything from him. There's no reason this divorce should be ugly."

"You'd think so, but it's not always the case. Just check out your Compton's."

"And what am I going to find in the encyclopedia that has anything to do with my divorce?"

"Freedom always costs," Lois summed up. "Though getting rid of that control freak is worth almost any price."

"This isn't all his fault. I've done some things that I'm not proud of either."

"Do any of those things include Lexis?" Lois probed gently.

"Why would you ask that?" Felicia said, unable to look her friend in the eye.

"Come on, Felicia, you may not have made any announcements, but your body language is screaming out the news. Whenever you two are in the same vicinity, it's pretty clear that something's going on between you."

"Is it really that obvious?"

"Don't get me wrong, you're still your highly professional self, but anybody who's observant or who cares about you can tell. Is Lexis the reason for the divorce?"

"No, not really."

"That sounds convincing. Have you two done the wild thing?"

"Only once," Felicia admitted, unable to keep from laughing.

"I won't ask for all the gory details, but you have to tell me one thing," Lois said, holding her two index fingers about six inches apart. Smiling, Felicia answered Lois's inquiry by pulling her hands another two inches apart.

"The brother is so lean. Who knew he'd be packin' a wallop?" Lois commented as they both burst out laughing. So amused were they that neither woman heard Stephanie return to the office to retrieve her forgotten briefcase. Instead of making her presence known, Stephanie quietly positioned herself outside Felicia's door to find out what all the laughter was about.

"If Lexis is that gifted, why did you do it only once?"

"I thought you didn't want any of the details."

"I lied," Lois laughed. "Give up the four-one-one. Let's start with where."

"In Martinique."

"You and Lexis went to Martinique together? How did you pull that off without Trace knowing?"

"We didn't go together. I was there on vacation, and Lexis just showed up."

"And where was your husband?"

"We had an argument, and Trace left for New York."

"So while he was in-flight, you and Lexis got busy."

"If you want to put it that way, yes. I have to tell you, Lois, he changed my life."

"He's that good, huh?"

"It wasn't the sex, though it was great," Felicia said, smiling at the memory. "Making love with Lexis made me look at myself differently. For the first time I felt like I was in charge of my life, that I was my own woman."

"That must have been one hell of an orgasm," Lois said, not getting the laugh she was expecting. "So why only once?"

"Things got complicated," Felicia said, getting quietly but visibly distraught.

"Hey, girl, if this is upsetting you, we don't need to talk about it."

"No, I need to tell someone. I've been carrying all this around for so long, sometimes I feel like I'm losing my mind."

"Felicia, you aren't the first woman who tripped out on her husband when her marriage was falling apart."

"It's not that. I got pregnant."

"Oh, shit. Did you tell him?"

"I didn't know which 'him' to tell."

"You had an abortion?"

"Yes."

"And neither of them knows?"

"No."

"So you did what you had to do."

"That's what I keep telling myself."

"Look, I have a meeting at CBS," Lois said, glancing at her watch. "If you need to talk, I'll be up late. You be strong tonight. Don't let Trace bully you into anything you don't want to do, and definitely don't say anything to him at this late date."

Hot copy, Stephanie said to herself as she quietly scurried back to her office. She couldn't believe what she'd heard out of Felicia's own adulterous little mouth. She stored the information away, knowing that it was only a matter of time before it came in handy.

"You've already filed? Without telling me?" Trace asked, slamming his glass down on the table. He was caught totally off guard by Felicia's announcement.

"That's why I'm here now."

"I thought this was supposed to be a temporary separation."

"We've done everything we can to save this relationship, Trace. When I came back from Martinique, we went to counseling. It didn't help, but we kept limping along for months until I finally moved out. It's over, Trace. Our marriage is over."

"I don't have time to get divorced," Trace pointed out angrily, unwilling to face the truth. "I'm in the middle of an important case."

Felicia shook her head in disbelief. Even when it came to the dissolution of his marriage, Trace put his career first. "Believe me, I wish it could wait, but it can't."

"What's the rush, Felicia?"

"I need to get on with my life."

"A life with a new lover?"

"No. I just want my freedom."

"You have your freedom. We haven't lived under the same roof for months. I don't see why this matter can't wait until I have the time and energy to give it my full concentration."

"And I don't see why this 'matter' has to be a big deal. We have no children. There are no custody issues," she said, keeping her cool.

"And I know you're glad about that," Trace remarked sarcastically. Trying to get Felicia pregnant had turned out to be a miserable failure. Trace still couldn't understand why she hadn't conceived during or right after the cruise, but she hadn't, and to make matters worse, she'd gone on the Pill shortly thereafter. Now, with divorce on her mind, Trace had to face the fact that he would never share parenthood with Felicia. "What about alimony or the property settlement?"

"There's no need for alimony, and I'm sure we can come to an equitable property agreement. I want to make this as painless as possible for both of us."

"What about WJ and A?"

"What about it?" Felicia asked, suspiciously.

"I do have a financial stake in the company. It seems to me that it should be on the table with everything else we own."

"Trace, I was hoping that we could dissolve our marriage quietly and without hurting each other any more than we have to," Felicia sputtered, outraged by his suggestion. "But if you want to go toe-to-toe on this, fine. Just understand that Wilcot, Jourdan and Associates is not negotiable."

"I guess we'll just have to see about that."

"Why are you being so difficult?"

"Because I don't want a divorce. So if you're hell-bent

on giving up on our marriage, be prepared to give up *everything*."

Felicia stormed out of his place. She had been such a fool to think that they could get through this divorce with a friendship intact. She should have known that because dissolving their marriage was her idea, Trace would make the situation as difficult and uncomfortable as possible. Lois's warning had been right on target; her freedom was going to cost her, but Felicia had not been prepared to pay with her company.

She walked out into the night air and flagged down a cab. Felicia climbed into the backseat, not knowing where to go. She didn't want to go home. The idea of being alone right now was totally unappealing. She needed to be around people, keep her mind occupied. The last thing she wanted was to be flooded with memories of the man who for over ten years had been her lover and husband, and who now had become her enemy.

"Where to, lady?"

"Seventy-third, between Columbus and Central Park West," Felicia said, giving the driver Lois's address. "No, wait," she said, changing her mind. "Make that One-sixteenth Street and Seventh Avenue."

Traffic was light, and they made it uptown to Harlem in less than fifteen minutes. The cab dropped Felicia off in front of Graham Court, and after the night guard buzzed her in through the wrought iron gate, she walked through the courtyard and into the building. She rode the elevator up to the fifth floor, silently second-guessing her decision to come. Within seconds of her knocking, the door flew open, revealing a pleasantly surprised Lexis Richards.

"Hey, what's up? Come on in." Felicia stepped into the apartment and immediately regretted her impulse to stop by. The lights in the living room were off, and the room was bathed in candlelight. The mellow sounds of South African guitarist Jonathan Butler filled the air, and an open bottle of wine sat on the coffee table. Lexis was obviously entertaining.

"I'm sorry for dropping in on you like this, but—"

"You were in the 'hood and decided to swing by," he finished.

"Something like that. You're busy, I'll call you in the morning."

"It's cool. I was just sittin' here by myself, chillin'."

"Are you sure?"

"Positive. Pull up a pillow," Lexis said as he pulled out another wineglass for Felicia. "How's everything at the office?"

"Busy. I brought you by some clippings on *Praline Livin'*. The buzz going around town is very good, and we're still another few months away from opening."

"Bet. Now, why don't you tell me what's really up?" Lexis insisted.

"What do you mean?"

"I can hear it in your voice. I can see it in your face. You either did something or want to tell me something, but you don't know how."

Felicia sat back and marveled at how well Lexis knew her. In all the years she and Trace had been married, he still could not read her feelings and moods the way Lexis could.

"I finally filed for divorce today."

"Is everything cool?" Lexis asked, trying to contain his own enthusiasm.

"If you're asking me if I feel okay about my decision, the answer is yes."

"What about Trace?"

"He's a different story. I just left his place. Things got pretty ugly."

"You rocked his world. You didn't expect him to just sit back and take it, did you?"

"Take what? The truth that our marriage is over? Yes, as a matter of fact I did. What I didn't expect was him trying to take away my company."

"He said that?"

"He told me that if I was giving up on our marriage I'd better be prepared to give up everything," Felicia said, unable to keep the tears at bay any longer.

Lexis reached over and gathered her up into his arms. "Baby, don't worry. He's just sellin' wolf tickets."

"He meant it and he'll do it, not because he really wants my business but because he wants to control me. Lexis, I can't lose WJ and A. It's all I have."

"Why are you so worried? Your people have money."

"I'm thirty years old. This is *my* problem. *My* responsibility, not my parents'."

"If you do need some help, I'm here," Lexis promised.

"Why is he doing this?" she asked, grateful for Lexis's support and happy to be back in his arms.

"Because he's a chump who doesn't like to lose."

The two sat in silence, both thinking about the impact Felicia's decision would have on their lives—both individually and together. Lexis couldn't help hoping that tonight marked a new beginning for him and Felicia. He was tired of being patient, tired of being her friend. He wanted more. Much more.

"Trace asked me if I had a new lover. I didn't know what to say," Felicia said.

"One slammin' day in the sun is all we had. You have nothing to confess and certainly nothing to feel guilty about."

"But I do," Felicia said softly. "Lexis, shortly after we got back from Martinique, I found out I was pregnant."

"Why didn't you tell me?"

"I didn't tell you or Trace because I didn't know who was the father."

"But it could have been mine?"

"Yes."

"Then I deserved to know."

"I'm sorry."

Stony silence was Lexis's response.

"It was the hardest decision I ever had to make, but considering the circumstances, I couldn't stay pregnant. Can you understand that?"

"Yeah, I got it—your body, your choice. What I can't understand is why you totally dissed me. We could have dealt with this together. I would have supported your decision either way."

"I'm sorry. I should have trusted you."

"Felicia?"

"Yes."

"What if you knew the baby was ours? Then what?"

"I would have definitely told you, but beyond that, I honestly don't know. We really didn't know what was happening between us then."

"And now?"

"I still don't know what's going on," she said softly. "But I'm ready to find out."

35

Miss, the gentleman at the bar sends this with his compliments," the waiter announced, presenting Gabrielle with a bottle of Peter Michael Point Blanc wine and a note. Gabrielle unfolded the cocktail napkin and saw what she assumed to be the giver's name and phone number. She turned to the bar and returned the wave of Christophe Dylan, a popular and sexy soap opera hunk.

"That's no bottle of Ripple," Felicia remarked with a whistle. "Point Blanc ninety-three—we're talking eighty-five dollars a bottle in a place like this."

"Shall I pour?" the waiter inquired.

"Please tell Mr. Dylan, thank you, but I can't accept his generous gift," Gabrielle replied, turning her attention back to the menu.

"Looks like a cold front has descended over the bar," Lois said in jest.

"I can never decide what to eat," Gabrielle admitted, ignoring her. Gabrielle was well aware of her reputation as an ice princess, and it was just fine with her.

"Everything is good here," Felicia assured her, "particularly the lamb."

"I don't eat red meat anymore. I wonder what the specials are today?" She was stalling until the waiter arrived. With luck, there would be something she found appetizing among the verbal listing of today's specials.

"Turn your menu over. They're on the other side," Lois said.

Time for Plan B. "Be right back." Gabrielle excused herself and walked over to the table diagonally across from theirs. Sitting alone was a man, immersed in a copy of *Advertising Age,* totally oblivious to his surroundings. As Gabrielle got closer, her lips stretched into a smile.

"Excuse me. I'm sorry to interrupt, but what are you eating?"

"Veal medallions with lemon and capers in a Chardonnay sauce," the man said, looking up from his magazine. A flicker of recognition registered in his eyes before he jumped up from his seat and warmly embraced the model. "Gabrielle Donovan!"

"Jack Hollis?"

"It's been ages since I've actually *seen* you. I must say, your photos do not do you justice. You look wonderful!"

"Thanks. So do you." It was true. He looked terrific.

"How have you been—other than busy?" Jack asked.

"Very well. And you? How's business?"

"Good, though advertising is a strange new world."

"I'd heard you'd closed your design firm a few years ago. Things are going well?"

"We've made a few inroads. Come join me. We can finish catching up," Jack offered hopefully.

"I'm sorry, I can't. I'm here for a business meeting."

"Why don't I wait for you, and we can have dessert together?" he suggested, determined not to let Gabrielle slip through his fingers again.

"Are you sure? We'll be here at least an hour."

"No problem. I just got served and I have plenty of work to keep me busy."

"Okay then, you're on."

Jack watched Gabrielle return to her table and turned back to his meal, only to find he was no longer hungry. It had been a long time since the anticipation of spending time with a woman had caused him to lose his appetite. But, as Jack figured out years ago, Gabrielle was no ordinary woman.

"I'll have the veal medallions with lemon and capers," she announced to the waiter.

"I thought you didn't eat red meat," Lois said.

"Veal is the other white meat."

"No, that's pork," Lois corrected her with a laugh.

"I swear, Gabrielle, we've eaten together at least fifty times over the years, and I have yet to see you order from the menu," Felicia observed.

"You can't tell what the food is going to be like just by reading it off the menu. I like to see what I'm getting," Gabrielle replied, reciting her well-practiced explanation. "Besides, if you pick your tables right, you can meet some very interesting dishes," Gabrielle added, smiling back at Jack.

"My, my, my, how things change. A minute ago you were blowing off Christophe Dylan. Now look at you, flirting with some stranger," Felicia teased.

"First of all, Chris is a jerk; and second, that's no stranger. I've known Jack Hollis for years."

"As in the Hollis/Henderson Group?" Lois asked.

"Yes. He and his friend have a small advertising company."

"He's being modest. Jack and his partner Fritz Henderson are quickly becoming known as the Rodgers and Hammerstein of the advertising world. Their firm is the talk of the block, and Jack's one of the most sought-after art directors in the business," Felicia informed her.

"Successful *and* fine. Is he single?" Lois asked.

"Very. And based on his reputation as a ladies' man, plans to stay that way for a long time," Felicia replied.

"I thought he was gay," Gabrielle remarked.

"Girl, don't you read the papers? He's in and out of 'Page Six' all the time. Jack's considered the heir apparent to JFK Jr.'s recently abdicated throne. How do you know him?" Felicia asked.

"He dated Stephanie."

"I'm sorry, but I can't see Jack Hollis with Stephanie, not with her funky little attitude," Lois remarked. It was common knowledge that Lois and Stephanie disliked each other. The two had managed to carve out a shaky truce in the office, but when she and Felicia were together, Lois didn't pull any punches.

"All right, Lois, that's enough," Felicia suggested tactfully.

"You're right, slamming an employee in front of a client is a no-no, but Gabrielle knows the deal. She lived with the woman."

"Yes, and she still has to work with her."

Not for much longer if I have any say-so, Lois thought. Stephanie Bancroft was one associate Wilcot and Jourdan could definitely do without.

"Speaking of work," Felicia continued, "Jonathan Demme is shooting a new movie, and he has a small part he swears you'd be perfect for. I think it's a great opportunity. I talked it over with Lois, and she agrees. She's also willing to represent you if you're interested."

"But I've never acted before," Gabrielle said lamely.

"Once upon a time you never modeled before, and now look at you. You're at the top of the heap," Felicia remarked.

"Modeling is one thing. Acting is an entirely different matter," Gabrielle said.

"It's just a small part."

"How much dialogue would I have to learn?"

"That I don't know. I'll tell you what, I'll call and have the script delivered. We'll decide later."

"I've already decided. I'm not interested," Gabrielle replied resolutely. She was intrigued by the idea of acting, but acting meant scripts, and scripts meant reading. Gabrielle was unwilling to take the risk.

"Why don't you take a few days to think it over?" Lois suggested.

"I don't have anything to think over. Just tell him thanks, but no thanks. Well, ladies, if our business is concluded here, I have a date for dessert."

"I'm not gay. I have never been gay, nor do I have any interest in being gay anytime in the future," Jack announced with a chuckle.

"I'm sorry. I had to ask," Gabrielle explained, relieved that she hadn't offended him.

"Where did you get an idea like that?"

"Stephanie," they answered together, before breaking up with laughter.

"I guess she was much more pissed off than I thought," Jack said.

"And then some. I'm glad to hear it isn't true."

"Oh, it's definitely not true, and it is my sincere hope that I have the chance to prove it to you one day," Jack said, giving Gabrielle one of his promise-laden smiles.

Over tiramisu and coffee, the two caught up on each other's lives. Jack filled Gabrielle in on the milestone events these past three years, mainly the start-up of his successful business, and Gabrielle entertained him with war stories from the fashion front. As he chewed on the last bite of his dessert, Jack was struck by his good luck that the elusive Ms. Donovan had reappeared just when things were becoming dreadfully dull with his current arm piece, Corona, a twenty-year-old pop star on the rise.

"Do you believe in kismet?" Jack inquired, turning on the Hollis charm.

"Kismet?"

"You know, fate. I believe that life is predetermined. That what is supposed to happen will," he explained with a flirtatious smirk on his full lips.

"For example, the two of us meeting up like this again?" Gabrielle asked, returning the smirk.

"Yes," Jack answered, locking eyes with hers.

At that moment the waiter approached, breaking the tension that had suddenly engulfed the room. While Jack tallied the check, Gabrielle took the opportunity to study this man who with every passing minute was becoming more and more appealing. From his hair to his smile to his body—if she had to come up with one word to sum up the physical attributes of Jack Hollis, it would be "magnificent."

"Gabrielle?" Jack called out, interrupting her thoughts.

"Sorry, I was having an out-of-body experience," she joked weakly, trying to hide her humiliation at being caught staring.

"I see," he answered, amused by her obvious embarrassment. "Are you psychic as well?" he asked, helping her out of her chair. "Can you tell me what I'm thinking right now?" Jack challenged as he drew his magnificent hands through that magnificent hair and smiled that magnificent smile.

Gabrielle felt a rush of warm blood invade her face. She knew exactly what he was thinking. It had nothing to do with psychic intuition. It was much more basic than that.

She threw back her head and released a throaty laugh. Gabrielle knew exactly what he was thinking, because, after all, great minds think alike.

"Learning lines will be no problem. I'll help you," Bea told Gabrielle.

"I'm just not interested in acting right now."

"Look at all those child actors who can't read yet. They still manage. Somebody helps them memorize their script."

"That's the point, Bea. I'm not a child."

"What about Lois and Felicia?"

"They're disappointed, but they understand, not like Stephanie. Even though she tried not to show it, she was pretty mad about me refusing to let her write my authorized biography."

"Trust me, you haven't heard the last of this. I have a feeling that if Stephanie really wants to write this book, she's going to keep on hounding you until you give in."

"She can try, but the answer will still be no. Until I can read my own biography, nobody else is going to write it."

"Are you thinking about trying tutoring again?" Bea questioned.

"Yeah. I was thinking of hiring a private tutor. You know, someone who will come to me in secret. What do you think?"

"I think it's a good idea, as long as they sign a confidentiality statement. But I don't see how you can fit it in right now, not with this calendar shoot and swimsuit special coming up," Bea responded, hoping that her argument made sense.

"I suppose you're right," Gabrielle agreed. "I've somehow managed to keep things together this long. I guess tutoring can wait a little longer," she added, resigned to the fact that she might never learn to read.

"I'm proud of you, Gabrielle. You've been through an awful lot in your short life. You've been dealt some rough blows, but you just keep moving on and up."

"I've been given a lot of good things, too, even if they didn't always last," Gabrielle said softly in a reflective afterthought.

"Are you talking about Doug Sixsmith?"

"It's not what you think. I'm over him, though not as quickly as he obviously got over me. It's pretty apparent that he just didn't love me the way I thought he did."

The sad look on Gabrielle's face only added to Bea's guilt for writing the letter that terminally severed their relationship. When she had sent Doug the note, under Gabrielle's signature, telling him that their relationship was over and to never contact her again, Bea honestly felt that she was doing the right thing. Doug had hurt Gabrielle terribly with his wild accusations. He didn't see the effect his hateful words had on Gabrielle for weeks after their breakup. She sat around her room like a zombie, not eating, not sleeping, not working. Doug Sixsmith had nearly destroyed Gabrielle, and though Beatrice could still see a shadow of pain lingering behind those lovely blue eyes when something reminded her of him, Gabrielle was well on her way to forgetting him.

That's exactly why Bea didn't pass on any of Doug's phone messages or give her his letter when it arrived in the week following their breakup. Bea didn't care how sorry he might be or how much he claimed to love her and want her back; Gabrielle had had enough hurt and heartache at his hands.

"Hi, John," Gabrielle said into the receiver that linked her apartment with the front desk downstairs. "How nice. Please send them up."

"Visitors?"

"No, flowers, and I think I know from whom."

"Oh?"

"I have a feeling these are from Jack Hollis. I ran into him at lunch today. We had a nice talk," Gabrielle said as she opened the door. When she returned, she was carrying five dozen pink roses artistically arranged in a crystal Orrefors vase.

"Would you read the card to me, please?" Gabrielle requested, putting the flowers on the dining room table.

" 'Thanks for making dessert so sweet. Let's get together soon to continue our kismet adventure. Love, Jack.' What's this about a kismet adventure?"

"It's just a joke," Gabrielle said, smiling at the memory.

"I haven't seen you smile like that in a long time, young lady. Is there something going on here that I should know about?"

"Not yet, maybe not ever. I like Jack, but I guess I'm still a little gun-shy."

"I know Doug hurt you very badly," Bea said, putting her arms around Gabrielle's shoulders. "But one day, when the time is right, you'll fall in love again. I promise."

36

Dead? How can he be dead? I just talked to him a couple of days ago," Stephanie asked Harry's secretary in disbelief. "What happened?"

"Heart attack. It was all so sudden. He just keeled over yesterday at the breakfast table. Poor Harry."

Poor Harry? He's dead; nothing bothers him anymore. What about me? Stephanie had the hottest tip she'd had in a long time, and Harry Grain was too dead to hear it, let alone print and pay her for it. Was there no justice in this world? How could Harry die without clueing her in that he was even sick? *Some people are so fucking thoughtless!*

"I'll be in with Carl if you need me," Stephanie said, referring to the paper's editor. *Carpe diem. Seize the moment,* she thought. Harry's sudden departure meant his job was wide open, and Stephanie had no intention of leaving until she put her own bid in to replace the man. She practically sprinted through the newsroom to get to Carl's office.

"Carl?" Stephanie asked, sticking her head in the editor's door.

"Visa, come on in. I'm glad you're here. I was planning to get in touch with you myself this afternoon."

"Really?"

"Yes, I know you're as upset as the rest of us about the loss of Harry Grain."

"In more ways than one, Harry's death leaves a void in all our lives."

"Harry spoke very highly of your work. He seemed to think that you have all the instincts necessary to be a fine celebrity reporter."

"If I do, it's only because those instincts were honed under Harry's tutelage. He was the best teacher a young reporter could ever hope to have."

"Visa, I'd like you to take over 'The Grain Harvest' column—on a trial basis—one column a week for the next six months. After that, we'll see how things are going. If they go as well as I hope, 'The Grain Harvest' will become yours. We'll even rename it."

"I'm honored, though slightly intimidated. Harry left some big footprints to fill," Stephanie said, quickly calculating the man-hours necessary to continue her work at WJ&A and write the column. She immediately abandoned the task, knowing that if taking this job meant that she had to work around the clock, she'd do it.

"I'm confident you'll find a way to blaze your own trail."

"I will definitely do my best to leave my mark. You can count on that," she promised.

Stephanie waltzed into the Mad Hatter, stepped up to the bar, and ordered herself a split of the house champagne. She had a lot to celebrate. Not only was the additional income going to come in handy, this job was just what she needed to get her plan in motion. Now that she had complete editorial control over "The Grain Harvest," Stephanie's plan to keep Gabrielle's personal life in the papers could begin in earnest.

This was her first time in the Mad Hatter since the initial months following her breakup with Jack Hollis. Prior to coming, Stephanie had thought she was finally over Jack, but now, sitting at the very bar where they met, the memories—both pleasant and painful—came crashing back. It was evident by the ache in Stephanie's heart that even after nearly three years, she still missed him. She'd had a few marginal relationships in the years following Jack, but none could fill the black hole his absence had created in her life.

Stephanie threw a few peanuts into her mouth and ground them into paste. She swallowed, gulping down with them any self-pity or anger she still harbored over Jack. Nothing was going to spoil her great afternoon. She had a second job doing what she loved—writing—and a new personal goal—authoring Gabrielle's biography. Now, if she could just find a place to live and a new man, life would seem almost fair. When her drink was delivered, she lifted the glass and silently congratulated herself for her recent good fortune.

"Celebrating?" asked the guy sitting on the stool next to her. Stephanie looked into the face of a rather plain, though not unattractive man. All in all, his face was common, rather forgettable, in fact, except for his eyes. Stephanie had never seen such strange and eerie-looking eyes before. They were the color of a pale-blue aquamarine, with very small pupils that had a way of gazing through you. If the eyes were the window to one's soul, then this man appeared spiritless.

"Yeah," Stephanie said, anxious to share her good news with someone. "I just accepted a new job. One I've wanted for quite a while."

"Congratulations. It's good to hear that at least one person in this city has a job they like."

"I take it you don't."

"Not most days."

"What do you do?"

"I'm a photographer."

"What do you shoot? Weddings? Bar mitzvahs?" Stephanie asked. He seemed like the type you'd find working at the portrait studio at Sears, though those spooky eyes of his could scare even Pugsley Addams.

"Nah, I don't do crap like that. I'm more of what you might call a celebrity photographer, you know, part of New York's paparazzi."

"Really? What's your name?"

"Howie Joseph. And you are?"

"Stephanie."

"Pleased to meet you," Howie said with all sincerity, his eyes locking on Stephanie's for a split second, before she looked away. "Why are you celebrating by yourself?"

"It's like that sometimes."

"Let me buy you a drink. An attractive woman like you shouldn't have to celebrate happy times alone."

"Thank you. In fact, why don't we grab a table? You can sit down and tell me all about yourself. One never knows when one will need a good photographer, does one?" Stephanie remarked with a sly grin.

Stephanie and Howie carried their drinks to a secluded corner in the back of the bar. After several hours of conversation and drinks, Howie's eyes appeared less spooky and Stephanie began to find him creatively appealing. Howie Joseph and Stephanie Bancroft had a lot in common. Both the photographer and the writer planned to establish their own celebrity by chronicling the lives of the already or about-to-be famous. Both were desperate to be recognized for their work and to feast on the fruits of fame. But perhaps the greatest thing Howie and Stephanie had in common was their uncanny ability to dismiss any discomfort or pain that doing their respective jobs might cause others.

By evening's end the pact between them was sealed. Both had found their professional soul mates. Not only did they agree to work together to help further each other's career, Howie had the solution to Stephanie's housing problem—the second bedroom in his apartment. They left the Mad Hatter together, headed back to Brooklyn to pick up Barclay and pack up a few of Stephanie's belongings, and took them over to Howie's apartment in a gritty part of Brooklyn known as Dumbo (Down Under the Manhattan Bridge Overpass), a haven for artists, photographers, actors, and writers. The apartment had two bedrooms and one usable bath; the other Howie had turned into a darkroom. It was sparsely furnished—a couch, coffee table, and a couple of chairs in the living room, a bed and dresser in each bedroom.

"How can you afford this place?" Stephanie inquired. The unit was a virtual mansion by New York standards.

"Well, for one thing, it's rent-controlled, and I also kind of lied to you in the bar," Howie admitted. "I do shoot weddings and bar mitzvahs, even birthday parties when I'm forced to."

"Well, roomie, stick with me and those times will fade like an old Polaroid. From now on we're on the celebrity watch."

"You're sure about this?"

"You just keep me supplied with exclusive photos, and we'll be okay. Remember, though, nobody can know that we're working together."

"Not a problem. Keeping secrets is a skill I mastered long ago."

"I hope, for your sake, you're as good as you say."

"I am," Howie told her matter-of-factly. "Now, when do we get started?"

"Tomorrow's soon enough for me."

"Great. I'd like to get out and see what the elusive Mrs. Bessette-Kennedy is up to."

"Forget Carolyn. There's a model I want you to concentrate on for a while."

"I like models. Which one?"

"Gabrielle Donovan."

"Yes!" Howie shouted joyfully. "Following Gabrielle around will be my pleasure. She's with First Face, right? I'll need to get some leads on her schedule."

"Don't bother. I can get you all the information you need."

"How do you know Gabrielle?"

"We have mutual friends. Just make sure you get me some good stuff. I want pictures of everything. I want to know where she goes and who she sees when she's not working. If she's jogging, I want a picture. If she's out partying, I want a picture. Hell, anything short of her sitting on the toilet, I want to see it captured on film."

"Why all the interest in Gabrielle?"

"Here's our first secret: I have big plans for us, Howie. We're gonna put together a nice little book on Ms. Donovan—a book that, if done right, will bring us both a lot of money and recognition. Only, nobody knows this yet, not even Gabrielle, so let's keep it that way. Now, are you interested? Do you think you can get me what I need?"

"You don't worry about that. I'm good, and I'm persistent. I can sniff out a celebrity shot from a mile away."

"Well, can you sniff me out something to eat? I'm starving."

"No problem. One ham and cheese, coming up."

While her new roommate and business partner headed

for the kitchen to fix her a sandwich, Stephanie checked out the view from the living-room window. Today had turned out to be a damned good one. Everything was looking up. She now had a place to live—granted it wasn't the snobby East Side, but it was clean and affordable—plus she was surrounded by fellow artisans. And Howie Joseph was just what she needed to set her plan in motion. If a picture was worth a thousand words, the combination of Howie's pictures and her words had to be priceless.

37

I've decided it was time to take matters in my own hands," Jack announced to Gabrielle over the phone.

"And those matters would be . . . ?" Gabrielle asked, smiling into the receiver.

"You and me. It's been two weeks since we met at the restaurant, and we still haven't spent any time together. To remedy this unacceptable situation, I checked with your assistant and mine and managed to clear both our calendars on Tuesday."

"You're just a take-charge kinda guy, aren't you?"

"That's right. So tell me what you'd like to do, and I'll make it happen."

"Plan anything you like."

"Anything?" Jack asked with a mischievous lilt to his voice.

"Within reason," Gabrielle stipulated lightheartedly.

"Okay, just be ready to have some fun," Jack warned, his imagination already in overdrive. Gabrielle Donovan, with her well-deserved reputation as the sweet but untouchable snow maiden of the supermodel set, represented the one thing Jack loved best about a beautiful woman—a challenge.

Early Tuesday morning Gabrielle's intercom buzzed, rousing her from a sound slumber. She opened her eyes and looked at the alarm clock. Slowly the glowing blue numbers came into focus. It was 7:28.

"Hello," she whispered into the intercom, her voice still groggy with sleep.

"Sorry to wake you, Ms. Donovan, but there's a Mr. Hollis in the lobby."

"Now?" Gabrielle asked, trying to clear the cobwebs from her mind. How had she managed to forget that Jack was coming over this morning? "John, please ask Mr. Hollis to wait ten minutes, and then send him up," she requested.

Gabrielle had twelve minutes, tops, to make herself look presentable. She wasn't going to be able to work any miracles in such a short span of time. Jack would just have to be impressed with a clean body and fresh breath, she decided as she raced into the bathroom. When she emerged, wearing a long terry bathrobe and a headful of damp hair, her doorbell was chiming.

"Good morning," Gabrielle said, opening the door.

"Morning," Jack replied brightly, stepping into Gabrielle's apartment. He was wearing a trench coat and carrying two white deli bags and the newspaper. Jack would look perfectly normal for a breezy fall morning, had it not been for his footwear. He was wearing black-leather slippers. "You look surprised to see me."

"The time we were supposed to get together seems to have slipped my mind," Gabrielle said, ignoring Jack's shoes for the moment.

"I left it on your answering machine last night."

"I didn't get in from Palm Springs until very late. I

haven't checked my messages. Let me hang your coat," Gabrielle offered, taking the coffee and bags from Jack.

Jack pulled off his trench coat, revealing the perfect outfit to go with his slippers. He was wearing a burgundy bathrobe, closed and belted over navy-striped pajama bottoms. A small triangle of Jack's naked chest peeked out from his robe.

Gabrielle burst into laughter. "I know there's a logical explanation for your attire."

"You said to plan my dream date. Well, *my* dream date begins with you and me lazing around in our pajamas, drinking coffee, and reading the paper together. So here I am. Elated to see that not only are you dressed for the occasion, but that Walt Disney and I have something in common."

"I'm missing the connection here," Gabrielle admitted.

"We both have our own Sleeping Beauty," Jack explained with a flirty wink.

"Well, Walt, welcome to the Magic Kingdom," Gabrielle said, picking up breakfast and leading Jack to the kitchen.

"This is quite a place you have here. I'm not sure which is more impressive, the tasteful decor or the incredible view," Jack commented. Gabrielle's apartment was simply but elegantly decorated in the cool, soothing colors of white, taupe, and gray. Dominating the room was a wall of floor-to-ceiling windows, and from this vantage point Jack had a commanding view of the East River, Roosevelt Island, and the Queensborough and Triborough bridges.

"Thank you, but no decor in existence can compete with the New York skyline."

"Ain't that the truth," Jack said, accepting his cup of coffee from Gabrielle. He sat down at the table and reached for the paper.

"What part do you want to start with—Sports? Arts and

Leisure? Take your pick," he said, offering Gabrielle the newspaper.

"I can't read the paper first thing in the morning," Gabrielle explained. "Usually I let the 'Today' show deliver the early news. Do you mind?"

"Not at all. Turn it on."

Gabrielle walked over to a small color television and turned it on to NBC. She returned to the table, picked up a cinnamon roll, and began nibbling around its edges. Al Roker filled the screen, delivering his always humorous and sometimes accurate weather report. When he finished, he threw the show back to Bryant Gumbel, who announced his next guest, Doug Sixsmith, author of the new thriller *Ride the Fire*.

Seeing Doug on the screen, Gabrielle nearly choked on her roll. She hadn't seen or heard his voice in six months, not since the day their life together came to a crashing halt. Doug looked tired, but he still had his easygoing good looks and genuine smile. She sat silently staring at the television, not hearing a word of what he was telling Bryant and the show's millions of viewers.

"Weren't you two an item a while back?" Jack asked casually.

"Yes, but that's ancient history."

"Why did you break up?"

"Career pressures," Gabrielle covered up lightly.

Jack took a long sip of his coffee and listened as Bryant wrapped up his interview with Doug. "So, any unresolved feelings on either part?" Jack was confident that this wimpy wordsmith presented him no real competition, but he wanted to know just what he was up against.

"Not at all. It was clear to both of us that we didn't belong together."

"That's all I needed to hear," Jack said, flashing a winning grin.

"You must have your mom wrapped around your finger with that smile," Gabrielle commented.

"I have to admit it got me out of a few jams now and again, with Mom, but believe me, it didn't move my old man in the least."

"Does your family live in New York?"

"My dad died of cancer when I was twenty-three, and my mother followed two years later. They were both only children, like me, so I have no extended family to speak of."

"Sounds like we have something in common."

"And I'm sure we're bound to discover more. Now I'm going home to change. I'll pick you up around noon, and we'll have lunch at one of my favorite spots before having some fun."

"Good, I'm ready for some fun." Gabrielle was through being serious when it came to men. If her relationship with Doug had proved anything, it was that love was for other people.

"This brewery is one of your favorite lunch spots, huh?" Gabrielle chuckled, wiping a smudge of mustard from Jack's chin. To her surprise, he had brought her to the Chelsea Pier Sports Center, located on the Hudson River.

"Best hot dogs this side of Yankee Stadium," he revealed. "Ready to hit a few?"

Gabrielle followed him out of the Chelsea Brewing Company and onto the driving range. Jack helped her pick out a driver from a variety of rental golf clubs and purchased a range card before traveling down the narrow walkway to an empty stall. The whoosh of clubs slicing the air, followed by the sharp whack of iron hitting ball echoed throughout the area.

Jack positioned Gabrielle so she faced the vinyl curtain that separated one practice tee from another and gave her a quick lesson on the art of the golf swing. "See, just nice and easy," he said as he launched his ball two hundred and ten feet across the Astroturf-covered pier. Gabrielle watched as a new ball popped up on its tee from the ground while the ATM-like machine automatically deducted the cost of another ball from the range card. She laughed aloud. Only in New York City would one find this high-tech addition to such a traditional, time-honored game.

"Go on, try it," Jack urged. Gabrielle pulled the club back behind her head and swung hard. The momentum of her swing caused her to twist around a full three hundred and sixty degrees. Gabrielle burst into laughter as she noticed that her ball had not left the tee. Jack's standing there shaking his head only made her laugh harder.

"I think there's something missing in my technique," she quipped.

"I'd say so. Let me show you," Jack said as he walked around and stood behind her. Pressing the front of his body against the back of hers, he wrapped his arms around her, capturing Gabrielle in a straight-arm embrace.

"God, you smell delicious," he said, getting caught up in the fresh scent of her hair. Momentarily forgetting her golf lesson, Jack took the opportunity to lightly kiss her neck and nibble her right ear. "You want a nice, smooth stroke," Jack whispered seductively in her ear. His close proximity and warm breath caressing the sensitive nerves in her ear was sending shivers through her body. Just as he intended, Gabrielle was finding it difficult to concentrate on his instructions. Suddenly the lesson was cut short by four quick, successive flashes. Someone had just taken their picture.

"Hey, what's going on here?" Jack demanded, turning around to find a small crowd of spectators.

"I told you that was Gabrielle Donovan," one of the golfers commented.

"It is you, isn't it?" shouted a woman. "Please, just one picture?" she pleaded.

Gabrielle looked at Jack and, with a slight shrug of her shoulders, motioned the woman over. Several pictures and autographs followed as the golfers took advantage of having one of the world's most famous models in their midst.

"Sorry about that," Gabrielle apologized once they were in Jack's Range Rover.

"Don't apologize. It was time to leave. You were causing too much of a disturbance."

"Sometimes fame isn't all it's cracked up to be," Gabrielle admitted.

"I'm not talking about the autograph hounds, I'm talking about that dreadful swing of yours. You were kicking up enough wind and dust to qualify as a tornado," Jack teased, patting her thigh. "Feel like doing a little shopping?"

Jack left the West Side and headed across town to SoHo, stopping at a trendy boutique on Spring Street. There, waiting for Gabrielle in the dressing room, was a sleek and sexy cocktail dress, hose, and a pair of classic fuck-me high-heeled pumps, all handpicked and paid for by Jack.

"I figured you'd want to change for dinner," he explained, "so I took the liberty of picking something out for you."

Gabrielle emerged from the dressing room wearing the tight red dress with a sheer illusion midsection. The dress traced every curve of her body, leaving nothing to the imagination. It was beautiful and daring, and obviously pleasing to Jack's discerning eye.

"God, you are hot," he exclaimed, proud of his choice of both dress and woman.

"How did you know my size?" she inquired. While this

attention-grabbing outfit was not something she'd pick out for herself, Gabrielle appreciated Jack's effort to surprise her.

"I looked up your particulars in your agency book. Damn, am I a lucky guy or what? I get to walk in with gorgeous you on my arm. Come on, let's get out of here," he said, anxious to show her off.

Jack Hollis was a true believer that clothes didn't make the man—his woman did. He would also be the first to admit that a woman's physical attributes were important to him. Beauty and love were forever interwoven as far as Jack was concerned. He was an artist, after all. He made his living creating aesthetically pleasing designs. He appreciated symmetry and the grace and natural flow of pretty things. How could he not be attracted to and desire a beautiful woman?

They headed over to The Niche, one of several trendy, high-profile restaurants in Manhattan where celebrities and wannabe celebrities often gathered to nourish their bodies and egos. They were stopped just as they were about to enter by a photographer who asked to take their picture. Jack happily obliged by pulling Gabrielle close and smiling broadly for the camera.

Jack had requested one of the tables in the center of the room, a table reserved by people who wanted to be noticed. The couple sat talking and munching on appetizers until they were interrupted by yet another fan requesting an autograph.

Gabrielle looked at Jack, her eyes filled with apology. "Go on," he prompted her with a smile. He didn't mind the intrusion at all; in fact, he rather enjoyed it. In no way did Jack feel slighted or emasculated by her celebrity. He felt just the opposite. To have a supermodel like Gabrielle

Donovan on his arm obviously meant that he must be at the top of *his* game.

Gabrielle quickly signed the man's napkin and sent him away happy. She turned her attention back to Jack, who was smiling broadly. "Why are you smiling?"

"Because I like the way you handle yourself with your fans."

"And I like the way you handle all these interruptions," she observed. "Most men don't really understand this part of it—you know, the autographs, the gossip," Gabrielle told him.

"I hope you know by now that I'm not most men."

"That is becoming increasingly clear," Gabrielle said, giving Jack a flash of the famous Donovan smile.

Jack leaned into the table and kissed her boldly, ignoring the public attention they were drawing. Gabrielle slowly pulled away, embarrassed but fully aware of the delicious urges her body was experiencing. There was an undeniable physical attraction between the two of them. It was a sensual pull that ached to be satisfied.

"I think it's time to leave," Jack announced.

The drive back to Gabrielle's was full of companionable chatter and laughter, layered over a healthy undercurrent of sexual tension. All too soon they found themselves standing in the hallway outside Gabrielle's apartment.

"Are you sure this date is over?" Jack asked, biting his bottom lip in a sexy, impossible-to-say-no-to manner. "How about some coffee?"

"I suppose that's the least I can do," Gabrielle said, smiling as she pushed the door open. "Why don't you put on some music?" she suggested on her way to the kitchen.

Jack smiled at her suggestion. In his mind, the perfect mood music would be "Let's Get It On," by the magnificent Marvin Gaye. Rather than tinker with the nuances of seduction, Marvin Gaye's music was straight and to the point. But tonight was not about bold sexuality, Jack reminded himself as he placed Kenny G on the CD player. Tonight was about romantic discovery, and for that nothing beat the soulful whine of a saxophone. Jack dimmed the chandelier, letting the city lights help set the mood.

Gabrielle returned carrying a tray laden with coffee and almond biscotti.

"Come sit down," Jack requested, patting the sofa cushion next to him. Gabrielle obliged, and Jack put his arm around her, pulling her close. "You are so damn sexy," Jack whispered, turning Gabrielle's face to his. His tongue gently parted her lips and began to explore her warm mouth, while his fingers combed gently through her hair.

Jack began nibbling at her ears and neck. Slowly he pushed her back on the sofa, gracefully positioning the two of them so they were both on their sides, belly to belly. Jack ran his hands over Gabrielle's back, arms, and breasts. Their kisses grew more and more ardent, each of them getting caught up in their bodies' wonderful sensations. Gabrielle could feel Jack's hardness press against her.

Jack took his mouth away long enough to lock his eyes with Gabrielle's as he unzipped Gabrielle's dress and swiftly unhooked her bra, releasing her breasts from their lacy confinement. He took her already stiff nipples into his mouth and tenderly bathed them in his warm saliva. She was not sure which was more powerful, the seductive tug of her nipples moving in and out of his luscious, warm mouth or the blatant sensuality that was smoldering behind those hazel eyes. Gabrielle heard herself moan as the ache in her pelvis intensified.

"Wait," she said huskily as she forced herself to sit up. Gabrielle had not been intimate with another man since Doug, and even though her body desired to be touched and penetrated, she was hesitant to proceed. Shouldn't they spend more time together before becoming intimate? Shouldn't she wait until her heart wanted him as much as her body?

"Yes, baby, what? Tell Jack what you want," he moaned, momentarily waylaid, but confident that his tried-and-true powers of persuasion would succeed.

"It's our first date," she tried to reason lamely.

"So let's make it one to remember," Jack replied, before devouring her lips again. His burning kiss immediately pulled Gabrielle's defenses down. She no longer had the power to resist him. She took his hand and led him back into her room and to her king-size bed. Together they fell on the bed, lost in their unleashed passion.

Quickly they both stripped off their clothes and lay naked on top of the covers. Jack devoured her, his mouth and hands moving wildly over the length of her body. He placed his finger inside Gabrielle and, feeling her wet lust, put on a condom and climbed on top of her. "I want to fuck you so bad," he told her. "Tell me you want me in your pussy, too," he moaned.

Jack's crude language both annoyed and excited her. She'd grown accustomed to Doug's loving words and gestures. Never had he spoken to her in such graphic sexual terms. But this was not Doug. This was Jack, and his raw passion and vocal intercourse gave their coupling an energetic, slightly pornographic tilt. Gabrielle found herself responding to Jack more with her body and less with her emotions. This was not about her love life. This was about her sex life. This was about releasing inhibitions and satisfying the hunger that had burned in her body for months.

"Yes. I want you," she told him. Her body believing her mouth, she pushed her hips closer to his. Hearing her words, Jack quickly penetrated her, and together their bodies found a mutually satisfying rhythm. They rocked back and forth, loudly expressing their pleasure. Gabrielle found herself letting go and focusing on the delightful friction the joining of their bodies created. It wasn't long until she exploded into orgasm, accompanied by a low, lusty wail.

"Oh, fuck yeah, baby," he moaned. As the words left his mouth, Jack's body went taut as he came with a powerful orgasm that seemed to go forever. He collapsed on top of Gabrielle and then rolled over, his breath still short. "Oh, my God, that was fantastic," he said. "It was like sitting in a Lamborghini and going straight from first to fifth gear before blasting off."

"Do you always describe your orgasms?" Gabrielle asked, amused by Jack's analogy.

"I guess so, though I never really thought about it," Jack explained, reaching for his pants and pulling out a pack of Marlboros. "Do you mind?"

"I didn't know you smoked."

"Only when I'm really stressed and after great sex."

"Are you telling me you're stressed out?" she teased.

"What do you think?" he asked, confident that Gabrielle was just as satisfied as he. Jack prided himself on being a skilled and imaginative lover.

"How about lighting up out on the terrace?"

"Fair enough," Jack said as he pulled on his pants. He gave Gabrielle a quick kiss and then walked outside to smoke. Gabrielle stretched out and tried to sort through her feelings. As proud of herself as she was for taking this final step away from Doug, she couldn't help comparing her new lover to her old. The two were such totally different men. Jack Hollis was tall, sexy, and handsome. He pursued her with outrageous flattery and coy flirtation. Doug was an all-American intellectual who, much more timid in his approach, had captured her heart and mind with intimate talks and quiet laughter. Jack was unpredictable, exciting, and fun-loving, while Doug was as comfortable and dependable as a rumpled bed at the end of a long day.

Her attraction to the advertiser encompassed much more than just the man. Jack made her feel grown up and womanly. He kept her wired and tense—an edginess brought on by the new sensation of pure sexual desire. He was an energetic and lustful lover, and what he lacked in romantic soulfulness he made up for in erotic excitement. Doug was warm, and smooth, and loving. He made her feel safe, protected, cherished.

Gabrielle had loved Doug with everything she knew how to give, and in return he had broken her heart. And though she had just made love to Jack, she knew she wasn't in love with him. But that fact, instead of pulling her away, made Jack all the more attractive and Gabrielle all the more interested.

38

"What a bitch!" Stephanie shouted as she hung up the phone. "She claims she can't meet with me because she has a shoot with Miguel, but I know she's just trying to avoid talking about the book."

"Forget about her," Howie Joseph suggested. "Why don't you blow off work for the rest of the day and stay home? I'm going to develop this latest roll."

"I hope you got some good stuff."

"We'll see. Yesterday was mostly your regular date stuff. The guy she was with looks familiar. I know I've seen him before, but I can't place him."

"Probably some equally stupid male model," Stephanie commented sarcastically.

"I get the distinct impression that you don't like this girl," Howie said.

"I don't like ingrates, especially those who reach the top and then forget the people who got them there. People like that deserve to fall from grace with a nice loud thud."

"And maybe a handprint on their back?"

"You only get what you have coming."

"Remind me to stay on your good side."

"You'd be smart to do so," Stephanie replied tersely. "Now, let's see what poor sap she's suckered into her life this time."

"I don't fucking believe this!" Stephanie screamed at the top of her lungs. She picked up her beer and flung it across the room. The glass bottle hit the wall and shattered into pieces. Having momentarily vented her anger, Stephanie cleared the coffee table and laid the pictures side by side. One by one, she picked up the black-and-white photos of Jack and Gabrielle and began to inspect them. From Jack grinning like a fool as Gabrielle swung a golf club to the two of them mugging for the camera in front of The Niche, Howie's camera had chronicled what appeared to be the perfect date.

Stephanie didn't know what irked her more, the fact that they looked like such the happy twosome—smiling, teasing, obviously enjoying each other—or the sad realization that in all the time she'd dated Jack, they'd never done "couple" things together like this, and never had Jack looked at her the way he was looking at Gabrielle—with eyes full of admiration and pride.

Since their breakup Stephanie had tried, with little success, to accept the fact that she and Jack would never be a couple again. Each time his name was linked with a beautiful model or starlet, the news would tug at her heart until the story of *their* breakup was circulated. She then would go on about her life, holding her breath until the next time. But Jack's apparent relationship with Gabrielle was simply too much to take.

"You two won't get away with this," Stephanie hissed at their images. "Step aside, you two backstabbing fucks, and watch me work."

* * *

Jack slipped quietly into the studio. Miguel was working, and he didn't want to break the photographer's concentration. Miguel was standing on the top of a three-rung stepladder, shooting down into a large white bathtub. Jack edged his way in closer to the action. Inside the tub, Gabrielle lay on her back, immersed in water. Her arms were tucked under her head, lifting it up and out of the water. Gabrielle's bronze mane, streaked with gold, was fanned out above her body. The studio lights reflected off the water, making her hair look as if it were strewn with tiny diamonds. Except for a gold G-string, Gabrielle's body was naked and completely painted gold. She was the personification of the world's most precious metal.

"Okay, I think we've got it," Miguel said, putting down his camera.

"Thank goodness. Any longer and they'll be calling this the golden prune shot," Gabrielle joked as she stepped out of the tub into a waiting bathrobe. "You're going to have to airbrush out at least a thousand wrinkles."

"It was worth it. You look fabulous. This calendar is going to be a knockout." Miguel felt just as excited as he sounded. Gabrielle fueled Miguel's imagination. The work they did together was magic and could be considered nothing less than art.

"You can put me down for one."

"Jack! How long have you been here?" Gabrielle asked.

"Long enough to see you at work. I'm impressed."

"I'm going to get cleaned up and into some dry clothes before I catch pneumonia," she said, leaving the two men to chat while she dressed.

"We have to dash," she announced fifteen minutes later. "I have to pop by First Face to autograph some swimsuits for the Pediatric AIDS Foundation's charity auction."

"See you later, baby," Mig said, giving Gabrielle a hug

and kiss. "Once the slides are developed, I'll give you a call so we can start choosing the best shots."

Jack and Gabrielle walked arm in arm out of the studio and into the dusk. They'd walked only a few steps when Jack stopped, grabbed Gabrielle up in his arms, and kissed her hungrily.

"Wow! What was that for?"

"I can't tell you how turned on I got seeing you painted up like that. You looked so incredibly sexy."

"I guess that shot goes in the calendar."

"Well, even if it doesn't, it's planted in my memory forever. You are extraordinary. How can someone so beautiful be real?"

"But I am real. All this other stuff is just hype. I'm not like the pictures you see," Gabrielle told him as he attempted to flag down a cab.

"Oh, I definitely like the real thing much better," he said, kissing her again.

Once Jack and Gabrielle were inside the taxi and on their way, Stephanie stepped out of a doorway across the street and headed for the subway. Several passersby stared at the tears streaming down her cheeks but opted to say nothing. Stephanie continued walking, too miserable to care.

39

Don't forget you're doing 'Nightline' tomorrow," Felicia told Lexis as they snuggled together before getting up to start their day. Since she'd filed for divorce, she and Lexis had been together constantly, though discreetly, not wanting to give Trace any fuel for the divorce proceeding.

"On what topic am I supposed to be representing the entire black race this time?" Lexis asked with a sleepy yawn.

"'Hollywood and History: Telling the Complete Story.'"

"I don't think Ted Koppel wants me to get started on that subject."

"It will be great publicity for *Praline Livin'*," Felicia pointed out.

"We're still on for tonight's premiere?"

"Definitely. I'll meet you at the theater. So, are you nervous?"

"Should I be?"

"Yes. Releasing a film during the Christmas season is a big deal. If the trades are any indication, you're in for some major success. That certainly would make *me* nervous."

"You really think it's that good?"

"Better, though I still think you should have done a love story."

"I told you, romantic flicks aren't my thing. The only love story I want to direct is happening right here," Lexis said, gently pushing the tip of her nose.

"I must admit, it's a story you tell very well," Felicia said as she kissed him on the lips before rising.

"Wait. Don't go yet. I have a proposal for you."

Felicia sat up and looked at him. He couldn't possibly be thinking about marriage; she wasn't even divorced yet. Even if she were, Felicia wasn't ready for a step like that.

"Don't worry, it's not that kind of proposal," he said, once again sensing her thoughts. "It's business."

"What kind of business?"

"I've been rapping with MarMa pictures about going into a limited partnership with a select group of black investors to create a small but funky movie studio called Sepia Films. My company would be one of its mainstays, but we'd bring in other black producers and directors. MarMa would kick in some venture capital and act as our distributor. Of course, they'd be gettin' a reasonable chunk of the profits."

"What a great idea!"

"We'll be able to green-light our own projects and tell our stories the way they should be told, not the way we're *told* they should be told."

"And every story about black people won't have to involve drugs, gangs, guns, or silly sidekicks?" Felicia said.

"And the brother wouldn't be the first to die in every movie."

"I think you're onto something," she said, laughing.

"Damn right I am."

"Why haven't you mentioned this before tonight? How could you keep news this exciting to yourself?"

"I wanted to get everything nailed down before I told

you. Felicia, if this thing works out the way I think it will, I want you with me all the way. I want you to head up all the publicity and marketing. Of course, you'll own a piece of the action as well."

"This is all very exciting, but I already own a company."

"I know, baby, but think about it. You'd be making history with the first *black-owned* film studio. Plus, you could beat that dog husband of yours by simply closing the doors of WJ and A and starting fresh. Lois and practically everybody you have working for you could come along."

"My company is a black-owned firm, with a damn good reputation of its own."

"I know, but instead of helping white folks make more money, you'd be concentrating on helping your own people."

"I'd like to think by successfully managing all my clients—black and white—I am helping my people," Felicia said, getting annoyed.

"Felicia, I really want you to be a part of this. We'd be working together all the time, bringing our vision to the world."

"Why can't you simply contract your work out to WJ and A?"

"Because we'd need your full-time attention. Getting this off the ground is going to be too intense for us to be just another client."

"Let's not get ahead of ourselves. Let's see how the deal shakes out."

"I swear it's gonna happen. Just think about it. You'll be able to meet all the MarMa bigwigs at the premiere party tonight after the screening."

"I'll be there, and I promise to give your proposal some thought, but not now. I have to get to my office," Felicia told him. Lexis's proposition was intriguing. The idea of being an integral part of such an exciting and historic business venture was tempting, and, as Lexis pointed out, it would be a fine kick in the teeth for Trace.

Then why do I feel like I'm being controlled again? Whether it was his intent or not, Lexis sounded suspiciously like Trace, not taking her business seriously and certainly not respecting the amount of work she'd put into it to make it a successful firm.

But Lexis isn't Trace, she reminded herself. Lexis didn't want her to shut down the business so she could stay at home and tend to his every whim. He wanted to use her expertise and professional acumen to further his dream. But whatever the reason, wasn't that just as selfish?

"Another great idea, Felicia," Peter Montell declared.

"Thanks, Peter. Once you—"

"Excuse me, Ms. Wilcot, Lois Jourdan from your office is on the phone," Peter's secretary interrupted. "She says it's urgent." The word immediately got Felicia's adrenaline pumping.

"Lois, what's wrong?" Felicia asked.

"Don't freak out or anything, but it's Trace. His office has called several times wanting to know if you know where he is. Apparently he didn't show up for work yesterday or today. And there's no answer at his apartment."

"That's strange."

"Could he be traveling?"

"Not without letting his office know. Trace doesn't do things like that. I'm going home. If they call again, tell them they can reach me at the apartment in fifteen minutes."

"Trouble?" Peter Montell asked, seeing the concern on Felicia's face.

"I hope not, but I have to run. I'll wait to hear from you. Thanks, Peter."

Felicia rushed back to her apartment and immediately called Trace's office to get a firsthand account of the situation. His secretary filled her in, revealing that Trace had not been seen or heard from in two days. Felicia promised to call around to friends and family and let Trace's secretary know whatever she found out.

After phoning several of their friends and his tennis club to no avail, Felicia called the hospitals in the area. She was relieved to learn that Trace had not been admitted. Finally she dialed the police precinct near his apartment, only to learn that her estranged husband had been arrested for allegedly robbing a cabdriver and had been sitting in a jail cell the last two days.

Felicia hurried down to the precinct and took the officer in charge to task. Twenty minutes later, after she'd finally convinced him of the officer's blunder, Trace was released with a halfhearted apology, and Felicia ushered her somber and humiliated husband out of the police station and back to their former home in Brooklyn Heights. They rode in silent outrage, each trying to grasp the reality of what had just happened. It wasn't until they were safely within the privacy of the brownstone that they began to discuss the situation.

"What happened?"

"I was on my way to the corner deli when a police car rode up beside me and told me to stop. The two officers got out and asked me for some ID. I didn't have any. When I tried to get them to tell me what I'd been stopped for, they told me to shut up and turn around so they could frisk me. When I refused, they threw me up against the car, handcuffed me, and took me down to the station."

"Why on earth would they think you tried to rob a taxi driver?" Felicia asked.

"Because I fit the description—a five-foot-seven-inch black man with a beard, wearing a black-leather jacket," Trace said angrily.

"Trace, you're over six feet, clean-shaven, and your jacket is brown."

"That obviously didn't matter."

"This is too ludicrous to believe. Didn't you tell them who you were?"

"I tried to explain the situation, but they somehow found it difficult to believe that this 'boy' could actually be a lawyer."

"Why didn't you call somebody? Everyone was worried sick."

"I was too embarrassed to call my office, so I tried to call my cousin Stan at home, but he wasn't there. Apparently the NYPD is as serious about that one phone call as they are about staking out Dunkin' Donuts," Trace explained with dry sarcasm. "Since I had no identification, they weren't about to let me go. I guess they thought they were doing their duty, getting another perpetrator off the street."

"This is all so frightening. If an educated, articulate, reasonable man like you gets treated like this, what do they do to the other folks?"

"Just about every man in that jail was black or Hispanic. How many were there on bogus charges like me?"

"This has got to stop. It happens too often and with no repercussions. Like when Harris got stopped and questioned for window-shopping on Madison Avenue, or when the police stopped Cliff and harassed him for walking 'funny.' Since when is it a crime to have a limp in New York City?"

"The irony of the situation is that those guys are two of the most successful traders on Wall Street. They're both brilliant and both can buy and sell the average policeman six, seven times over, but they still can't walk down the street minding their own business without being hassled," Trace added furiously.

"And people wonder why black men are so angry."

"You know, I never thought anything like this could happen to me. I did everything I was supposed to do," Trace said, his voice full of hurt and confusion. "I went to the right schools, read the right books, played the right sports, but that wasn't enough. Underneath the suit and tie, the fat investment portfolio, and the Ivy League education, I'm still just a common thug to these people," he said in a voice that, in all their years together, Felicia had never heard. His words resonated with the hurt and anger of a man who'd been robbed of his ego, his self-respect, his dignity. Felicia watched as the mighty, cocksure man she knew as Trace Gordon disappeared. Only the physical remnants of the man remained. It was a sight that broke Felicia's heart.

Seeing him crumble before her left Felicia with only one course of action. She took Trace into her arms and held on for dear life. Any dissonance between them was replaced with the empathy and understanding that only two people who have shared a considerable part of their lives together could share.

"Those cops accomplished in forty-eight hours what nobody has done in the almost forty years I've been alive. I was humiliated to the point that for the first time in my life I felt like a nigger," Trace said after a long silence.

"It seems that when some people think we're getting too big for our britches, they feel the need to knock us back down to size."

"So they held me in that piss-hole just to put an uppity nigger in his place? That's insane," Trace responded angrily.

"I guess now you understand that racism is still a reality of this world." Felicia was encouraged to hear some of the fire return to his voice.

"You talk like I don't know that racism exists."

"On the surface you do. You feel it in the subtle slights you receive from women who clutch their handbags when you walk by or security guards who follow you around stores for no apparent reason—"

"Or when an associate in the firm where you're a partner demands to see your ID because you're wearing workout gear instead of a suit," Trace interrupted.

"Or having some woman with collagen-enhanced lips and a frizzy perm tell you that you're really pretty for a *black* woman. Those kind of things you hear so often you don't even feel outraged anymore."

"I think you could safely say that I've had my share of racist experiences."

"You have, but for the most part we don't feel racism like most black folks do. We were raised in a world where money and power kept the bigots at bay. We ceased being black in the eyes of most white people the minute they determined that we didn't live in a certain place or speak in a certain way, or that we could stand as their intellectual and social equals—"

"Or superiors. Those cops knew that I wasn't some petty thief. They kept me in that cage because I was something much worse—an educated black man who had the nerve to be more successful than they were."

"I guess at sometime in our life we all get the wake-up call."

"Wake up to what? To the inane idea that despite the fact that I bust my ass every day of my life to make sure I live a life that counts for something, I shouldn't be *too* successful because I'm black?"

"No, wake up to the fact that white people control the game because they make the rules."

"I don't know if I can play the game anymore. Two days

ago I walked out of my house a man, confident that I could conquer the world. Today I left that jail feeling like a fucking eunuch," Trace said wearily.

"You're not a eunuch. You're a strong, virile black man who will not allow the life to be sucked out of him by some billy-club-wielding jackass wearing a badge. You did nothing wrong, they did. Once you've had time to sort this thing through, you might want to make that point to the NYPD in a big way. Being the fabulous lawyer you are, I'm sure they'll get the message loud and clear."

"Feli, I can't do this alone. I need you. Will you stay here with me, tonight?" Trace pleaded, trying to contain his tears.

"Of course I will," Felicia said. Seeing Trace hurt like this tugged at her heart and made it impossible to say no. "Why don't you get out of those clothes and take a shower. I'll fix you some hot tea and cook dinner. You must be hungry."

"Thank you," Trace said, staring deep into Felicia's eyes. "I have been such a fool," he said sadly, resting his head momentarily on her shoulder before trudging heavily down the hallway to the bathroom.

Felicia headed to the kitchen to make dinner. When she put the chicken in the microwave to defrost, the digital clock on the oven caught her eye. It was 8:57. She'd completely forgotten Lexis's premiere. She picked up the phone and dialed his beeper number. Within three minutes the phone rang.

"What the hell happened to you?" Lexis screamed into Felicia's ear. His anger began to dissipate as he listened to her explanation. "Man, that's some sorry shit. I feel for the brother."

"How did it go?"

"We turned it out, baby. Too bad you had to miss it.

Why don't you come on over to the party? It's just getting started."

"I can't, Lexis. I'm here with Trace. I told him I would spend the night."

"You what!"

"He's pretty upset. I couldn't let him be alone."

"Sure he's torn up now, but give him a couple of days and he'll be right back to the same punk who was trying to snatch your company. I can't believe you're letting him play you like this."

"He's not playing me, but I do owe him."

"Why?"

"Because this was the man I made a home with for almost ten years. Tonight he had the scare of his life, and I refuse to let him go through it alone."

"Maybe it's about time he realized that he can't hide behind his Harvard degree and his house in the Hamptons forever. Maybe what Trace got was what he needed—a kick in the ass to wake him up to the fact that he's a black man livin' in a world where he ain't liked and ain't wanted, despite his extensive knowledge of fine wines."

"I think he learned that lesson the hard way, which is exactly why he needs me. Trace's entire world is falling apart. I can't just turn him away."

"I'm tryin' not to hear this, Felicia."

"And I'm trying not to argue about it. I'm sorry I missed the premiere, but this is an extenuating circumstance that could not be avoided."

"Well, I need you, too, so you make the choice. It's either him or me."

"This isn't necessary, Lexis, but if you can't understand that—"

"Understand what? That you can't let go of the man who's been controlling your life for years?"

"I'm not holding on to Trace. I'm just helping him through this rough spot," Felicia tried to explain.

"This is the kind of thing that brings people together. You were in the process of emotionally distancing yourself from him and now—*bam!*—you're right back in the mix. I can't wait forever, Felicia. I won't."

Felicia heard the sound of the dial tone singing in her ear before she could open her mouth to respond. She hoped like hell that Lexis was wrong about her getting emotionally caught up again with Trace, but she was also afraid he might be right.

40

Hi, Doug. This is Zoe. You don't know me, but I'm a friend of Gabrielle Donovan. We work together."

Doug's ears and heart perked up at the mention of Gabrielle's name. "Yes?"

"I'm calling because I'm very worried about her."

"Why? What's wrong?" Doug asked, concern coloring his voice.

"This is a delicate situation, since you two no longer date," the woman began.

"Just come out with it," Doug said impatiently. If something was wrong, he wanted to know without going through all this hemming and hawing.

"Ever since Gabrielle's been seeing Jack Hollis, she's really changed. She's out partying all the time, showing up late for bookings, short-tempered and difficult to work with. The word is that Gabrielle's doing drugs and boozing it up pretty good."

This news crushed Doug. He would never have dreamed that the Gabrielle he knew and still loved would get caught up in alcohol and drugs. She knew damn well that substance abuse was the quickest way to ruin her career.

"Does Greg von Ulrich know this?" he asked. Saying Greg's name aloud was painful. Doug had realized long ago what a fool he'd been to suspect Gabrielle of sleeping with him.

"To be honest, I don't know."

"I find it hard to believe that Greg von Ulrich would ignore any talk about his top model using drugs."

"If you don't believe me, you can see for yourself. They'll be at the MarMa party tonight at Nell's."

"I don't know what I can do to help. As you said before, Gabrielle and I are no longer a part of each other's lives."

"You're right. I'm sorry. There's just one other thing—"

"Yes."

"I think he might be hitting her. I don't know it for a fact, I just know she's had some weird bruises lately. I thought you'd want to know," the caller said and hung up.

Doug sat in silence, holding the phone as the dial tone turned into a recording telling him to hang up and dial again. The thought of Gabrielle caught up in the seamy side of stardom disturbed him greatly. Was he to blame? Was Beatrice right? Had the pain he caused Gabrielle by his foolish mistake driven her to hanging out with some abusive, lowlife playboy, doing drugs and flushing her professional integrity down the toilet? Blame or no blame, he couldn't let this continue.

Stephanie sat holding the picture of Jack and Gabrielle, smiling like a fool. It had been a stroke of genius to pretend to be a model and lay that bogus story on Doug. She could tell from the moment she mentioned Gabrielle's name that he was still stuck on her. She wasn't quite sure if Doug had bought the drugs-and-booze story, which is why she'd added the business about the bruises. It was the perfect touch. She'd bet her next paycheck that Doug would show up at Nell's tonight gunning for Jack. And when he did, Howie would be there to capture the fireworks on film. But this time the news wouldn't stop at her column. Because this was a big party by a major feature-film company, the television cameras would also be rolling, catching any shenanigans between the three on videotape. It was time to spread the wealth. The more newspapers and tabloid programs picked up the news on Gabrielle, the sooner the public would be clamoring for the story behind all these headlines.

"Say good-bye, Gabrielle. Your days as Miss Goody Two-shoes are over. From now on the world is going to see you for what you really are—a selfish, conniving bitch," Stephanie promised as she slowly tore the picture to shreds.

"Isn't there anything we can do to stop this?" Gabrielle asked. She and Jack were in the limo on their way from the *Praline Livin'* screening to the premiere party, when Jack presented her with the latest *Star Diary*. Her calm had quickly turned into anger thanks to another fabricated story by Visa Lee.

"It's really not that bad," Jack said, taking a good look at the pictures that accompanied the article. His eye first fell on the photo of the two of them outside the restaurant. Jack was pleased with the way he looked in the photo—appealing, confident, out on the town with one of the world's most beautiful women. They made a striking twosome. The second picture showed them both smiling, cuddled up at the driving range. "This is a great picture of the two of us," he commented before reading the article to her.

*It appears that the reigning ice princess of the supermodel set, **Gabrielle Donovan**, has suffered a major meltdown. Word has it that she's being squired around town by boy toy and advertising guru **Jack Hollis**, her first public romance since dumping bestselling novelist **Doug Sixsmith** for her boss, **Greg von Ulrich**. According to sources,* *it's too soon to know how far this liaison will go. Mr. Hollis, known for his on-again-off-again romances with any famous woman who will have him, may decide to drop Gabrielle for the next flavor of the month. Stay tuned as this model saga continues.*

"I wouldn't worry about this," Jack told her, happy to see his name in bold ink. "You know it's not true, and the bigger a stink you make about it, the bigger a deal it becomes."

"It is a big deal when people I care about get hurt."

"Look, I don't know or care what happened in the past, but this kind of stuff doesn't bother me at all. It's the price you pay for being a celebrity."

"It's a high price."

"Forget this. What you need to do is go to the MarMa party and have some fun."

"Wouldn't you rather go home, order Chinese, and watch a good movie instead?"

"No way. *Everybody's* going to be there. You should, too."

"Give me one good reason why."

"A little thing called your acting career, maybe."

"Why is everyone trying to make me into an actress? I'm a model—and a damn good one." Gabrielle had not told Jack of the requests she'd turned down from several directors to appear in their movies. The idea of acting for a living was still far too intimidating for her to consider seriously.

"Acting is a natural transition from modeling. Look at Isabella Rossellini, Cybill Shepherd, Andie MacDowell," Jack pointed out.

"Good for them, but I'm still not sure it's what I want."

"Still, being in the loop can only help if you eventually decide that it is. You gotta keep your options open, Beauty."

"Okay, you win. I'll go, but only because you want me to."

"Well, if you're into pleasing me, I have one more request," Jack said as he smothered Gabrielle with a wet and sexy kiss. She just had enough time to repair her makeup before the limo pulled up in front of Nell's.

"You look sexy as fuck. I don't know how I'm going to be able to keep my hands off you," Jack whispered in her ear as the paparazzi's cameras flashed. Gabrielle was wearing the dress Jack picked out for her—a ten-thousand-dollar Ralph Lauren design. The pewter-colored gown, covered in beads that twinkled like diamonds, was nearly transparent and draped low under the arms, allowing a revealing side peek at her breasts.

"You're sure this dress isn't a little much? Or maybe not enough?"

"No way. It's memorable. You want to stand out in this crowd. Look what that little leather-and-safety-pin Versace number did for Elizabeth Hurley's career," Jack told her as their names were checked off the guest list and they walked through the crowd and into the party. Sprinkled among the two hundred or so people were well-known actors, models, and rock stars. They all stood milling around the club, drinking, talking, seeing, and being seen. Jack proudly piloted Gabrielle over to the bar.

"What would you like to drink?" he asked.

"My usual."

Jack ordered Gabrielle's ginger ale with a twist of lime and a sidecar for himself. They carried their drinks back into the center of the room and were soon joined by Lois Jourdan and Lexis Richards.

"Happy holidays. Enjoying the party?" Lois asked.

"We just got here," Gabrielle said.

"So did we."

"Lois Jourdan and Lexis Richards, this is Jack Hollis."

"I like your work. I thought *Praline Livin'* was phenomenal," Jack remarked.

"Thanks for the props," Lexis said.

"Where's Felicia?" Gabrielle asked.

"She was otherwise occupied," Lexis explained, the tightness in his voice obvious.

"Gabrielle, Lexis has been talking my ear off about you. He thinks you'd be perfect in his next movie," Lois said, getting away from the subject of Felicia. "I keep telling him that since you've already turned down Penny Marshall and Martin Scorsese, he's going to have to do some fancy talking."

"And I keep telling her that you're a born actress and I'm just the director to bring out your hidden talents," Lexis responded. "I mean, I'm not trying to dis Penny or Marty, but they obviously didn't have the right vehicle. I think I do."

"I didn't realize you'd turned down parts in those movies," Jack commented, surprise all over his face. "Why?"

"Like Lexis said, they weren't the right parts."

"I'm still working on the treatment, but I'd love for you to do a screen test when the script is finished," Lexis said.

"I'll think about it," Gabrielle said, unwilling to commit to anything.

"Bet. I'll be in touch," Lexis promised as he and Lois headed off to chat with actor Samuel L. Jackson and the president of MarMa.

"I can't believe you turned down the chance to work with two such *huge* directors," Jack said. "They make hit films. They could have made you into a movie star."

"Eva, over here," Gabrielle called out to her friend, ignoring Jack's comment. She had no desire to try to explain her reasons for ignoring the movie industry's invitations into their exclusive club.

Within seconds Jack and Gabrielle were joined by model Eva G. and her date, Pic, the bass player for the rock group 8-Track. Pic had an incredible sense of humor and kept them all laughing hysterically over his stories of life on and off the road. Gabrielle was grateful for the entertainment, as it kept Jack from pressing her further about her nonexistent acting career.

"What's your name again?" asked the burly man at the door.

"Doug Sixsmith. I was invited tonight, but I RSVP'ed my regrets. Well, I changed my mind."

"Oh, yeah, you're that writer guy. Go on in," the bouncer said, parting the velvet rope that separated the stars from the stargazers.

Doug hurried into the club and immediately began to look for Gabrielle. After his initial pan of the room, he was certain that he would not find her. This party was the epitome of everything Gabrielle detested about the celebrity side of her business. The room was full of women sheathed in tight, attention-grabbing dresses and men in their casual yet carefully constructed power fashions. Gabrielle hated these phony types who were ever ready to flash their insincere smiles and recite their padded résumés.

He was about to leave, satisfied that the mysterious phone call was a gross exaggeration, when he spotted Gabrielle standing with Eva G., some skeezy-looking guy in leather jeans, and a man whom he presumed to be Jack Hollis. They were all hunched over and laughing hysterically. Immediately his heart skipped a beat. Despite the fact that she was dressed like an expensive call girl, Gabrielle was still the most exquisite woman he'd ever laid eyes on.

Doug winced slightly as he saw Jack speak to Gabrielle, his words prompting her to quickly drain her drink and hand him her empty glass. His eyes continued to watch as Jack handed Gabrielle his drink, from which she took a healthy swig, made a face, and broke into laughter. Doug clenched his teeth as Jack indiscreetly rubbed Gabrielle's behind and then headed off toward the crowded bar.

Doug was astounded. In all his time with Gabrielle, he'd never seen her even finish an entire drink, let alone gulp one down and grab another. From the drinking to her dress, Gabrielle had changed. The caller was right to call him. Jack Hollis had corrupted Gabrielle and was leading her down the path to disaster. Doug had to talk some sense into her. He only hoped she would listen.

"Good evening," he said, sauntering up to the group. "Gabrielle, Eva, it's nice to see you again."

"I remember your face," Eva said, "but I forgot your name."

"Doug Sixsmith."

"That's right. You're Gabrielle's friend, the writer. This is Pic," Eva said, introducing her date.

"Nice to meet you."

"Hey, dude, how's it going?"

Gabrielle, shocked to see Doug, found herself quickly draining the rest of Jack's drink. She coughed slightly as the alcohol spilled down her throat. What was Doug doing here? This was the last place she'd ever expect to find him. He hated these stupid parties as much as she did.

"Gabrielle, how are you?" Doug asked.

"What are *you* doing here?" she asked, sounding much more abrupt than she intended.

Doug felt himself bristle at her inhospitable tone of voice. "I was invited. MarMa bought the film rights to my novel."

"How nice. A bestseller and a movie. I guess nothing slows you down, does it?" she said with sarcasm.

"Working keeps my mind off other things. Have you read it?"

"No, I've been busy," Gabrielle answered sharply. She couldn't believe that Doug was taunting her like this in public. He'd read her letter. He knew damn well she couldn't read his book, even if she wanted to.

"Well, maybe you'll get around to it," Doug said, disappointed that, just as she had promised she would in her note, Gabrielle had totally written him out of her life.

"Don't count on it," she said nastily.

"Excuse us, Pic and Eva, I'd like to speak to Gabrielle for a moment," Doug said as he took Gabrielle's arm and led her to a quieter corner of the room. Unaccustomed to the rush of alcohol through her system, she stumbled slightly.

"You're drunk," he accused.

"I am not drunk. I had one drink."

"I just saw you drain your glass and send your boyfriend off to get you another, a request he was all too eager to oblige, I might add."

"It was ginger ale."

"I can smell the alcohol on your breath. Then you finished off a second drink while I was standing right in front of you. Who knows how many you had before I got here?"

"That was Jack's, and I drank it because I was shocked to see you," Gabrielle explained, speaking slowly. "I haven't had anything else all night, but even if I did, it's okay. I'm over twenty-one. You of all people should know that."

Doug ignored her reference to her disastrous birthday. "Gabrielle, what's happened to you? You've changed. Look at the way you're dressed. The Gabrielle I knew might wear something like that on the runway, but not out in public. Hell, the woman I knew wouldn't even be here tonight."

"You don't know me at all, remember?" Gabrielle said fiercely, repeating the same words he'd used.

"Obviously something is very wrong," Doug said. "I've heard about the changes in your behavior—late for work, temper tantrums. I've even heard talk of your using drugs. You never used to act like this. At least not when you were with me."

"But I'm not with *you* anymore, am I? And where are you getting this crap from anyway?"

"I have my sources."

"Oh, what, *Star Diary*? I forgot, that's where you get all your news. Well, once again you've been misinformed. I didn't drink or do drugs then, and I don't now. And as far as what I wear when I go out, don't worry about it. You don't have to be seen in public with me anymore," she said angrily and started to walk away.

Doug grabbed her arm and pulled her back to him. Aware of the photographers' flashbulbs going off, he tried to lead her downstairs near the restrooms. "Don't walk away from me. We need to talk."

"I think we talked enough the *first* time you accused me of something you'd read in a tabloid."

"I'm sorry about that. I should have known better. I wanted to apologize, but your letter—"

"You read what I had to say and figured once a liar always a liar," she interrupted.

"Please, can't we go somewhere and discuss this?"

"It's a little late for that now. I'd appreciate it, though, if you could keep what I told you to yourself."

"Why would I want anybody to know? I do have some pride."

"I guess the revelation would be a huge source of embarrassment to you, wouldn't it? Hanging out with a *dumb* model was bad enough, but something like this would really tarnish your esteemed intellectual reputation," Gabrielle said bitterly, misunderstanding his comment. At least she knew that while he was ashamed and unwilling to share his life with her, Doug was obviously amenable to keeping her secret.

"I'm sorry, I didn't mean that," Doug said. "If you remember, in the letter I—"

"Let's just drop this. I've moved on. Why don't you?"

"I see who you've moved on to. Hollis is totally wrong for you. I've checked him out, He's nothing but a trophy collector, and you're his latest acquisition."

"As usual, you've got it all wrong. I'm the one with the prize," she retorted. Gabrielle was well aware of Jack's reputation and the fact that he enjoyed being seen in public with her. She also knew that he treated her with the utmost respect and that when they were together he made her feel as if she were the only woman in the room.

"What the hell is going on here?" Jack interrupted. "I've been looking all over for you," he told Gabrielle, handing her a glass of ginger ale.

"This is between me and Gabrielle. Mind your own business," Doug told him.

"Gabrielle *is* my business," Jack declared.

"Jack, let's just go," Gabrielle pleaded, seeing that they were drawing a crowd.

"You'll never be happy with him, Gabrielle," Doug warned.

"Man, take another look. Surely you can see that this beautiful lady is not only happy but totally *satisfied*."

"Would you please quiet down," Gabrielle interjected again.

"You son of a bitch," Doug said and took a swing, his right fist connecting with the left side of Jack's jaw. The blow caused Jack to momentarily reel backward. Regaining his composure, he came straight at Doug with a left hook to his right eye. The two scuffled, while the television cameras from "Entertainment Tonight," "Extra," and "Inside Edition" recorded every last punch. Howie happily stood by catching all the action frame by frame. He was going to make a bundle on this stuff. As part of Stephanie's plan, he would sell several of these pictures to magazines and tabloids across the country and around the world, saving the very best, of course, for *Star Diary*.

"Stop it, both of you!" Gabrielle screamed. As security guards and others rushed to the scene, Gabrielle, frustrated, embarrassed, and completely disgusted, tossed her drink on the two men and walked out of the club. They could tear each other to shreds as far as she was concerned.

"I come bearing dinner and a thousand apologies," Jack said as Gabrielle let him into the apartment. Despite the fact that it was already dark outside, he was wearing large sunglasses to hide the ugly bruises on his face from last night's sparring match. He was also carrying an armful of newspapers and a brown paper bag containing several cartons of Chinese food. "Am I forgiven?" he asked meekly.

"I suppose so," she said, returning to her jigsaw puzzle.

"Good," he said kissing her. "Today's been rough enough."

"Felicia tells me we're all over the place. Every newscast, every paper, and of course every tabloid—print and television—has us featured as their top entertainment story," she said while searching for the top of *Il Duomo*.

"Yeah, see for yourself," Jack said, plopping the newspapers down in front of her.

"Jack, I've never seen you upset over being in the newspaper. What's going on?"

"We lost the Nissan account. The president said he couldn't trust the image of his company with a guy who doesn't care about his own."

"Ouch."

"Ouch is right. I lost a lot of money today. How about you? Any fallout from last night?"

"Well, I haven't heard from any of my endorsement companies yet, but I did get a lot of ribbing at my shoot today, particularly about the photo of me pouring my drink on the two of you," she said.

"Did you see the headline in *Celebrity Watch* that said 'Punch Is Served'? You have to admit it was pretty funny. But the best one was the *Daily News* headline, 'Sucker Punch'" Jack said, causing them both to chuckle.

"I never thought I'd be laughing at something the tabloids wrote about me. All jokes aside, Jack, what got into you last night?"

"I don't know, seeing that guy with his hands on you again—I didn't like it."

"I told you, it's over between Doug and me."

"Maybe for you, but I saw the way he looked at you. He's still in love with you, Gabrielle."

"I doubt that, but even if he is, I don't love him anymore," Gabrielle said, fighting the contradictory emotions her heart was suggesting.

"Prove it. Marry me."

"What?"

"You heard me. Marry me. I love you, Gabrielle," Jack told her, himself amazed by what he'd just said. It was true. The unthinkable had happened. The one thing Jack always vowed he would never do—commit himself to one woman.

Jack's surprise proposal shocked her into silence.

"I think this is where you say, 'I love you, too.'"

"How could you want to marry me now?" she asked, momentarily ignoring his comment. "We've been dating only three months. You don't really know me."

"Yes I do. You're gorgeous, bright, funny, sensitive, and

sexy as hell. I know you're a perfect size six, wear a size-nine shoe, and prefer going barefoot indoors. You can't go to bed without brushing your teeth, and you can't get going in the morning without at least two cups of coffee. I also know that your hair smells like wildflowers after you shower and that you make the sweetest little sigh right after you come."

"Okay, so you know a few things."

"Ah, but I know a lot more. I know that you really loved that jerk and that he hurt you big time, and now you're scared to get involved in another serious relationship. I know you think this marriage proposal is premature, but I also know that you are the most perfect woman I have ever met, and I'm crazy about you."

"Don't put me up on a pedestal, Jack. I'm the last person who belongs there," Gabrielle told him softly. "I'm nowhere even *close* to being perfect."

"Maybe not, but you're perfect for me," Jack said, pulling her to him. "So tell me yes, Beauty. Say you love me and you'll marry me."

"There's so much I love about you, Jack," Gabrielle admitted softly. "I'm just not sure that I'm *in* love with you."

"That's enough for now—as long as you think you could fall in love with me eventually. Do you?"

Instead of speaking, Gabrielle bathed his face in a sprinkle of kisses. Lip to lip, she and Jack walked into the bedroom and made hungry, aggressive love. Both properly satisfied, they dropped back into the pillows. Jack, too drowsy to smoke his usual cigarette, cuddled up to Gabrielle and settled in for the night. "Think about it. I'm the man you need. I'm the man who can make you happy," he said and drifted off to sleep.

41

Gabrielle untangled herself from Jack's body, put on her bathrobe, and walked quietly out to the living room. It was four o'clock in the morning. She stood at the window, looking down on the city.

Now that she was famous, the early hours before dawn were Gabrielle's favorite time of day. During this time, when all the world was still, she felt momentarily liberated—no longer held captive by her illiteracy. While everyone slept, she had no expectations to fulfill or public image to uphold; she was alone without fear of exposure.

These past few days had been so full of drama. Seeing Doug again after all this time was difficult. Their conversation at Nell's had clearly dashed any secret hope that they would get back together. Doug's words and actions made it apparent that he would never be able to cope with her celebrity and the gossip and speculation that swirled around her public image. Once again Doug had approached her readily believing the lies instead of relying on his personal knowledge of her. Doug really didn't seem to know her at all.

Oh, but he does, Gabrielle reminded herself. In the letter she'd dictated to Beatrice, she had told Doug her entire life story and begged him to forgive the confusion and pain her illiteracy had caused them. Knowing Doug the way she *thought* she did, Gabrielle had expected him to understand. Instead Doug simply dropped her from his life with no further contact.

All this time she hadn't understood why Doug had never acknowledged her confession. The reason became all too clear at Nell's: Loving an illiterate was too much of a burden for an intellectual like Doug. How would it look should the word get out that Doug Sixsmith, award-winning journalist and bestselling author, was involved with a woman who couldn't read a word he wrote?

Jack, on the other hand, wanted to get as close to her as a man could get to a woman. She still couldn't get over Jack's proposal. Standing there in the dark, Gabrielle tried to sort out her emotions toward this man who wanted to marry her.

You don't love Jack, not the way you loved Doug, Gabrielle's heart told her. *True,* she argued back, *but isn't that to be expected?* Doug was her first love. *I may not be in love with Jack, but I do love him,* she argued further. Moreover, Gabrielle respected and truly liked him as a person. And after her bitter experience with Doug, she now trusted friendship much more than love.

Gabrielle stepped away from the window and curled up on the sofa. While combing through the fringe of a throw pillow, she began to seriously consider Jack's proposal.

Why not marry him, Gabrielle asked herself. Jack loved her. He was incredibly handsome, successful, and, most important, he seemed to understand and even embrace her public life. And after all the hell her celebrity had caused between her and Doug, Jack's infatuation with her fame was indeed a blessing. He could make her happy. And she would do her best to return that happiness.

I will marry Jack, she decided. But first Gabrielle

would tell him the truth. She refused to let her illiteracy destroy another relationship.

Gabrielle walked back into her bedroom and crawled under the sheets. Softly she rocked Jack's shoulder until he opened his eyes and rolled over to face her.

"Do you really want to marry me?"

Jack sat up and rubbed his eyes, trying to wake up. "More than ever."

"Then there's something about me you need to know. Jack, I can't read or write very well."

"What? You're dyslexic?"

"It's not that simple—"

"No, it's not that big a deal. I don't care if you don't read or write as well as you'd like. You have so much more going for you, Beauty. Obviously you know enough to become successful at whatever you've wanted to do."

"Except maybe an acting career."

"Is that the reason you turned down those parts and don't want to do the screen test for Lexis Richards?"

"Yes."

"Do you know how many actors and celebrities are dyslexic? Cher, Tom Cruise, Whoopi Goldberg, and Walt Disney—the list goes on and on."

"It doesn't bother you?" Gabrielle inquired, thinking that Jack was telling her the same things her mother had.

"What bothers me is that you would even for a moment consider not marrying me because of it. I'm sure this dyslexia thing has complicated your life in ways I can only imagine, but it's nothing to be ashamed of. So you have a learning disability. Why would I let something so inconsequential stop me from marrying you?"

Gabrielle didn't know how to reply. Jack was determined to blame her illiteracy on dyslexia. *Does it really matter why he thinks I can't read?* she asked herself. The important thing was that he now knew that she was unable to read and he still loved her, which was much more than she could say for Doug. Instead of worrying about his reputation, Jack was worried about losing her.

"So, am I hearing a yes?"

Gabrielle looked deep into Jack's eyes. Here was a man who knew she couldn't read and still wanted her. Here was a man who was offering her the opportunity to live a full life despite her deficiencies. "Yes," she said, tears welling up in her eyes.

Jack swooped her up in his arms and kissed her with great happiness. He was being truthful when he told Gabrielle her dyslexia didn't matter. It was an invisible inconvenience, one that he was sure could be tricky and annoying at times, but one that nobody else needed to know about. As far as Jack could see, Gabrielle's problem would not alter their life together in any discernible manner. "When?"

"How about Christmas Eve?"

"Are you kidding me? That's tomorrow."

"I'd never kid about anything as serious as becoming Mrs. Jack Hollis."

"God, I love the sound of that! But don't you want the big, fancy wedding with all the trimmings?" Jack asked.

"The last thing I want is my wedding to be a media circus. I want a quiet, private ceremony right here at home."

"That's all the convincing I need."

"Let's do it, then. We tell no one, promise?"

"What about Bea?" Jack asked.

"Of course I'd like Beatrice there. I couldn't possibly get married without her. What about you? Will you ask Fritz to be your best man?" Gabrielle asked.

"He's the only man for the job."

"Why don't we surprise them?" Gabrielle suggested. "We'll tell them when and where to show up, but not why."

"I can't wait to see the look on Fritz's face when he realizes I'm actually getting married."

"That's another reason for a small wedding. I don't think I could get married in a church where the groom's side is full of crying women wearing black armbands," Gabrielle teased.

"I was merely marking time, waiting for you," Jack said, kissing her forehead.

"We do have another problem," Gabrielle announced. "I'm scheduled for a major publicity tour to promote my new calendar and video. I'll be on the road for weeks. I don't know when we'll be able to have a honeymoon."

"And I'm headed to Europe next week, so even if you were free, I'm not. But I promise you, Beauty, when we can both get away, we'll take a proper honeymoon."

"Look, the sun is coming up," Gabrielle said, jumping up and rushing out onto the terrace. Jack, wrapped in a sheet, joined her there. Together they stood in awe and watched the sun rise over the city. "It's the start of a beautiful new day," Gabrielle said, reflectively.

"The start of a beautiful new *life*," Jack whispered, taking her in his arms.

Jack and Gabrielle spent a frenzied morning preparing for their wedding. By midday they had contracted a baker and a florist, and Jack had pulled a few strings with a friendly judge, not only to grant them a marriage license and waive the twenty-four-hour waiting period, but to preside over the nuptials as well.

"I'll meet you back here at five-thirty," Jack said as he headed out the door.

Gabrielle walked back into the kitchen, picked up the phone, and dialed Beatrice's number. She'd briefly debated going down and telling her in person, but she decided to call instead, afraid her excitement would give the surprise away. "Good morning," she said when Bea picked up.

"Good morning. What's up?"

"I'm having a little holiday celebration tonight. Can you come?"

"Where's Jack? Aren't you planning to spend Christmas Eve with him?" Beatrice asked.

"He'll be over later."

Beatrice was surprised and pleased that Gabrielle was requesting her company. Gabrielle spent most of her very limited free time with Jack. Even though she lived only one floor away, Beatrice was reluctant to drop in or call, afraid she might be interrupting the two.

"I'd love to. Where and what time should I meet you?"

"Here at six o'clock."

"Sounds good. What should I wear?"

"Anything that makes you feel pretty. I'll see you at six. Don't be late," Gabrielle said and hung up the phone before Beatrice could ask any more questions. Checking Beatrice's name off of her mental "to do" list, Gabrielle moved on to the next item—a wedding dress. What would she wear for a last-minute wedding? She took a trip into her bedroom to find out.

Gabrielle opened the door and walked into her closet in search of something appropriate. Suit after suit, dress after dress ended up in the discard pile on her bed. Gabrielle was just about to give up in despair when she pulled out the perfect outfit. It was a stunning cocktail dress designed by none other than Maynard Scarborough. It was white and had a tank-style bodice in transparent mesh with sparkling beaded accents. Gabrielle went deeper into her closet and dug out a pair of matte-silver Manolo Blahnik pumps. From her jewelry box she selected a pair of dangling pearl earrings that had once belonged to Helene.

That task completed, Gabrielle called downstairs to the spa and made an appointment at two-fifteen to have her nails done. Next she pulled on a pair of jeans and a crisp white T-shirt, grabbed her jacket and purse, and headed out the door. She had some serious shopping to do.

"Mr. Hollis is downstairs," the doorman announced at 5:35.

"Thanks, John. Please send him up." Gabrielle opened the door to find Jack holding a large bouquet of calla lilies and white roses, their stems tied with a white satin ribbon.

"Wow!"

"Wow, yourself," Gabrielle replied. Jack was dressed in a navy-blue double-breasted Armani suit. Under his jacket he wore a light-blue mandarin-collar shirt with very subtle burgundy stripes.

Jack whistled in admiration as he stepped inside and handed Gabrielle the flowers. The living room had been transformed into a floral wonderland, and soft candlelight flickered everywhere. Even the Christmas tree had been dressed in white poinsettias, with twinkling lights peeking from within the branches. A small wedding cake sprinkled with fresh flowers sat proudly on the dining-room table, surrounded by crystal champagne flutes and a bottle of Dom Perignon, chilling in a silver ice bucket.

"Merry Christmas," Jack said, handing Gabrielle a small package. She might not have been able to read the name, Tiffany & Co., on the lid, but she surely recognized the trademark blue box tied with white satin ribbon.

"I want to tell you something before we go through with this," he said. "I know that you're not in love with me right now, but that's okay. I promise to do whatever it takes so you'll never regret your decision."

Gabrielle was visibly moved by Jack's words. She knew

he was taking a big chance by making her his wife now. She opened the box slowly, her breath escaping in admiration when she saw the exquisite ring inside. Jack had chosen a magnificent six-carat, pear-shaped diamond sitting in the center of two large sparkling trilliants, all set in platinum. It was a showstopper—a ring that told the world that she was loved and treasured by a successful and generous man.

"It's like a perfect teardrop of happiness," she whispered.

"Even though ours is probably one of the shortest engagements in history, I couldn't let you go without a proper ring. Here, let me put it on," Jack said, removing it from the box. "Gabrielle Donovan, will you marry me?" he asked, slipping it on the appropriate finger. It fit perfectly.

"Yes," she said, reaching up to meet his lips with hers. "I do adore you, Jack. And I respect, admire, and trust you. I can't believe that you still love me in spite of my 'problem.' Love like that can't go unreturned forever."

"Did Doug know about your dyslexia?"

"Yes."

"I knew he was an asshole, but I didn't realize what a big one. I do owe him a huge favor, however. Because of his stupidity, you're about to become my wife."

"I don't want to talk about Doug. He's the past. Today's all about the future," Gabrielle told him.

"And speaking of which, there are a few things we need to work out before our guests arrive," Jack said.

"Such as?"

"Where are we going to live?"

"Good question. Well, we have three choices—your place, my place, or we buy a new place."

"Since yours is bigger, why don't we move into it for the time being? Once we catch our breath, we can decide where we might like to live."

"That sounds fine. I can put some things in storage to make room for your belongings," Gabrielle offered.

"That was easy enough."

"There's one other thing. I'd like to keep my name professionally."

"Changing your name is not an issue, but I'd like our kids to take my name."

Kids? She and Jack had never discussed children. He had no idea how she felt about becoming a mother. Should she tell Jack about Tommy now, before they got married? Would he be able to handle another confession, particularly one so devastating? "How many kids do you want?" she asked tentatively, opting not to disclose her secret.

Before Jack could answer, the doorman buzzed again, informing Gabrielle that Fritz Henderson was in the lobby. When Jack opened the door minutes later, both Fritz and Beatrice stood outside. Once they were over the threshold, it became quite clear to both of them that this was to be more than just a simple holiday celebration.

While they waited for the judge to arrive, Gabrielle took Beatrice to the side for a quick chat. "I guess you figured out what's going on," she said.

"Are you sure about this? Last time we spoke about Jack you said you weren't interested in another serious relationship—and now you're getting married."

"I know it's sudden, but it's what I want."

"Are you in love with him?"

"No, but I love him enough. Jack knows how I feel, and it doesn't matter."

"What kind of a man marries a woman knowing she doesn't love him? Why is he rushing you into this? Doesn't that make you wonder about his motives?"

"Actually, it was my idea to get married today."

"And what about Doug?"

"Bea, don't do this. Don't ruin my wedding day."

"The reason you aren't in love with Jack is that you still love Doug. I know you do."

"I'm marrying *Jack*," Gabrielle said, lowering her voice even more. "At least he's willing to accept me just as I am."

"You told him?" Beatrice asked. "He knows you're—"

"Sort of. He thinks I'm dyslexic."

"Where did he get that idea?"

"I don't know. When I told him I couldn't read or write, he assumed it was because I was dyslexic. Who cares, as long as he knows and I don't have to pretend with him?"

"Ladies, Judge Murphy is here," Jack announced.

"Bea, please be happy for me," Gabrielle pleaded.

"That's all I ever wanted, honey, for you to be happy," Beatrice said, sounding more accepting than she felt. She kissed Gabrielle and followed her into the living room. Flanked by Fritz and Beatrice, Jack and Gabrielle stood in front of the judge and the ceremony began. In less than five minutes Gabrielle Donovan and Jack Hollis were husband and wife.

After photographing and toasting the bride and groom, Beatrice found a seat and sat down. She felt physically ill. Everything had backfired in her face. How could Gabrielle do this to her? How could she not discuss her plans or feelings about this man who was now her husband? It pained her to think that Gabrielle would never find true happiness with this man she didn't love.

If she's not happy, it's all because of me, Beatrice chastised herself. *If I hadn't come between Gabrielle and Doug, at least she would have married a man she really loved and who really loved her.*

42

You've seen her on the cover of *Sports Illustrated* not once, but twice. Her first calendar sold out in three days, making it the bestselling calendar ever. And she's got a special on the Lifetime network tomorrow night. Put your hands together for my next guest, the very fine Miss Gabrielle Donovan!"

The crowd was in a frenzy, circling their arms wildly as late-night-talk-show host Craig Arthur led the audience in his trademark chant. Gabrielle, resplendent in black, walked slowly onto the stage. She really hated doing these talk shows. She was always afraid that some research assistant would dig up her past and serve it up to her in front of millions of curious viewers. Craig gave her a brief kiss and hug and led her to the interview sofa. Gabrielle sat deep into the gray couch and waited for the admiring crowd to settle down.

"I don't know about you, but for me 1997 looks like a very good year," Craig said in jest as he flipped through the calendar, setting off a frenzy of testosterone-related *woof-*ing. "Is it fair that one woman should look so good twelve months of the year?"

Gabrielle smiled modestly at his compliment. "The truth is, people don't see me before the stylists and makeup people work their magic."

" 'Fess up now, what's it like to be considered one of the ten most beautiful women in the *world*?" Craig asked, referring to the most current issue of *People* magazine.

"It's flattering, but not really accurate," Gabrielle explained. "I'm somebody's creation. An image. I'm not the photo on the page. You probably wouldn't even recognize me on the street without all the glamour getup."

"Maybe not the street, but what about the boardroom? People are calling you Gabrielle, Inc. You've got your own swimwear line, cosmetic deals, this calendar, and now a television special."

"I can't model forever. I have to have something to fall back on when all this is over."

"What about acting? Word is you've turned down parts in some very big films. Just not interested?"

Gabrielle sat back and crossed her arms in front of her. To those fluent in body language her subtle change in position signaled that she was uncomfortable with the subject matter. "I can't honestly say that I'm not interested. I'm just not ready to act yet."

"But aren't you about to go one-on-one with Erica Kane of 'All My Children'?"

"It's a cameo. I'm just playing myself in a couple of scenes with Susan Lucci. Hardly a stretch. Now, why are you trying so hard to talk me out of modeling? Don't you think I have at least a few good years left?" Gabrielle countered coyly.

"I'd say so. What's the hardest thing about your job?"

"The traveling. I've been to Europe three times this past month. I've been back and forth across the U.S. at least four times in between."

A collective "ahh" came up from the audience.

"Now, wait," Gabrielle protested good-naturedly. "I know getting paid to travel to exotic places all the time sounds glamorous, but believe me, it's no fun when you can't remember what country you're in, the airline has *once again* lost your luggage, and your body clock is still set for a time zone you haven't been in for days," she explained. "Plus, it gets lonely on the road."

"How can any woman as superfine as you have trouble finding a willing male in any country?"

"I'm no different from most women out there. I wasn't looking for just *any* man," Gabrielle said demurely. "I was looking for the *right* man." Once again applause and barks of approval filled the studio.

"My sources tell me that you've found Mr. Right. Rumor has it you recently got married."

"For once the gossips got it right," Gabrielle said, smiling. "In fact, my husband is here with me."

"Let's bring him out. I know *I* want to meet the man who is bad enough to claim you as his own," Craig said, motioning Jack out of the wings and onto the stage. Jack stood close to Gabrielle, grasping his wife's hand in his.

"I'd like you all to meet my husband, Jack Hollis," Gabrielle announced.

"Sit down, man, you got some 'splainin' to do," Craig told Jack in his best Ricky Ricardo accent. "How did you manage to pull this off? We didn't even know you two were engaged."

"It was a *brief* engagement," Gabrielle revealed. "We got engaged early Christmas Eve morning and married that night at home. It was really private and *very* special."

"Come on, Jack, tell us how you managed to capture the heart of this lovely," Craig said, flipping through Gabrielle's calendar for emphasis.

"Fate and luck," Jack said, male pride bursting out all over his face.

"No, I'm the lucky one," Gabrielle interjected. "Jack has to deal with a lot being married to me," she said, sharing a knowing smile with her husband.

"What? You snore or something?" Craig asked, setting the audience's laughter off again.

"No. I'm talking about the travel, the gossip, the demands on my schedule—everything. He's the sweetest guy in the world," Gabrielle told the audience.

"We'll find out more about the secret marriage of supermodel Gabrielle Donovan—or should I say Mrs. Jack Hollis—when we come back," Craig told his television viewers over the thundering applause. "Gabrielle, why don't you take us into the break? Just read what's on those cards John is holding up there."

Gabrielle suddenly felt very warm. She was sure that the boom mike above her was picking up the sound of her pounding heart, alerting the millions of people watching that she was panicked. She stared straight ahead into the footlights, unable to see any of the audience, still applauding madly. John stood less than twenty feet from her, holding the cue cards and pointing to the contents—words that meant nothing to her. She sat staring at those cards, her eyes frantically searching for a word she recognized, anything to give her a clue.

Is this how it's going to happen? she thought. *I'm going to get caught right here in front of millions.* Her plan had always been that if she ever got caught in this kind of situation she'd simply faint, drawing attention away from her inability to read. Her plan, however, had not factored in a national television audience. *How am I going to get out of this?* she asked herself, gripping Jack's hand.

Jack sat on the couch, unsure what to do. Should he take

over and read the cards for his wife? But wouldn't that draw more attention and make people more suspicious? Jack squeezed Gabrielle's hand, silently relaying his support, while praying that she would find a way to extricate herself from this sticky situation and avoid embarrassing them both.

"Craig, I have a confession to make," Gabrielle said softly.

Craig sat staring at his guest, wearing a puzzled expression on his face. Gabrielle sat before him looking totally serious and very uncomfortable. The audience sat spellbound, hushed in anticipation of some juicy news.

"I'm really embarrassed to admit this," she said softly, "but I can't read those cards."

"What the hell?" asked the show's director from the control room. "Camera two, push in, push in. Give me a closeup."

"I can't even see them. I don't have my contact lenses in," Gabrielle explained.

Craig Arthur looked directly into camera two. "You heard it here first. America's number-one glamour girl is blind as a bat. We'll be right back. Quick, how many fingers am I holding up?" he laughed, teasing her as they went to break.

Once they were off camera, Gabrielle snuck a relieved look at Jack, who winked back proudly. He was impressed with her ability to rebound so gracefully. He gave his wife a kiss on the cheek. For a flash she had been tempted to reveal her secret and finally unload the monkey she'd been carrying around on her back all these years, but when it came down to it, she just didn't have the nerve.

With precision aim, Stephanie turned off the television from across the room with her sneaker. Using the remote, she turned off the VCR. She routinely taped talk and entertainment-news shows in hopes of uncovering tidbits to use in "The Visa Lee Report." Stephanie circled the room several times and then sat down on the edge of her bed, trying not to hyperventilate.

Mrs. Jack Hollis? Oh, God, no. Oh, God, no, she repeated in her head. Stephanie stood up and, wringing her hands, once again paced the room. She hadn't believed the gossip, mainly because Gabrielle's travel schedule had been so intense lately, there'd been no time for her to get married. *He couldn't have married her. He's mine. But he did. Damn it, he did.* Stephanie couldn't hold her misery inside any longer. What started as a slow wail from her toes resonated through her body and was released as a loud, woeful sob. She cried in self-pity, in resentment, and in hatred. The one thing she'd ever wanted, Gabrielle Donovan had kept from her. She walked over to the mirror and peered at her mascara-stained face, red and bloated from her tears. Taking a deep breath, she pulled herself together and made a promise to the woman in the looking glass. This final act of betrayal could not be tolerated, and it most definitely would not be ignored.

Doug turned off his television and walked over to the window. He wished he'd followed his first instinct and not watched tonight's show. Who was he kidding? There was no way he would pass up any opportunity to see Gabrielle again, even if it was only on a twenty-one-inch television screen.

He had so many strong feelings for this woman, the most overwhelming being regret. Doug so regretted his words and actions on Gabrielle's birthday. He should have been more forceful after the breakup and ignored Gabrielle's requests that he stay out of her life. And finally, the fiasco with Jack Hollis. His biggest mistake of all was the night at

Nell's when he'd driven Gabrielle away and straight into Jack's waiting arms.

"'He's the sweetest guy in the world,'" Doug said aloud, mimicking Gabrielle's words. "*You* certainly weren't, you asshole," he yelled at his reflection in the window.

So often, in the back of his mind, he'd heard Gabrielle's voice telling him not to let go, that she still loved and needed him. Doug had listened to that voice, letting himself believe that they were meant for each other, that once again fate would eventually bring them back together. Now, with the announcement of her marriage to Jack Hollis, Doug knew that he'd merely been indulging in wishful thinking. With tears streaming down his cheeks, Doug forced himself to acknowledge the truth: He and Gabrielle were over, and as soon as forever came and went, he would finally stop loving her.

43

Gabrielle forced herself to stop tapping her fingers as she rode nervously along Sixth Avenue in the backseat of the Lincoln Town Car. Why had she agreed to appear on the MTV Video Music Awards? The last thing she wanted to do was get up in front of an audience of millions and present the award for best rap video. Especially when neither Bea nor Jack was available to coach her through it.

It's not like you've never done a television show before, she reminded herself. *True, but it's the first time after that near-disastrous episode on "The Craig Arthur Show."*

That event three weeks ago had shaken her confidence and left her full of anxiety about future television appearances and uncertain of how much longer she could continue to keep her illiteracy hidden without losing her mind. Her public faux pas was also the reason she'd abruptly canceled her guest appearance on "All My Children." The show's producers, while not happy, seemed to take it in stride, quickly replacing Gabrielle with her friend and colleague Eva G., but the tabloids, particularly *Star Diary,* chose to rely on speculation and innuendo to write their stories.

As her car pulled up to the side entrance of Radio City Music Hall, Gabrielle exhaled loudly in an attempt to squelch her fears. Arming herself with the Donovan smile, she grabbed her evening bag, exited the limo, and walked toward the door in a hail of flashbulbs.

"Ms. Donovan, I'm Fred," the guest-relations assistant greeted her at the door. "This way, please."

Gabrielle followed Fred through several winding corridors and into the dressing room, where she found the makeup and hair people waiting. Just as they began to work on her, the producer, script in hand, popped in to greet her.

"Gabrielle, good to see you again."

"You too, Alex. How's it going?"

"You know how these things are—controlled chaos. In fact, I've got a little problem and need your help."

"Oh?"

"Queen Latifah's people just called. Her flight is delayed, and she's not going to make it in time to do the first award presentation, so I need to move you into her spot with Gwyneth Paltrow."

"But . . . I . . . I only know *my* lines," Gabrielle pointed out. She could feel the panic begin to inch through her body, wrap around her diaphragm, and squeeze the air from her lungs. Why did this have to happen to her? Why couldn't they choose someone else?

"Not to worry. Just read off the TelePrompTer. You've seen these award shows before. It's the rare presenter that *doesn't* read their lines—let alone read them well."

"I think Gwyneth can handle it on her own, don't you? You don't need me."

"But I do. Everything is set up for two presenters, so here's the new script for you to look over. Trust me, it's really not a big deal."

Gabrielle took the paper and forced a "no problem" smile as the producer left, glad he could not hear the words that were screaming silently inside her. *It is a big deal, goddamn it! It's a humongous deal. Just read. Just read. So damn easy for you to say, but impossible for me to do.* With a live audience of hundreds and a television audience of millions, Gabrielle knew that she couldn't afford another public slipup. The press would start asking questions, and sooner or later she and all her lies would be exposed.

Gabrielle felt light-headed and closed her eyes, trying to steady herself. Instead of finding her equilibrium, she was bombarded with the terrifying image of standing mortified at the podium while the audience howled wildly as she stuttered through the unfamiliar lines. *I can't do it again. I can't,* Gabrielle thought as she tried to catch her breath.

"Are you okay?" the makeup girl asked, seeing the panic in her eyes.

"I only know *my* lines. I can't do this again," she repeated aloud as she bolted from the chair. Gabrielle ran to the exit, oblivious to the puzzled looks of the other celebrities and production crew. She felt the fiery heat of embarrassment creep up her face and stain her cheeks, reminding her of another time she'd run out on a job. In three years she'd come so incredibly far, but at this moment Gabrielle felt as if she hadn't progressed at all. The public might perceive her as a top model at the height of her profession, but she still felt as insecure and unemployable as the teenager who'd run away from her job selling muffins.

Gabrielle burst through the exit door before stopping to catch her breath. Tears were flowing, blurring her vision as she searched up and down the street for her car and driver. After several fruitless minutes Gabrielle hailed a cab and instructed the driver to take her home. The cabdriver, alerted by the whimpers emanating from the backseat, stole a look at the famous face in his rearview mirror. Instead of the glamorous, confident supermodel he'd come to recognize, he saw the crumpled face of a frightened child wrapped up in her own arms, rocking pitifully to and fro.

Jack walked into the apartment and closed the front door behind him. The apartment was silent, signaling that Gabrielle was either still asleep or already up and out. He carried his overnight bag into the bedroom. The bed had not been slept in, leaving Jack to pause in wonderment and concern. He put his bag down and picked up the telephone.

"Morning," Bea greeted him.

"Good morning, Bea. I just got back from L.A. and was wondering if you knew where my wife was."

"Gabrielle spent the night here, Jack. In fact, she's still asleep. She had a rough day yesterday, and since you were out of town, I suggested she camp out here."

"Is she okay? What happened?"

"She had a panic attack just before the MTV Video Music Awards and walked out."

"Panic attack over what? Does this have something to do with her dyslexia?"

"Yes, but I think maybe she should explain everything to you. Shall I wake her?"

"No, let her sleep. I'll see her when she gets up."

Jack hung up and immediately ran down to the newsstand and picked up several daily newspapers, including *Star Diary*. He stopped by the Greek deli for coffee before returning home to see just what he'd missed while in Los Angeles.

By the time he'd finished Page Six and Liz Smith's column, he knew that Gabrielle had abruptly left Radio City

Music Hall, reneging on her commitment to be a presenter, but he learned little else. It wasn't until he read *Star Diary* that he got the full dish, with the usual side order of unconfirmed speculation by "sources close to Ms. Donovan."

> *It appears that supercool supermodel **Gabrielle Donovan** is creating diva moments faster than McDonald's can make french fries. You remember how she so rudely canceled her guest appearance on "All My Children" at the ninth hour, making her persona non grata in Pine Valley (not to worry, dear, fill-in Eva G. did a marvelous job). Now it appears that the model pulled another no-show at last night's MTV Video Music Awards. My sources tell me that when asked to fill in for the delayed Queen Latifah, Gabrielle refused and left the building in a huge huff, insinuating to those within earshot that she had no desire to share the podium with actress Gwyneth Paltrow. Please, Ms. Donovan, isn't it about time you checked your ego at the door?*

Jack folded the tabloid in half as he thought about what he'd read. He knew instantly that this episode was not about his wife's ego, but more about her lagging confidence. Perhaps it was time for Gabrielle to come clean with the public about her dyslexia. The secret wasn't worth all the aggravation. Besides, he was here for her now and could support her through any fallout. She didn't have to depend on the out-of-touch, albeit well-meaning advice of some senior citizen. Together, as husband and wife, they could turn her learning disability into a positive social statement—a statement that garnered them both lots of attention, placed them squarely among elite celebrity couples, and tightened the marital knot that bound them together. Jack smiled as he pictured the two of them hosting elaborate fundraisers and appearing in public-service campaigns produced by his agency. Yes, they could definitely use Gabrielle's problem to their advantage. Just as soon as the time was right, when his wife got over this latest episode and regained her confidence, he was going to convince her as well.

44

"Two pink lines mean yes, one means no," Gabrielle reminded herself as she awaited the results of her home pregnancy test. She'd waited three months in vain for her period to appear, but it was time to face the fact: She was pregnant.

While she waited for the drugstore test to tell her what she already knew, Gabrielle took time to think about the way her life was unfolding. Despite the fact that both she and Jack had been on the road the greater part of their seven-month marriage, the two of them had settled into an easy and very comfortable union. Their life together was happy and mutually satisfying.

Gabrielle had finally stopped worrying about falling in love with her husband. It wasn't important anymore. If it happened, it happened. Unless Jack was a better actor than she thought, they both seemed quite content with the way things were.

Gabrielle might not have married the great love of her life, but she got something just as important from her relationship with Jack—peace of mind. With his love and support she was slowly regaining her confidence and feeling better about her career. Jack's knowing that she couldn't read made home a safe haven for Gabrielle. She didn't have to make excuses or pretend when she was with Jack. Sharing her secret had given her security, a treasured friendship, great passion, and now a baby.

But do I want this baby? she asked herself, looking at the two-lined test strip. Gabrielle had decided long ago that she would never bring a child into this world. Her decision was made, not because she didn't love children or desire motherhood, but because Gabrielle had never believed she could be a *good* mother. How could she read her child a bedtime story or help out with homework? How could she work and communicate with a child's teacher or doctor? And what was the likelihood that a child of hers might also be illiterate? How could Gabrielle subject her own flesh and blood to the kind of humiliation and degradation she'd known all her life?

More than anything, Gabrielle feared that she would place her child in constant jeopardy because of her inability to read prescription doses, danger warnings, and the like. How could she compromise the safety of her own child? Wasn't the death of one child at her hands enough?

Now that you're pregnant, you must tell Jack, Gabrielle's conscience reminded her. *You can't keep Tommy a secret forever.* Impossible, she decided. As understanding as Jack might be about her "dyslexia," asking him to understand this tragedy was asking too much. Gabrielle would take the secret of Tommy Montebello to her grave.

Besides, things were different now. She was older, and Jack would be there to protect their child. He could help their child avoid the heartbreak that she herself had endured. They'd also have to hire someone to help out when she went back to work. They would employ the smartest, most competent nanny they could find; better yet, a nurse. Suddenly Gabrielle felt better about this pregnancy, knowing that her baby would be surrounded by people to love and take care of him or her. And she mustn't forget Bea. Beatrice would make such a fabulous grandmother.

Gabrielle heard Jack's key in the door, and she scurried to hide the pregnancy test.

"How are you, Beauty?" Jack asked as he swooped into the room and kissed his wife.

"Lonely. I've missed you," she admitted, kissing him back.

"Me, too. Got any plans for this evening?" Jack asked, attempting to make a meal of her earlobe.

"Nothing special."

"Then how about we order in some Thai food, get naked, and have a feast in bed?"

"Before the feast, could we have a little discussion?"

"About?"

"About the honeymoon you promised me. I've been working nonstop, and I'm tired. Let's go somewhere. Just the two of us."

"Where would you like to go? Paris, maybe?" Jack suggested.

"No," Gabrielle said, sounding more abrupt than she intended. Paris held very special memories for her, all inappropriate to relive on her honeymoon with another man. "To be honest, I'd love to go somewhere close. I'm tired of sitting on airplanes for hours on end."

"How about New England? Killington, Vermont, would be perfect."

"But it's July. Isn't Killington a ski resort?" she asked.

"In the wintertime. In the spring and summer it's wonderful. Lots of fresh air. Green grass. Wildflowers. You'll love it," Jack assured her.

"Sounds perfect. Can we go soon? Like in the next week or two?"

"I'm really tied up with the Nabisco account right now—"

"Jack, please. I don't ask for much. I need to get away *now*. Can't you work something out?" she insisted.

"Okay, since it's obviously very important to you, I'll talk to Fritz and try to clear my schedule," Jack promised.

"Try?"

"Okay, I'll definitely clear it."

"Thank you," Gabrielle said, giving her husband a big kiss.

"What about your screen test with Lexis Richards?"

"I'm not sure I'm going to do that anymore."

"Why not? I thought we agreed. You know Beatrice and I will help you with your lines."

"I just have the feeling I'm going to get very busy in the next few months. I'm not sure I can fit filming a movie into my schedule."

"Why don't you do the test? You can always decline the role, but at least this way you keep your options open," he suggested.

"We'll talk about it later." Gabrielle was grateful for a legitimate excuse to once again delay her entry into acting. She knew that Jack and Lexis would understand her reason for not doing the screen test after she told them she was pregnant. "Just promise me that you won't tell anyone about our plans. I don't want our honeymoon to turn into a photo-taking free-for-all."

"My lips are sealed."

"Well, my darling, unseal them and kiss me," Gabrielle demanded as their lips melted together. Then, abruptly she pulled away. "Jack, promise me that nothing will get in the way of our taking this trip."

"Promise." Jack was anxious to get away with his beautiful wife as well. This honeymoon was the perfect opportunity to broach the subject of Gabrielle's going public with her dyslexia. He was convinced that once she did, she would be able to realize her full potential as a model and actress, and she'd love him forever for being the one to free her from her invisible shackles.

Stephanie sat in the Wilcot, Jourdan & Associates staff meeting wondering how much longer she was going to have to endure this bullshit. Granted, with two partners and a staff of eight, these meetings had come a long way from the days of she and Felicia sitting face-to-face, but they were still tedious as hell. Stephanie was now the most senior associate, and, unfortunately, Felicia had stayed true to her word and given her more challenging assignments. Working two jobs, while lucrative, was exhausting.

Even though "The Grain Harvest" had officially become "The Visa Lee Report," Stephanie was reluctant to leave until she had the manuscript to Gabrielle's life story in her hot little hands. Until her plan to smear Gabrielle into submission bore fruit, she was stuck in this office, required to follow the orders of these two dingbats.

Stephanie definitely had far more fun writing her gossip column than pumping out press releases. Her alter ego, Visa Lee, and Howie were having a ball collecting juicy tidbits and revealing photos of their celebrity subjects. Their collaboration was working out nicely, and, thanks to Howie, Stephanie was building quite a collection of exclusive photos and stories for Gabrielle's biography.

While Lois and Felicia whined on about the status of their clients, Stephanie began a new list of setups for Gabrielle. An affair perhaps? That might cause a few fireworks in the Hollis household. Stephanie put a big star by that one and continued to think.

She needed something that did more damage to Gabrielle's good-girl public image. Nothing so far had made a big enough dent in her "little darling" persona. The "diva moment" reports around the canceled soap opera and awards show hadn't had the prolonged impact she'd hoped for. To date the biggest stir had come after the fight at Nell's. Never before had her fans thought of Gabrielle as a party girl. *That's it,* Stephanie decided. It was time for Gabrielle to step into the volatile world of celebrity parties. If the combination of sex, drugs, and rock 'n' roll couldn't do serious damage to a reputation, nothing could.

"Okay, that takes care of Laurence Fishburne, now let's move on to In the House Filmworks," Felicia said. "With the mammoth success of *Praline Livin'*, Lexis Richards's next film is generating a huge amount of interest. *Soul Survivor* could be the film that makes him a major Hollywood player."

"Everybody is talking about it, particularly if he'll be the one to finally snag Gabrielle Donovan," Lois remarked.

"Good. As long as the talk is positive, I'm happy. Now, to keep that chatter going, we want to blanket the media with stories about our client. Every time I turn around, I want to see, hear, or read about Lexis Richards."

"I guess you'll be handling this one personally, right, Felicia?" Stephanie asked with a casual snideness to her tone.

"As a matter of fact, our newest associate, Timberly, will be taking over Lexis's account on a day-to-day basis. I'll be concentrating more on overall strategy." Felicia would never admit to anyone, with the exception of Lois, that it was too difficult for her to work as closely with Lexis as she had in the past.

Since the incident, Felicia and Trace's divorce had taken a backseat to the rebuilding of Trace's shattered self-image. Just as Lexis had predicted, the arrest had brought the couple back together, effectively putting a grinding halt to any romance between her and the director. Just how temporary an alliance it was still remained to be seen, as Felicia found herself wondering if perhaps her marriage was revivable after all.

"Stephanie, I need you to call and cancel all of Gabrielle's appearances for July third through the ninth," Felicia said.

"Is she sick or something?"

"No, she's going on vacation. She and Jack are finally taking a honeymoon, and they want it kept very hush-hush."

A Fourth of July honeymoon, Stephanie mused. *This could be interesting. There's got to be something I can do to add a few fireworks to the trip.*

"You can send out the press release on her Model of the Year nomination for the VH1 Fashion Awards. I made a few changes, and it's back on your desk," Felicia continued.

"What if we need to talk to her once this release goes out? How can we reach her? You know, for a quote or something," Stephanie asked, trying to gather information without drawing suspicion.

"It will have to wait. She and Jack don't want to be reached."

"If that's all, I'll go start canceling Gabrielle's appearances," she said.

"That's it."

Dismissed, Stephanie headed straight for her office and picked up the phone. If Felicia wouldn't tell her where Gabrielle was going, she knew who could. Quickly Stephanie dialed Bea's phone number and waited impatiently for her to answer. Finally, after the sixth ring, she picked up.

"Hello."

"Bea, it's Stephanie."

"Hello, dear, how are you?"

"I'm okay, though I have a little problem and could use your help."

"Oh?"

"My apartment is being fumigated, and I was wondering if I could camp out at your place? Just for one night."

"Sure, honey. When?"

"Thursday. Thanks, Bea. Hey, you know what would be fun? Maybe Gabrielle can come down. We can have a slumber party. It will be like old times in Brooklyn," Stephanie suggested.

"She and Jack will be out of town," Bea revealed, trying to remember any such slumber party in the brownstone.

"Where are they off to?" she asked casually, trying to save herself from having to spend any more time with Henny Penny than absolutely necessary.

"They want to get away by themselves for a short time."

It was clear that Beatrice was not about to break any confidences, so Stephanie didn't push the subject. She'd find out all in due time. "Oh, that's too bad. See you Thursday."

"Bea, you look tired. Why don't you go to bed? There's no need to stay up on my account," Stephanie told the woman.

"I think I will turn in. You're sure you don't mind sleeping on the sofa in my office?"

"I'm fine, really," Stephanie said, patiently waiting for Beatrice to vacate the room.

"Okay, then, good night," Bea said, shuffling off to bed.

Stephanie waited ten minutes for Beatrice to settle into bed before beginning her search. She sat down and quietly rifled through the papers on the top of the desk, finding her bills and other personal correspondence but nothing about Gabrielle's trip. In one of the file drawers she found a multitude of folders containing fan letters, autographed pictures, and personal-appearance requests. In the other drawer she found newspaper clippings chronicling most of Gabrielle's career accomplishments.

Giving up on the desk, she stood up to move on to the closet. Inadvertently her thigh pulled open a narrow drawer located on the underside of the desk. She drew it open to find several photographs, some ballpoint pens, and a calendar book. Stephanie pulled out the calendar and leafed through the pages. She grabbed a piece of paper and jotted down a few dates and places Gabrielle would be in the future. She turned to the dates in question and found exactly what she was looking for.

Vermont? What a cheesy honeymoon. Jack always was a cheap bastard. Stephanie jotted down the address before happily shoving the appointment book back into the drawer. Hearing the distinct sound of metal scraping against wood, she once again removed the datebook and ran her hand through the inside of the drawer. Her fingers got tangled up in a silky cord, and when Stephanie removed her hand she was holding a gold skeleton key dangling from an orange tassel. *I wonder what this is for,* she thought curiously as she peered around the room.

Stephanie got up from the desk and quietly opened the closet doors. There were several winter coats and other seasonal clothing hanging in the closet. On the floor, toward the back of the space, was a wooden chest. Stephanie pulled the chest into the room and inspected the lock. It made no difference that the key in her hand was too small, because the chest was not locked. She lifted the lid and dug around inside. The smell of cedar wafted up and assaulted Stephanie's nostrils.

Trying to ignore the repugnant smell, Stephanie lifted out a blanket and several wool sweaters. Further rummaging produced a few personal trinkets—what looked to be some sort of sailor's cap and an eight-by-ten pearwood box with a keyhole meant to be joined with the key in her hand. Bingo!

Stephanie quickly unlocked the box and poured its contents onto the carpet. Scattered before her was a band from an old cigar, a set of black onyx rosary beads, a sealed letter, and several old photographs of Beatrice and a young man wearing a uniform. Stephanie studied the pictures. *So old Mother Superior did have a life a long, long time ago.* Stephanie put down the photos and picked up the letter. She was shocked to see that the envelope was addressed to Gabrielle at the brownstone residence. Even more surprising was the fact that the sender was Doug Sixsmith.

Now, this is interesting, Stephanie thought. *Why would Beatrice have an unopened letter from Doug to Gabrielle locked up and tucked away in her closet?* Even more puzzling to Stephanie was why the letter had not been read. *Jesus, if you're going to go through the trouble of stealing a letter, you should at least read the damn thing,* she thought as she flipped the envelope over and over through her fingertips. *By the same token, to happen upon a mystery this intriguing and let it go without further investigation would be just as stupid.*

Carefully she broke the seal, lifted the letter from the eggshell-colored envelope, and quickly read Doug's letter. By the letter's end it was finally clear what had really happened between Gabrielle and Doug.

Stephanie laughed aloud as she realized that she and Beatrice were now partners in crime. While her story in *Star Diary* had provided the catalyst for their breakup, Beatrice had made sure they stayed that way. Stephanie's laughter stopped abruptly when she realized that had Beatrice kept her meddling paws out of things, maybe Gabrielle wouldn't have married Jack.

She tucked the letter into her overnight bag before returning everything to its rightful place. Stephanie snickered to herself as she climbed into the sofa bed. Why in heaven's name did Beatrice keep this letter? Why hadn't she destroyed it or simply had it returned to sender? Why? Because, thank God, Beatrice was too unbelievably stupid to be true.

45

From the creek running behind their accommodations to the invigorating Vermont air, Gabrielle adored everything about Killington. She particularly loved their rented house. Its triangular shape reminded Gabrielle of a contemporary Swiss chalet. The front was faced in cedar shingles, while the entire back of the chalet was glass, giving them full view of the surrounding woods. The house was delightfully secluded, their nearest neighbors being over three miles away, giving Gabrielle the privacy she so desperately craved.

Inside, the chalet was split into two levels. Upstairs was a huge loft with the master bedroom and bath, while downstairs held the living room, kitchen, a smaller bedroom, and a half bath. A huge stone fireplace dominated the living room, adding to the rustic yet contemporary decor. Ceramic tiles lined the floors, scattered with several colorful cotton rugs. The place was furnished in a mix of rattan and Shaker-style furniture. Several fans hung from the high, slanted ceiling.

Gabrielle and Jack were curled up together on the couch. More for ambience than warmth, logs crackled in the fire. Oil lamps were lit around the room and upstairs on the banister of the loft, making the house look as if the stars had come inside for the evening. This was the first night of their week-long honeymoon, and both were feeling completely relaxed.

"I love you," Jack whispered in her ear.

"If I shaved my head, would you still love me?"

"Of course I would. We just couldn't share the same bed until your hair grew back," Jack told her.

"Jack!" Gabrielle said, playfully hitting him in the shoulder.

"I'm sorry, you wouldn't be the same without those curls."

"What if I got fat?" she asked, getting up and heading into the kitchen.

"I can't even picture you pudgy," Jack said, unwilling to imagine his wife being anything other than drop-dead gorgeous. The Hollises were known in the press as one of the world's "beautiful" couples, along with John Jr. and Carolyn, Will and Jada, Tom and Nicole. It was a reputation that Jack thrived on. If Gabrielle were to be disfigured in any way, would he still love her? Of course, would be his first reaction, but truthfully, deep down inside, could he be sure?

"Can you picture me fat now?" Gabrielle asked, walking back into the room with a bundle of dishtowels tucked under her shirt. She looked as if she were at least seven months pregnant. She stood in front of her husband, giving him her best runway poses so he could see her make-believe bulk from various angles. "So, what do you think? Does a little extra weight become me?"

"What's going on here?" Jack laughed, still not quite catching on.

"I'm pregnant," she told him, watching closely as the news sank in.

"You can't be pregnant."

"Here, open this," she said, handing him a small envelope.

Still stunned, Jack opened the pouch and pulled out what looked like three Q-tips with pink stripes. "I couldn't believe it either, so I checked—three times. You see, we are having a baby!"

"This is fabulous. It's terrific!" he yelled, giving his wife a bear hug. He wanted to have children with Gabrielle, though he hadn't counted on starting quite so soon. Now that she was expecting, their timing couldn't have been more perfect. With the announcement of her pregnancy, Jack was fully convinced that Gabrielle would now be his forever.

"I take it you're okay with this?" Gabrielle asked, laughing.

"Of course I am. This is the start of a long line of Hollis/Donovan offspring." Jack sighed contentedly.

"Just how many kids do you want?"

"Two. Maybe three. I hated being an only child, especially after my parents died," Jack told her before putting his lips to her stomach. "Hi, Cashew, this is your dad."

"Cashew? What kind of name is that?"

"I don't know, I just figured the baby is about the size of a cashew nut right now."

"It's cute, I like it—for now. But what about real names?"

"If it's a boy, I'd like to name him Kyle Alexander, after my father, and for a girl, Hillary, just because I've always liked the name."

"I like Kyle, but Hillary Hollis? That's a mouthful."

"You have a better suggestion?"

"Kylie Helene. Kylie, after your dad, and Helene, after my mom."

"I don't care what we name her as long as she looks like you," Jack said, pulling Gabrielle close. "I love you."

Floating in an emotional whirlwind, Gabrielle had never felt closer to Jack than she did at this moment. "And I love—"

"Shh," he interrupted. "Don't say it until you really mean it. I know it will happen one day, but not today, not when we're caught up in the emotions of becoming parents," he told her. The fact that she was willing to have his baby was more revealing than those three little words could ever be. This child provided an everlasting bond between them, one that nothing and no one could ever break.

"Three Jenn Lane. This is it!" Howie announced.

"This tiny little cracker box is where she's spending her honeymoon?" Stephanie said in disbelief. It looked nice enough, but it was certainly minuscule. Stephanie shook her head in disgust. According to *Forbes*, Gabrielle had made over $7.2 million last year, and still she rented this dumpy little cheese wedge for her honeymoon? Gaby had a lot to learn about the lifestyles of the rich and famous.

"Now what?" Howie asked.

"Now you're going to drive me back to our house and then come back here and watch the place. If they leave, I want you to look around, check the doors and windows, see where we might be able to get in. Also, bring me back their garbage."

"What do you have in mind?"

"We're going to give Mr. and Mrs. Hollis a surprise wedding reception. One that it looks like they hosted themselves," Stephanie revealed. She'd worked everything out while on the six-hour drive from New York to Vermont. Celebrities were famous for throwing wild parties and trashing places that didn't belong to them. By the time she and

Howie got done with the place, it would look as if the frat party of the century had just ended. Once this hit the news, Gabrielle's reputation as the industry's good girl would die a tortured death.

Howie dropped Stephanie off at the small cabin they'd rented six miles away. He loaded up his knapsack with his camera equipment and headed back to the chalet. He parked his Aerostar van down the road and hiked into the woods. The photographer walked about a hundred feet, until he found an inconspicuous spot where he could see but not be seen. Howie was there less than twenty minutes when he saw Jack and Gabrielle leave the house and pile into their Range Rover. He waited for them to clear the area before leaving his perch and venturing down to the house.

Howie took a slow tour around the property, not only looking for points of entry and the presence of an alarm system but also taking a few snapshots along the way. He started around back and found a sliding patio door that led outside to the deck. Howie tried pushing the door open. It was unlocked and moved less than an inch before refusing to budge anymore. He peered inside and saw a thick dowel sitting in the floor track, preventing any further movement.

Howie walked back around to the front of the house. Besides the door there were four large windows, too high off the ground to make entry possible. He tried the front door; it was locked also. On further inspection he realized that the lockset was not substantial, nothing that a quick jimmy couldn't open. Howie returned to the side of the house and pulled the plastic bags out of the garbage cans, climbed into the van, and headed toward the house he and Stephanie shared.

"Well, let's see what we've got here," Stephanie said, dumping the garbage from the Hollises' chalet onto the kitchen floor. Among the paper towels, yogurt containers, empty food cans, and the like, three small wands caught her eye. "Hot damn, Howie, we've hit the jackpot!" Stephanie screamed, holding up her find.

"What the hell are those?"

"Home pregnancy testers. It looks like Gabzilla is knocked up."

"Those certainly explain these," Howie said, holding up a box of unopened condoms.

"I hope she gets as big as a house and her nose swells up to the size of a pear. What is this?" Stephanie asked as she unraveled a scrap of paper. "'Beatrice called.' I wonder what Henny Penny wanted? I thought the whole idea of this little getaway was so the honeymooners could spend some time alone together."

"They won't be alone much longer."

"Howie, I just got a great idea. You know those photos you took of Gabrielle and Salvatore Ciccone at the Fashion Plate?"

"The ones where he's planting a nice juicy one on her for donating some of her outfits to hang in the restaurant?"

"Yeah."

"Let's dig them out. Maybe we could stir up a little speculation over who's the father of Gabrielle's baby. He's pretty famous for knocking up glamour girls."

"You really are the master of inference, aren't you?"

"No. I'm merely the master of my fate."

"*Our* fate," Howie emphasized.

"Yes, our fate. Now, let's get into town. We have to shop for party supplies."

"We can do that in the morning. It would be a shame to let these things go to waste," he said, holding up the box of discarded Trojans.

Why not? Stephanie thought as she accepted Howie's

kiss. Though he was not at all gifted, his dick stayed hard and he didn't smell or drool. And God knows, all this plotting against Gabrielle had Stephanie keyed up and wired. She needed to release some of this tension, and it was either screwing Howie or going for a jog. The way Stephanie figured, if she was going to have to break a sweat, she might as well do it in bed.

Beatrice didn't even wait for the dial tone before hanging up on Gabrielle. When Gabrielle called to invite Bea up to the cabin to celebrate her pregnancy, the news upset Beatrice for a variety of reasons. First, as much as the idea of being a grandmother appealed to her, Gabrielle was much too young to have a baby. She had miles to go with her career before settling down to raise a family.

Also, Beatrice was sure that having a baby so early in their marriage was Jack's idea. He knew that his wife didn't love him, and this was an attempt to rope Gabrielle in and keep her tied to him forever. Why couldn't Jack just disappear? Then things between Bea and Gabrielle could get back to normal, and Gabrielle would once again depend on and need her as she had before he'd insinuated himself into their lives.

46

"I want you to get over to the house this morning and stake it out. Take the cellular so you can call me when they leave. I'll drive over so we can 'decorate.' Make sure you pack lots of film and the video camera," Stephanie said, barking out her orders. "And don't forget to take back their garbage and all the trash we've collected from the neighboring houses."

"We got pretty lucky finding all those beer cans."

"God bless college students. No wonder so many flunk out of school. They're too busy partying. Now, do you understand the plan?"

"What's there to understand? They leave, we go in and trash the place, making it look like they had the party of the century. I take pictures, you take video. How hard can it be?"

"It's not, that's the beauty of it. This plan is so simple, it's foolproof. Now, don't forget to wear your gloves, and for God's sake, don't steal anything. If we want to screw up Gabzilla and Jackoff's reputations, this thing can't look like a robbery."

"I understand why you hate her, but why Jack?"

"Let's just say that a long time ago, Jack Hollis tried to

fuck me. And the way I see it, one good fuck deserves another."

Howie left the house and headed for the chalet, while Stephanie made sure everything was packed, both for the party and their getaway. Once everything was captured on film, she and Howie planned to hightail it back to Manhattan. After loading the car, Stephanie cleaned up the house, taking great care to dust everything in order to eliminate any fingerprints. Once her task was completed, she sat down and began sorting out which juicy facts to save for "The Visa Lee Report" and which to share with her colleagues around the country. She decided to save the pregnancy as an exclusive for herself and release all but the best photos to her competitors.

In less than an hour Howie called to inform her that Jack and Gabrielle were gone. After one last check Stephanie left the house, careful not to touch anything. Within minutes she was at the chalet. They quickly unpacked the car, and while Stephanie parked down the road and out of sight, Howie proceeded to break into the house.

He tried to jimmy the lock, but it was equipped with an unseen dead bolt, preventing his credit card from slipping through. Not wanting to waste time, he pulled out his pocket knife and quickly unscrewed and pulled off the knob, retracting the lock mechanism with his gloved finger.

"Hurry up!" Stephanie called out in a quiet shout. Howie replaced the doorknob, but in the interest of saving time didn't bother to screw it back completely.

Once in the house the two quickly went about their work. First they smeared the walls, doors, and furniture with cake, yogurt, raw eggs, and party dip. Howie drew a large heart across the sliding patio door and filled it with the words JACK AND GABRIELLE, FOREVER in red spray paint, while Stephanie sprayed the place with colorful liquid string. In a two-person parade, Stephanie walked around the house sprinkling bags of potato chips on the floor as Howie followed behind her, grinding them into the tile. They decided to wash down the chips with Jack's favorite brandy and several vigorously shaken bottles of champagne. Howie and Stephanie opened the bottles, sending a shower of foam all over the room and a river of alcohol onto the floor, saturating the carpets.

While Howie busied himself by spraying Cheez Whiz in the VCR, Stephanie was lighting up the Marlboros, taking a couple of drags and then putting the cigarettes out in the sofa cushions, leaving burn marks in the cotton upholstery.

"It's show time," Howie announced, grabbing the broom. He put on a Van Halen CD and proceeded to entertain Stephanie with an exuberant performance on his makeshift guitar. As he jumped and danced around the house, Howie managed to knock pictures off the walls and break vases and other knickknacks, including several of the oil lamps, releasing their highly combustible fluid around the room. For an added touch, he yanked out the phone lines.

After quickly littering the loft with trash and beer cans and defacing the kitchen with graffiti messages like JUST MARRIED, and TOGETHER FOREVER, Stephanie and Howie stopped to admire their work. The two exchanged high-fives, pleased by the results. They'd done a fine job. The chalet was an absolute mess.

"All right, let's take the pictures and get out of here," Stephanie said. She retrieved the video camera from its carrying case and began taping the house from top to bottom, while Howie took still photos of the rubble.

"I think we have enough," Stephanie said.

"I want to get some shots from upstairs," Howie informed her while he reloaded his camera.

"Make it quick," Stephanie ordered. Just as the words left her mouth, Stephanie heard a car turn into the driveway. She peeked out of the window and saw Jack walking toward the house. "Get down here, *now!* He's back."

Stephanie's words sent Howie flying down the stairs. "Shit! Shit! Shit!" she whispered frantically. "What are we going to do?"

"Just shut up and don't panic," Howie said, taking charge. "We'll just have to play this by ear."

They could hear Jack progressing down the gravel walkway toward the house as they ran over to the sliding door to escape. Howie removed the dowel, while Stephanie fumbled with the lock. It was stiff and would not budge. Hearing the key turn in the front door, the couple dashed into the kitchen to hide just as the door flew open.

"What the hell happened here?" Jack said as he walked inside, closing the door behind him. Stepping carefully through the debris, he waded deeper into the chalet and surveyed the damage.

As he continued to look around, his eye caught the message written in spray paint on the patio door. Obviously a group of jerks had found out that he and Gabrielle were here and decided to throw a wedding reception without them. Thank goodness his wife was in town at the spa for the next few hours. He'd have time to get this mess cleaned up before she got home.

"Don't touch anything until you call the police," Jack said aloud, hoping to give anyone who might still be lurking the impression that he was not alone. He picked up the poker from the fireplace and took a quick tour of the house. As he walked toward the kitchen, Howie and Stephanie, crouched under the counter, stopped breathing, afraid of giving themselves away. Just as he was about to round the kitchen counter, the breeze stirred the wind chimes on the front porch, causing them to sing. The noise caught a jittery Jack's attention, and he returned to the living room.

"He's calling the police," Stephanie whispered to Howie. Panic was written clearly on her face. Howie held his index finger up to his lips, signaling her to remain quiet.

"Shit," they heard him say. "They ripped the fucking phone out of the wall." He'd have to use the phone in the car.

But first he needed to sit down. Satisfied that he was alone, Jack walked over to the sofa and found a dry spot. His hands were shaking as he reached over and picked up the half-smoked pack of cigarettes. He didn't care if he had promised Gabrielle he'd stop smoking; this situation demanded a cigarette. Jack fired up the Marlboro and took a long, deep drag. He was much more disturbed than he'd realized. This incident had revealed to him the dark, dangerous side to celebrity life. *What if Gabrielle had been here alone? What if this had taken place after the baby was born? Who knows what could have happened?*

Jack took another deep drag on his cigarette and thought about all he had to lose. He had everything he wanted—a successful business, a glamorous and famous wife, and now a baby on the way. Life was perfect. But to keep it that way, things were going to have to change. Bodyguards, alarms, watchdogs—he'd do or buy whatever it took to keep his family safe and the life he'd built intact.

"What's he doing?" Stephanie whispered, her voice barely audible.

Howie answered with a shrug of his shoulders.

"We have to get out of here," she mouthed.

Howie shook his head in agreement and listened hard. Hearing no movement or noise coming from the next room, Howie motioned for Stephanie to stay still as he quietly picked up the dowel.

The two of them heard Jack stirring in the living room. Howie pointed to Stephanie and then to the door. Stephanie tiptoed over to the door and slowly slid it to the right, causing a low, rumbling sound.

The sound of the door opening startled Jack. He took the half-smoked cigarette from between his lips, threw it down, and ground it into the floor, not realizing that his foot had not touched the glowing butt. "Who's there?" he called out, reaching for the poker. Jack stood up, inadvertently kicking the cigarette butt onto the edge of the cotton throw rug. He walked around the couch and took two steps toward the kitchen, when he felt the dowel connect with his forehead before he fell to the ground and passed out.

"Howie, let's go," Stephanie screamed from the back door. The dowel still in his hand, Howie turned to run, not noticing the smoldering rug. He ran through the kitchen and out the door. Stephanie had already retrieved the car and was waiting for him. Howie jumped into the passenger seat, and they roared off the property and down the winding access road that would eventually connect them with the highway.

"Whoopee!" she responded in glee. "Damn, that was exhilarating, but a little bit too close for comfort."

"We got some great shit!" Howie told her. "I can't wait to see the headlines on this one."

"You don't think anyone saw us leaving, do you?" Stephanie asked.

"Nah, in the two days I spent watching the place, I never saw one single person."

They drove on, passing a pair of attractive young women looking for a ride. "Don't even think about it," Stephanie warned him. Howie snuck a glance at the hitchhikers in his sideview mirror and noticed a taxicab pass them, heading in the direction they'd just left.

"Shit. We have to go back," Stephanie exclaimed, slowing down.

"Are you out of your fucking mind?"

"I left the camera bag behind the couch in the living room," Stephanie said.

"Screw the bag, it's not worth it."

"It is if you don't want to get caught. There's a tag on that bag with our fucking address on it," Stephanie said as she quickly pulled off onto the shoulder, made a U-turn, and headed back toward the chalet.

When Jack came to, the house was already engulfed in flames. He tried to get up, but his head hurt and he felt woozy. Smoke was everywhere, and Jack could barely see his own hand in front of him. Coughing and gasping for every breath, he slowly pulled himself across the floor, his progress impeded by the overwhelming smoke and debris. He made his way to the front door and tried turning the knob. Thanks to Howie's burglar skills, the doorknob kept spinning in his hand, refusing to catch and release him from this burning hell.

Overcome by smoke, Jack collapsed near the front door. He heard a voice he recognized screaming out Gabrielle's name.

"No Gab. Help me," he pleaded, before breaking into a coughing fit.

"Jack, is that you?" Beatrice asked. "Is Gabrielle with you?"

"No Gab. Help," he repeated, gasping for air and collapsing.

Bea could see the flames dancing in the windows at the front of the house. She lightly touched the doorknob. It was very warm but still touchable. That meant that the fire was close but hadn't made it all the way to the front door yet. She wrapped her hand in her shirttail and reached for the knob. She tried to turn it, but it wobbled around and then fell off in her hand. Beatrice tried, for what seemed like a lifetime, to replace the doorknob.

"Jack," she called out. Bea got as close to the door as she comfortably could and listened. She could no longer hear Jack's voice.

"Jack?" she called. *"Jack?"* she called again, louder. Hearing nothing, Bea once again backed away from the house and headed toward the road. Beatrice saw a van approaching and attempted to flag it down. The van momentarily slowed up, long enough for Bea to notice that the license plates had been removed, and then kept on going.

"That was Beatrice," Stephanie shouted, ducking her head. "What the hell is she doing here?"

"Screw Bea. Did you see the house? It looked like a fucking incinerator," Howie said as his camera clicked away.

"Fuck taking pictures, Do you think Jack got out?"

"Damned if I know, but we definitely can't stick around to find out."

"I hope he did, because if not, we're in one hell of a lot of trouble," Stephanie remarked as she raced down the road. At the first phone they encountered, she stopped and Howie called to report the fire. Once back in the car, they drove in silence the rest of the way home.

Bea watched the car drive away, not believing that it hadn't stopped. She hurried back toward the house, wondering if Jack was still alive. As she came up alongside the Range Rover, she heard the phone ringing. Bea opened the passenger-side door and picked up the phone. "Hello," she said into the receiver.

"Bea? Is that you?"

"Yes."

"What are you doing in the car? Where's Jack?"

"He's . . . in the house. Gabrielle . . . there's been an accident."

"Is Jack all right? What happened?" Gabrielle asked, fear consuming her.

"I'm not sure, honey, but there's no time to explain. Just come quick."

Bea hung up and dialed 911, trying hard to forget that a few days before, she'd made a wish for Jack to disappear. Damn. Be careful what you wish for.

47

Gabrielle, Beatrice, and Fritz Henderson stood huddled together at the foot of the Chelsea Pier waiting for the sun to rise over the Hudson River. It was sadly ironic that the people standing with Gabrielle on this warm and somber August morning were the very same witnesses who had stood with her on her wedding day. Only this time they were together again to say good-bye to her husband.

Gabrielle tightly grasped the small vial in her hand. Because Jack had no family and she wanted to avoid any further publicity, she'd decided to cremate his body and in a final tribute, sprinkle a small amount of his ashes off the pier where they'd had their first date.

Looking across the river, Gabrielle found herself hoping that with the sunrise she would wake up from this horrible nightmare once again a wife instead of a widow. She and Jack had had so little time together, and already she was forced to say good-bye. His death was so senseless and unnecessary. Of all the emotions that were coursing through her at this moment—guilt, remorse, fear—it was the anger that Gabrielle tried to squelch before it welled up and took hold of her. She was angry at God for taking away yet another important person in her life, leaving her alone and forcing her to yet again rework the road map of her future. She was angry at Jack for going back to the chalet instead of joining her at the spa as she'd requested. But most of all Gabrielle was angry at herself for allowing Jack to die in that fire knowing that his wife and the mother of his unborn child was not in love with him.

As the sun rose over the Hudson, Gabrielle began to sob. Beatrice handed her a fresh Kleenex and held her until she could collect herself. "Thank you both for being here with me. Is there anything you'd like to say before we—" Gabrielle asked, unable to continue without crying.

"Jack, you were my best friend and business partner," Fritz stepped in, his voice shaky. "I've known you since the third grade, and throughout the years we've been like brothers, always there for each other. And I know that this past year was one of your best. I'd never seen you happier or more positive about your future.

"It won't be the same without you around, buddy. Hell, *I* won't be the same, but I am grateful for the time we did have. I love you, Jack, and don't worry, I'll be here for Gabrielle and the baby. And don't worry about the company. I'll make sure it grows into a business your kid will be proud to inherit."

"Jack, you and I didn't know each other well, but we had one thing in common—we both loved Gabrielle very much," Beatrice followed sadly. "Though your time together was brief, you made her very happy. For that I thank you. I'll look after your wife and child the very best I can. May you rest in peace with the Lord."

"Jack, I promise to keep your spirit alive for our baby. I'll make sure your child grows up knowing what a good and kind man you were. You'll stay in both our hearts forever. Good-bye, love," Gabrielle said simply, her heart too full of grief and guilt to say any more. With shaky hands, she un-capped the vial of Jack's ashes and scattered them over the Hudson River. As the fine gray dust hung in the air before descending slowly into the water, the three recited the Lord's Prayer. After several minutes of silent reflection, Gabrielle, flanked by both Bea and Fritz, walked back to the car, each lost in private and personal memories of the man to whom they'd said farewell.

"Here's your Motrin," Gabrielle said, handing Beatrice the bottle of pills and a glass of water. Like all of Gabrielle's medications, the bottle's label was color-coded, identifying the contents. "I hope they help."

"Thank you, honey. They'll do fine until I can get my prescription refilled."

"I'm sure all this stress is what's making your back hurt."

"Honey, I'm fine. Now, stop fussing over me. You're the one who's nearly five months pregnant. I should be tak-ing care of you. Are you all right?"

"Yes. I'll just be glad when the memorial service is over and all these people go home."

"You must be exhausted. You've been up since very early this morning. Why don't you lie down awhile? Your guests will understand," Beatrice suggested with concern. For a woman who's belly was full of life, Gabrielle herself looked lifeless.

"Do you know what the worst part of all this is?" Gabrielle asked, lost in her own thoughts and ignoring Bea's advice. "Besides the fact that Jack will never see his baby?"

"What's that?" she asked softly.

"I never told Jack that I loved him," Gabrielle said, breaking into tears.

"Oh, yes, you did, sweetheart. When you told him that

you were carrying his child, you let him know. Jack knew you'd never go ahead with this pregnancy unless you did indeed love him."

"This is all my fault."

"That's nonsense, Gabrielle Donovan," Beatrice said sternly. "You had nothing to do with this. Don't you dare blame yourself."

"It's true. Jack is dead because I insisted on taking a honeymoon. If we had stayed at home, none of this would have happened and my baby would still have its father," Gabrielle wept as she folded into Beatrice's arms.

"Oh, honey, don't do this to yourself," Beatrice said, rocking Gabrielle gently and wanting desperately to help her, but having no clue as to how. As much as her heart went out to Gabrielle and her baby, Beatrice could not deny the satisfaction she felt once again having Gabrielle all to herself. Widowed, pregnant, and illiterate, Gabrielle needed Bea now more than ever.

"What's the latest from the police?" Ruthanna asked Felicia in a hushed voice. They were out in the kitchen with Gabrielle's other friends, away from the rest of the folks who had come to pay their respects to Jack's widow. Each was full of questions about the tragedy, and, as Gabrielle's official spokesperson, Felicia found herself on the receiving end of their inquiries.

"According to Gabrielle, they're still pursuing their main theory that some local kids broke into the chalet and had a party. Apparently they break into unoccupied vacation homes all the time."

"But her house was obviously occupied," Jaci remarked.

"The police think that they were fans. I guess the fact

that it was a so-called celebrity's house made it too enticing to pass up," Felicia responded.

"And what about the fire?" Greg von Ulrich asked.

"The fire department has determined from the heavy burn marks on the rug that the fire started near the couch. Apparently, from the soot scrapings, there was some kind of accelerant used, more than likely the oil lamps."

"But who or what lit it?" Lois queried.

"They don't know. At face value it looks like a party that got out of hand, but because of Jack they're not ruling out arson and murder."

"They think someone actually tried to kill him?" Stephanie asked, pushing her way into the huddle.

"Even though he died of smoke inhalation, they found a large contusion on his head. They think it's possible that Jack surprised the vandals and they panicked, knocked him out, and then set the fire to cover their tracks," Felicia informed the others.

"Do they have any suspects?" Stephanie asked casually, willing herself to stay cool.

"So far only the guy who called in the fire, but apparently he's disappeared."

"Couldn't the police trace the phone call?" Ruthanna asked.

"They did. It was traced to a pay phone about two miles from the chalet. The detective said that they dusted it for fingerprints, but nothing usable came up," Felicia revealed.

"So that's it? Jack might have been murdered, and they have no leads," Greg remarked as Gabrielle and Beatrice reentered the room.

"None. They found a partially melted camera bag in the living room, but any identification was totally burned away."

"I just hope, for Gabrielle's sake, they catch the monsters who did this," Jaci said, voicing everyone's thought.

"Howie, how the fuck did all this happen? The plan was so simple. Jack wasn't supposed to die," Stephanie remarked following the memorial service.

"It was an accident. We left the house a mess, but Jack was the one who torched the place."

"He'd still be alive if he hadn't come home so early."

"How do you know that? Who's to say that he wouldn't have gotten hit by a car later that evening? Jack Hollis died because it was his turn. End of story."

"Maybe."

"Did you find out anything about the investigation?" Howie asked anxiously.

"Some good, some bad. The good news is that the police have no way of identifying the camera bag. The bad news is that the person who called in the fire is the prime suspect right now."

"That would be me."

"Don't worry. They've got nothing. No prints. No leads. Nothing."

"But what about Beatrice? What if she knows it was us who drove by her?"

"Believe me, she hasn't got a clue. Besides, even if she did figure it out, I know something that's sure to keep her big mouth shut." Stephanie briefly filled Howie in on Beatrice's ill-advised attempt to keep Doug and Gabrielle apart. "Do you think Gabrielle would ever trust Beatrice again? I think not. So, you see, nothing and no one is going to get in the way of us writing Gabrielle's biography."

"You still want to go ahead with this?" Howie asked.

"Hell yes. We've come too far to turn back now. This

entire Killington fiasco has actually turned out to be a blessing. Gabrielle has been front-page news ever since the fire. Felicia's going crazy trying to keep up with all the press requests. The public can't get enough of the poor, grieving widow and pitiful mother-to-be."

Howie had to respect Stephanie's ability to bounce back with such total resilience. Having accepted the fire and Jack's death as an unfortunate turn of events, she was ready to press forward. Stephanie Bancroft refused to let anything block her chosen path to success.

"Just promise me, no more setups."

"We don't need any more. It's time to strike a deal while the iron is hot."

"That's exactly why I sent our proposal to a friend of mine. He's the assistant to Russell Shockley, the editor of Target Press. He promised to make sure it got seen."

"Target Press is just another tabloid publishing house. They specialize in those fast and dirty tell-all books. I want this to go through a legitimate publisher. That's why it has to be an *authorized* biography," Stephanie argued.

"Do you really think that's going to happen? Gabrielle doesn't seem to be at all interested in this project."

"I just have to give Gabzilla a little time to get over her grief. I don't want to appear unsympathetic to her situation, now do I?"

"As long as we destroy the pictures," Howie reminded her. "It's too dangerous to keep them."

"We need them for the book," Stephanie insisted.

"Are you crazy? We can't use these photos in the book for the same reason we couldn't use them in the newspaper: Nobody else has pictures of the house before and during the fire. If we use them, we might as well pave a yellow brick road right to our front door for the police to find us."

"Okay. Get rid of all the prints and negatives in the file. *Burn* them," Stephanie suggested, collapsing into laughter. She was laughing not only because of her joke, but because she had a set of the Killington photos hidden away. Despite Howie's reservations, she was definitely holding on to those photos. When all this hubbub blew over, who knew where they might end up taking her?

48

With Howie away to photograph Arnold Schwarzenegger and Maria Shriver's appearance at Planet Hollywood, Stephanie opted to stay at home and have a good cry. Three months had passed since the tragic incident, and, contrary to her outward show of bravado and indifference, she was still deeply disturbed by Jack's death. Despite what Stephanie had told Howie, or even herself, she'd never hated Jack. She couldn't. He was the only man she ever genuinely loved, and the idea of having played a part in his death was devastating.

Still, a small part of Stephanie was almost relieved that Jack was dead. Her relief was rooted in the knowledge that with Jack's death she would finally be released from this dungeon of unrequited love. Losing Jack through death seemed much more tolerable than losing him to Gabrielle through marriage. The pain of constantly being reminded that Jack had never loved her in any way that even remotely resembled his feelings for Gabrielle was much crueler than knowing that she'd never see or speak to him again.

Stephanie cracked open a bottle of tequila and put the tape of "The Craig Arthur Show" in the VCR. She wanted to see Jack alive again and for one last time relish the memories of when the two of them were together. Stephanie fast-forwarded the tape to the part where Craig signaled Jack to join him and Gabrielle on stage. As Jack walked out onto the set, Stephanie's tears began to flow. He looked so handsome, so vibrant, so alive. It was hard to believe that he was gone.

She let the tape run, blocking out Gabrielle and focusing on Jack. In her tequila-induced fog, Stephanie allowed herself to fantasize that she was on the show plugging her book and announcing her marriage to Jack. Stephanie replayed Jack's entrance several times before acknowledging Gabrielle's presence. She decided to watch Craig Arthur's entire interview with the model. Eight minutes later, she turned off the television in disgust.

"What a crock she's feeding these people. 'I wasn't looking for just *any* man. I was looking for the *right* man.' Like Jack, you bitch. Being with *me* made him the right man, didn't it? 'I can't read those cards . . . I don't have my contact lenses in.' Blind bat— Wait a minute," Stephanie interrupted herself. "Gabrielle doesn't wear contacts. That witch has twenty-twenty vision. Why would she lie about wearing contact lenses and then say she couldn't read the cue cards? This just doesn't make sense," Stephanie told herself.

Stephanie jumped up and turned the VCR and television back on. In the search mode she quickly rewound the tape to the bantering right before the break. She paused the machine again right after the host had requested that Gabrielle take them into the break.

She could see the fear in Gabrielle's eyes. It was clear, if you were looking for it. Gabrielle was petrified. But why? Stephanie turned her attention from Gabrielle to Jack. He looked strange as well. Almost as if he were frightened for his wife. *I smell a rat.*

All the man had asked was for Gabrielle to read the cue cards. What about such a simple request would scare her into lying on national television? Was it stage fright? Was she worried about screwing up her lines on live TV? It's not as if Gabrielle hadn't done a million of these stupid shows before. Stephanie had booked most of them herself.

"So what are you hiding, Gabzilla? What has you looking like you've seen a ghost?" Stephanie rewound the tape again and watched the interlude for a third time. *This just didn't make sense. Nothing was requested or said that even an idiot like Gabrielle couldn't handle. So what's the deal? Unless . . . Could it be she really can't read?*

"Nah," Stephanie said, answering her own question. She got up and paced the room. *I've seen her reading books and commercial scripts. How could she not be able to read?*

Barclay hopped off his perch on the windowsill and sauntered over to the couch. He stretched and began rubbing himself up against Stephanie's legs. "Barclay, cut it out. I'll feed you in a minute," she told him.

"But Bea *is* always helping her learn her lines," she thought aloud as Barclay continued to distract her. "Barclay, I said I'll feed you in a minute— Feed the cat! That's it!" Stephanie shouted as she picked up the cat and made her way into the kitchen and began going through the cabinet.

She pulled out a tin of Barclay's food and examined the label. The brand name, Amoré, dominated the sticker, but there was no picture or drawing of a feline to distinguish it as cat food. Still, anybody who could read the words "tuna and ocean whitefish entrée for cats" would know that the contents of this can were not meant for human consumption.

"She was making lunch out of cat food!" Stephanie informed Barclay. Stephanie recalled the very first time she and Gabrielle had met in the kitchen of Beatrice's brownstone. In her mind she could see the condiments lined up on the kitchen counter and Gabrielle's shocked expression as Stephanie had thanked her for feeding the cat.

"Remember how weird she got? She just ran out of the room in the middle of our conversation." The more she thought about it, the more occasions Stephanie could point to in which Gabrielle had very slickly avoided reading—like how she drew pictures on her shopping lists. She never wrote down phone messages, or read the newspaper, or did any of her own paperwork. "Barclay, I don't think that stupid man-stealing bitch can read!"

Stephanie finished feeding the cat and flew into the bedroom to change her clothes. She searched through a pile of back issues of *Star Diary* and grabbed the last edition that featured Gabrielle prominently on its front cover. She stuffed the newspaper into her bag and, with one final shot of tequila, ran downstairs to hail a cab. Stephani was 97 percent sure that her hunch was right. Gabrielle was hiding something big, and she was going to get to the bottom of this mystery.

"Send her up, John," Gabrielle instructed the doorman. It was after 10 P.M., and she assumed that Stephanie was here on an errand for Felicia. She certainly couldn't be making a social call. Following Gabrielle's marriage to Jack, their relationship had become visibly strained. Though she took great pains to camouflage it, Stephanie's resentment was apparent. And now, after Jack's death, Gabrielle found it particularly difficult to be around her.

"So, Gaby, how the hell are you?" Stephanie asked when the door opened, purposely using the one nickname that Gabrielle absolutely despised. Uninvited, she swept past Gabrielle into the apartment, nearly knocking her over with her large leather tote bag. Usually, on the rare occasions that she did see Gabrielle, Stephanie showed much more deference, but tonight, thanks to her discovery and half a bottle of tequila, she just didn't give a damn.

"Do come in, Stephanie," Gabrielle said, after the fact. "Can I take your bag?" she asked, disregarding the woman's obvious attempt to annoy her.

"No thanks." Stephanie wanted her ammunition close by in case their impending conversation didn't yield the desired results. "You're huge," Stephanie observed rudely. "Are you sure you haven't got twins in there?"

"I'm sure. What exactly can I do for—"

"Where's Mother Superior?" Stephanie interrupted, ignoring Gabrielle as she sat down and made herself comfortable.

"I guess downstairs in her own apartment. Look, Stephanie, I don't mean to be rude, but I have lines to learn."

"And you're going over them by yourself?" she asked, her voice full of manufactured surprise.

"Excuse me?" Gabrielle asked, her bewilderment obvious.

"It's just, well, I know Henny Penny always helps you learn your lines."

"Well, tonight I'm on my own. So, if you'll tell me what you're here for, I can get back to work."

"I see," Stephanie said, continuing to ignore Gabrielle's obvious attempts to get her to move on. "Say, I saw a story on you in both *Vanity Fair* and *Vogue* this month. You're all over the place," Stephanie said, not expecting or receiving a reply. "Felicia certainly is earning that big fat retainer you pay her."

"Felicia does a great job, and she works hard for me. You do, too," Gabrielle added in an obvious afterthought.

"I'm glad you realize that I've helped you, too,"

Stephanie responded, jumping at the opportunity to use Gabrielle's words to her own advantage. "You have to admit that because of me you not only met Felicia but Miguel Reid and Jack," she said with a sweet-and-sour smile.

"I'm grateful for any help you've given me."

"It's good to hear that, because I have, in the infamous words of the Godfather, an offer you can't refuse."

"And that would be?"

"You and I have been friends for a long time now. We practically grew up together with Beatrice in the brownstone. There's nobody better—"

"Stephanie, where is this all going?"

Irritated that Gabrielle had interrupted her carefully prepared recitation, Stephanie blurted out, "I want you to authorize me to write your biography."

"Haven't we been through this already? For God's sake, Stephanie, I'm only twenty-two years old. My life is a short story. I haven't lived long enough to fill an entire book."

"Are you kidding me? Madonna, Michael Jackson— they both had several biographies on the bookshelves before they were thirty. All the big celebrities do."

"I'm not interested."

"Gabrielle, don't you get it? The whole world has an unquenchable thirst when it comes to you. This book could make you even bigger than you are now. And to be honest, it would really help me, too."

"Look, I'd like to help you, but the answer is *no*."

"Just like that? You won't even take time to consider it?"

"I'm sorry." There was nothing for her to consider. Gabrielle knew that there was no way she could allow anyone, let alone Stephanie Bancroft, to write her life story. She couldn't afford to have some writer flinging open the closets of her past and finding the skeletal remains of a life she was desperately trying to put behind her.

Outwardly Stephanie was fighting hard to keep her cool, but inwardly she was seething. She was holding a first-class ticket on the bullet train to success, and she wasn't going to let Gabrielle derail her now. If Felicia Wilcot could ride Gabrielle's coattails to the top, so could she. "Time to pull out the big gun," Stephanie said under her breath as she bent down and pulled the paper out of her tote bag.

"Pardon me?"

"I said time for me to run, but before I go, have you seen this? It's the early edition of tomorrow's paper," Stephanie lied, holding up the newspaper. Gabrielle recognized it as one of the more popular supermarket tabloids. Her face was on the cover, as it had been countless times these last few years.

"I really don't have time for this."

"Maybe you should make time. You won't believe what they're saying about you."

"I don't pay attention to those rags."

"Go ahead. Read it," Stephanie insisted, pushing the paper into Gabrielle's hands. She watched the model closely, looking hard for any sign that might confirm her suspicions.

"You of all people know I don't read this crap," she said, throwing the paper to the floor to emphasize her point. Gabrielle felt a sick, tingling feeling spread through her body. Stephanie was on some sort of fishing expedition, and that stupid newspaper was her bait.

"According to this, you don't read much of anything."

Gabrielle froze. Her stomach felt like a cement mixer, churning its contents into a concrete mass that weighed heavily in her belly. *How did she find out? What else does she know?*

"Since you won't *read* it or can't *read* it, let me *read* it for you," Stephanie continued, pronouncing the word "read" with wicked emphasis. "'Illiterate Supermodel Has Secret Past.'" With pleasure, Stephanie watched the undeniable look of dread flicker ever so briefly in Gabrielle's eyes. *It's true. The bitch can't read. Now it all made sense—the books on tape, always memorizing everything, never writing anything down, the ignored notes and lame excuses. They all made perfect sense.* "I told you you'd be amused."

"I can't believe you came here to show me a story some reporter made up to sell papers," Gabrielle raved on, hoping she sounded more convincing than she felt.

"So, it's not true. You can read."

"Of course I can. I have to read things like scripts, speeches, and contracts all the time. How could I do my job if I couldn't read, Stephanie? In fact, I have a script for a commercial right here I need to learn—"

"Don't you mean a storyboard? I think instead we sit down and start going over your biography—the one *I'm* going to write."

"For the last time, you're not writing my life story. Not now. Not ever."

"You listen to me, Gabrielle Donovan. I've spent the last three years of my life promoting you into a fucking superstar. Well, now it's your turn. You, whether you like it or not, are going to help me finally realize my dreams."

"I think you give yourself too much credit."

"You know, Gaby, I always thought you were kinda dumb, but now I realize you're just plain stupid."

Gabrielle's face stung just as if she'd been slapped. "I am not stupid," she said defiantly.

"Oh, yeah? Well, that headline—pure bullshit. I made it up, and you fell for it. But now you've really got my interest piqued. You can't read. What else are you hiding?"

"Leave."

"Fine. I'm gone. But understand this, Gabrielle: With or without you, I'll write this book. Now, with you, it's sure to be a kinder, gentler story. In fact, who says we even have to mention this whole little reading thing? Without you, well, that's an entirely different story. I can't guarantee complete accuracy, because—I have to tell you—unauthorized biographies are so much more of a pain in the ass to write. I'll have to dig up childhood friends, old teachers, and enemies, too. It's an incredible amount of work."

"Get out of here, Stephanie."

"I'll give you a few days to come to your senses, and then I take matters into my own hands," she replied, turning to leave.

Gabrielle sank slowly to the floor. Her head was reeling, and she felt as if she was going to vomit. How could she possibly allow Stephanie to blackmail her into writing her biography? But if she didn't agree, Stephanie would seek her revenge to the fullest, investigating every dark corner and putting her own evil spin on each story or nuance of a story she found. And that would not be the end of it. The media vultures would get into a feeding frenzy over the multitude of stories that would contradict the web of lies Gabrielle had so carefully woven throughout the years.

How would people react when they found out that the famous Gabrielle Donovan, supermodel and successful businesswoman, was nothing more than an illiterate sham? A more terrifying thought occurred to Gabrielle: What if Stephanie found out about Tommy? If that story ever got out, the ramifications could be unthinkable. What if, based on that tragic incident, the authorities deemed her an unfit mother and took her baby away?

Stephanie had to be stopped.

49

Gabrielle continued to knock frantically on Beatrice's front door. Just as she was about to turn around and go back upstairs to call, she heard movement on the other side of the door.

A confused and groggy Beatrice peered through the peephole. Startled into wakefulness by the blatant distress on Gabrielle's face, she threw open the door. "Honey, come in. What's wrong. Is it the baby?"

"The baby's fine. It's me. I can't take it anymore," she sobbed and collapsed into Bea's arms. "She knows, and she's going to tell if I don't—"

"Who knows what? What's happened?" Bea asked.

"Stephanie. She found out that I can't read!" Gabrielle cried out.

"How?"

"I don't know, but either I let her write the biography or she's going to destroy me. Bea, why is she doing this to me? Not now. Not after everything that's happened already. And not with the baby due in six weeks."

"Some folks don't need a reason to be cruel."

"I can't do it, Bea. I can't spend the rest of my pregnancy defending myself against my own lies," she cried miserably.

"What are you going to do?"

"I'm calling Felicia," Gabrielle said, picking up the phone. It was going on 11:30 P.M., but this was an emergency.

"That's good. I should have thought of that. Felicia will know what to do," Bea said. She waited as they talked, wondering why Stephanie would want to hurt Gabrielle like this.

"She's coming over for a strategy meeting tomorrow morning at ten," Gabrielle announced, no longer crying but feeling dazed and unfocused. "She agrees that whatever Stephanie has planned is going to need some sort of public cleanup."

"You look worn out. Why don't you try to get some sleep?"

"I think I will. I'm feeling kind of weird."

"Come on, honey, I'll walk you back upstairs," Beatrice said, leading Gabrielle toward the door and back up into her own apartment.

Gabrielle had just retired to her bedroom when the phone rang. Bea quickly picked up the receiver, not wanting the ringing phone to disturb her rest.

"Beatrice, it's Stephanie. I need to talk with Gabrielle."

"It's late, Stephanie. Gabrielle is resting right now and can't be disturbed," Bea said tersely.

"Who spit in your Cheerios?"

"I heard about your visit with Gabrielle tonight. I think you're despicable for trying to blackmail her, and I can't believe you would do something like this to a friend."

"And you of all people would surely recognize a despicable act toward a friend."

"Don't play games with me, Stephanie."

"Bea, this is no game. This is serious business. I found

your *mailbox*. You know, if you put it out in the open, *everybody* might get their mail."

"How dare you snoop around my house!" Beatrice reprimanded, feeling much less forceful than she sounded.

"Please, cut the indignation—at least until you can give me a legitimate reason why you have a sealed letter written to Gabrielle from Doug Sixsmith locked away in a box, in a chest, deep down in your closet."

"That letter is none of your business."

"I didn't see *your* name on it. Don't you know that tampering with the U.S. mail is a federal offense, punishable by law?"

"What do you want, Stephanie?" Beatrice asked in a weary voice. There was no point left in denying her actions, and she'd rather Stephanie know the truth than create and spread her own twisted version.

"For starters, I want to know why you kept this letter?"

"It's very simple. I was afraid if I gave it to Gabrielle, she'd get hurt all over again."

"Why would you think that? Doug's letter was dripping with regret and self-condemnation."

"I didn't read the letter, and you shouldn't have either. I'm not proud of what I did, but I honestly thought I was doing what was best for Gabrielle."

"Always protecting your girl, aren't you, Bea? Anyway, that's water under the bridge. It's time for you to help *me* out."

"Help you out how?"

"By convincing Gabrielle to let me write the authorized version of her biography."

"I can't do that."

"Okay, fine, but I can't promise that I won't mention to her that you were responsible for keeping her and Doug apart."

"She doesn't want you or anybody else writing a book about her. Nothing I say can make her change her mind."

"You underestimate your influence, Beatrice. Gabrielle trusts you to protect her and help her make the right decisions, or at least she did," Stephanie said, the implication clear. "With everything she's been going through, you don't want to disappoint her, too, do you?"

Stephanie was right, there was only so much pain and disappointment a person could bear before falling apart. The news that Beatrice had intentionally sabotaged her relationship with Doug might be the apple that tipped Gabrielle's emotional cart. Beatrice had no choice but to go along with Stephanie. She couldn't afford the risk to Gabrielle's well-being, not with the baby's birth so close.

"I'll talk to her, but I can't promise you anything."

"Look, this book is practically written. All it needs is a little fine-tuning by Gabrielle. It *will* be published, and when it is, for once Stephanie Bancroft will get what she deserves. Now, are you with me or against me? Before you answer, just think about what being against me is going to mean."

"I said I'd try."

"Good. And don't worry, as long as you cooperate, your secret is safe with me. We're partners now, Bea. You look out for me, I look out for you. Oh, and by the way, I'm holding on to the letter for safekeeping, because if Gabrielle doesn't agree to do this book, before you can say 'special delivery,' this letter will be plastered all over the front page of every newspaper in town. Understand?"

"Yes."

"Good. Oh, Bea, one last thing. Who's the sailor in the picture?"

Bea replied by slamming down the phone. Stephanie had to laugh. First Gabrielle, now Beatrice, and Felicia next.

All her ducks were lining up nicely in a row. She couldn't wait until it was time to take aim and fire.

"Deena, when Stephanie gets in, please tell her I want to see her immediately," Felicia requested as she walked through the front doors of Wilcot, Jourdan & Associates.

"She's already here."

"Good. We can get this over before the rest of the staff shows up. Please buzz her and ask her to be in my office in five minutes."

Twenty minutes later, Stephanie came strolling into Felicia's office. "I heard you wanted to see me."

"Fifteen minutes ago. Please close the door," Felicia requested sharply.

"I was finishing up a press release," Stephanie explained without apology.

"Stephanie, I'm not going to beat around the bush about this. Gabrielle called me last night."

"Yes."

"She says you dropped by to insist that you be allowed to write her biography."

"I think her hormones must be working overtime. I didn't insist on anything. I simply suggested that perhaps it was time she gave the public what they've been clamoring for— a book about her life. I also mentioned that, considering our history together, I would be the perfect one to write it."

"And you didn't issue her any threats or ultimatums?"

"As a matter of fact, I did," Stephanie answered defiantly. She was tired of sucking up to this bitch. Those days were over, beginning right now. "And you know what else I told her?" she asked with a wild look in her eyes. "I told her that I knew a big, fat, juicy secret about her, and if she didn't let me write the book, I was going to tell the whole world. Maybe that's the part she took as an ultimatum."

"Not only did you attempt to solicit a client for personal gain, you tried to use blackmail to accomplish it. Your behavior is unprofessional and unacceptable. You're fired. Clear your office and be out of here this morning by ten."

Stephanie responded to Felicia's statement with a loud chuckle. "Like I really care about this stupid job. Though you're a fine one to talk about soliciting clients."

"If you have something to say, say it."

"What do you think your husband would say if he found out that not only did you have an affair with one of your clients, but also an abortion?" Stephanie asked as she sat back and watched Felicia's face fall apart.

"Go pack your things, Stephanie," Felicia hissed. "And I'm warning you, you'd better keep your filthy lies to yourself."

"Oh, Felicia, don't get your panties in a bunch. We can work something out. Here, you take these," Stephanie said, handing Felicia two sheets of Wilcot, Jourdan & Associates letterhead. "Now, you make sure that Gabrielle shows up at this press conference and reads—oh, silly me—*memorizes* this statement, and the two gentlemen in your life need not know a thing."

"What makes you think anybody is going to show up at a press conference *you* call?"

"Take a good look at that. You're the one doing the inviting. Everybody knows that if Felicia Wilcot calls a press conference, something important must be going on."

"Have these already gone out?"

"Didn't you teach me that if you want people to attend, you must give them plenty of notice? I faxed most of them out this morning. The rest are being hand-delivered. Believe me, I've done everything necessary to ensure that we have maximum attendance. I did learn from the master, you know."

"Stephanie, get out of my office before I call security and have them bounce your ass out of here."

"First a friendly warning: If you or Gabrielle even think about canceling this press conference or not showing up, the front page of every tabloid in America will be screaming out the secrets you two are trying so hard to hide. I have lots of connections, and I'm not afraid to use them."

Felicia waited for the door to close behind Stephanie before she broke down. How did she find out about Lexis and the abortion? She had confided only in Lois, who would never betray her confidence. *How she found out isn't important,* Felicia told herself. All that mattered at this point was what Stephanie planned to do with the information.

What a mess. Another breaking scandal was not what she needed now, not with both men in and out of the papers—Lexis with his movie success and Trace with this lawsuit pending against the New York Police Department. Felicia wished she'd listened to Lois and fired Stephanie a long time ago. Now she had to figure out some way to deal with her, and she'd have to do it fast. The press conference was three days away.

"That's the secret she's holding over me," a much calmer Gabrielle said, telling Felicia of her illiteracy. Bea sat nearby holding her hand. A victim of Stephanie's treacherous threats herself, Felicia knew exactly what Gabrielle was going through.

"I'm shocked, to say the least," Felicia remarked. "How? I mean, all these years and I had no idea."

"I've been illiterate a long time. I'm very good at hiding it and compensating for my lack of skills. Beatrice is the only other person who knows, and she's my lifeline to the literate world."

"That's why I've never seen you order from a menu,"

Felicia commented, remembering incidents throughout their relationship that corroborated her story.

"Or read any of my press clips or anything you give me without taking it home first. The list goes on," Gabrielle elaborated.

"But you're rich, and famous, and beautiful—you don't look or act like an illiterate person," Felicia remarked.

"I could say the same about you—that you don't look or act like the typical black person. Just like it's unfair for me to stereotype all African Americans, you shouldn't try to pigeonhole all nonreaders. Illiterates come in all shapes, sizes, colors, and tax brackets. It's an equal-opportunity disability."

"I'm sorry, I didn't mean to do that. I guess I'm just bowled over by this."

"There are some other things I need to clear up before we figure out what to do about Stephanie. I want you to know everything."

"Okay," Felicia responded.

"First of all, I didn't live the dream life my press kit claims. My father was not in the military. The truth is that he abandoned us the day I was born. I was raised by my mother, who made her living as a waitress—not a surgical nurse—in between her six marriages. She loved me very much, and more than anything she wanted me to be a famous model."

"Believe me, Gabrielle, there are very few celebrities whose real life matches their press bio," Felicia told her.

"There's more. Much more," Gabrielle remarked as she reflected a moment before continuing. "When I was thirteen, my mother and I were living in Raleigh-Durham, North Carolina. My mom had just gotten divorced again, and we were strapped for cash, so I baby-sat some of the neighborhood kids whenever I could to help out. One of my regular jobs was watching Tommy Montebello, a little boy who lived down the street. I would baby-sit every Thursday after school. Tommy was a really cute kid and so sweet. I really loved him." Gabrielle paused to steady herself. She found herself trembling as the memories came rushing back. Bea patted her hand in support, curious to hear the rest of this story.

"On this one particular Thursday, Tommy went outside in the yard to play with two little boys from down the street. About five minutes later he came back carrying a small package of cookies and asked if he could eat them. See, he was very allergic to nuts, so they were real careful about what he ate," Gabrielle explained as she began to cry softly. "I recognized the package—they were double-chocolate-chip cookies; my mom bought them all the time. I asked him if they had any nuts in them, and he said no."

Beatrice and Felicia sat, sympathy written all over their faces. They didn't know the exact details, but it was evident where this story was headed. "How old was Tommy?" Felicia asked.

"Five. That's right, I took the word of a five-year-old."

"Are you okay, honey?" Beatrice inquired. "Are you sure you want to go on?"

"I'm okay," Gabrielle assured them through her sniffles. "Anyway, I told him it was okay to eat them, and he went back out to play. About five minutes later, one of the boys came running over to tell me Tommy had fallen down and wouldn't get up. I went outside, and he was on the ground gasping for air. His face and throat were swollen. He couldn't breathe. By the time the ambulance came, he was already in shock." Gabrielle began weeping miserably. Bea put her arms around her, crying also. This story explained so much—like why Gabrielle was so fearful about being a good mother.

"There were nuts in the cookies," Felicia commented softly.

"When they examined the package, listed among the ingredients in small print were pecan shavings," Gabrielle revealed as she began to cry harder.

"But you honestly thought they were just chocolate-chip cookies," Felicia probed.

"Yes. I'd eaten dozens of those same cookies myself—there were no chunks of nuts in them. But had I been able to read the package, I'd have known about the pecans and Tommy wouldn't have—" Gabrielle sobbed, unable to continue.

"Oh, dear," Bea remarked, her ears sadly hearing what Gabrielle was unable to say.

"What happened afterward?" Felicia asked.

Gabrielle took a few minutes to collect herself before continuing. "It wasn't enough that I'd made such a terrible, terrible mistake; I lied about it. I told everyone—the paramedics, Tommy's mom, my mom—that I had no idea when or where he got the cookies. I told them that one minute he was out on the swing set with his friends and the next thing I knew he was passed out on the lawn. So everybody believed that his death was an accident—one I had nothing to do with. Even his mom didn't blame me. She gave me the Wizard of Oz snow globe. It belonged to Tommy, and I've kept it to this day so I would never forget what I did." Felicia, Gabrielle, and Beatrice sat crying, silently mourning Tommy Montebello.

"Gabrielle, it *was* an accident," Bea reassured her. "It was a common mistake with a truly unfortunate outcome. Foods in this country are terribly mislabeled. Most literate people don't read the ingredient lists. They simply take the packaging at face value."

"There's one thing I don't understand," Felicia said.

"Why didn't your mom insist that you learn to read after such a terrible incident?"

"Remember, I lied to her, too. All she knew was that one of the other kids shared his cookies with Tommy. She had no idea that I'd given him permission to eat those cookies. I wanted to tell her and insist that she put me in some kind of reading program, but I was too ashamed. I didn't want her to be disappointed in me. We moved a few months after that anyway.

"So, that's everything. All my secrets are out in the open," Gabrielle remarked as she pulled herself together. "The question is: What do we do with them now?"

"Do you think Stephanie could be bluffing?" Bea asked, not really believing it.

"I don't think so," Felicia said, pulling out the press release. "She's invited the media to a press conference at which you will introduce her as your authorized biographer. I'm expecting an avalanche of phone calls when I get back to the office."

"Maybe you should just let her write the book," Bea suggested, following up on Stephanie's demand. "Then at least you'd have some kind of control over the contents."

"I may have no other choice. Ooh," Gabrielle said, putting her hands to her stomach and shifting uncomfortably in her seat.

"Are you okay?" Felicia asked.

"I think so. I've been having these periodic twinges. Probably gas."

"Gabrielle, you can't let this upset you. You just have to forget all this and put it behind you."

"Bea, there's no more room. All these secrets and tragedies that I've been putting behind me now have my nose pushed to the wall. There's nowhere else to go."

"It sounds like you've made a decision."

"Actually, I've made two. I want to stop hiding and get on with my life—like doing the screen test. I've decided to try my luck at acting. Jack wanted me to do it, and deep down I want to as well. I've been acting all my life. How could I not be good at it?"

"You said you made two decisions," Bea said.

"I have. Felicia, we're going to have that press conference. I'm tired of running. It's time for the world to know the truth."

"You're going to let Stephanie write the book?" Felicia asked.

"Yes. I hate the idea of giving in to her, but, as Bea pointed out, at least I'll have some control."

"Are you sure you want to do this?" Beatrice asked. She was uncomfortable with the idea of Stephanie's getting her way, but at the same time relieved that Stephanie would be pacified.

"I don't have any choice, Bea. I can't take the risk that the same thing that happened to Tommy could happen to my baby. Once the truth comes out, I can finally learn how to read without having to sneak around, afraid of being discovered."

"Stephanie really has us all right where she wants us, doesn't she?" Bea remarked bitterly.

"Looks that way. I definitely hate the idea of giving in to Stephanie, but if Gabrielle feels comfortable with her decision, then let's get everything out in the open and deal with it," Felicia remarked, thinking not only of Gabrielle's situation but of her own. "I do think we should take control of the press conference. Stephanie doesn't have to call the shots on everything," she suggested.

"I think I'm in labor," an alarmed Gabrielle announced. "My water just broke."

"It's too soon. You have another month and a half."

"I know. What's wrong? Why is the baby coming now?" Gabrielle cried.

"Don't panic. You're going to be okay," Felicia said, trying to keep everyone calm. "I'll call an ambulance and her doctor. Bea, why don't you throw a few things in a bag. And you, Mommy, sit there and stay calm."

Within ten minutes Gabrielle was on her way to Lenox Hill Hospital. Bea accompanied her in the ambulance, while Felicia went back to the office to prepare for the onslaught of calls she was going to receive once the press learned that Gabrielle was having her baby.

Felicia called her colleagues in the hospital's public-relations department to clarify the procedures for press inquiries, before being transferred to the nurses' station on Gabrielle's floor. The head nurse was able to verify that Gabrielle had been checked in and that her condition was still being evaluated.

As she expected, Felicia had a pile of messages waiting for her. They were mainly from the media Stephanie had invited this morning, wanting more details. Felicia, hesitant to explain why the event might be delayed, decided to return the calls later, once she had more information on Gabrielle's condition.

"Felicia, Lexis Richards is on line two," her secretary interrupted.

Felicia took a deep breath before picking up the handset. "Hi," she said.

"Whoa, you sound hassled."

"It's been a rough morning."

"I hope I didn't catch you at a bad time, but I have to talk with you about Sepia Films," Lexis said, his tone all business.

"What about it?"

"It's a go. We have a few more details to hammer out

with MarMa, but before the end of the year we'll be ready to make an announcement."

"That's great. I'm happy for you," Felicia said with genuine delight.

"Thanks. The question is: Are you in?"

"I don't know. I guess we really need to sit down and have a serious discussion."

"I heard that. We have a lot of *business* to rap about. I've waited long enough, Felicia. Time has run out. Either you know what you want or you don't."

"It's not that simple."

"No, baby, it ain't that complicated. You've got to decide. It's him or me. And if it's me, we go public with our relationship. We tell the world that you're more than just my publicist, you're my woman. If you can't, well, then I guess that's it."

"Can we get together and discuss this?"

"Yeah, we can talk, but no more hiding behind Trace or anybody else."

"I'll meet you at my place tonight at ten," she said and hung up the phone. Mired in the swamp of deception, Felicia felt as if she were going nowhere. Guilt had plagued her marriage and had all but destroyed her relationship with Lexis. In the end, she had no idea who, if anybody, she'd wind up with, but at least she'd be rid of this remorse and her life would be her own again. Before she could change her mind, Felicia dialed Trace's office. She asked Trace to meet her at his apartment for an early dinner. She had finally reached the bridge, and it was time to cross.

"Stephanie's office looks like a ghost town," Lois said, sticking her head into Felicia's office. "Don't tell me you finally gave that girl the boot."

"You got it."

"What did she try this time?"

"Not much, just a little blackmail. She knows about Trace and Lexis. Lois, you didn't . . ."

"Don't even go there, girl. It wasn't me. Who else did you tell?"

"Nobody. Only you."

"Then the only way Stephanie could have found out is if she overheard us the night we talked in your office. What does she want so bad that she has to resort to blackmail?"

"She wants to be Gabrielle's authorized biographer."

"I hope Gabrielle said no."

"She wanted to, but Stephanie has something on her, too."

"Damn, this is getting ugly. What does she have on Gabrielle? I mean, despite what the gossip rags report, she seems like your ultimate Girl Scout."

"This information stays in this room until the press conference," Felicia said, closing her door. "Gabrielle is illiterate."

"What?"

"I know, I couldn't believe it either."

"That explains her reluctance to jump into acting."

"And other things. I don't understand how a person grows up not knowing how to read. It must feel like you're living in a foreign country."

"I guess. But I'm missing something here. Why does Stephanie need to blackmail *you* in order to write Gabrielle's biography?"

"I'm the one holding the press conference for the big announcement."

"Oh, that little evil hussy really does have this all thought out, doesn't she? When's the press conference?"

"The release she's already sent out says the end of this

week, but now I'm not sure. Gabrielle went into labor this morning."

"I thought she had another five or six weeks to go."

"The baby said otherwise."

"Have you told Stephanie things are going to be delayed?"

"I'm afraid to. She threatened to use her media contacts with the tabloids if we didn't toe the line."

"That might explain this," Lois said, handing Felicia a pink phone-message slip. "I found this on the floor in her office."

"This is from that reporter Visa Lee of *Star Diary.*"

"Look again. This is *to* Visa Lee. Now, what do you think Stephanie is doing with a phone message to that reporter?"

"Unless she *is* that reporter," Felicia said.

"Looks like Stephanie has a few secrets of her own."

"You know, all this makes sense. All those little leaks and erroneous stories on Gabrielle and our other clients in *Star Diary.* Though this message doesn't actually prove that Stephanie is Visa Lee."

"Well then, we'll have to find a way to prove it. Let's grab dinner and come up with a plan," Lois suggested.

"I can't. I'm going over to talk to Trace. I'm going to tell him everything."

"What about Lexis?"

"He knows about the pregnancy already."

"At this late date, why even tell Trace?"

"Because maybe if I'd been honest with him in the first place, I could have saved my marriage." Felicia finally said aloud the thoughts she'd been recently thinking.

"Felicia, are you considering going back to him?"

"Trace isn't the same selfish, egotistical man he used to be. The incident with the police made him take a really hard look at himself. He's come out of this a much more considerate and thoughtful man. He's a lot like the man I fell in love with years ago."

"And what about Lexis? I thought you loved him."

"I do, but Lexis and I don't share the history Trace and I do."

"Yeah, but history has a way of repeating itself. Has it ever occurred to you that he's being just as controlling and manipulative as he's always been? Has it crossed your mind that he's using this police thing to hold on to you?"

"I don't think so."

"If Trace is who you want, then that's your decision to make, but really think about what you're doing," Lois advised, ending the discussion. She felt strongly that Felicia was headed in the wrong direction, but she knew it was up to her friend to find out for herself. "Getting back to Stephanie, there is another benefit to your coming clean."

"Please tell me. I need all the incentive I can get."

"Have you considered the fact that if both Lexis and Trace know the truth, Stephanie no longer has anything to hold over your head? Same thing for Gabrielle. If she's decided to air all her dirty linen in a book, fine, but who says Stephanie has to write it? Why can't she get somebody legit to write it? If Gabrielle thinks that Stephanie is going to play fair at this late date, she's dreaming."

"Lois, you're absolutely right. Who says we have to go along with Stephanie just because she says so?"

"You don't."

"I have to go. I need to talk to Beatrice. There might just be a way to beat Ms. Bancroft at her own game," Felicia announced.

50

Felicia walked into the brownstone to find both dinner and Trace waiting for her. "This is some spread," she commented. He'd taken the time to stop and pick up dinner on his way from the office. Not only did he have all her favorite dishes, but in the center of the table was a vase full of peonies, her favorite flower—another sign of the thoughtful changes that had taken place in Trace since his arrest.

"I'm glad you called," he told her, kissing her lightly on the forehead as he helped her into her chair. "It gives me the chance not only to spend some time with you, but also to discuss something that's been on my mind for a while now."

"We do have a lot to talk about," Felicia commented.

"We could flip a coin and see who goes first."

"You go," she suggested, curious to know his thoughts.

"I guess I should begin by telling you how much I appreciate everything you've done for me lately. I feel like I've been through hell, and the only reason I got back was because you were here to lean on," Trace said. Felicia smiled in response and patted his hand. "I realize now that without you in my life, I can't be whole."

"What are you saying, Trace?"

"I'm saying that I'm tired of being in this state of limbo. I want us to be together again, sharing our lives as a married couple."

"I've been thinking a lot about us also," Felicia admitted. "I've been wondering if maybe I didn't give our marriage the chance it deserves."

"Does that mean you want us to be together, too?" Trace asked, hope tingeing his voice.

"The thought has crossed my mind lately, but before we even discuss the possibility, I think that we have to be honest about our past," Felicia said, determined to tell the truth.

"I agree," Trace replied. "If we're going to try again, we have to do it with a clean slate. I know that I could be a controlling bastard sometimes, but believe me, it was only because I was afraid of losing you."

"You knew that I loved you."

"I knew you *said* you loved me, but I didn't believe it. In my mind, if you really loved me you'd want to be home, raising our family, and taking care of your man, not building a business. You once asked me if I was jealous of WJ and A. Even though I wouldn't admit it to you then, the answer is yes. I was jealous because, as time went by, it became your life. I felt like I didn't count anymore. That's why I grew to hate the company."

"Then why did you want to make it an issue in our divorce?"

"I didn't want your business, I wanted you. I thought if it came down to a choice between me and your company, there might be a chance you'd choose me. I also figured if you did choose the business, my owning half of it would be one way to stay in your life."

"Isn't it amazing how the fear of losing love can kill it just the same?" Felicia offered softly.

"I've done some really stupid things in the name of love—like trying to get you pregnant on that cruise. I'm ashamed to admit that I punched holes in your diaphragm," Trace revealed.

"You did *what*?" Felicia asked, not believing what she'd heard.

"I wanted us to have a child, and you kept putting it off. I knew that once you were pregnant, you'd see that you really did want to start a family."

"Trace Gordon, that was the most despicable, hurtful, *unforgivable* thing you have ever done," Felicia said furiously. The thought of all the pain and heartache his selfish trick had caused forced Felicia into immediate decisiveness. They were through. Trace was never going to change, and she was never going to be happy in this relationship.

"Why are you getting so upset? It didn't work."

"You're wrong. I did get pregnant."

"That's not possible. I'd have known," Trace insisted.

"The pregnancy was short-lived."

"You had a miscarriage?" Trace asked, unwilling to entertain any other ideas.

"No, I ended the pregnancy on my own."

"How could you? You knew how much I wanted a baby."

"Obviously not. Not once did I think you'd stoop to lying and cheating to get your way. Do you have any idea what you put me through? I beat myself up every day for being so careless. And the guilt over aborting this child nearly drove me crazy. I felt like such a monster for cheating you out of fatherhood."

"You're damn right you cheated me. You cheated both of us," Trace said angrily.

The two sat at the table in silence, each disturbed and disappointed in the other. The air of reconciliation had evaporated, replaced by a chilly fog of angry confusion. Trace could feel his chances slipping away, but he refused to stop trying.

"Look, it might have been unfair to sabotage you like that—"

"Might have been?"

"Okay, it *was* unfair, but is it wrong to love a woman so much that you want to see that love re-created in your child? What did I do that was so damn unforgivable?"

"What you always do—try to force me into denying myself and my own desires. You want me to suffocate my dreams so I can concentrate on yours. That's not a marriage. That's not sharing. That's a sick control."

"I don't want to control you. I want to *love* you," Trace insisted. "Felicia, let's not lose sight of what's important. We started off this conversation both admitting that we wanted to give our marriage another try. There's so much we can share if we take the chance. We can still have a family and be happy together. So let's just forgive and forget our *mutual* mistakes and move on."

"Some things are just too difficult to forgive, and others can never be forgotten."

"I'm telling you, Felicia, I've changed. I'm not the same man I was before."

"If that's the case, I'm happy for you, Trace. Change is good. Change is what keeps a person vibrant and alive."

"Then we do have a chance?" he asked hopefully.

"No, because you see, I've changed, too. The woman I am nearly died with you. I can't take that chance again. I want to live my life, not yours."

"I can still take your company away. You'll be running home to Daddy in no time," Trace threatened, his hurt turning bitter.

"You go ahead and try, but I won't be running home to

Daddy. I'm running home to *me*. Good-bye, Trace," Felicia said. Their eyes locked for a brief moment before Felicia turned and walked out of the brownstone. She felt a certain lightness to her step, a feeling that came with the realization that she was finally free. Felicia flagged down a cab and headed uptown on her way to meet Lexis.

As Felicia walked through her front door, her phone was ringing. She said hello into the receiver, only to find Stephanie on the other end.

"So what's the deal?" she demanded. "I can't get ahold of Gaby or Beatrice, so I decided to call the hired help."

Felicia decided to ignore Stephanie's slight. "Gabrielle has agreed to let you write the book—"

"For someone who doesn't know her ABC's, she's a smart girl."

"But the press conference will have to be postponed," she said tightly. That snide comment made Felicia all the more determined to keep Stephanie from succeeding. "Gabrielle went into labor this morning. She's in the hospital."

"She's having a baby, not heart surgery. I don't see a reason to postpone anything," Stephanie protested.

"Stephanie, be reasonable, she's already agreed to let you write the book. At least let her have these first few days with her baby without a media circus," Felicia argued.

"You want me to be reasonable, fine. We'll move the announcement to the hospital. I'm sure they have some place we can hold the press conference. Have someone call me," she demanded and hung up without saying good-bye.

Felicia hung up feeling wonderfully devious. If the plan she and Beatrice had concocted worked, Stephanie Bancroft was going to be terribly unhappy come Friday afternoon. Felicia was still smiling when the doorman called to announce that Lexis was on his way up.

"Hi," she said, standing in the doorway of her apartment.

"Hey," Lexis replied. They both grinned, causing much of the awkwardness that had built up between them to vanish. "You seem to be in a much better mood than you were earlier," he commented.

"I am. It's amazing how good taking control of your own life can make you feel."

"Whoa, this sounds deep. What's goin' on?"

"I just came from Trace. We had a long and very honest talk about our marriage."

"You told him everything?"

"I'd intended to, but then he told me that he'd intentionally tried to get me pregnant. I thought he had changed, but it's pretty obvious that he hasn't. Trace and I are through, Lexis."

Lexis got up and walked over to the window. "I've heard this song before," he said, his voice devoid of emotion. He was in no mood to have his feelings crushed again.

"This time it's for good. I know what I want now."

"What do you want, Felicia?"

"You," she said, smiling. "I'm ready to go public with our relationship."

"Yes!" Lexis said, swooping Felicia up in a jubilant hug. "I guess you'll have to wait until the divorce is final before you officially move in. But hell, I've waited this long, what's another few months?"

"Before you go crazy on me, there's something else you need to know."

"Yeah?" Lexis said, not liking the tone of her voice.

"I don't want you to misunderstand my intentions. I'm not ready to move in with you or take any major steps toward anything serious."

"I thought things had already gotten pretty serious

between us. Why do you keep yanking my chain?" Lexis asked, feeling as if he'd been sucker-punched.

"I have some very strong feelings for you, Lexis, but I am not ready to make any long-term commitments."

"You got burned once. That doesn't mean it will happen again. You can't be afraid, Felicia. You gotta put your desire above your fear."

"One of the reasons I stayed so long in my marriage was that I was afraid of being out here alone. I went from my father's house to my husband's house without time in between to learn how to survive on my own."

"You built a thriving business by yourself. If that's not a case of survival of the fittest, tell me what is."

"But there was always some man around to take care of me in case I failed. If Papa didn't bail me out, Trace would. Having that kind of safety net allowed me to take chances I might not have otherwise. All my life I've used other people—my parents, my husband, even my clients—to validate me, to tell me I was smart, and strong, and beautiful. It's time for me to accept responsibility for my own growth and happiness."

"I guess this means Sepia Films is out one vice president," Lexis said.

"At least for now, but I'm quite willing to work on a per-project basis."

"In that case, you're hired to promote my next film."

"I'll get on it right away. What's it about?"

"It's a love story," Lexis said, smiling.

"I thought you didn't do love stories," Felicia pointed out, returning his grin.

"I usually don't, but then I got an idea about these two people who can't seem to get it together long enough to say hello, but aren't about to say good-bye."

"How does it end?"

"I don't know yet. It's still in development."

"Just as long as Angela Bassett plays the lead."

"How long do you think this transformation is going to take?" Lexis asked, drawing Felicia close.

"Could be months, could be years. I'll keep you posted."

51

Beatrice returned home from Lenox Hill Hospital feeling both exhilarated and exhausted. Helping Gabrielle deliver her baby was the single most important task she'd ever performed. Through this incredible experience Beatrice had finally become a participant in the circle of life, and, as with most people, she found birth—like death—to be a life-altering experience.

The bittersweet birth of Kylie Helene Hollis had given Beatrice a mighty lesson in maternal love. She learned that loving a child meant sacrificing one's own needs and desires. Gabrielle, a mother for less than forty-eight hours, already understood that. She was willing to forfeit her sterling reputation to protect the well-being and happiness of her daughter.

Just as Gabrielle was willing to alter her life for the sake of Kylie, Beatrice knew she had no choice but to do the same. Now that Gabrielle had decided to let the world know her secret, everything was going to change. It was time for Bea to release Gabrielle from her protective cocoon and allow her to become an independent woman. The only way to accomplish this was to tell the truth. Beatrice decided to begin with Doug Sixsmith.

Bea sat at her desk staring at the phone. She was reluctant and embarrassed to make the call. She had no idea what she was going to say or how she was going to explain the predicament she was in, but in her heart Beatrice knew that Doug was the only person who could help Gabrielle.

Beatrice slowly dialed his number. After several rings an answering machine picked up. The coward in Bea was grateful that she could leave a message and postpone this conversation. She asked Doug to call her back soon, explaining that it was an emergency. She didn't want to alarm him, but time was of the essence.

Doug stood in the door of his bedroom, dripping water on the carpet. He rushed out of the shower to answer the phone and was stopped in his tracks by the urgency in Beatrice's voice. There could be only one reason she was calling him after all this time.

He'd wanted to contact Gabrielle after the death of her husband, but so much time and distance had come between them. Though he still loved her, Doug opted not to rock the boat. Things were back to where they were before their chance reunion on the *Bellezza del Mare*. Work remained the only constant in his life, and he'd finally come to peace with the fact that he was destined to live a life full of professional achievement and personal failure.

He dried off and quickly got dressed, debating whether he should return Bea's phone call. Curiosity won out. As he dialed her number, Doug found himself eager to hear news of Gabrielle.

"Hello, Beatrice. This is Doug Sixsmith."

"Thank you for returning my call."

"I'm surprised to hear from you."

"I thought you'd like to know that Gabrielle had her baby—a little girl."

"That's great. They're both doing well?" Doug asked. He found the news depressing. Another monumental event had taken place in Gabrielle's life without him.

"Physically they're both fine, but Gabrielle desperately needs you."

"She said that?" Doug asked, hope rising in his chest.

"No. She has no idea that I'm calling you."

"If that's the case, I think you'd better look elsewhere. Last time I tried to help Gabrielle, disaster struck."

"There is no one else. You're the only one."

"Why don't you tell me what's going on?"

"Gabrielle is being blackmailed by Stephanie Bancroft." Doug listened intently as Beatrice explained the bare facts of the situation. By the time Bea was finished, Doug was furious, but still unwilling to get involved.

"If Gabrielle has already decided to let Stephanie write the book, why are you calling me?" he asked.

"She only agreed because she thinks that if she works with Stephanie she'll have more control over the contents. We both know that won't be the case. That's why *you* have to write this book."

"Bea, I'll be glad to give you the names of some other writers, but I can't be a part of this. Gabrielle has told me on more than one occasion to stay out of her life. I'm sorry she's in trouble, but I don't think I'm the guy to come to her rescue," Doug replied, ignoring his impulse to get involved.

"She still loves you," Bea blurted out.

"What?"

"She never stopped, not even when she was married to Jack."

"That's a nice fantasy, but we both know it's not true," Doug said, refusing to acknowledge his heart's hiccup. "She made her feelings about me quite clear. It's all down in black and white."

"Gabrielle didn't write that letter, I did."

"Why wouldn't she write it herself?"

"For the same reason she couldn't read the note you left on her birthday—Gabrielle is illiterate."

"I've seen her reading with my own eyes," he said, his mind disbelieving his ears.

"She was covering up, but there isn't time to go into that now. The truth is, the letter she dictated was not the letter I wrote. She wanted to tell you the truth and ask you for another chance. I didn't want you to hurt her again, so I told you the relationship was over for good. That's also why I didn't give her your letter or tell her you called."

"You meddling old woman," Doug exploded. "How could you do that to us? You let her go on believing that I didn't love her and was so repulsed by her confession that I couldn't even bother to acknowledge her feelings? You don't think that hurt her even more?"

"I realize that now, and I am sorrier than you can ever imagine, but I honestly thought I was protecting her. Doug, you have every right to blame and despise me, but not Gabrielle. She doesn't know any of this."

"Are you planning to tell her?"

"Yes, before the press conference, I hope," Bea said.

"What press conference?"

"Tomorrow at one o'clock in the hospital auditorium, Gabrielle is going to announce her illiteracy and introduce her biographer. I'm hoping that it will be you. Stephanie shouldn't be allowed to profit by hurting other people. Will you help us?"

"Tell me something. Has Gabrielle told you that she still loves me?"

"Not in so many words," Bea admitted. "Does it matter?"

"I don't know. I have to think about this," Doug replied honestly.

"Please think fast. You'll be saving her life."

But what about my own? Doug thought, hanging up the phone. Beatrice's confession was in one way a gift, giving him hope that a future with Gabrielle might still be possible. But by helping her would he merely be helping himself to more heartache?

52

That's right, Felicia Wilcot. I'm calling to leave a message for Visa Lee. Tell her today's press conference has been pushed back to two o'clock."

"That ought to do it. If Stephanie is Visa Lee, she'll be late for her own press conference," Lois said.

"And what am I going to do if she is?"

"I don't know, but it should involve some sort of public flogging."

"She's already in store for a little humiliation today," Felicia divulged.

"Sounds like Ms. Bancroft's boat is sinking fast."

"Like the *Titanic*."

The hospital auditorium was teeming with reporters and camera crews milling about, munching on refreshments, waiting for the conference to begin. Already seated in the front row were representatives from the Literacy Volunteers of America and several new readers and their tutors. Also in attendance were Greg von Ulrich, Jaci Francis, and Ruthanna Beverly. Doug, tied up in an unscheduled meeting with his agent, walked through the auditorium doors just minutes before the start of the program.

"I guess this will be her kid's first press conference," a reporter from *US* magazine remarked.

"Maybe," Doug replied. It was clear that these reporters had no idea of the magnitude of Gabrielle's impending announcement. He was not even sure that she realized the impact her confession was going to make, not only on her life, but on the lives of thousands of others. After years of being a fashion model, Gabrielle Donovan was about to become a role model for a massive group of people whose hidden shame kept them silent and too embarrassed to seek help.

Beatrice spotted Doug as he walked into the auditorium and breathed a sigh of relief. With him on their side, Bea knew that everything would be okay. She hoped that Gabrielle felt the same. Felicia and Bea had decided not to mention anything to her, on the chance that Doug might change his mind.

"Have you seen Stephanie?" Lois whispered to Felicia backstage.

"No, have you?"

"Nope. Looks like we've caught a big fat rat in our trap."

Promptly at one, Felicia walked to the podium standing front and center on the auditorium stage. Gabrielle stood in the wings with Beatrice, nervously awaiting her cue. This was no doubt the most frightening thing she'd ever done, but, strangely, it was also one of the most exciting.

"You know, in a perverted kind of way, I owe Stephanie."

"You owe her nothing. Trust me, she's going to get what's coming to her," Bea said before Felicia's voice interrupted her.

"Ladies and gentlemen, I'm Felicia Wilcot, and on behalf of Gabrielle Donovan, I'd like to thank you for coming this afternoon. We have several exciting announcements to make today. First, I'm sure you've heard by now the reason we're holding this press conference in the hospital. Three days ago, on November tenth, at twelve-eighteen in the afternoon, Gabrielle Donovan gave birth to a five-pound, eleven-ounce, baby girl named Kylie Helene Hollis. The birth was by cesarean, and both mother and daughter are doing quite well."

"Can you spell that?" shouted a reporter.

"K-Y-L-I-E," Felicia said.

"Who was Gabrielle's labor coach?"

"Her friend and personal assistant, Beatrice Braidburn."

"Can we see Kylie?"

"Not at this time. Out of respect for mother and daughter, that's all the information we will release right now."

"That's it? Don't we get to speak with Gabrielle?" asked a reporter from the Associated Press.

"Ms. Donovan has asked me to read you the following letter, after which she will answer a few questions." In a soft and moving voice, Felicia read the statement that she and Gabrielle had carefully prepared.

" 'My dear friends and fans: Through the years, in my role as a spokesperson for various companies, you have often heard me say that each of us has special talents, which make up for our human deficiencies. Since many of you here in this room have written so kindly about my talents, I'd like to tell you briefly about one of *my* deficiencies. I am illiterate. Simply put, I cannot read or write.' "

A collective gasp reverberated around the auditorium. Mouths were agape as pens flew busily across the reporters' pads. Doug stood among the journalists taking it all in, hoping that his colleagues would be kind and realize the strength it took to make this admission.

Backstage Beatrice silently squeezed Gabrielle's hand in a show of support as Felicia continued to read.

"'For me and millions of others in this country, the education system broke down. We slipped through the cracks. We learned to survive in this world of words by taking advantage of our special talents. We get through life manipulating others into doing what all literate people can do for themselves—read a recipe, fill out a job application, understand a bus schedule, or write a letter to someone we love.

"'Unless you have been there, you can't know what it is like to live as an illiterate. Imagine being a fugitive on the lam, where not a day goes by that you don't worry about getting caught. Imagine being labeled lazy, a quitter, a failure—not because you're stupid, but because you're too ashamed to admit you can't read, too ashamed to ask for help. Imagine being constantly on your guard, able to relax fully only at night, just before you fall asleep. Imagine that your evening prayer is always the same, "Thank God I made it through another day without being found out."

"'But keeping such a secret takes its toll. In so many ways my life has been a lie and I, a fraud. I am tired of pretending. I am tired of hiding. This afternoon I begin living the truth, so tonight my prayer can be different.

"'Throughout these past few years, I have come to appreciate and rely on your kindness and support. Now I need your understanding. Please help me, and those that follow, to get over our embarrassment and shame so we are free to learn. Please don't taunt us. Teach us. Thank you.'

"Ladies and gentlemen, Gabrielle Donovan," Felicia announced, discreetly wiping away her tears. As Gabrielle walked to the podium, the auditorium remained quiet, shocked into silence by this amazing admission. Everybody in the room was trying to digest and put into perspective what they'd heard. From the rear of the auditorium, Doug, tears in his eyes, began to applaud, an action that was replicated by the rest of the room.

Led by Greg von Ulrich, the members of the audience, one by one, rose from their seats, giving Gabrielle a standing ovation. She stood, basking in the glow of their acceptance, grateful for the love and support. She felt as if the entire world had been lifted off her shoulders. She was no longer ashamed. She was free, and it felt wonderful.

"Thank you," she said softly into the microphone. "I'd be happy to answer your questions." The auditorium erupted into a collage of reporters' voices shouting out questions. Felicia stepped to the mike in an effort to control the chaos.

"Please, one at a time," she requested as she pointed to a reporter in the front row.

"How have you managed to hide this for so long?"

"I learned very early to trust my instincts and to invent new solutions to problems. Most of all, I learned how to get others to help me do what I needed done."

"Can you give us an example?"

"To avoid being found out, you learn to be creative. On buses and trains I memorized the number of stops between my home and my usual destinations, or asked the bus driver to tell me where to get off. I grocery-shopped by looking at the pictures on the labels. If I got sick and needed medication, I memorized the doctor's instructions and then color-coded my medicine bottles so I knew which was which. When I had to fill out forms, I'd bandage my hand and ask a stranger for help. There are a million tricks," Gabrielle told her audience.

"You're considered one of the most successful young businesswomen in your industry. How can you be so smart and not know how to read and write?"

"Intelligence and illiteracy are not synonymous. Because I can't read, I find other ways to educate myself. I learn a lot by being a good listener. I listen to radio shows and to books on tape. I learn by watching TV and going to the movies. I build my vocabulary by listening to people speak and then learning the words I didn't know."

"Have you ever tried to learn to read?"

"Several times, but something always got in the way. Either I moved, or my tutor left, and then I got too recognizable. It's not easy hiding something like literacy lessons when you live in a fishbowl."

"Gabrielle, why are you going public with this?"

"Because I'm tired of pretending. Because I'm hoping that by my going public, others like me will be encouraged to seek help as well. But the most important reason is my daughter. For Kylie's sake, it's time for me to learn to read."

Stephanie burst through the auditorium doors just in time to hear Gabrielle's comment. It was immediately clear that the press conference had been going on for quite a while. She stood in the middle of the aisle and looked at her watch; it was 1:53. She was sure her secretary had said that the press conference began at two.

Felicia saw Stephanie step through the double doors. Following Gabrielle's last answer, she walked back up to the podium and addressed the audience. "I know this is a lot to digest, and you must have a million questions, but in the interest of time we'll move on. There are press packets available for you on your way out. They contain a copy of Gabrielle's statement and a more in-depth press release. Those of you who wish to talk with Gabrielle further may contact my office. Right now, we have one last announcement to make."

"I should have brought two notepads," quipped a reporter in the front row.

"We are well aware that today's revelations and events in the recent past have raised a great deal of public interest in the entirety of Gabrielle's life. For this reason, Gabrielle has decided to coauthor her biography," Felicia told the audience.

Stephanie stood in the middle aisle bursting with anticipation. Finally her moment to stand in the spotlight had arrived. Out of the corner of her eye, Stephanie saw Doug Sixsmith standing toward the front. *Step aside, Dougie, your competition has arrived.*

"I'd like to introduce you to the coauthor of the Gabrielle Donovan story, a writer whose work is synonymous with integrity and truth . . ."

Felicia is really laying it on thick, Stephanie thought as she began her way to the stage. She quickly ran through her remarks, not wanting to stumble when she got to the podium. She was about to ascend the stage stairs when the bomb dropped.

". . . Mr. Doug Sixsmith."

With one foot on the bottom stair, Stephanie stopped in her tracks. The smile on her face quickly metamorphosed into a horrific grin. *What the fuck is going on here?* As Doug climbed onto the stage and approached the microphone, Stephanie realized that she'd been double-crossed. They'd set her up. *They won't get away with this,* she promised herself as she turned on her heels and slipped out the side door.

Gabrielle stood on the stage, just as shocked as Stephanie. Who had decided that Doug would write her book, and why hadn't it been discussed with her? If she had been consulted, Gabrielle would have told them in no uncertain terms that Doug Sixsmith would be the last person she'd consent to write her biography.

"Doug, John Newman from *Time.* Will this book be a tell-all?"

"It's too early to say what it's going to be, but I can say

what it won't be," Doug answered. "It won't be a trashy, name-dropping, mudslinging exposé."

"Gabrielle, how do you feel about working with your ex-boyfriend on such a personal project?" a reporter from the *National Enquirer* asked.

"He's a great writer. Isn't that all that counts?" Gabrielle commented graciously, avoiding Doug's eyes. "Doug and Felicia will be happy to answer the rest of your questions, but I'm afraid I have to go to my daughter now. Thank you all very much."

While Doug and Felicia remained at the podium, Beatrice and Lois joined Gabrielle, and together they walked to her room. "Why didn't someone let me in on the surprise?" Gabrielle asked.

"We weren't sure until the last minute whether Doug would agree to do it," Beatrice explained.

"Did you see the expression on Stephanie's face when Felicia announced Doug's name?" Lois laughed. "She looked like the Joker from *Batman*." The trio walked into Gabrielle's room, only to find Stephanie sitting in wait.

"I can't believe that you all were stupid enough to try and stick it to me like that. You know what this means, don't you?" Stephanie asked the group.

"Let's just cut to the chase and have you tell us," Lois replied smartly.

"It means I'm still writing this book and everybody's secrets get spilled."

"Sorry, Stephanie. There's nothing you can hold over our heads anymore. In case you missed it, Gabrielle just made a public announcement about her illiteracy," Bea said smugly.

"And Felicia has already dealt with Trace and Lexis," Lois piped up, "so it looks like your game of blackmail is finished."

"It ain't over until the fat lady sings, and that means you, Beatrice. I think it's time these two heard your song. Why don't you share your juicy secret with Gabrielle?" Stephanie asked. All eyes turned to Beatrice, who felt herself growing first terribly agitated and then totally calm.

"Why don't you go first? I hear you have a few secrets of your own," Bea challenged, looking directly into Stephanie's eyes with a steely stare. Stephanie was caught off guard. What was Bea talking about? Did she know about Killington? "Why don't you tell us how you manage to make everyone's life miserable under two personas," Bea continued.

Stephanie tried to keep her relief in check. Apparently Henny Penny had figured out that she was Visa Lee. Who gave a rat's ass about that now? She was almost through with that gig anyway. Once this book came out, she would be too busy with her new career to continue. "Don't tell me you're a fan of 'The Visa Lee Report'?"

"Not hardly. I don't covet trash in any form."

"*You're* Visa Lee?" Gabrielle gasped. "You're the one who's been writing all those terrible things about me?"

"Guilty as charged. And I sincerely want to thank you for your cooperation. Thanks to you, my column has developed quite a following."

"Do you know what your lies did to me? To my life, you lying, scheming, ungrateful bitch?"

"*I'm* the ungrateful bitch? You should be thanking me for keeping your name in the headlines."

"Thanks for nothing."

"Nothing? Your life is the fucking fairy tale it is because of *me*. Do you know how it felt to see *you* marry the one man *I* loved, knowing that I introduced you? Or every day watching you rise to the top, knowing that *I* was the one who made it all possible? All I asked was for a little help in return, and what do you do? Stab me in the back. So don't talk to me about being ungrateful and dishonest, you sanctimonious bitch. We had an agreement, and you welched on it."

"This was all done without my knowledge, but now that it's happened, I think it was a damn good idea. You're the one living the fairy tale if you think for one second that you're going to write my biography," Gabrielle argued back.

"Don't be so sure about that. You haven't heard the last from me. Not by a long shot," Stephanie promised. "And before you blame me for all your misery and heartache, talk to your personal assistant over there. Ask her how she 'personally assisted' Doug Sixsmith out of your life," she said, throwing the words into Gabrielle's face before storming out of the room.

Stephanie's inference dropped a grenade in their midst, releasing a foggy silence into the room. Realizing that Beatrice and Gabrielle needed privacy to maneuver through this emotional minefield, Lois headed out the door in search of Felicia.

Both women, tentative about delving into the truth, set Stephanie's accusation aside for the moment. Bea turned to look at Gabrielle. She could see confusion in the girl's eyes. It was time to level with her about the letter. "Honey, why don't you get in bed? It's been a rough afternoon."

"I can't believe the nerve of that woman. After everything she's done to me to try and destroy my reputation, *she* has the audacity to feel betrayed."

"I know Doug will do a great job—" Bea said.

"What on earth possessed you and Felicia to think that I could ever work with Doug Sixsmith? Despite what I just said to Stephanie, I have no intention of writing my grocery list, let alone my life story, with that man," Gabrielle said, her anger becoming apparent.

"Don't be so hard on him, Gabrielle. Doug just found out you were illiterate yesterday when I told him."

"Don't lie for him. He told me to my face that he read my letter."

"He read *a* letter, but it wasn't the one you thought you sent. I'm ashamed to admit this, but I wrote a different letter, one telling him to stay out of your life. I also never gave you the note he wrote in return or told you about his phone calls," Bea said softly. Gabrielle sat silently for a moment, stunned by Beatrice's admission.

"What did his letter say?"

"I don't know. I didn't read it."

"Where is it?"

"Stephanie has it. She spent the night over at my place recently and found it while going through my things."

"First you stole the letter, then Stephanie. And here I thought you were both on my side," Gabrielle said angrily.

"I am on your side. I was trying to protect you. I love you like you're my own daughter."

"My mother would have never done anything like this to me."

"Gabrielle, please. I'm so dreadfully sorry for interfering."

"You did more than interfere. You nearly destroyed my life, and because of you Jack is dead," Gabrielle accused her angrily.

"How can you blame me for Jack's death?" Bea was shocked by her allegation.

"He'd be alive today because we would have never gone to Vermont together in the first place."

"Gabrielle, whatever I did, I did out of love," Bea pleaded, begging for understanding.

Gabrielle's voice turned cold. "Your kind of love I don't need."

The women were interrupted by a soft tap on the door. The nurse entered, pushing Kylie in the isolette. "Here's your roommate," she announced.

"Thanks, Velma," Gabrielle said as she got off the bed to check on her sleeping daughter. Conversation between the women ceased until the nurse left the room.

"Gabrielle, I would never do anything to intentionally hurt you or Kylie. You have to know that. I love you both, and I want to take care of you."

"I put my life in your hands. I will not make the same mistake with my daughter's."

"Don't say that. I know you love me, too."

"I can't love someone I don't trust," Gabrielle said, recycling the very words that Doug had said to her. "I want you to go, and I don't want to see you again," Gabrielle said, tears streaming down her cheeks.

"Don't do this, please, honey. All I have is you and the baby," Bea pleaded.

"Not anymore," Gabrielle said and turned away.

Beatrice took one last look at Gabrielle and Kylie before leaving the room. She wandered down the corridor toward the elevator in a daze. Bea was shattered, but she had no one to blame but herself. If she had only trusted Gabrielle to have enough love in her heart for both of them, she'd still have her family. Instead, she was alone.

The elevator doors opened and Beatrice stepped forward, barreling into Doug Sixsmith. The contact caused her to drop her leather patchwork handbag. Bea's wallet, eyeglass case, prescription medicine, and several loose coins spilled out across the corridor floor. Doug reached down and gathered up Beatrice's belongings, put them back in her purse, and handed the bag to the distraught woman. As she burst into heart-wrenching sobs, Doug put his arms around Beatrice and led her over to a nearby bench.

"I've ruined everything," she sobbed.

"You told her the truth?"

"Yes. She said she never wants to see me again."

"She's been through a lot lately. I'm sure she didn't mean it."

"She has every right to hate me. I hate myself for all the pain I've caused her."

"We've both hurt her, and it's going to take time for her to sort her feelings out."

"You don't understand. I did much more than just keep you two apart. I stole her independence."

"What are you talking about?" Doug asked.

"I was the only person in this entire world who knew that Gabrielle was illiterate, but did I do anything to change that? No. I helped her come up with a thousand different reasons why she shouldn't get tutoring, but I had only one reason—I was afraid that if she learned to read, she wouldn't need me anymore."

"You had to have helped her somehow," Doug said, trying to comprehend the magnitude of Bea's actions.

"She tried those phonetic learning tapes once. At first she did very well. She got excited, and I got frightened, so when she started having trouble, I made her feel comfortable about quitting."

"Of course she was excited," Doug said. "Imagine you were paralyzed and then one day you felt this twinge in your legs. The doctor tells you that soon you'll be able to walk without the crutches you've become so dependent on. Suddenly you realize that a whole new world is about to open up for you."

"But that's the part that scared me. I was her crutch. Once she could read and function on her own, why on earth would she still need me?"

"That's a chance we're both going to have to take," Doug told her.

"Will you talk to her? Will you try to make her see how much I love her?"

"I'll do what I can, but I'm not sure she wants to have much to do with me either."

Gabrielle heard a faint tap on her door, but offered no acknowledgment. She wanted to be alone to sort through her emotions. Beatrice's bombshell had left her feeling angry and betrayed. How could Bea watch her suffer, knowing full well that she could stop her pain at any time? And poor Jack. Would he still be alive had Beatrice been honest and forthcoming? Gabrielle wasn't sure she would ever forgive Bea.

"Gabrielle?" a voice that made her heart skip called out. Gabrielle looked to the door and saw Doug, holding a bunch of purple irises, enter her room. The sight made her smile and brought fresh tears to her eyes.

"Come in."

"Is this a bad time?" he asked tentatively.

"It's fine." Gabrielle watched as Doug walked across the room and placed the flowers on her bedside table. Before coming over, he stopped at the isolette and gazed down at Gabrielle's daughter.

"I see that another cover girl has made her way into the world," he remarked lightly, his back to Gabrielle. He didn't want her to see the range of emotions moving across his face. "She's beautiful, Gabrielle. You do good work."

"Thank you."

Doug took one last look at the daughter that should have been his and turned to face Gabrielle. "I bought this for her," he said, handing Gabrielle a four-piece wooden puzzle of a soft, fuzzy lamb. "I figure it won't be long before she's ready for the wonderful world of jigsaw."

"Thank you," Gabrielle repeated, finding his gesture sweet, but still too confused to say more.

"Are you okay? I know this afternoon must have been rough on you."

"A little."

"For a bunch of jaded reporters, they all seemed pretty supportive," Doug said, trying to fill the clumsy silence.

"I'm happy about that."

"And for what it's worth, I'm very proud of you. What you did took a lot of courage. You're going to help a lot of people."

"Thank you, but I wasn't trying to be a hero. I just want to finally learn how to read," she replied self-consciously.

"About the book. If you're uncomfortable with the idea . . ."

"I need some time."

"I understand. You must be tired," Doug said, feeling very ill at ease. "I'll go so you can get some rest," he said, looking into her lapis eyes.

"Thanks. I'll have Felicia get in touch with you about the book," Gabrielle informed him, looking away. She knew that she sounded curt and professional, but Beatrice's revelation was too new and her emotions too jumbled. She didn't know how to behave around Doug at this moment.

"Fine. You take care," Doug said, not taking his eyes off her. Another few awkward seconds went by before he turned and left the room. Gabrielle took several deep breaths. On the third exhale, Doug burst back through the door.

"I'm sorry, but I can't leave here without knowing the truth. Gabrielle, why didn't you tell me you couldn't read?"

"At first I was ashamed, and I thought you would be, too. And then, after my birthday, I sent you a note explaining everything, or at least thought I had, but—"

"Bea told me about your letter. Believe me, it's the only reason I stayed away," Doug said.

"I don't know if I'll ever be able to forgive her."

"Try to put yourself in her place. She thought she was protecting you from me."

"It wasn't all your fault. If I had told you the truth, things might have worked out differently. Still, Bea had no right to interfere like that."

"Maybe not, but at least she owned up to her actions. You've got to give her credit for that."

"I'll think about it."

"Will you think about something else?" Doug asked, reaching for her hand. He was amazed by how comfortable and right it felt in his. "Would you think about forgiving me. I was so stupid for believing that idiot reporter Visa Lee's lies."

"You mean Stephanie's. Visa Lee is her pen name."

"All this confusion between us is because of Stephanie Bancroft?"

"Not all of it. She had help."

"You can't lump Bea and Stephanie together. What Beatrice did was wrong, but she acted out of love. Stephanie was just being a jealous bitch."

"I'd like to say she was all done, but I think she's planning to write a book about me."

"Not if I can help it," Doug promised. He paused for a moment before continuing and searched her eyes with his. "Gabrielle, do you think there's a chance, however remote, for us to try again?"

"So much has happened. It could never be the same."

"I know that things are different," Doug said, nodding at the hospital bassinet. "We'll take it nice and slow. Just give it some thought?"

Gabrielle nodded in agreement as Kylie's hungry cry filled the room.

"I guess that's my cue to get out of here," he said, resisting the temptation to run his hand through her unruly curls.

"Thanks for the flowers and the puzzle for Kylie. She'll love it."

"My pleasure. I'll call you soon?"

"Okay."

"See you later, sweet potato," he said to Kylie. Doug and Gabrielle shared a smile, both remembering the many times they'd spoken that familiar line. Suddenly the stiffness between them melted, leaving a pool of possibilities before them. Doug departed, leaving Gabrielle alone with her daughter and her memories. He walked down the corridor with other things on his mind. It was time to pay Stephanie Bancroft a visit.

53

Call your friend at Target Press and see if we can get an appointment with Russell Shockley," Stephanie ordered Howie the minute she walked into the apartment.

"I thought you wanted to work with a legit publisher. What happened?" he asked, noticing the ferocious look in her eyes.

"I got hoodwinked. They found out I was Visa Lee and set me up. By the time I got to the press conference, Gabrielle had made her big confession and then announced that Doug Sixsmith was going to write her book."

"Her ex-boyfriend?"

"Yeah. She didn't even let Jack's grave get cold before she hooked up with old lover boy."

"What about your professional reputation?"

"I've rethought my position. Forget journalistic legitimacy. Plenty of biographers are raking in big bucks writing unauthorized books. Hell, without the Kitty Kelleys of the world, the true lives of people like Jackie Onassis, Elizabeth Taylor, or Frank Sinatra might never be revealed. Now, go make that call."

Howie returned shortly with a wide grin on his face.

"You're one lucky lady. You have an appointment at Target today at six-thirty. He's leaving for vacation tomorrow, but he remembered our proposal and wants to talk before he goes."

"Perfect. Are you going with me?"

"Nah. I'm working the premiere of Tom Hanks's new flick. You can handle Shockley without me, can't you?"

"Howie, don't ask stupid questions."

The least I can do for Gabrielle is get her letter back, Beatrice thought as she knocked on Stephanie's front door. Within seconds she heard the sound of Stephanie's grumbling as she approached.

"Beatrice, what a surprise, What happened? Gabzilla throw you out of your apartment?"

"I came to talk to you. May I come in?" Beatrice said, trying to sound civil. After everything Stephanie had said and done, it was difficult.

"Sorry, the place is a mess. Next time why don't you call before you come barging over." There was no way that Stephanie could let Beatrice into the apartment now, not with the Killington pictures spread on top of the coffee table. She'd pulled them out, along with other photos they had of Gabrielle, to put together a representative sampling for her meeting at Target Press.

"I'm used to your mess," Bea said, pushing her way inside. She had not come all this way to let Stephanie stop her now. Beatrice was determined that Gabrielle would finally see Doug's letter.

"Make this quick, Bea," Stephanie said, as she placed herself between Beatrice and the coffee table.

"I want Gabrielle's letter back."

"Sorry, you know what they say: 'Possession is nine tenths of the law.'"

"I'm not leaving until I get it," Bea insisted, just as the phone began to ring.

"Don't make me throw you out," Stephanie responded, ignoring the phone. The answering machine picked up, and the two women could both hear Russell Shockley leaving a message. Stephanie ran to the phone. "Get lost. Now!" she shouted to Bea before picking up the receiver.

Bea, with no intention of going anywhere, walked over to the sofa and sat down. She was shocked to see at least two dozen photos of Gabrielle scattered across the coffee table. What was Stephanie doing with all these pictures? She picked up a photo of Jack and Gabrielle and was about to reach for another when the image of the Killington house caught her eye. She picked up the stack and quickly leafed through it. The first two photos showed the vandalized vacation house. Bea gasped when she saw the last two photos. They were of the back of the chalet engulfed in flames.

How and where had Stephanie gotten these photographs? And why hadn't she turned them over to the police? Bea was still mulling the questions over in her mind when Stephanie snatched the photos from her hand.

"You just can't keep your big nose out of other people's business, can you?" Stephanie barked.

"Where did you get these pictures?" Beatrice asked in a tone that was not to be ignored.

"If you must know, I received them in the mail."

"Who sent them to you?"

"I don't know. They were sent anonymously to my office at the paper," Stephanie lied, taken aback by Beatrice's sudden assertiveness.

"Do the police know you have these?"

"My source asked me not to contact the police."

"I thought you said they were mailed to your office."

"There was a note attached," Stephanie countered weakly.

"Why wouldn't your source want the police to have these? They might help solve this case."

"I don't know, but I've had enough of your inquisition," Stephanie said, as she walked over to the bookcase and pulled an envelope from between two books. "Here, take your stupid letter and get out of here." Stephanie was getting nervous. *Damn this old bat. Why did she have to show up when these photos were out in the open?*

"You're lying," Beatrice said, taking the letter and putting it in her purse. "If you received those photos legitimately, you would have printed them in your column. There's no way you would pass up these pictures unless you were afraid to use them."

"You're way off base, old lady," Stephanie said tensely. "You have your letter, so beat it."

"Did you take these pictures yourself?"

"How could I? A, I'm not a photographer, and B, only *you* knew where they were going."

"That's true. But *you* spent the night snooping around my apartment. If you found the key to my pearwood box, then you must have found the calendar book where I kept all of Gabrielle's travel arrangements," Beatrice accused the woman. Judging from the panic-stricken look in the back of Stephanie's eyes and the flushed rims of her ears, Beatrice knew she'd hit the nail squarely on its head.

"I have to give you credit, Henny Penny, you're much brighter than you look."

"Why don't you tell me everything?"

"Damn it, there's nothing to tell," Stephanie insisted. "I've been keeping notes on everything that happens to Gabrielle professionally and personally for months now. I went up to Vermont to take a few pictures of the lovebirds on their honeymoon for inclusion in my book. End of story."

"Don't lie to me, Stephanie. You didn't go to Vermont to take pictures. You went to the house determined to ruin Gabrielle's honeymoon. You were the one who broke in and trashed the chalet. There were no college kids, no strangers—only you."

"Why the hell would I go through all that trouble?"

"Because you're jealous of Gabrielle—jealous that she married Jack and that she's rich and famous. That's the only reason you want to write this book—to capitalize on Gabrielle's fame and gain some of your own."

"Is that really so terrible? She gets everything she wants—men, money, work. I get nothing. So what if I found a way to grab a little glory for myself?"

"Glory through murder?"

"I didn't kill anyone," Stephanie sputtered, outraged by the accusation.

"You set the house on fire with Jack in it," Bea accused.

"It was an accident. I admit we tried to make it look like they'd had a big party. I planned to report it in my column, but that's all. I never meant for anybody to die."

"You left him in a burning house. What did you expect would happen?"

"It wasn't on fire when we left," Stephanie said in her defense.

"You might not have killed Jack, but you certainly set him up to die. You won't get away with this. Whatever book you plan to write, you'll be writing it in jail."

Beatrice stood by disconcerted as Stephanie broke into a throaty laugh. Her bewilderment turned to fear as the look in Stephanie's eyes seemed to grow increasingly bizarre. Beatrice felt as though she were cornered by a wild animal. Slowly, she began backing away in the direction of the door.

"Where do you think you're going?" Stephanie said, standing in front of her. Purposefully walking toward Bea, she forced the woman to the couch. Beatrice fell back onto the sofa with a heavy thud.

"I'm going home."

"To call the police?" Stephanie asked. Beatrice remained quiet, afraid to say or do anything. "Go right ahead and turn me in. We can bunk together in the same cell."

"That will never happen."

"Sure it will. Think about it. Was it just coincidence that you were the one who discovered the fire? You, the only person who knew where they were staying?"

"Why would I want to hurt Jack?"

"Because you were afraid of losing y   ⋮ precious Gabrielle."

"Nobody will believe that story."

"Everybody knows that you have a history of keeping Gabrielle away from the men in her life. Doug was just a boyfriend. Who knows how far you'd go to get rid of her husband?"

"That's absurd."

"I told you we were partners. I meant it. You turn me in and I'll name you as my partner in crime. I think 'accomplice' is the term the police use."

She was so clever. Not only had she managed to blackmail Beatrice, Stephanie had managed to make her a conspirator in this miserable incident. But she hadn't bet on one thing: Bea didn't give a damn anymore. She'd already lost Gabrielle and Kylie. There was nothing left to lose.

"I'm willing to take that chance. I'm almost sixty-seven years old. Going to prison means nothing to me. But come hell or high water, I will not let you get away with hurting Gabrielle. You'll have to kill me to keep me from turning you in, and we both know you won't do that."

The idea that Beatrice was willing to go to jail or even die for Gabrielle enraged Stephanie. She responded to Bea's statement with a hard, swift slap to her jaw. While Beatrice sat momentarily stunned by the strike, Stephanie hurried over to the desk and pulled out a black revolver. She approached Beatrice again, waving the gun in front of her. Beatrice inhaled loudly. She'd pushed Stephanie too far.

"I wouldn't be so sure about that," Stephanie said. She could see that the woman was clearly petrified. To keep her that way, she was careful not to let Bea get a good look at the gun. From a reasonable distance it looked like a deadly killing instrument. In reality, it was Howie's water pistol.

"Don't move," Stephanie ordered as she circled the couch and stood behind Beatrice. Holding the toy revolver to Bea's head with one hand, Stephanie quickly stripped off her pantyhose and proceeded to tie Bea's arms behind her at the wrist. She didn't bother tying up her feet, knowing that without the use of her arms, Bea would not be able to raise her hefty body from the couch.

"Don't do this, Stephanie. You're already in enough trouble."

"Shut up! I didn't kill Jack, and I'm not going to jail for vandalizing a house," Stephanie said furiously.

"If that's the truth, tell the police."

"They won't believe me, just like you don't. Besides, I have a better idea. Since you're so willing to take the rap for all of this, you can."

"How so?"

"You'll see. Don't go away," Stephanie chuckled snidely. She walked down the short hall to the back of the apartment and opened her bedroom door. Immediately, the cat sprang from the room. Barclay wandered into the living room and hopped up onto the windowsill behind the sofa to nap.

Stephanie returned to the living room carrying a tripod and video camera. She set the tripod up opposite the couch and bolted the camera in place. She looked through the viewfinder and adjusted the camera so that Beatrice's head and shoulders were loosely framed by the background of the room. She checked to make sure that Bea's arms, still tied behind her back, did not stand out suspiciously. This confession could in no way look coerced.

"What is that for?" Bea asked, her voice trembling.

"You're going to give me a *believable* confession to the Killington fire. Keep it short, and don't try anything funny. Oh, be sure to add that you're sorry and you can't live with what you've done. That's always a good touch. Here we go. Action!"

"I—uh—I, I can't do this," Bea faltered.

"You can do it. You *will* do it," Stephanie barked, waving the gun in Bea's face.

While Stephanie rewound the videotape, Bea took a minute to put her thoughts together, drew in a deep breath, and began. "Gabrielle, I know I've hurt you badly, and for that I am so very sorry. What I'm about to tell you will only hurt you more, but you deserve to know the truth about everything.

"I didn't want Doug to come between us, so I found a way to eliminate him from the picture. For a while things were normal again, but then Jack came along. He ambushed me with your surprise marriage and pregnancy. I resented him for taking you away from me, so I came up with a plan to get rid of him, too." Beatrice paused, and Stephanie prompted her to continue by pointing the revolver at her.

"I didn't mean to kill him. I only meant to sour the relationship between you by ruining his reputation. I paid some kids to destroy your vacation house. It was expensive, and I had to use my credit card to get a cash advance, but I knew

I could get the money back by selling the story to one of the tabloids. I thought if the public believed that Jack was irresponsible and immature, so might you. But Jack came back too soon. One of the kids knocked him out, and he dropped his cigarette on the floor. That's what started the fire. His death was an accident.

"I'm so sorry for everything, Gabrielle. I know that you and Kylie will be all right, and that Doug will take good care of you. He's a good man. Give him another chance to prove it. I hope in time you will find it in your heart to forgive me. I can't live with myself knowing all the pain I've caused you. I love you more than life itself. Good-bye."

"Very touching. Now, that wasn't so hard, was it?"

"When are you going to send this to her?" Bea asked wearily.

"I'm not. Oh, didn't I tell you? This is a combo confession/suicide letter. I'm not sending it anywhere. The lucky person that finds your body will find this with it."

"Suicide?"

"That's the way it has to be. For one thing, it makes the confession that much more convincing. For another, I don't have a choice. You know too much, and frankly, I can't count on you to keep your mouth shut. Now, where's your purse?"

"On the floor."

Stephanie retrieved Beatrice's handbag and emptied it onto the coffee table. Using a Kleenex, she picked up Bea's bottle of Valium. "These will be perfect," she declared. "We're going to make your back pain disappear forever."

"You'll never get away with it."

"Sure I will. If the police haven't linked me to the fire by now, they never will. And now that they have your very convincing confession, the case will be solved and I can write my book and get on with my life."

"You have it all figured out, don't you?"

"Pretty good for something I whipped up on the spur of the moment. I'd love to chat with you, but I have a meeting." Stephanie went into the kitchen and returned with a tall glass of orange juice and a garlic press. Again handling the bottle with a tissue, she poured the pills into a small yellow mound on the table and began crushing the tablets, several at a time. Stephanie poured the powdered Valium into the glass of juice and carefully mixed the drink with the handle of the press.

"I want you to drink this, and don't do anything stupid like spitting it out," Stephanie warned.

All conversation and action were halted by a knock on the door. "Shit," Stephanie said, pulling the gun out of her waistband. She pointed it at Beatrice, signaling her to remain silent.

"Stephanie?" Doug Sixsmith called out after several unanswered knocks. What the hell did *he* want? For a moment she thought about not answering, but decided to let him in, just in case she needed an alibi.

"One minute. I just got out of the shower," she called. It took all of Stephanie's strength to help Beatrice from the couch. She hurried to the bathroom at the back of the apartment and motioned for her to sit on the toilet as she rummaged through the clothes hamper. She pulled out a pair of socks and stuffed them in Beatrice's mouth. "Don't try anything stupid," she whispered. She pulled her bathrobe over her clothes and wrapped her hair in a towel before going back into the living room. Stephanie scurried to clean up the apartment. She picked up the empty pill bottle and Doug's letter with a Kleenex and put them in her pocket. Next she quickly shoved Bea's belongings and the garlic press back into the purse and stuffed it under the sofa. She gathered up the photographs and pushed them under the couch as well, leaving the table clear but for an innocent-looking glass of orange juice.

"Stephanie, open up," she heard Doug demand as she unbolted the camera and collapsed and carried the tripod into the kitchen and leaned it up against the refrigerator.

"I'm coming," Stephanie called out, hiding the camera behind a large potted plant as she opened the door. "Fancy seeing you here. Shouldn't you be out interviewing some of Gabrielle's old reading teachers or something?" she asked nastily.

"I want to talk to you."

"I don't have time to chat right now. I have a meeting with my publisher."

"What I have to say will take just a minute," Doug said, pushing into the apartment. "I found out today that besides your public-relations career, you're also a columnist."

"So what? There's no law against freelancing."

"No, there isn't. But there is a law against the kind of malicious lies you turn out under your bogus byline."

"I stand by my sources and my reports, particularly those involving Gabrielle's many lovers."

Doug refused to get riled. "Whatever book you're planning to write about Gabrielle, you and your editor had better go through it *twice* with a fine-tooth comb. If there's a single libelous remark in there, you can be sure that Gabrielle will sue you for every bloody cent you earn, and then some."

"*If* she can read it," Stephanie sniped.

Before Doug could respond, they were interrupted by a crash. The loud noise startled Barclay the cat from his perch, and he scurried across the floor toward the bedroom. At first Stephanie thought it was Beatrice trying to signal for help, but she quickly realized that the noise had come from the kitchen, caused by the tripod hitting the floor. It was time to wrap things up before Beatrice got any bright ideas.

"Sounds like you have a bad case of professional jealousy to me," Stephanie remarked caustically.

"I'm warning you, Stephanie."

"And believe me, my knees are knocking. Before you go, take this," Stephanie said, walking over to the desk and scribbling something on a piece of paper. As Doug watched Stephanie traipse across the room, his eye quickly caught a glimpse of leather patchwork sticking out from under the couch.

"Here," she said, handing him a scrap of paper and reclaiming his attention.

"What's this?"

"My autograph." She smirked. "This will save you the embarrassment of having to ask later."

"Kiss my ass," Doug said, crumpling the paper and throwing it back at her before slamming the door behind him.

Stephanie had no time to enjoy her snappy comebacks. She had little more than an hour before her scheduled meeting, and she still had to get Beatrice to drink the juice and then take her home. She carried the glass into the bathroom and removed the socks from Bea's mouth.

"Now, where were we?" Stephanie held the glass to Beatrice's lips. "Cheers," she said as the woman slowly drank the lethal concoction. Bea accepted her fate, afraid of doing anything that might further jeopardize Gabrielle or Kylie.

"Good girl," Stephanie said, watching Beatrice drain the glass.

"May I have a glass of water?" she requested, coughing.

"I guess that's as good a last request as any." She got Bea some water and held the glass as she drank, washing away the bitter taste the poisonous cocktail had left in her mouth.

"Enough."

"I'm going to get myself together. I'll drop you by your apartment on my way to Target Press," Stephanie said very matter-of-factly. Beatrice was astounded by her audacity. A moment ago Stephanie had literally been pouring death down her throat, yet she acted as if they'd just had tea together. What kind of monster was she?

"Can you untie my hands now?" Bea asked.

"Sorry. I don't want you to stick your finger down your throat." Stephanie pulled on a new pair of pantyhose, ran a comb through her hair, and was back in the living room within five minutes. Quickly she collected the photos and Bea's belongings and put everything in her big tote, along with her manuscript. Checking to make sure the prescription bottle and letter were still in her jacket pocket, she motioned to Beatrice. "Let's get the lead out."

By the time the cab arrived at the apartment building, Bea looked languid and relaxed, like a woman who'd had one too many drinks at happy hour. "Wait for me. I'll be back in a couple of minutes," Stephanie told the driver as the two women stepped out of the taxi. Arm in arm they walked into the building. "Don't get brave on me," Stephanie hissed in whispered warning, poking the toy weapon discreetly into Bea's side.

Luckily, the doorman was not at his post, and Stephanie hurried through the lobby. She pushed Beatrice down the hall and rang for the freight elevator. The two women got off on Bea's floor and walked the corridor in silence. Stephanie found Beatrice's keys and let them into the apartment. As quickly as Bea's large and cumbersome body would allow, Stephanie took her into the bedroom and helped her into the bed. Twenty minutes had gone by since she'd taken the medication, and her breathing was becoming increasingly shallow.

Stephanie pulled on a pair of gloves, put the videotape on the nightstand, and propped Doug's letter up on top of the cassette. She carried the pill bottle into the bathroom and placed it on the counter. To make the scene look authentic, Stephanie filled Bea's glass from the tap, drank the water, and set it down next to the bottle.

Stephanie walked back into the bedroom and found the woman nearly asleep. Considering everything taking place at this moment, she felt surprisingly calm. It was a shame that things had to end like this, but Stephanie was too close to achieving her goal to let an old lady get in her way.

"Sleep tight," she called out as she left the apartment. Stephanie rode the elevator back down and calmly walked through the lobby and into her waiting taxi.

54

Doug's advice took root in Gabrielle's conscience. He was right. Beatrice was the only family she and Kylie had left, and despite her behavior, her motives were pure. She picked up the phone and dialed Bea's number. It rang several times before Beatrice, in a very groggy voice, picked up the phone. "Bea, is that you?"

"Gab, show shorry," she said almost incoherently.

"Are you okay?"

"No tape. No tape."

"Bea, you're not making sense. You sound funny. What's wrong?"

"Peels—"

"Peels? I don't get it." *Peels, peels . . .* "Pills!" Gabrielle shouted, finally understanding. "Bea, did you take some pills? Bea, did you hear me? Did you take any pills? *Bea?* Answer me!"

Gabrielle heard the receiver drop and began to panic. She disengaged the line and ordered an ambulance to the apartment. She then tried to ring Felicia, but to no avail. In a panic she dialed Doug.

"Doug, thank God you're there."

"I just walked in the door. What's wrong?"

"It's Bea. I called and she sounded strange. She said something about pills, and then she dropped the phone."

"You don't think she—"

"She was extremely upset when she left. Who knows? I called nine-one-one."

"I'll head right over. I'll call and let you know what I find out."

Doug arrived just as the paramedics were wheeling Beatrice out her door. "What happened?"

"Looks like a drug overdose," the medic answered.

"Is she going to be all right?"

"She's in pretty bad shape. We found the empty bottle, but I don't know exactly how many pills she took. With any luck, we got here in time. You know her?" he said.

"She's my girlfriend's mom. What hospital?"

"We're taking her over to Bellevue."

Doug walked into Bea's apartment and went directly to the phone. He dialed Gabrielle's room number at Lenox Hill, hanging up after several rings. He waited a few minutes and tried again. Still no answer. *Strange*, he thought. Doug picked up the phone again and this time dialed the hospital operator.

"I'm sorry, sir, Miss Donovan has been discharged." Doug hung up not sure what to do. Deducing that Gabrielle was probably on her way home, he decided to wait. He sat on the couch, emotionally exhausted by the enormity of this situation.

"Beatrice!" Gabrielle shouted as she burst into the apartment, carrying her daughter. Doug stood up to greet her. "Where is she? Is she all right?"

"The paramedics took her away about five minutes ago. Apparently she took an overdose of pills."

"Oh, God, no! Is she—" Gabrielle stopped short, unable to verbalize her fearful thought.

"She's not dead, but she is unconscious. They took her to Bellevue."

"Let's get over there," Gabrielle insisted.

"Gabrielle, that's not a good idea," Doug explained gently. "The emergency room is no place for a newborn. Why don't you stay here and let me go to the hospital? I promise to call you as soon as I hear any news."

"But I want to tell Bea that I'm sorry and I love her."

"And you will—later. In the meantime, I'll tell her for you."

"Okay, but call me the minute you know something."

"I will."

While her daughter slept, Gabrielle's mind continued to sort though the grave circumstances. Try as she might to come up with a sensible answer, she continually returned to the ultimate question: Why?

Gabrielle knew that Bea had been terribly upset when she left the hospital, but the idea that she might try to kill herself had never crossed her mind. Over the years, Gabrielle had seen Beatrice in a full gamut of moods, but never depressed to the point of being suicidal. Why would she try to kill herself? Had her angry words brought Bea to the brink of death?

Surely Beatrice, knowing how much this would haunt her, must have left some sort of explanation. Gabrielle thought back to their brief phone conversation, trying to recall something that might help her understand all this. *She said something about a tape,* Gabrielle remembered. She got up and headed to the office to look around for an envelope or an audiocassette with her name on it. Finding nothing in the study, she walked across the hall to Beatrice's bedroom. From the doorway Gabrielle looked around. Other than

Bea's purse lying on the bed, nothing looked unusual or out of place. She continued scouting the room until something caught her attention. Gabrielle walked over to the nightstand and picked up the envelope. She recognized her name written in Doug's handwriting. *I thought Bea said Stephanie had this,* a puzzled Gabrielle remembered.

She put down the letter and picked up the video. There was no label or identifying marks on it. She hurried back into the living room and opened the cabinet containing the television and VCR. Gabrielle pushed "Play" and sat down to watch. Beatrice's image came up on the screen, and as her words began to fly around the room, Gabrielle began feeling light-headed and downhearted.

Gabrielle watched the tape with tears falling down her cheeks. She sat in disbelief, unable to accept the horrible admissions Beatrice was making. Caught up in the misery of this emotional tragedy, she almost didn't hear Doug come in.

"Well?" she asked, bracing herself for bad news.

"Things are still touch and go. They've done everything they can for the time being, but she still hasn't regained consciousness," Doug reported gently. He waited several seconds for a response, but instead got only silence. "Gabrielle, honey? Did you hear me?"

"I heard you," Gabrielle managed to say.

"Are you okay?"

"Not really," she said, before bursting into hysterical tears.

"Baby, what can I do to help?" Doug asked, feeling helpless and inept.

"I found a videotape she left me. She said she wanted to kill herself because—" Gabrielle paused, unable to continue.

"Take your time."

"Because she killed Jack," Gabrielle wept.

"Beatrice actually admitted this on tape?"

"See for yourself," Gabrielle said as she turned on the VCR. Together she and Doug watched Bea's confession in stunned disbelief. "This answers a lot of questions," Gabrielle said.

"Actually, it creates more in my mind. Something just doesn't hit me right," Doug said as he rewound the tape. Gabrielle, unable to sit through another screening, took Kylie into the bedroom. Doug stayed on the couch, watching intently for whatever was causing the red flags to wave in his head. Midway through, he paused the machine and called for Gabrielle.

"I'll admit that you have some interesting material here," Russell Shockley said from across his desk. "But why should we publish your biography, particularly when Gabrielle Donovan has just announced that she's coauthoring her own?"

"The answer is very clear," Stephanie said calmly. "She and her ex-lover are writing the book together. The details of her life will be so sugarcoated, it might as well begin with 'once upon a time.' I, on the other hand, will be able to give readers the *real* deal. I have information and photos that are totally exclusive—photos I haven't even used in my widely read column in *Star Diary.*"

"You brought examples?"

"Yes," Stephanie said, pulling out several photographs she and Howie had catalogued over the months. Included were never-before-seen shots of Gabrielle with Jack, with Doug, and with various celebrities, including several with Salvatore Ciccone. "There's a great deal of speculation that Salvatore is really the father of her child," Stephanie offered. "You can see by these select photos that they were definitely close."

"I like the exclusivity angle, but I don't see how this will make much impact against Gabrielle's telling the world how she made it to the top of the modeling world without knowing how to read," Russell said, still unconvinced.

"There is something else. Something very big," Stephanie said, trying to save this deal.

"Talk to me."

"Take a look at these," Stephanie said, handing Russell the photos of the Killington house. Silently she congratulated herself for having the good sense to ignore Howie's advice and keep a set. Once Beatrice and her confession were found, the case would be closed and Stephanie would be free to use these pictures in her book. "Do you recognize this place?"

"Where did you get these?" Russell asked.

"Gabrielle's personal assistant, Beatrice Braidburn, gave them to me for safekeeping," Stephanie said, feeling progressively more comfortable with her lie.

"Where did she get them?"

"She didn't say, and I didn't ask. At the time I was Gabrielle's publicist and had no thoughts of writing my own book, but things changed. How fortuitous for both of us that this very legitimate source dropped these pictures into our lap."

Russell Shockley stood up and extended his hand. "If we're going to head off the competition, we have to move quickly. How quickly can you give me a complete manuscript?"

"Is right now soon enough?" Stephanie asked, pulling the manuscript from her bag.

"Well, Ms. Bancroft, it looks like we're in business."

"Oh, yes, we most definitely are."

"You found something?" Gabrielle asked, emerging from the back room.

"Maybe. Watch this tape again and really listen to what Beatrice is saying," Doug said as he pushed the "Play" button. Following Bea's sign-off, he paused the tape, leaving her image looming on the television screen.

"Here's what I don't understand. Why would she use her credit card to pay those kids? Since when do delinquents accept credit?"

"She said she used it to get a cash advance," Gabrielle corrected.

"But why would she make such a point about it? And even if Bea did set this whole scenario up to ruin Jack's reputation, I can't believe she'd try to sell it to a tabloid. Why not let the mainstream media simply report the story? Wouldn't that give the whole thing more credibility?"

"Maybe, but only the tabloids would pay for the story," Gabrielle pointed out, staring at the television screen. "Hey, that looks like Barclay."

"Who?"

"The cat peeking over Beatrice's left shoulder."

"That's the same cat I saw go flying across the room when I visited Stephanie earlier this evening. So Bea must have been at Stephanie's at some point, too."

"You don't think that Stephanie—"

"That's exactly what I think." Doug was now certain that Beatrice was not admitting any wrongdoing, but instead leaving a bounty of clues that would lead them to the real culprit. "It all makes sense now. What credit card have we all come to hate?"

"Visa. Everywhere *she* wants to be," Gabrielle replied, her eyes growing wide with realization.

"Visa Lee, a.k.a. Stephanie Bancroft, tabloid writer. This whole story about ruining Jack's reputation and souring your relationship sounds much more plausible when you think of Stephanie as its originator."

"Then why would Bea confess to everything and try to kill herself?"

"Bea must have confronted her. That's why Stephanie had her make this tape," Doug said.

"And if Bea dies after leaving this confession, Stephanie gets off scot-free."

"Exactly."

"Could she really be that evil?"

Before Doug could respond, they were interrupted by Kylie's hungry cry. Gabrielle took her into Beatrice's bedroom to nurse. As she sat feeding the baby, a thought occurred to her. "We don't have any hard proof that Stephanie is responsible," she called out into the other room.

"What was that?" Doug asked, stopping in the doorway. There was something profoundly moving about seeing the woman he loved feeding her newborn daughter. "I'm sorry. I didn't hear you."

"We have no real proof that Stephanie is responsible for any of this."

"Not at the moment, but I think we have enough to call the police and let them—"

"What's wrong?" Gabrielle said, looking up from the baby and following Doug's eyes. He had stopped talking and was staring at the bed.

"When Beatrice was at the hospital, she dropped her purse and I helped pick up her belongings. I swear I saw the same bag at Stephanie's, shoved under the couch. But why would she go there of all places? Beatrice was upset after talking to you. Stephanie would be the last person she'd seek out."

"To get this, maybe?" Gabrielle said, pulling Doug's letter out of her pocket. "Bea told me that Stephanie had the letter you sent me, but I found it here on top of the videotape."

"That would explain it."

"At the hospital, do you remember if her pills were in her purse? She always carried them with her," Gabrielle asked.

"There was a prescription bottle, but I can't be sure if they were the same pills."

"What are you thinking?" she asked, noticing the look of contemplation that had overtaken his face.

"You said she always carried the pills around with her. Look at her bag. It's still zipped up. Doesn't it seem odd to you that a person bent on committing suicide would take a bottle of pills out of her purse, zip it back up, and then go into the bathroom? It's just a bit too neat."

"So if her pills are still in her purse . . ."

"Then she was given something else, somewhere else, and then brought back here."

"See if the pills are inside," Gabrielle suggested.

Using his handkerchief, Doug emptied the contents of Beatrice's handbag onto the bed. They found no vial of pills scattered among the rest of the contents, but they did find something inside that was suspiciously out of place.

"What is that?" Gabrielle asked.

"It's a garlic press," Doug said as he examined the press without touching it.

"Why would Beatrice be carrying around a garlic press?"

"I think we might be a tad closer to having some hard evidence," he answered, bending his nose down to meet the bowl of the press. It smelled like medicine. "No garlic, but if we're lucky, a good set of fingerprints."

"You're right, Doug, it's time to call the police."

55

Well, partner, looks like we've arrived, despite a few bumps along the way," Howie said, knocking the neck of his beer bottle against Stephanie's.

"This is only the beginning. I've decided our next subject should be Kathie Lee Gifford," Stephanie announced. "She's just too fucking chipper to be true. I bet she's hiding more dirt than a Hoover vacuum cleaner."

"I'm impressed. You're all ready to serve up your next victim."

"Yes, but for now I'm gonna savor the sweet taste of today's dessert—Gabrielle à la mode," Stephanie said, laughing at her own joke.

"So you think you're ready for fame and fortune?"

"Are you kidding me? I've been ready all my life," Stephanie remarked as a knock sounded on the front door, "and I can't wait to show Gabzilla how it's done."

Stephanie sauntered over to the door and took a quick look through the peephole. Two men, one tall and black, the other short and blond, stood outside her door with the rumpled authority of two cops. "Yes?"

"NYPD," the short blond announced, holding his badge up to the peephole.

Stephanie stepped away from the door and took a minute to calm herself before opening the door.

"Can I help you?"

"Stephanie Bancroft?"

"Yes."

"You're under arrest for the kidnapping and attempted murder of Beatrice Braidburn."

"This is obviously some sort of mistake," Stephanie retorted with false bravado. "You have no idea who you're dealing with. Ever heard of Visa Lee? *Star Diary*?"

"You have the right to remain silent," the blond detective continued, ignoring Stephanie's comment as his partner handcuffed her.

Stephanie did remain silent, not only because it was her right, but because she was trying desperately not to panic. She had to think straight. If they knew about Beatrice, it wouldn't be long before they figured out that she was behind the Killington fire and blame her for Jack's death, too.

As the detective finished reading Stephanie her Miranda rights, Howie sat at the table formulating his own plan. Forget Kathie Lee Gifford. The next head Stephanie served on a platter would be his. Howie knew instantly that when push came to shove, she would rat him out without second thought.

"Howie, call me a lawyer. Preferably one who knows what the hell he's doing," Stephanie demanded. "And make sure you stick around where I can find you," she called out as the detectives escorted her through the door.

Alone in the apartment, Howie hung his head in defeat. The warning in Stephanie's voice was explicit: They had ridden to the top of this mad rollercoaster together, and Stephanie Bancroft had no intention of going down alone.

56

November 3, 1998

When she walked through her front door, both Kylie and Doug were stretched out in front of the fireplace, sound asleep. The flickering flames bathed the room in a golden glow. She stared tenderly at the two of them, engraving on her memory the picture of the two people she loved most in the world.

"Hi," Doug called out quietly, his voice groggy with sleep. "How'd your tutoring session go?"

"Great. I'm making a lot of progress, though I spent the last half hour tonight signing copies of our book for my tutor and ten of her closest friends."

"What do you expect when you're the coauthor of a bestselling book?"

"I expect to help a lot of people, since most of the proceeds go to the Tommy Montebello Literacy Foundation."

"I have to tell you again how proud I am that you named your foundation after Tommy. It was very generous of you."

"It was the very least that I could do. He and his family deserve the recognition and much more."

"But I know how hard it was for you to go public with his story."

"It was worth it. At least everything is out in the open. Anything new here?"

"You got several calls. Lois left a message for you to call her about your rehearsal schedule for *Soul Survivor.*"

"I have to admit that as apprehensive as I was about doing the screen test for Lexis, I'm looking forward to shooting the picture."

"I'm not sure if I like the idea of you doing love scenes with Jonathan Bradley."

"Hey, Jonathan may be a Hollywood heartthrob, but his face doesn't make *my* heart skip a beat. Yours does," Gabrielle said, smiling.

"Felicia wants you to call her, and Gil from the prosecutor's office phoned. The case has gone to the jury, and he's expecting a quick verdict. It looks like Stephanie's trial could be over in the next day or two."

"I hope they nail her to the wall."

"The case against her is strong, especially with Bea's testimony. Between arson, kidnapping, and murder, I think we can safely count on Stephanie and her picture-taking accomplice being put away for a very long time," Doug said.

"That will give her plenty of time to stew over the dismal failure her book turned out to be. I still can't believe that Target Press published it even after Stephanie's arrest."

"It's all about the money, though the publisher, Russell Shockley, won't have much left once the lawsuits are settled."

"I don't know about Salvatore, but I didn't sue for the money. I sued because I didn't want Kylie growing up thinking that the things said in Stephanie's book were true.

Stephanie wanted so badly to be somebody famous. In the end, she's famous all right, but for all the wrong reasons," Gabrielle said.

"I feel absolutely no sympathy for that woman. In fact, I've had enough of Stephanie Bancroft to last a lifetime."

"Ain't that the truth. How about Kylie? Have you had enough of her this evening as well?" Gabrielle asked, happy to move on to a cheerier subject.

"No way. We had a wonderful time together. We read a few books, watched a few videos, and took about fifteen laps around the living room. I'd say she has this walking thing down," Doug said, grinning. "Bea called to check on us, but I assured her that I had everything under control."

"You know how grandmothers worry." Gabrielle took Kylie from Doug's arms and put her in the nursery.

"Are you through cuddling for the evening?" she asked, sitting down on the floor next to him.

"Not a chance." Doug gently pulled Gabrielle to him and kissed her softly.

"I have something for you. Something I never dreamed I'd be able to give you," Gabrielle said as she handed Doug an elegantly wrapped box. "Go on. Open it."

"It's Kylie's first birthday next week, not mine."

"Not every gift needs an occasion," Gabrielle said as Doug untied the ribbon and opened the box. Under the tissue paper, buried under a blanket of delicious-smelling rose petals, were several large white puzzle pieces.

"I could use a little help here, Jigsaw," Doug requested after several unsuccessful attempts to solve the puzzle. "Otherwise it might be Kylie's sweet sixteen before I get this together."

"Amateur." Gabrielle sighed happily, and in less than a minute assembled the puzzle. She took a deep breath and, for the first time in her life, began to read her own hand-writing:

My dearest Doug,

*Life is strang. Now that I can rite them, there are no
words to tell you how much I love you and how much
your love meens to Kylie and me. Plese don't ever stop.*

*Love forever,
Gabrielle*

Doug found himself crying as he focused his attention on Gabrielle. He didn't notice her halting recitation, as it was his heart, not his ears, doing the listening.

"This is the first love letter I've ever written," she told him as her tears flowed.

"It's the first one I ever received that mattered," he answered, pulling her into a loving embrace. "You and Kylie mean everything to me. There is no way I could, would, or will ever stop loving you."

Safe in Doug's arms, with no more secrets and lies between them, Gabrielle felt her soul quiet and at peace. For the first time in a very long time, all was right with the world.